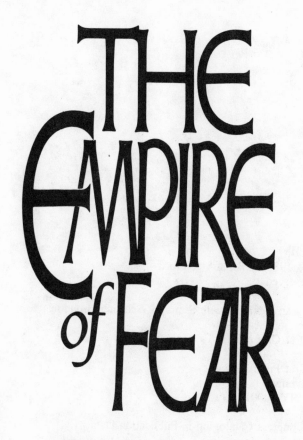

THE EMPIRE of FEAR

BRIAN STABLEFORD

Carroll & Graf Publishers, Inc.
New York

Published by arrangement with Simon & Schuster, London

First Carroll & Graf edition 1991

Carroll & Graf Publishers, Inc.
260 Fifth Avenue
New York, NY 10001

Library of Congress Cataloging-in-Publication Data

Stableford, Brian M.
    The empire of fear / by Brian Stableford.
        p.   cm.
    ISBN 0-88184-742-9
    I. Title.
PR6069.T17E46   1991
823'.914—dc20   91-22766
                                                    CIP

Manufactured in the United States of America

For my wife Jane
without whose support and encouragement
such a book as this would never have been
thought of, let alone written

CONTENTS

Part One:
THE FRUITS OF PASSION
page 1

Part Two:
THE SHADOW OF ETERNITY
page 33

Part Three:
THE BREATH OF LIFE
page 105

Part Four:
THE SEASON OF BLOOD
page 183

Part Five:
THE BLOOD OF MARTYRS
page 267

Part Six:
THE WORLD, THE FLESH AND THE DEVIL
page 351

Acknowledgements
page 389

PART ONE

The Fruits of Passion

'A man who loves a vampire lady need not die young, but cannot live forever'

(Walachian proverb)

ONE

It was the thirteenth of June in the Year of Our Lord 1623. Warm weather had come early to Grand Normandy and the streets of London were bathed in sunlight. There were crowds everywhere and the port was busy with ships, three having docked that day.

One of these ships, the *Freemartin*, had come from the equatorial regions and had produce from the mysterious heart of Africa, including ivory, gold and the skins of exotic animals. She had also brought back live animals, for the prince's menagerie in the Lions' Tower. Rumour spoke of three more lions, a snake as long as a man was tall, and brightly-clad parrots which the sailors had taught to speak. There was talk, too, of secret and more precious goods – intricately-carved jewels and magical charms – but such gossip always attended the docking of any vessel from remote parts of the world.

Beggars and street urchins had flocked to the dockland, responsive as ever to such whisperings, and were plaguing every seaman in the streets, as anxious for gossip as for copper coins. The only faces not animated by excitement were those on the severed heads atop the Southwark Gate. The Tower of London, though, stood quite aloof from the hubbub, its tall and forbidding turrets so remote from the streets that they seemed to belong to a different world.

Edmund Cordery, Mechanician to the Court of Prince Richard, was at work in his garret in the south-west turret of the White Tower. Carefully, he tilted the small concave mirror on the brass device which rested on his workbench, catching the rays of the afternoon sun and deflecting their light through the hole in the stage, and then through the system of lenses which made up the instrument before him.

He looked up, then stood and moved aside, directing his son, Noell, to take his place. 'Tell me if all is well,' he said, tiredly. 'I can hardly focus my eyes.'

Noell closed his left eye and put the other to the microscope. He turned the wheel which adjusted the height of the stage. 'It's perfect,' he said. 'What is it?'

'The wing of a moth,' his father replied.

Edmund scanned the polished tabletop, checking that the other slides were in readiness for the demonstration. The prospect of the Lady Carmilla's visit filled him with a complex anxiety which he resented. Even in the old days, she had not come often to his workroom, but to see her here now would perforce awaken memories which the occasional glimpses which he caught of her in the public parts of the Tower and on ceremonial occasions did not recall.

'The water slide is not ready,' Noell said. 'Shall I . . . ?'

Edmund shook his head. 'I shall make a fresh one when the time comes,' he said. 'Living things are fragile, and the world which is in a water drop is all-too-easily destroyed.'

He looked further along the bench-top, and moved a crucible, placing it out of sight behind a row of jars. It was impossible – and unnecessary – to make the place tidy, but he felt it important to conserve some semblance of order and control. He went to the window and looked out, over the Cold-Harbour Tavern and St. Thomas's Tower, at the sparkling Thames and the distant slate roofs of the houses on the further shore.

From this high vantage-point the people in the precincts of the Outer Ward seemed tiny. He was higher above them than the cross on the steeple of the church beside the Leathermarket. Edmund's gaze dwelt on that distant symbol. He was by no means a devout man, but such was the agitation within him that he crossed himself, murmuring the ritual devotion. As soon as he had done it, he chided himself for his weakness of spirit.

I am forty-four years old, he thought, *and a mechanician. I am no longer the boy who was favoured with the love of the lady, and there is no need for this trepidation.*

This private scolding was a little unjust. It was not simply the fact that he had once been Carmilla Bourdillon's lover which provoked his anxiety. There was the microscope on the bench. There was the fact that he was followed whenever he went about the Outer Ward, so that his every chance meeting had come under scrutiny. If that were not enough, there was the ship from Africa, whose master had undertaken a mission for the Invisible College while fulfilling Richard's demand for new lions for his collection.

But he had lived with danger for many a year, and had schooled himself to stay calm. Lady Carmilla was a different matter. His relationship with her had been a genuine affair of the heart, and it pained him that she was now doing Richard's work, becoming an intermediary between prince and mechanician. The fact that an intermediary had been brought in at all was an overt sign that Edmund had lost favour. He hoped that he would be able to judge by the lady's reaction how much there really was for him to fear.

The door opened, and she entered. She half-turned, dismissing her attendant with a brief gesture. She was alone, with no friend or favourite in tow. She came across the room carefully, lifting the hem of her skirt a little, though the floor was not dusty. Her gaze flicked from side to side, over the shelves with their bottles and jars, the furnace, the turning-machine, and the numerous tools of the mechanician's craft.

To many, vampires and commoners alike, this would have seemed a room full of mysteries, redolent with unholiness – like the alchemist's den which the unfortunate Harry Percy had made for himself while he was an unwilling guest in the Martin Tower. The Lady Carmilla probably saw no very great difference between the work of the wizard earl and that of the mechanician, but it was always difficult to judge what the opinion of vampires was regarding the multifarious quests for knowledge which common men nowadays pursued. Her attitude was cool and controlled. She came to stand before the brass instrument which Edmund had recently completed, but only glanced at it before raising her eyes to stare fully into his face.

'You look well, Master Cordery,' she said, calmly, 'but you are pale. You should not shut yourself in your rooms now that summer is come to Normandy.'

Edmund bowed slightly, but continued to meet her gaze.

She had not changed in the slightest degree since the days when he had been intimate with her. She was already four hundred and fifty years old – not a great deal younger than Richard – but her beauty had not begun to fade. Her colour was very white, as was common in the vampires of northern Europe, and had that lustrous purity – almost a silvery sheen – which was the unmistakable badge of immortality. No mole or wart, no scar or pockmark, could mar the perfection of a vampire face. Her eyes were a deep liquid brown and her hair was jet black, in striking contrast to her skin. Vampires very rarely retained fair hair after conversion, even when they had been born with it. Her lips were gently rouged.

He had not stood so close to her for several years, and he could not help the tide of memories rising in his mind. For her, it would be another matter: his hair was greying now, his skin beginning to crease; he must seem an altogether different person. But as he met her gaze it seemed to him that she too was remembering, and not entirely without fondness.

'My lady,' he said, his voice quite steady, 'may I present my son and apprentice, Noell.'

Noell blushed, and bowed more deeply than his father.

The Lady Carmilla favoured the youth with a smile. 'He has the look of you, Master Cordery,' she said. To Noell, she added: 'In the days before you were born, your father was the handsomest man in England. You are very like him, and should be proud.' She returned her attention then to the instrument. 'The designer was correct?' she asked.

'Yes, indeed,' he replied. 'The device is most ingenious. I would dearly like to meet the man who thought of it. It taxed the talents of my lens-grinder severely, and I think we might make a better one with greater care and skill. This is a poor example, as one must expect from a first attempt.'

The Lady Carmilla sat down, and Edmund showed her how to apply her eye to the instrument, and how to adjust the focusing-wheel and the mirror. She expressed surprise at the appearance of the magnified moth's wing, and Edmund showed her the whole series of prepared slides, which included other parts of insects' bodies, and thin sections cut from the stems and seeds of plants.

'I need a sharper knife and a steadier hand, my lady,' he told her. 'The device shows all too clearly the clumsiness of my cutting.'

'Oh no, Master Cordery,' she assured him, politely. 'These are quite pretty enough. But we were told that more interesting things might be seen. Living things too small for ordinary sight.'

Edmund explained the preparation of water-slides. He made a new one, using a pipette to take a drop from a jar full of dirty river-water. Patiently, he helped her search the slide for the tiny creatures which human eyes were not equipped to see. He showed her one which flowed as if it were almost liquid itself, and tinier ones which moved by means of cilia. She was captivated, and watched for some little time, moving the slide very gently with her painted fingernails.

Eventually, she asked: 'Have you looked at other fluids?'

'What kind of fluids?' he asked, though the question was quite clear to him, and disturbed him.

She was not prepared to mince words. 'Blood, Master Cordery,' she said, softly. Her past acquaintance with him had taught her respect for his intelligence, and he half-regretted it.

'Blood clots very quickly,' he told her. 'I could not produce a satisfactory slide. It would take more skill than I have yet acquired. But Noell has made drawings of many of the things which we *have* studied. Would you like to see them?'

She accepted the change of subject, and indicated that she would. She moved to Noell's station, and began sorting through the drawings, occasionally looking up at the boy to compliment him on his work. Edmund stood by, remembering how sensitive he once had been to her moods and desires, trying hard to work out exactly what she might be thinking. Something in one of her contemplative glances at Noell sent an icy pang of dread into his gut. He did not know himself whether it was anxiety for his son, or jealousy.

'May I take these to show to the prince?' asked the vampire, addressing the question to Noell rather than his father. The boy nodded, too embarrassed to construct a proper reply. She took a selection of the drawings, and rolled them into a scroll. She stood up, and faced Edmund again.

'The court is most interested in this apparatus,' she informed him. 'We must consider carefully whether to provide you with new assistants, to aid development of the appropriate skills. In the meantime, you may return to your ordinary work. I will send someone for the instrument, so that the prince may inspect it at his leisure. Your son draws well, and must be encouraged. You and he may visit me in my chambers on Monday next; we will dine at seven o'clock.'

Edmund bowed to signal his acquiescence; it was, of course, a command rather than an invitation. He moved before her to the door and held it open for her. He exchanged a brief glance with her as she went past him, but her expression was distant now, and inscrutable.

When she had gone, something taut unwound inside him, leaving him relaxed and emptied. He felt strangely cool and distant as he considered the possibility that his life was in peril.

It was not even my invention, he thought, angrily. *After so many years of careful treason, so much endeavour to find the secret of their nature, am I to be thought too dangerous to live only because I have seen what another man has devised? Or have they changed their minds about our scholarly endeavours, and decided to keep watch on all of Francis Bacon's friends, and the Earl of Northumberland's magi too?*

He watched Noell while the boy carefully put away the slides which they had used in the demonstration. He had enjoyed these last few weeks, since his son had joined him in his work. As the Lady Carmilla had said, Noell *was* very like his father, though he had not yet grown to his full stature, and his mind was only beginning to quicken with that inquisitiveness and ingenuity which had made Edmund Cordery what he was.

Alas!, thought Edmund, *I had hoped the day might come when I no longer need protect thee from the truth of my pursuits. Now, perhaps, I must send thee away, and trust thee to the hands of another tutor.*

Aloud, he said only: 'Be careful, my son. The glass is delicate and sharp in the edge; there is danger of injury on either side.'

TWO

When the twilight had faded Edmund lit a single candle on the bench, and sat staring into the flame. He had been turning the pages of Antonio Neri's *Arte Vitraria*, which had made the secrets of the Venetian glassmakers known throughout Europe, but he had found himself unable to concentrate on the text. He put the book aside, and poured dark wine from a flask which he kept in the room. He did not look up when Noell came in, though he heard the door open and close; but when the boy brought another stool close to his and sat down, Edmund offered him the flask. Noell seemed surprised, but took it, then found himself a goblet, poured a measure, and sipped carefully.

'Am I old enough to drink with thee, then?' he asked, with a hint of bitterness in his voice.

'You are old enough,' Edmund assured him, deliberately using the less intimate form of address. 'Beware of excess and never drink alone. Conventional fatherly advice, I believe.'

Noell reached across the bench so that he could stroke the barrel of the microscope with slender fingers. He had not had much of fatherly advice, conventional or otherwise. Edmund had thought it prudent to keep him at a safe distance from treasonous activities, and from dangerous thoughts.

'What are you afraid of?' Noell asked, matching his father's form of speech, so that they addressed one another not as parent and child, but as equals.

Edmund sighed. 'You are old enough for that, too, I suppose?'

'I think you ought to tell me.'

Edmund looked at the brass instrument, and said: 'It might have been better to keep a machine like this a secret among common men, at least for a while. Some clever Italian mechanician, I dare say, eager to please the vampire lords and ladies, showed off his invention as proud as a peacock, avid for their applause. Doubtless the trick was bound to be discovered, though, now that all this play with lenses has become fashionable; and such a secret could not be kept for long.'

'You'll be glad of eyeglasses when your sight begins to fail,' Noell told him. 'In any case, I can't see the danger in this new toy.'

Edmund smiled. 'New toys,' he mused. 'Clocks to tell the time, mills to grind the corn, lenses to aid human sight. Turning-machines to make screws, coin-presses to mark and measure the wealth of the Imperium. All produced by common craftsmen for the delight of their masters. I think we have succeeded in proving to the vampires how very clever modern men can be, and how much more there is to know than is written in the pages of the Greek and Roman sages.'

'You think that the vampires are beginning to fear us?'

Edmund poured wine from the flask and passed it again to his son. 'They have encouraged scholarship because they thought it a fit distraction; a deflection of our energy from resentful and rebellious ideas. They never looked for the kinds of reward which our learned men have begun to reap. Great changes are remaking the world: changes wrought by artifice and discovery. But an empire of immortals loves constancy. Vampires mistrust the new, whenever it rises above mere novelty. Yes, the vampires are becoming anxious, and justly so.'

'But common men, without immunity to pain, disease and injury, could never threaten their dominion.'

'Their rule is founded as much in fear and superstition as in their nature,' Edmund said, quietly. 'To be sure, they are long-lived; they suffer only a little from diseases which are fatal to us; and they have marvellous powers of regeneration. But they are not invulnerable. Their empire is more precarious than they dare admit. After centuries of strife they still have not succeeded in imposing vampire rule on the Mohammedan nations. The terror which keeps them in power in Gaul and Walachia is based in ignorance and superstition. The haughtiness of our princes and knights conceals a gnawing fear of what might happen if common men lose their reverence for vampirekind. It is difficult for them to die, but they do not fear death any the less for that.'

'There have been rebellions against vampire rule in Gaul and Walachia. They have always failed.'

Edmund nodded. 'But there are three million commoners in Grand Normandy,' he said, 'and less than five thousand vampires. There are no more than forty thousand vampires in the whole Imperium of Gaul, and no greater number in Walachia. I do not know how many there might be in Cathay, or India, or in the heart of Africa beyond the Mohammedan lands, but there too, common men must outnumber vampires very greatly. If commoners no longer saw their masters as demons or demigods, but only as creatures more sturdily made, the vampire empires would be frail. Vampires say that the centuries through which they live give them a wisdom which common men can never attain, but that claim has become increasingly difficult to believe. All but a very few of the new things in the world are the work of common men: Dutch ships and Dutch looms, Norman cannon and Norman glass. Our arts mechanical have outstripped their arts magical, and they know it.'

'Would not the vampires argue that such devices are only useful to make the world more comfortable for common men – that our mechanical arts are but a poor substitute for the magical power to remake ourselves, which they have and we do not?'

Edmund looked carefully at his son, with a certain pride. He was glad that the boy knew how to handle a disputation. He had given Noell to other teachers at an early age, thinking it best to keep himself apart from the boy. In these last few weeks of closer association, though, he had seen much in the boy's conduct which reminded him of his own habits and inclinations, and it had pleased him – affection for his son had never been lacking in him, but circumstances had not allowed him to bring it to a proper fruition. It seemed likely that they never would. Perhaps this was his only opportunity to pass on that fraction of the knowledge he had gleaned which he had never dared trust to another.

He hesitated. But there could be no harm – could there? – in a discussion and disputation such as scholarly men engaged in for amusement.

'Vampires have a power,' agreed Edmund, 'which we call a magic power. But what do we mean by a magic power? Is it magic when we design the sails of a ship so that it makes headway against the wind? Is it a magic power which is in the vacuum which we use in pumps to draw water from our mines? Is it magic which allows silver to dissolve in mercury as sugar dissolves in water? All these tricks were magic when they were shown to people who did not known how they were done. Magic is simply that which we do not yet understand.'

'But a vampire is very different from a common man,' insisted Noell. 'It is a difference of the soul, nothing to do with mechanical art. The soul which animates the body of a common man is much less powerful than the soul which animates a vampire body, and no mere physick will grant it that power.'

'*No mere physick,*' echoed Edmund. 'And yet, I wonder. That wizard earl, Harry Percy, who was locked in the Martin Tower for so many years, laboured to make an elixir of life which would make us all the equal of the vampires. Richard's knights looked on in amusement, and called him the mad earl – but they watched him very carefully for all that. Richard was fascinated by his experiments in prophecy and his studies of alchemical texts. Had Percy's researches ever come close to the means by which the vampires make themselves, they would have killed him most expeditiously.'

'The Gregorians believe that vampires are the devil's creation,' said Noell. 'They say that the vampires hold sabbats at which Satan appears, and that vampires are more powerful than common men because they are possessed by the souls of demons, which Satan puts into their bodies when they have renounced Christ and sworn to do evil.'

Edmund was momentarily alarmed by this speech. It was not wise to speak *that* heresy within the Tower walls, for fear of being overheard. Pope Gregory's condemnation of the vampires might be reckoned a more damaging rebellion against their rule than any armed insurrection, and the vampire princes knew it. They had been quick to force a new pope to condemn Gregory as the foulest of heretics, and had now gone so far as to place a vampire on the throne of St. Peter, but they had not entirely stamped out the notion of their demonic status, and perhaps never would. It was such a fine and lurid story – the kind of forbidden slander in which every man delighted, whatever he might really believe.

'The orthodox view is that the vampire estate was ordered by God, as were the estates of common men,' Edmund reminded his son. 'The Church now tells us that the vampires were granted long life upon the earth, but that this is as much a burden as a privilege, because they must wait all the more patiently to enjoy the bounty of Heaven.'

'Would you have me believe that?' asked Noell, who knew well enough that his father was an unbeliever.

'I would not have you believe that they are devil's spawn,' said

Edmund, gently. 'It is unlikely to be true, and it would be a pity to be burned as a heretic for casually speaking an untruth.'

'Tell me then,' said Noell, 'what you do believe.'

Edmund shrugged, uncomfortably. 'I am not sure that it is a matter for belief,' he said. 'I do not *know*. Their longevity is real, their resistance to disease, their powers of regeneration. But is it really magic that secures these gifts? I am prepared to believe that they carry out mysterious rituals, with strange incantations, but I do not know what virtue or effect there is in such conduct. I often wonder whether they are certain in their own minds. Perhaps they cling to their rites as common men in Europe cling to the mass, and the followers of Mohammed to their own ceremonies, out of habit and faith. Clearly, they know what must be done to make a common man a vampire, but whether they understand what they do, I cannot tell. Sometimes, I wonder whether they are as much the victims as we of that superstitious terror which they try to instil in us.'

'Do you believe, then, that there *is* an elixir – a potion which might make every man safe from all disease and injury, and delay death for many centuries?'

'The alchemists talk of a secret wisdom which was known long ago in Africa, of which the vampires are now the custodians, but I do not know whether to believe it. If it were only a magic brew which made vampires, I think the secret might have escaped long ago.'

Noell stared at the instrument which was before him, lost in contemplation. Then he said: 'And do you think that this device might somehow reveal the secret of vampire nature?'

'I fear that Richard thinks so. He is very uneasy. The Imperium is troubled, and it is said that the *Freemartin* has confirmed rumours of a plague in Africa which can kill vampires as well as common men.'

His tone was very sombre, and he was surprised when Noell uttered a small laugh.

'If we discovered the secret, and *all* became vampires,' he said, lightly, 'whose blood would we drink?'

It was a common remark – the kind of ironic jest which children liked to ask of one another. Edmund was tempted, for a moment, to be flippant in his turn, and turn the whole conversation in a humorous direction, but he knew that was not what the boy intended. Noell's laugh had been a sign of embarrassment – an apology for introducing an indelicate subject. But if one had to talk about vampires, one could hardly avoid the topic of blood-drinking, however indecent its mention was supposed to be. Carmilla Bourdillon had not been ashamed to speak of it – why should the boy?

'It is another thing which we do not understand,' he said. 'It makes us uncomfortable. It is not for ordinary nourishment that a vampire takes the blood of men; it does not serve them as bread or meat, and the amounts they need are tiny. And yet, they *do* need it. A vampire deprived of blood will go into deep sleep, as though badly injured. It also gives them a kind of pleasure, which we cannot wholly understand. It is a vital part of the mystery which makes them so terrible, so unhuman . . . and hence so powerful.'

He stopped, feeling embarrassed, not so much because of conventional ideas of indecency, but because he did not know how much Noell understood regarding his sources of information. Edmund never talked about the days of his affair with the Lady Carmilla – certainly not to the wife he had married afterwards, or to the son she had borne him – but there was no way to keep gossip and rumour from reaching the boy's ears. Noell must know what his father had been.

Noell took the flask again, and this time poured a deeper draught into his cup. 'I have been told,' he said, 'that humans find a special pleasure too . . . .when they offer their blood to be drunk.'

'Not true,' replied Edmund, awkwardly. 'The pleasure which a common man takes from a vampire lady is the same pleasure that he takes from a common lover. It might be different for the women who entertain vampire men, but I suspect that the unique pleasure which they claim to experience has more to do with the fact that male vampires so rarely make love after the fashion of common men. Then again, the mistresses of vampires have the excitement of hoping that they may become vampires themselves. They seem to be . . . favoured . . . in that respect.' Edmund hesitated, but realised that he did not want the subject dropped, now it had been broached. The boy had a right to know, and perhaps might one day *need* to know. He remembered how the Lady Carmilla had looked at the boy when she told him that he was like his father.

'But perhaps it is true, in a way,' Edmund went on. 'When the Lady Carmilla used to taste my blood, it did give me pleasure. It pleased me because it pleased her. There *is* an excitement in loving a vampire lady, which makes it different from loving an ordinary woman . . . even though a vampire lady's lover very rarely becomes a vampire – and never simply *because* he is her lover.'

Noell blushed, not knowing quite how to react to this acceptance into his father's confidence. Finally, he seemed to decide that it was best to pretend a purely academic interest.

'Why are there many more vampire women than vampire men in London and the other Gaulish courts?' he asked.

'No one knows for sure,' Edmund said. 'No common men, anyhow. I can tell you what I suspect, from hearsay and by reasoning, but you must understand that it is a dangerous thing to think about, let alone to discuss. You must know that I have kept many things hidden from you, and I think you know why. Do you understand that there is danger in this, if we continue?'

Noell nodded. The boy took another sip from his cup, as if to signify that he was ready for *all* adult responsibilities. He was eager to learn, and Edmund was glad to see it.

Edmund set his own cup down, and drew breath, wondering how much Noell might already know, and how much his knowledge might be confused by colourful fantasies.

'The vampires keep their history secret,' said Edmund, 'and they have tried to control the writing of human history, though the spread of printing presses has made it impossible for them to stop the distribution of forbidden books. It seems that the vampire aristocracy first came to Western Europe in the fifth century, with the vampire-led horde of Attila, which conquered Rome. Attila must have known well enough how to make vampires of those he wished to favour. He converted Aetius, who became the first ruler of the Imperium of Gaul, and Theodosius II, who was then Emperor in Byzantium, before that city became part of the Khanate of Walachia.

'Of all the vampire princes and knights who now exist, the vast majority must be converts descended from Attila and his kin. I have read accounts of vampire children born to vampire ladies, but they are probably false. Vampire women are barren, and vampire men are much less virile than human men – it is well-known that they couple very rarely, though they summon their mistresses nightly to take blood. Nevertheless, the mistresses of vampires often become vampires themselves. Vampire knights claim that this is a gift, bestowed deliberately by magic, but I am not so sure that every conversion is planned and deliberate.'

He paused, then went on. 'It is possible that the semen of vampire men might carry some kind of seed which communicates vampirism much as the semen of common men makes women pregnant – perhaps as haphazardly. The male lovers of vampire ladies don't become vampires; the female lovers of vampire men often do; logic suggests the conclusion.'

Noell considered this, and then asked: 'Then how are new vampire lords made?'

'They are converted by other male vampires,' Edmund said. 'No doubt the conversion involves elaborate rites and incantations, and perhaps an elixir such as the Earl of Northumberland sought, but I suspect that the old descriptions of the vampire sabbat which the Gregorians bandied about may have a little truth in them, if we only assume that Satan's part is played by a vampire lord.' He did not elaborate, but waited to see whether Noell understood the implication.

An expression of disgust crossed the boy's face, followed by an expression of disbelief. Edmund did not know whether to be glad or sorry that his son could follow the argument through, but he was not surprised. The Gregorian accounts of the vampire sabbat, which described Satan enjoying unnatural sexual intercourse with his minions, were so thrilling as to be told and retold in scrupulous detail. Then again, there was a pillory outside the Lord Lieutenant's lodgings, where disloyal servants were sometimes lodged; it was common practice for those yeomen of the guard who were so disposed to visit the pillory by night, to use the hapless victim while his wrists and neck were pinned. This too would be common knowledge among the youths and servants of the Tower, and Noell could hardly help but know what buggery was.

'Not all the women who lie with vampire men become vampire ladies,' Edmund went on, 'and that makes it easy for the vampires to pretend that they have some special magic. But some women never become pregnant, though they lie with their husbands for years. I am not certain whether I should believe in the special magic.'

'It is said,' observed Noell, 'that a common man may also become a vampire by drinking vampire blood, if he knows the appropriate magic spell.'

'That,' said Edmund, 'is a dangerous myth. It is a rumour which the vampires hate, for obvious reasons. They exact terrible penalties if anyone is caught trying the experiment, and I know of no believable case of anyone who became a vampire by such means. The ladies of our own court are for the most part one-time lovers of the prince's knights – Richard, for all his legendary handsomeness, has never been interested in mistresses. We can only speculate about the conversion of the prince himself, which was probably a planned affair, done entirely for political reasons, but he is said to have been a favourite of that William who brought this island into the Imperium of Gaul in 1066. He seems to have been favoured above his father Henry, or that other Henry who was his great-grandfather, each of whom were made into vampires late in life. William may have been converted by Charlemagne himself.'

Noell reached out a hand, palm downwards, and made a few passes above the candle-flame, making it flicker from side to side. He stared at the microscope.

'Have you looked at blood?' he asked.

'I have,' replied Edmund. 'And semen. Common blood, of course – and common semen.'

'And?'

Edmund shook his head. 'They are not homogeneous fluids,' he said, 'but the instrument isn't good enough for detailed inspection. You've seen yourself how coloured haloes confuse the outlines of things, and the magnification is too weak. There are small corpuscles – the ones in semen may have long tails – but there must be more . . . much more . . . to be seen, if I only had the chance. By tomorrow, this instrument will be gone; I do not think I will be given the chance to build another.'

'You're surely not in danger!' protested Noell. 'You're an important man – and your loyalty has never been questioned. People think of you as being almost a vampire yourself. You are called alchemist or black magician, like the wizard earl! The kitchen girls are afraid of me, because I'm your son; they cross themselves when they see me.'

Edmund laughed, a little bitterly. 'No doubt the ignorant suspect me of intercourse with demons. Many avoid my gaze for fear of the spell of the evil eye. But none of that matters to the vampires. To the vampires, I am only a common man, and for all that they value my skills, they'd kill me without a thought if they suspected that I might have dangerous knowledge.'

Noell was clearly alarmed by this. 'Wouldn't . . . ?' He stopped, but carried on after a brief pause. 'The Lady Carmilla . . . wouldn't she . . .?'

'Protect me?' Edmund shook his head. 'Not even if I were her lover still. Vampire loyalty is to vampires.'

He stood up, then, no longer feeling the urgent desire to help his son to understand. There were things the boy could only find out for himself, and might never have to. He took up the candle, and shielded the flame with his hand as he walked to the door. Noell followed him, leaving the empty flask behind, but could not resist the temptation to ask one last question.

'But . . . she did love you, did she not?'

'Perhaps she did,' said Edmund Cordery, sadly. 'In her own way.'

THREE

Edmund left the Tower by the Lions' Gate, and crossed quickly into Petty Wales, looking behind him to see whether he was followed. The houses which extended from the edge of the wharf to the Bulwark Gate were in darkness now, but there was still a trickle of traffic; even at two in the morning the business of the great city did not come entirely to a standstill. The night had clouded over, and a light drizzle had begun to fall. Some of the oil-lamps which were supposed to keep the thoroughfare lit at all times had gone out, and there was not a lamp-lighter in sight. Edmund did not mind the shadows, though; he hoped that they might be to his advantage.

He discovered as he walked towards the wharf that two men were dogging his footsteps, and he dawdled in order to give them the impression that he did not care where he was going. When he reached the wharf, though, he was quick to find a waterman – the only one who was abroad at this ungodly hour – and gave him three penny pieces to row him across the Thames as fast as his boat could go.

Looking back, Edmund saw the two spies pause beneath a lamp. They were discussing whether to follow him. One looked along the wharf towards Traitors' Gate, but even the devil on horseback could not get to Tower Bridge, then back along the south bank to Pickle Herring Street, in time to catch him that way. It was too soon, though, to congratulate himself, because he knew that there might be agents of the Lord Lieutenant already waiting on the further shore.

He made his way to Druid Street with great care, listening for the sound of footsteps behind him They came, though this time there was but one man on his track. Once he entered the network of streets surrounding the Leathermarket he could easily give the man the slip, or so he judged, but he was growing weary of this pestilent attention. Whom the vampires destroyed, they first made mad with the prying of their catspaws, and he longed to draw his sword and have it out with the spy. But such precipitate action could only work to his disadvantage this night, and he hoarded his wrath for another time.

He knew the maze of filthy streets around the Leathermarket very well. He had been born in Crucifix Lane, and had lived in this district as a child. It was while he was apprenticed to a local clockmaker that he had learnt the cleverness with tools which had taken him into the Tower, to work with Simon Sturtevant under the tutelage of Francis Bacon. He had been the best of the apprentices, though he was honest enough to know that he could never have come to his present position of authority but for the interest taken in him by the Lady Carmilla. Her interest in the cleverness of his fingers and the strength of his back had been entirely different from the interest of poor Francis, who had hoped to be a vampire, but took one bribe too many, and lost even his position as Chancellor.

Edmund had a brother and a sister still living and working in this district, though he saw them very rarely. Neither one of them was proud to have a reputed magician for a brother, and though they were not Gregorians, they nevertheless thought that there was something unholy about his one-time association with the Lady Carmilla. He sent money to his sister, sometimes, because her husband was often at sea and she did not always find it easy to feed her children.

He picked his way carefully through the rubbish in the dark alleys, unperturbed by the sounds made by scavenging rats. He kept his hand on the pommel of the sword at his belt, but he had no need to draw it. The packs of rats which plagued the shores of the Thames would attack children under cover of dark, and sometime bit whores as they plied their trade, but they were too wily and cowardly to bother grown men.

Because the stars were hidden the night was pitch-dark, and very few of the windows which he passed were illumined by candlelight, but he was able to keep track of his progress by reaching out to touch familiar walls every now and again. Soon, he no longer heard the footsteps of his follower, and knew that he was safe.

He came eventually to a tiny door set three steps down from a side-street, and rapped upon it quickly, three times and then twice. There was a long pause before he felt the door yield beneath his fingers, and he stepped inside hurriedly. The door clicked shut again, and he relaxed, unaware until then how tense he had been.

He waited for a candle to be lit.

The light, when it came, illuminated a thin female countenance, crabbed and wrinkled. The crone's eyes were very pale and her wispy white hair was gathered imperfectly behind a linen bonnet.

'The lord be with you,' he whispered.

'And with *you*, Edmund Cordery,' she croaked.

He frowned at the use of his name. It was a deliberate breach of etiquette, a feeble and meaningless gesture of independence. The old woman did not like him, though he had never been less than kind to her. She did not fear him, as so many others did, but she considered him tainted. They had been bound together in the business of the Invisible College for nearly twenty years, but she would never completely trust him. To her, he would always be a vampire-lover.

She led him into the inner room where he had arranged to conduct his business, and left him there.

A stranger stepped from the shadows. He was short, stout and bald, perhaps sixty years old. He made the special sign of the cross, and Edmund did the same.

'I am Edmund Cordery,' he said. 'Are you the one who was appointed to take care of Richard's lions, and the other beasts, aboard the *Freemartin*?'

'Aye,' replied the other. 'It fell to me to take care of all the beasts.' The older man's tone was deferential, but not fearful. He emphasised the word *all* very faintly, with a certain irony in his voice. He seemed to Edmund to be an educated man, and no mere sailor.

'You have served Richard well – and the College even better, I hope,' Edmund told him, with careful courtesy.

'That I have,' said the other, 'though it was mad work which your friends asked me to do. I think you do not know what evil matters you are toying with.'

'Oh yes, sir,' said Edmund, coldly. 'I know, indeed I do. I understand that you are a brave man. Please do not think that your mission is undervalued.'

'I hope that you were not inconvenienced in coming to me here,' said the stout man.

'By no means,' Edmund told him, immediately taking his meaning. 'Two followed me from the Tower, but were left on the other bank. One came after me on the south shore, but it was easy to shake him loose.'

'That is not good.'

'Perhaps not. But it has to do with another matter, not with our business. There is no danger to you, I think, and if the creatures for the menagerie are in a good state, Richard will be generous. He loves his lions, ever since they named him Lionheart. He is proud of his reputation.'

The other man nodded uncertainly. 'When I was first told what you wanted,' he said, 'I was told that it was Francis Bacon who needed these things. I am unhappy to hear of his fall from grace. I have been asked to tell you that the College does not want you to take risks. I wish you would leave this gift with me, to be destroyed.'

'Destroyed! Why, man, you've risked your life to bring them here! In any case, it is not for you to guess what the College may want of me. I know that better than anyone *you* may have seen in London.'

The stout man shook his head. 'Forgive me if I appear to doubt you, sir,' he said, 'but I have seen one gentleman who is your friend. He is anxious, sir, most anxious for your welfare.'

'My friends,' Edmund replied, 'are sometimes over-careful.' His voice was stern, and he stared down into the smaller man's eyes, forbidding further disagreement.

The stout man nodded again. It was a gesture of resignation, a submission to authority. He pulled something from beneath a chair. It was a large box, clad in leather. A row of small holes was set in the side, and there was a sound of scratching from within which testified to the presence of living creatures.

'You did exactly as you were instructed?' asked Edmund.

The other nodded. 'Each time two died, two others were put in to feed upon the corpses. Because of this, and the business of feeding the python, there was hardly a . . . '

He broke off suddenly as Edmund reached out to the box, putting his hand upon the mechanician's arm. 'Don't open it, sir, I beg you! Not here!'

'There is nothing to fear,' Edmund assured him.

'You haven't been in Africa, sir, as I have. Believe me, *everyone* is afraid. They say that vampires are dying too, though there were no vampires to be found in the places we visited. Africa is a strange and frightful continent, Master Cordery. No man alive could go there and return believing that there is nothing to fear.'

'I know,' said Edmund, distractedly. ''Tis a different world, where all is upside-down, where the men are black and the vampires are not princes. I have told you what I think of your bravery; spare me, I beg you, your traveller's tales.' He shook off the older man's restraining hand, and undid the straps which sealed the box. He lifted the lid, but not far – just enough to let the light in, and to let him see what was inside.

The box contained two big black rats. They cowered from the light. Edmund shut the lid again, and fastened the straps.

'It's not my place, sir,' said the stout man hesitantly, 'but I really do not think that you properly understand what you have there. I've been in Corunna, and Marseilles. They remember other plagues in those cities, and all the horror stories are emerging again to haunt them. Sir, if any such thing ever came to London . . .'

Edmund tested the weight of the box, and found it light enough to give him no difficulty. 'It is not your concern,' he said. 'Your task now is to forget everything that has happened. I will communicate with your masters. The matter is in my hands.'

'Forgive me,' said the other, 'but I must say this: there is naught to be gained from destroying vampires, if we must destroy ourselves too. It is a tragedy too terrible to contemplate that half the common men of Europe might be wiped out, as the result of an intemperate attack upon our oppressors.'

Edmund stared at the stout man, angrily. 'You talk too much,' he said. 'Indeed, you talk a deal too much.'

'I beg your pardon, sir.' He cowered away from Edmund's anger, but he was obviously sincere in his anxiety.

Edmund hesitated for a moment, wondering whether to reassure the messenger with a fuller explanation, but he had learned long ago that where this kind of business was concerned, it was best to say as little as possible. There was no way of knowing when this man would next be required to speak of this affair, or to whom, or with what consequence. In any case, a fuller explanation was by no means certain to make the messenger rest any easier with his conscience or his fear.

The mechanician took up the box. The rats stirred inside, scrabbling with their small clawed feet. With his free hand, Edmund made the sign of the cross again.

'God go with you,' said the messenger, with urgent sincerity.

'And with thy spirit,' replied Edmund, dully. He left without pausing to exchange a ritual farewell with the old woman who lived in the house.

He walked quickly through the pitch-dark streets, with his free hand still resting on the hilt of his sword. This time, he walked across Tower Bridge, though he knew that there would be men there waiting for him. They would not dare to challenge him, but would simply follow him back to the entrance of the White Tower, and then, when he left it again, to his apartments near the Mount. They would report to the Lord Lieutenant that he had brought a box with him, but if men were sent to search for it in the hope of learning what it contained, they would not find it.

It was by Traitors' Gate that he gained entry to the Tower. He was as certain as he could be that whatever transpired during the next few days, it would not be by the same gate that he would quit the citadel, however much he deserved the appellation which it bore. His aim was to carry betrayal to such unprecedented lengths that he would place himself beyond the reach of the vampires' ordinary processes of vengeance.

FOUR

When Monday came Edmund and Noell made their way to the Lady Carmilla's chambers, which were in the gallery near to the Salt Tower.

Noell had never been in such an apartment before, and it was a great source of wonder to him. Edmund watched the boy's reactions to the carpets, the wall-hangings, the mirrors and the ornaments, and could not help but recall the first time he had entered the chamber himself. Nothing had changed here, and the rooms were full of provocations to stir his faded memories.

Younger vampires tended to change their surroundings often, addicted to novelty, as if they feared their own changelessness. The Lady Carmilla had long since passed beyond this phase. She had grown accustomed to changelessness, and had transcended the attitude to the world which permitted boredom. She had adapted herself to a new aesthetics of existence, whereby her private space participated in her own eternal sameness. Innovation was confined to tightly-controlled areas of her life, exemplified by the irregular shifting of her erotic affections from one lover to another.

The sumptuousness of the lady's table was a further source of astonishment to Noell. The knives and spoons which he normally used were silvered pewter, though the forks which his father had lately bought were solid silver, because imitations were not yet being made. Here, all the implements were silver, including the salt-cellars and casters. Instead of earthenware drinking vessels there were crystal goblets, and carved decanters for the wines. The oval gateleg table was covered by a fine linen cloth woven with a damask design. The one thing that Carmilla Bourdillon's table had in common with Edmund Cordery's was the glazed pottery made in Southwark, the plates and bowls being decorated with blue brushwork, representing entwined flowers.

The lavishness of provision for just three diners was something which obviously took Noell aback, and Edmund could see that his son was confused. At home, the boy would be served with his meal and expected to eat it, but here the table was set with a number of diverse dishes, from which he must choose. In the first course were included two soups, roast beef and pork, and a sallet. Edmund caught his son's eye, and let him watch while he took what he needed, so that the boy could copy him.

Although the constant movement of the lady's servants seemed to bother Noell a little, Edmund was pleased to see that the boy settled down quickly. When the second course was set out, with game and sweetmeats, he helped himself more casually.

Edmund had been very careful in preparing his dress for this occasion, fetching from his closet finery which he had not put on for many years. On official occasions he was always concerned to play the part of the mechanician, and dressed in order to sustain that appearance. He never appeared as a courtier, always as a functionary. Now, he was reverting to a role which Noell had never seen him play, and though the boy had no idea of the subtleties of his father's part, he clearly understood something of what was going on; he had earlier complained, in acid fashion, about the dull and plain way in which his father required *him* to dress. Edmund had dismissed his objections in a peremptory manner.

Edmund ate and drank sparingly, and was pleased to see that Noell did likewise, obeying his father's instructions despite the obvious temptations of the lavish provision.

When the second course was done with, the servants brought in more sweet things, including a sack posset flavoured with mace and cinnamon.

'Do you like it?' she asked, when Edmund took his first taste. 'I had the recipe from one who is a friend of yours: Kenelm Digby.'

Edmund raised his eyebrows. Kenelm Digby was only a few years older than Noell. He *was* a friend of Edmund's, but he was also a member of the Invisible College, and it was disturbing to hear his name mentioned. Kenelm was the son of Sir Everard Digby, who had been executed in 1606 for his small part in hatching the Gunpowder Plot – a bold but foolhardy attempt to destroy Prince Richard.

'I did not know that he had visited the court,' said Edmund, politely, though it was a lie. He wondered – as she may have intended him to wonder – whether the Lady Carmilla planned to make Digby her next favourite.

'The posset is excellent,' he assured her, pushing it to one side, 'but I have little appetite left, after so remarkable a meal.'

For a while the lady was content to exchange ordinary courtesies with her guests, but she came quickly enough to the real business of the evening.

'Our beloved Prince Richard,' she told Edmund, 'is quite enraptured by your clever device. He finds it most interesting.'

'Then I am pleased to make him a gift of it,' Edmund replied. 'And I would be pleased to make another, as a gift for your ladyship.'

'That is not my desire,' she said coolly. 'In fact, I have other matters in mind. The prince and the Lord Lieutenant have discussed certain tasks which you might profitably carry out. Instructions will be communicated to you in due time, I have no doubt.'

Edmund bowed in acknowledgement.

'The ladies of the court were pleased with the drawings which I showed to them,' said Carmilla, turning to look at Noell. 'You have a good hand. Would you like to be a portrait painter, and have pretty vampires to copy?'

'I think I would rather be a mechanician,' replied Noell.

'Of course,' she replied. 'After all, you are very like your father. Is he not, Edmund?'

'He has a way to grow, yet,' replied the mechanician.

The lady again addressed herself to Noell. 'Even Richard marvelled at the thought that a cupful of Thames water might contain thousands of tiny living creatures. Do you think that our bodies, too, might be the habitation of countless invisible insects?'

Noell opened his mouth to reply, because the question had been so obviously directed to him, but Edmund interrupted smoothly. 'There are creatures which may live upon our skin,' he said, 'and worms within us. We are told that the macrocosm reproduces in essence the microcosm of human being; perhaps there is a smaller microcosm within us, where our natures are reproduced again, incalculably small. The Earl of Northumberland has ideas upon this subject, I believe, and I have read . . . '

'I have heard, Master Cordery,' she cut in, 'that the illnesses which afflict common men might be carried from person to person by means of such tiny creatures.'

'The idea that diseases were carried from one person to another by tiny seeds is an old one,' Edmund replied, 'but I do not know how such seeds might be recognised, and I think it very unlikely that the creatures we have seen in river-water could possibly be of that kind. Galen tells us . . . '

'It is a disquieting thought,' she said, interrupting again, 'that our bodies might be inhabited by creatures of which we can know nothing, and that every breath we take might be carrying into us the seeds of change, too small to be seen or tasted. It makes me feel uneasy.'

'There is no need,' Edmund protested. 'Seeds of corruptibility take easy root in common flesh, but yours is inviolate.'

'You know that is not so, Master Cordery,' she said levelly. 'You have seen me ill.'

'It was a pox which killed many common men, my lady, yet it gave to you no more than a mild fever.'

'There are reports from the captains of Dutch ships, and from the master of the *Freemartin*, that the plague which has been raging in Africa has now reached the southern regions of the Imperium of Gaul. It is said that this plague makes little distinction between common man and vampire.'

'Rumours, my lady,' said Edmund, soothingly. 'You know how news becomes blacker as it travels. I doubt that this disease is half as bad as it is painted by travellers' tales.'

The Lady Carmilla turned again to Noell, and this time addressed him by name so that there could be no opportunity for Edmund to usurp the privilege of answering her. 'Are you afraid of me, Noell?' she asked.

The boy was startled, and stumbled slightly over his denial.

'You must not lie to me,' she told him. 'You are afraid of me, because I am a vampire. Master Edmund Cordery is a sceptic, and must have told you that vampires are not such marvellous magicians as some believe. But he must also have told you that a vampire lady can do you harm if she wills it. Would you like to be a vampire yourself, Noell?'

Noell hesitated before replying, but said: 'Yes, I think so.'

'Of course you would,' she purred. 'All humans would become vampires if they could, no matter how they might pretend when they bend their knee in church and thank God for making them what they are. And men can become vampires; immortality is within our gift. Thus, we have always enjoyed the loyalty and devotion of the greater number of our common subjects. We have rewarded that devotion in fair measure. Few have joined our ranks, but many have enjoyed the fruits of our favours. Even the nobles among the common men, which you call in England earls and baronets, have much to thank us for, because we are always generous to those we love.'

'I have told him the same thing, my lady,' Edmund assured her.

'I could not doubt it,' said the Lady Carmilla. 'And yet, had I asked you whether you earnestly desired to be a vampire, you would not have said yes. Am I correct?'

'I am content with my station, my lady,' said Edmund. 'It is all that I have desired. I am not nobly born, even among the common folk.'

'Of course,' she said. 'Your first delight was always to shape things with your hands, to work with metal and with fire, to make new things, and learn all you could of the mechanical arts. You have done well, Edmund, and I am sure that you have sung our praises to your son, and told him what excellent masters we are.

'Have you explained to him how the vampire princes rescued Europe from a Dark Age, and that as long as vampires rule, barbarism will always be held in check? No doubt you have told him, rightly, that our rule has not always been kind, and that we tolerate no defiance, but that we are just as well as hard. It would have been far worse, would it not, for Gaul to remain subject to those terrible mad emperors of Rome?'

'I fear, my lady, that my duties have made it difficult for me to supervise my son's education,' replied Edmund, 'but he has had the best tutors in the court to teach him Latin and Greek, and rhetoric and history.'

'And I am sure that he learnt his lessons well,' said Carmilla, turning again to face Noell. 'Even so,' she said, softly, 'there are men who would upset our rule, and destroy us – did you know that?'

Noell did not know how to reply to this, and simply waited for her to continue. She seemed a little impatient with his gracelessness, and Edmund deliberately let the awkward pause go on. He had seen that his interruptions would not dissuade her. Perhaps, he thought, there was a certain advantage in allowing Noell to make a poor impression.

'There is an organization of rebels,' the lady went on, 'ambitious to discover the mysterious way by which vampires are made. They put about the idea that they would make all men immortal, if only they could discover how it might be done, but this is a lie, and foolish. The members of this secret society seek power for themselves.'

The vampire lady paused to ask for a new bottle of wine. Her gaze wandered back and forth between the gauche youth and his self-assured father.

'The loyalty of your family is, of course, beyond question,' she eventually continued. 'No one understands the workings of society better than a mechanician, who knows how forces must be balanced, and how the different parts of a machine of state must interlock and support one another. Master Cordery knows how the cleverness of rulers resembles the cleverness of clockmakers, do you not, Edmund?'

'Indeed I do, my lady,' replied Edmund.

'There might be a way,' she said, in a strangely distant tone, 'that a good mechanician might earn a conversion to vampirism.'

Edmund was wise enough not to interpret this as an offer or a promise. He accepted a measure of the new wine, and said: 'My lady, there are matters which it would be as well for us to discuss in private. May I send my son to his room?'

The Lady Carmilla's eyes narrowed a little, but there was hardly any expression in her finely-etched features. Edmund held his breath, knowing that he was trying to force a decision upon her that she had not intended to make so soon.

'The poor boy has not quite finished his wine,' she said.

Edmund did not argue. She clearly did not want the boy to go yet.

'Why do you think, Noell,' she said, 'that so many common men are opposed to our rule?'

Edmund looked quickly at Noell, and saw that he was flustered. He wanted to deflect the Lady Carmilla's attention away from this perverse interrogation, but had already found that he could not do it with polite interventions. He wondered whether she was using the boy to provoke him, or whether she was simply indulging herself in cruel playfulness. She was capable of casual cruelty. None knew that better than he.

'Noell cannot know these things,' he said, his voice now sharper and more insistent. 'May I be allowed to make the explanation?'

She raised her eyes, as though in defeat. 'Very well,' she said, pretending displeasure.

'Common men,' said Edmund, 'believe vampires to be very cruel. They know that vampires are themselves almost immune from pain – that a vampire can become quite indifferent to pain, by an effort of will. They cannot help but be envious of this immunity, when tortures of every horrible kind are prescribed as punishments by law. They see men cast into dark and filthy dungeons, shackled and pinned. They see men flogged. They see hands struck off, and the stumps dipped in boiling pitch. They may not see prisoners stretched on the rack, or broken by the strappado, or torn with pincers, but they know that these things happen in the crypts beneath this very building. They may see executions on Tower Hill, and at Tyburn, if they have the stomach for it.

'You spoke earlier of Kenelm Digby, and whether you intended to or not, you reminded me what happened to his father, whose part in the plot against the prince was but a little one. He and three others, if you will recall, my lady, were lashed to hurdles and dragged by horses a full mile to the scaffold in St. Paul's churchyard, through streets crowded with onlookers. He was sorely bruised, and cut, and smeared with all manner of filth. No sooner had Sir Everard climbed the ladder, my lady, than Richard's loyal executioner cut the tightened rope by which he hung, so that he had not even time to become unconscious, let alone to choke to death. Then he was dragged, still bound, to the block, where he was castrated, and his belly cut so that the entrails could be drawn out. Then he was quartered, and his heart cut out to show to the crowd.

'I do not believe, as some have said, that when the executioner declared him an enemy of his own people, Sir Everard's dead lips pronounced the words "Thou liest!" but I know that he was a good man, who did not deserve to die thus because he gave unknowing succour to rebels.

'Common men, my lady, believe that such things could not happen, were they ruled by their own kind. Oh, they have heard of Nero and the other mad Romans, but they cannot credit that common men of

today, who know the meaning of pain, could subject their fellow men
to such ordeals. Christian men have little sympathy for the heathen
Turks, but they are sickened by tales of what the Walachian warlord
Vlad the Impaler did to his prisoners when he recaptured Byzantium.
When our own Richard fought the Saracens, and when Charlemagne
made treaty with Haroun al Raschid, things went differently, but these
days, which should have become less cruel, have instead become
blacker. Alleged Gregorian heretics burn daily throughout Gaul, and
when so many men are consigned to the fire, how can others be blamed
for wondering whether vampires might indeed be demons?

'That, my lady, is why so many common men detest you.'

Edmund glanced at Noell, then, and saw that his son wore an
expression of horror, fearful for the fate of a man who could say such
things to a vampire's face. But the Lady Carmilla was not horrified at
all. In fact, she laughed aloud, in apparent delight. 'Oh Edmund,' she
said, 'I had forgotten what it is to dispute with an honest man!'

'But father,' said Noell, 'you only describe what other men might
think, do you not?

'My lady knows,' said Edmund, gently, 'that I am no Gregorian. I
know that she is no demon in disguise. But she also knows that I pity
those who must burn to death for mere foolishness, and all those who
are hurt only for the sake of hurting them. I would that the world were
a kinder place, and I understand why some men think that it never can
be, while those who reign over us have no proper understanding of
that thing which truly rules all our lives.'

'Which thing is that?' asked Carmilla, no longer laughing.

'Fear,' my lady, said Edmund. 'Only fear. Fear of death itself, but
chiefly fear of pain. I think we could all bear to die, even though our
masters do not. But men find it hard to suffer pain, in the knowledge
that those who inflict such punishment could never be thus punished
in their turn.'

'We punish vampires who are guilty of crimes,' said Carmilla, flatly.

'Oh yes. You kill them, in the ingenious ways by which vampires
must be killed. But you do not make them suffer pain, because you
cannot. All of your kind are indifferent to pain, unless you choose to
feel it. Is that not so?'

'It is so,' she conceded. 'But will you tell me, Edmund, whether the
greater number of men are any happier in those lands where they are
ruled by common lords? You take leave to pity the Turks, but do
you not also pity those who were their victims when they ravaged
Byzantium? Is there no pain in the world of the Arabs, who likewise
cut off the hands of thieves, and execute murderers, and devise cruel
tortures – and keep slaves besides! There are no slaves in Gaul, save
only for felons and Mohammedans who serve as oarsmen in the galleys.'

'You are right, my lady,' said Edmund, 'to remind me that savages are savage. I have no doubt that matters in the heart of Africa stand as ill, though if what is said can be believed, common men may there rule over vampires. But the people of Gaul are Christians, who have heard that they must love one another, and you cannot blame those poor followers of Jesus who think the vampire princes have turned an uncaring ear to that message. They believe that kings who were common men, and understood pain, and were Christians besides, could never do the things which vampire princes do. Perhaps they are wrong, but they believe it.'

'And do you think that they might succeed in taking our place?' she asked. There was a sharper edge to her voice now.

'I think they might, my lady. Once, all the vampires of Europe were united by the cause of conquest, which took them far into the northern nations, extending the Imperium of Gaul to Denmark and these British isles, and taking Walachia's boundaries deep into Russia. Afterwards, the vampires of Gaul and Walachia were united by the threat of a common foe: the Turks. But the Turks are chastened now, and have retreated from Byzantium. Now is the time when the vampire-led nations will develop their own rivalries – and an empire divided is an empire which one day must fall.'

'By your own account,' she replied, coldly, 'the vampire race can never lack for a *common* enemy.'

Edmund smiled, and acknowledged the point by raising his wine-glass in salute. Then he glanced, briefly, at Noell, before trying to measure the mood to which the argument had brought the lady.

'I think my son has had wine enough, my lady,' he said. 'I will send him away, if you will permit. There is a matter I would discuss with you in private.'

Carmilla studied him for a few seconds, then waved a languid hand to signal her consent. Noell came quickly to his feet, and took an awkward leave, bowing and blushing. Edmund watched the boy go quite calmly, reacting not at all to Noell's last apologetic glance in his direction. Edmund knew that Noell would carry out his instructions, and dared not risk suspicion by any hint of an untoward farewell.

When Noell had gone the Lady Carmilla rose from her seat and went from the dining room into an inner chamber. Edmund followed her.

'Thou art presumptuous, Master Cordery,' she told him. He marked the change in the manner of address, and knew that the game was all but won.

'I was carried away, my Lady. There are too many memories here.'

'The boy is mine,' she said, 'if I so choose.'

Edmund bowed, but said nothing.

'And wilt thou be jealous of him?'

'Yes my lady,' said Edmund. 'I will. But I grow ever older, while he must take his turn to become a man such as I once was; and as for thee . . . why, the time will be no different, but just the same.'

'I did not ask thee here tonight to make love to thee. Nor was it my intention to begin the seduction of your son. This matter which thou wouldst discuss with me – does it concern science or treason?'

'Science, my lady. As you have said yourself, my loyalty is not in question.'

Carmilla stretched out upon a sofa, and indicated that Edmund should take a chair nearby. This was the antechamber to her bedroom, and the air was sweet with the odour of fine perfume.

'Speak,' she bade him.

'I believe that Richard is anxious as to what my little device might reveal,' he said. 'But I think you know well enough that a discovery once made is likely to be made again and cannot properly be unmade. Do you want my advice, Lady Carmilla?' He had changed deliberately to the less intimate form of address, and was perversely pleased to observe that she did not seem to like it.

'Do you have advice to offer, Edmund?'

'I do. Do not try to control the things that are happening in Gaul by terror and persecution. If your rule is as unkind as it has been in the past, you may open the way to destruction. Should the vampires of Grand Normandy be prepared to concede power gradually to a parliament of commoners, they might show the way to a better world; but if instead they strike out, their enemies will surely strike back.'

The vampire lady leaned back her head, looking at the ceiling. She contrived a small laugh. 'I cannot take advice such as that to Prince Lionheart,' she told him. 'He would not hear it. He rules, in his own estimation, by divine right, according to his code of honour. He is certain that the common people acknowledge the propriety of his claims.'

'I thought as much, my Lady,' Edmund replied, smoothly. 'But I had to say what was in my mind.'

'Common men have their own immortality,' she complained. 'The Church promises it, and you all affirm it. Your faith tells you that you must not covet the immortality which is ours, and we do no more than agree with you when we guard it so jealously. You must look to Christ for salvation. I think you understand that we could not convert the whole world if we wanted to. Our magic is such that it must be used sparingly. Are you distressed because it has not been offered to you? Are you jealous? Would you become our enemy because you cannot become our kin?'

'Prince Richard has nothing to fear from me, my lady,' he lied. Then he added, not quite sure whether it was a lie or not: 'I loved thee faithfully. I still do.'

She sat up straight, and reached out a hand as though to stroke his cheek, but he was too far away for her to reach.

'That is what I told Richard,' she said, 'when he said to me that thou wert a traitor. I said to him that I could test thy loyalty more keenly in my chambers than his officers in theirs. I do not think thou couldst delude me, Edmund.'

She rose to her feet, and came to him, and took his face between her hands.

'By morning,' she told him, gently, 'I will know whether or not thou art a traitor.'

'That thou wilt,' he assured her.

FIVE

He woke before her, his mouth dry and his forehead burning. He was not sweating; indeed, he was possessed by a feeling of desiccation, as though the moisture was being squeezed from his flesh. His head was aching and the light of the morning sun, which streamed through the unshuttered window, hurt his eyes.

He pulled himself up to a half-sitting position, pushing the coverlet back from his bare chest.

So soon! he thought. He had not expected to be consumed so quickly, but he was surprised to find that his reaction was one of relief rather than fear or regret. He had difficulty collecting his thoughts, and was perversely glad to accept that he did not need to do so.

He looked down at the cuts which she had made on his breast with her little silver knife; they were raw and red, and made a strange contrast with the faded scars whose criss-cross pattern told a story of unforgotten passions. He touched the new wounds gently with his fingers, and winced at the fiery pain.

I suffer, he thought, *but there is virtue in suffering which those who cannot suffer cannot know. Who feels no pain can feel no pity.*

He pitied his sleeping lover, and was proud to do it. 'We are martyrs both,' he whispered, very softly. 'Martyrs both.'

She woke up then, and saw him inspecting the marks.

'Hast thou missed the knife?' she asked sleepily. 'Wert thou hungry for its kiss? Thou may'st delight in its caress, for 'twas lovingly done.'

There was no need to lie now, and there was a delicious sense of freedom in that knowledge. There was a joy in being able to face her, at last, quite naked in his thoughts, and unashamed. 'Yes, my Lady,' he said, faintly. 'I had missed the knife. Its touch rekindled flames in my soul, where I had thought to find mere embers.'

She had closed her eyes again, to allow herself to wake slowly. She laughed. 'It is pleasant, sometimes, to return to forsaken pastures. Thou canst have no notion how a particular taste may stir congenial memories. I am glad to have seen thee again, in this way. I had grown quite used to thee as a grey mechanician. But now . . . the flush of youth is upon thy countenance.'

He laughed, as lightly as she, but the laugh turned to a cough and something in the sound alarmed her. She opened her eyes and raised her head, turning to face him.

'Why, Edmund,' she said, 'thou'rt as hot as fire!'

She reached out to touch his cheek, and snatched her hand away again when she found it unexpectedly strange and dry. A blush of confusion spread across her own silken features, removing just for an instant that magical glamour which marked her for what she was.

He took her hand, and held it, looking steadily into her eyes.

'Edmund,' she said, softly. 'What hast thou done?'

'I cannot be sure what will come of it,' he said, 'and I do not think that I will live to find out whether I have succeeded, but I have tried to kill thee, my Lady.'

He was pleased by the way her mouth gaped in astonishment. He watched disbelief and anxiety mingle in her expression, as though fighting for control of her features. She did not call out for help.

'This is nonsense,' she whispered.

'Perhaps,' he admitted. 'Perhaps it was also nonsense which we talked last evening. Nonsense about treason. Thou knowest only too well that it was a doomed man which thou took to thy bed. Why didst ask me to make the microscope, my Lady, when to make me a party to such a secret was to sign my death warrant?'

'Oh, Edmund,' she said, with a sigh. 'Thou couldst not think that it was I who decided it. I have tried to protect thee from the Lord Lieutenant's fears and suspicions. It was because I was once thy protector that I was made to bear the message. What hast thou done, my poor traitor?'

He began to reply, but the words turned into a fit of coughing.

She sat upright, wrenching her hand away from his enfeebled grip, and looked down at him as he sank back upon the pillow.

'For the love of God!' she cried, as fearfully as any true believer. 'It is the plague: the plague out of Africa!'

He tried to answer, wishing to congratulate her on her lucky guess, but could only nod his head as he fought for breath.

'But there was no sign of any sickness on the *Freemartin*,' she protested. 'They would have held the ship by the Essex coast, but there was no trace of plague among her crew.'

'The disease kills men too quickly,' said Edmund, in a shallow whisper. 'But animals can carry it in their blood for much longer, before they die.'

'You cannot know this!'

Edmund managed a small laugh. 'My lady,' he said, 'I am a member of that Fraternity which interests itself in everything which might kill a vampire. This information came to us in good time for us to arrange delivery of other animals, as well as those which brave Prince Richard demanded as symbols of his valour. When we asked for them, we had not in mind the means of using them which I have employed, but more recent events . . .' Again he was forced to stop, unable to draw sufficient breath to sustain the thin whisper.

The Lady Carmilla put her hand to her throat, swallowing as if she expected to feel evidence already of her infection.

'Thou wouldst destroy me, Edmund?' she asked, as though she genuinely found it difficult to believe.

'I would destroy you all,' he told her. 'I would bring disaster, turn the world upside down, to end your rule . . . we will not allow you to stamp out learning itself to preserve your cruel empire. Order must be fought with chaos, and chaos is come among you, my lady, ne'er to be subdued again. Where'er your kind will sup, 'twill be the blood of martyrs that is spilt. With all my heart, I curse your kind . . . despite that I have loved thee, lady mine.'

When she tried to rise from the bed he reached out to restrain her, and though there was no power left in him, she allowed herself to be checked. The coverlet fell away from her, to expose her breasts as she sat upright. Her skin had the polished brightness of a marble statue, such as those giants among common men, the Greeks, once made with such consummate artistry.

'The boy dies for this, Master Cordery,' she said. 'His mother too.'

'They are gone,' he told her. 'Noell went directly from your table to the custody of the society which I serve. By now, they are beyond your reach. Richard will never find them, for the true extent of his realm is less than the precincts of this castle. Common men may easily hide among common men, and you cannot find what you cannot truly see.'

She stared at him, and now he could see the beginnings of hate and fear in her stare. 'You came here last night to bring me poisoned blood,' she said. 'In the hope that this new disease might kill even me, you condemned yourself to death. What did you do, Edmund?'

He reached out again to touch her arm, and was pleased to see her flinch and draw away, because he had become dreadful in her eyes.

'Only vampires live forever,' he told her hoarsely. 'But anyone may drink blood, if they've the stomach for it. I took full measure from my two sick rats, and I pray to God that the seed of this fever is raging in my blood, and in my semen too. You have received full measure, my lady . . . and you are in God's hands now like any common mortal. I cannot know for sure whether you will catch the plague, or whether it will kill you, but this unbeliever is not ashamed to pray. Perhaps you might pray too, my lady, so that we may know how the Lord prefers one unbeliever to another.'

She looked down at him, her face becoming masklike in its steadiness, so that she was indeed like a statue of some unkind goddess.

'I trusted thee once,' she whispered, 'and I might have made Richard trust thee now, had thou not chosen to be guilty. Thou couldst have become a vampire. We might have shared the centuries; lovers forever.'

This was dissimulation, and they both knew it. Vampires did not love vampires. They could not; time, it seemed, killed that kind of love. Only mortal blood could feed a vampire, and a vampire must have that food. Edmund could not pretend to know why these things were true, but he did not doubt that they were. He had been Carmilla Bourdillon's lover, and then had ceased to be, and had grown older for so many years that now she remembered him as much in his son as in himself. Her promises were hollow, and she must have realised as he looked at her that she could not even taunt him with them. There was not a pang of regret to be wrung from him.

From beside the bed she took up the small silver knife which she had used to let his blood. She held it now as if it were a dagger, not a delicate instrument to be plied with care and love.

'I thought that thou still loved me,' she told him.

That at least, he thought, might be true.

He actually put his head further back, to expose his throat to the expected thrust. He wanted her to strike him – angrily, brutally, passionately. He had nothing more to say.

He knew that his motives had been mixed, and that he genuinely did not know whether it was merely loyalty to his cause which had made him submit to this extraordinary experiment, or whether there was in what he had done a fury against this perfect lady, who had outgrown his love.

It did not matter, now.

She cut his throat, and he watched her for a few long seconds while she stared at the blood which gushed precipitately from the wound.

I was right, he thought. *No pity at all.*

But then he saw her put stained fingers to her lips, knowing what she knew . . . and he realised that after her own particular fashion, she did still love him.

PART TWO

The Shadow of Eternity

'Then Jesus said unto them, Verily, verily, I say unto you, Except ye eat the flesh of the Son of man, and drink his blood, ye have no life in you.

'Whoso eateth my flesh, and drinketh my blood, hath eternal life; and I will raise him up at the last day.

'For my flesh is meat indeed, and my blood is drink indeed.

'He that eateth my flesh, and drinketh my blood, dwelleth in me, and I in him . . . '

(John 7:53–56)

PROLOGUE

The de-ciphered text of a letter received by Sir Kenelm Digby at Gayhurst in the summer of 1625.

Cardigan Abbey, June 1625

My friend,

I am not yet accustomed to the cipher with which you have entrusted me, but I shall not allow myself to be content with a short missive on that account. If this is the language of the Invisible College, then I am ardent to master it, for my one mission is to serve that College well. It is what my father hoped for me, and it is what I now must hope for myself.

I have found Cardigan very different from the other places where I have stayed. It seems hardly to be a part of the same realm as London, and one could easily believe that it lay altogether beyond the bounds of the Imperium of Gaul. To hear the ordinary folk talk – when they condescend to use the English which I can understand – one might think that this was still Ceredigion, the Kingdom of Elphin, where Taliesin was found. Of course there are no druids any more, nor bards either, but the motto of the Bardic Order is still quoted as if it carried the allegiance of all: Y Gwir yn erbyn y Byd; which means, The Truth against the World.

I suppose there are worse watchwords which a man might adopt.

The monks of the Abbey who are my hosts are certainly no Gregorians, and do not seem to hate the vampires, but they observe a privacy in their faith which all but disowns the authority of Rome – and hence ignores the pronouncements of the Borgia pope. There were Christian churches in Wales, so they say, before Augustine came to Britain to convert the Saxons, and the Saxons once converted then set out to slaughter the Welsh monks in the name of Rome. In a place such as this, a thousand years is not sufficient to wipe out the memory of a grudge; there is little writing here to make old news stale, and the tales passed down by word of mouth from father to son (or from abbot to novice) remain forever fresh in the telling.

I can only judge, from what I have seen here, that the Abbey is not flourishing – though I do not know how much this reflects the independent spirit of the monks. I dare say that if heresy-hunting Dominicans were sent here they might find cause for displeasure, but I cannot imagine that these amiable and pious men would bring down any reasonable wrath upon themselves. I think the lack of novices may have more to do with the general apostasy which has been rotting the faith ever since the vampires turned it upside-down, and made it plain to all Christendom that mere power is the governor of doctrine.

Whatever the reason, there are but twenty monks here, who employ a single bailiff to look after their business. One of the brothers must serve as almoner, and though he has three boys to help him in his work it does not seem to me that any of them is determined to take Holy Orders himself. There are no lay workmen in the Abbey, not even in the brewery, and the monks cultivate very little land of their own, leasing the rest of their small estate to tenant farmers. They have few visitors to put a claim on their charity, though they help a good many of the poor men and women of the town – which is called Aberteifi by all its citizens, save for the petty nobles and soldiers who live in the castle.

I pay for my keep here by performing certain duties within the monastery. I had initially hoped to make some contribution by the mechanical arts which I had begun to learn as my father's apprentice, but the monks have some tool-making skill themselves, and have no use for those pumps and turning-machines which were my father's pride and joy. The only trick which I have been able to put to use here is to show the monks how to make a weight-driven clockwork jack which will turn the roasting-spit before the kitchen fire, relieving the almoner's boys of the sometimes-painful task of acting as turnspit.

The outcome of this inspiration, has been that I am put to work in the kitchen, helping Brother Martin and Brother Innocent to prepare the prandium *and the* coena *each noon and evening. When the brothers are at vespers I am in sole charge of the kitchen, but by then the day's work is almost done, the bread having been taken from the ovens, and nothing left within but custards in pastry cases. My time is mostly spent in carrying water from the well, or in watching the cauldrons simmer.*

I do most of my studying in the library, which is a plain room but not uncomfortable. The forbidden books are kept in a cellar beneath a hidden trapdoor. I grow weary of my lessons in Latin and Greek, and the study of books which were written before there were vampires in Europe. I want to know my enemy, that I may learn to fight him, but Q insists that I must become a man of learning before I endeavour to set my learning to special use.

Q is a strange person, and I do not understand why my father ordered that I be given into his care. I know that my father was an unbeliever, and it seems remarkable that he should have appointed a monk to be my guardian, even a monk who is more than a little sceptical of certain items of dogma. It is not that I question Q's wisdom, for I am quite ready to believe that he is the wisest man in Gaul, but I cannot quite perceive his position within the Invisible College. He seems so detached and calm, less than fervent in his opposition to vampire rule.

Q is no more a Gregorian than the monks who live here, though he is no more a Roman either. He is a guest here, as am I, and has no special intimacy with our hosts by virtue of his cloth. He is an outsider, respected for his learning, but kept distant. He does not seem to mind this in the least, being a man much wrapped up in his own thoughts, and although he is not a big man

– I outweigh him by at least two stones, now that I am nearly full-grown – I think he is very strong of constitution and character.

I understand, now, why my father kept so much hidden from me. I know that it was to protect me that he would not let me share his secrets until the very end, and would not tutor me in treason. But the result of his carefulness is that I have grown up hardly knowing him at all, and I cannot discover what might have been in his mind when he laid down the instructions which you have faithfully followed. I would far rather be at G—— than here, though I know that if I were I would be inviting danger to your household as well as to mine. The fact that I am now parted from my mother makes things even harder to bear. Of course I am a man now, and no longer a child, but to find myself so utterly removed from all that I have known is a trial. Perhaps it is not right that I should air complaints before you, who lost your own father at a much earlier age; but I cannot help but wish, sometimes, that my father had met a martyrdom as manifest as the one which yours suffered. There is too much that I cannot fathom regarding his life and his motives.

I am anxious for action. I am beginning to think that I was not cut out to be a scholar, and though I know that you combine with ease the arts of the scholar and the skills of the fighting man, I do not know whether I dare try to be a man of so many parts. If it were to come to a choice, I think that I might rather be a swordsman, to pit myself against the vampires in open combat, than a cunning man striving to defeat them by stealth. That is not what my father imagined for me – but did my father know me any better than I knew him? How can I trust that he knew best what path of life I should follow?

I wish that I were not a hunted outlaw, so that I might go my own way, instead of looking to others to hide and take care of me. Sometimes, I look out over the sea, watching the herring-ships, and the fluyts which collect the lead from the nearby mines, and think of taking passage for some alien land, where no one has ever heard my name, there to make a career of adventuring. But you will doubtless think me foolish, and that the child in me is slow to yield to the man.

Even Q sometimes watches the ships with a curious light in his eye, and I have heard him say that the vampires' fear of the sea is one more nail in the coffin of their dying empire. He argues that the big sailing ships which ply the northern seas are marking out a new empire, which the land-loving vampires cannot own. Sometimes he stares westward as if he were looking across the world, to that lost Atlantis which some men believe might still exist on the far shore of the ocean, between Ireland and distant Cathay. The other monks, though, think he is mad to speculate about undiscovered continents, and I believe some of them are not yet reconciled to the belief that the world is round. When they look westward, their dreams are of lost cities and fortresses which are said to have been drowned by the sea in Elphin's time. There are many tales to be heard hereabouts of sea-sprites more beautiful than vampire ladies which haunt such lost estates, sometimes tempting foolish mariners to leap from

the safety of their decks to the merciless embrace of the sea. I have never heard
such sirens calling, though, and I trust that I never will.

But I must not trouble you with my discontents, which can only make you
weary. I hope that in future time I will write you letters with more substance
in them, and more of a cargo of joy. In the meantime, I beg you to see that
my mother is well cared for, and will let her know that I am hale and hearty
in my exile. I do not often pray, for I cannot bring myself to believe that the
prayers of men are anywhere in Heaven heard, but when I do, I pray for you,
and for my mother, and for the deliverance of England. If there is in truth a
God, I am sure that my doubting Him will not prevent His giving just attention
to my pleas.

Fare well.

N

ONE

In the cellar beneath the library of the Benedictine monastery at
Cardigan, Noell Cordery looked up from the book which he had been
studying. He rubbed his tired eyes. Although it was barely four o'clock,
and the summer sun still stood high in the sky, he was forced to read
by candlelight, because the room had no window. Indeed, the cellar
had no official existence; it was where the forbidden books were kept.

At one time, Noell had thought the cellar a fine place, and it had
given him a thrill of excitement to place himself in it, with the stone
concealing the trapdoor set firmly in place. It had seemed then to be a
place gravid with magic – magic as white, of course, as its whited
walls, but magic nevertheless. It had been stimulating to be among so
many fabulous secrets, inscribed on parchment by monkish hands
because they were too precious or too dangerous to be trusted to the
printing press.

Now, Noell had learned to see the room in a different way – less
magical, though arguably no less strange. Now, it seemed to him that
the windowed library up above was the storehouse of the world of the
orthodox Church, of belief lit by official wisdom. In that world were
vampires and common men, alike made by God, alike in adoring God,
each in their own particular way a chosen people. It was a world not
entirely happy, no doubt, but a world fundamentally at peace with
itself; a world reconciled to its order. Here, by contrast, was an underworld, dark and murky, where Gregorians and Gnostics, magicians

and alchemists could deposit their whispering voices and discords. In the world glimpsed in the pages hidden here, vampires were the spawn of the devil and common men helpless victims of their outrage – two races constantly at odds, destined to be at war until the Day of Judgement. This world was by no means peaceful, but was instead a veritable palace of Pandemonium, a riot of painful cries forlornly demanding justice, hearing no answer.

Noell no longer liked to read in the cellar. He could see little risk in removing books to the upper room, which was well-lighted, or even to his quarters in the outer court, beyond the private and sacrosanct bounds of the inner abbey. The existence of the secret room was undoubtedly known to every one of the monks, despite the fact that those not supposed to know would never acknowledge the fact. The monastery had few lay visitors, save for the bailiff who conducted its business affairs, and was rarely required to play host to the peripatetic friars who were the secret police force of the vampire-led College of Cardinals. Cardigan was one of the safest places in the nation – which was one reason why Noell was there – and its rules had come to seem overly protective. To his Benedictine hosts, though, the idea of breaking or bending a rule to take advantage of the leniency of circumstance was unthinkable. Obedience was the very core of their existence, and all rules had for them the same force as *the* rule: the *Regula Benedicti*.

As he watched the candle-flame flickering in the draught from the ventilation-holes, Noell allowed himself to be distracted from his studies, asking himself yet again why his father might have sent him to a place like this, placing him in the care of a priestly scholar like Quintus. He could not answer the question; his father's plan, interrupted by his death, remained unexplained.

He looked back at the book which he had been studying. It was the *Discoverie of Vampyres*, written by the Kentish gentleman Reginald Scot in 1591, following an earlier tract exposing the follies of witchfinding. It was the first substantial treatise on vampirism written in English, and treated with scalding scepticism many popular beliefs regarding the supernatural powers of vampires. It also contained a long speculative essay on the origins of the vampire race. Clearly Scot, a lay scholar who was also an expert in the cultivation of hops, had had access to other forbidden books, including the early editions of that encyclopedia compiled by many hands, *The Vampires of Europe*, and an English translation of Machiavelli's book of cunning advice to tyrants, *The Vampire Prince*.

Why, complained Noell, *could I not have been entrusted to the care and tutelage of a man like Scot? Even if he was a man of words, and not action, he was a man of bold words.*

Pale slanting sunbeams suddenly streamed in above him as the stone which sealed the cellar was drawn back. Guiltily, he bowed his head over the page, as though he were studying it assiduously, trying to give Quintus the impression that nothing in the world mattered to him more than Scot's argument to prove the case that vampirism originated in Africa, not in India as Cornelius Agrippa had asserted.

Quintus had brought him a cup of cool ale, which would no doubt have been very welcome had he been tending the cabbages and kale in the kitchen gardens, sweating in the sunlight. In the cold of the cellar, though, he would far rather have had hot tea.

'The bailiff has gone on his way,' said the monk. 'He brought news from the town. The galleon *Firedrake* limped into the fisherport at Milford Haven two days ago, battered by a great storm off the south of Ireland. She had been chasing the pirate Langoisse, and her captain claims that the pirate's caravel, dismasted and holed, went down off Cape Clear.'

'Langoisse!' exclaimed Noell, then added, dolefully: 'If 'tis true, there will be celebration in Swansea Castle . . . and when the news reaches London, Prince Richard will likely declare a public holiday.'

Langoisse was the hero – or villain – of many a broadside ballad. The romantic version of his life suggested that he had once been a French aristocrat, darling of the court at Versailles, certain one day to be inducted into the True Aristocracy, but that his enemies had conspired to have him cast down, wrongly convicted of treason. Sentenced to the galleys, he had one day struck a whip-man in protest against his brutality. He had been flogged near to death, and had sworn a curse against the entire Imperium of Gaul. Later, he had led a successful mutiny, and used the captured galley as a pirate ship against the merchant shipping of the Mediterranean. The French and Spanish had both sent ships to hunt him, but he captured one of the finest after a great battle, and became master of the seaways.

Noell had heard a different story in London. It was common knowledge in the Tower that the pirate's real name was Villiers. Like Noell, this Villiers had been brought up in the Tower, but had been taken into exile by his mother when his father was imprisoned. He had indeed gone to the court in Versailles, to ask the Emperor Charles to intervene on his father's behalf, but Charles had taken Richard's part in the quarrel. Later, when Richard had visited Charles's court, the emperor had tried unsuccessfully to reconcile the two. Villiers, claiming to have been insulted, had tried to challenge the Prince of Grand Normandy to a duel, though the law made all princes immune to such challenges. Some time after, while living in Paris, Villiers was charged with murder. Though he had been in low company of late, he may have been unjustly accused, perhaps by agents of Richard and perhaps by a vampire lady. In any case, he had gone to the galleys. He had indeed become a mutineer, and had taken his captive galley to Malta, where he had kinsmen who were important men in the Order of St. John –

the Knights Hospitallers. Although the knights of Malta were loyal to the Imperium of Gaul, and had made themselves great heroes in defending Europe against the Turkish fleet in a great siege, they were also known for being somewhat independent of spirit, and made their living by piracy when the need was there.

Sailing with the Maltese privateers, the man now called Langoisse had learned the arts of seamanship, and established a reputation of his own. The greater part of his piratical exploits involved stealing cargoes from unarmed merchantmen – the small galleys which plodded between the Mediterranean ports were no match for sailing ships in terms of speed. Nevertheless, Langoisse had always been enthusiastic to come into the rougher northern waters where he might prey on English ships, and in so doing offer insult to Prince Richard. Noell guessed that a careful count would probably show that this brave buccaneer had attacked far more herring-fishers than carracks, and had not grown greatly rich by his depredations, but the big slow ships of such navies as vampire princes kept could not put a stop to his activities. Their inability to catch him had been elevated into a legend by his own boasting.

Despite knowing this truer account, Noell considered Langoisse to be a hero. He was, after all, a true rebel against the vampire aristocracy of the Imperium of Gaul. He was a free man, who need not and would not bow the knee to blood-supping masters. The vampire empire was extensive, but its security on land contrasted with its fragility at sea, and on the oceans of the world men could fight vampires on almost equal terms, because vampires could drown as well as burn, and a vampire admiral who went down with his ship would surely die.

Because of this, Noell was troubled by Quintus's news. If Langoisse was dead, then Noell had to reckon it a tragedy.

'Perhaps he reached safety,' he said to the monk. 'The pirate must have more friends than enemies in Ireland.'

'Aye,' said Quintus. 'But that was a fearful wind blowing across St. George's channel, as we found when we caught the tail of it ourselves. Dismasted, he would not have been able to steer for Baltimore or Kinsale. On the other hand, the *Firedrake*'s captain has every reason to hope that the caravel went down, if he is not sure. He will not be lightly forgiven if Langoisse has escaped him – the bailiff says that the pirate had earlier taken a vampire lady from the wreck of the *Wanderer*, else he'd not have been caught in the storm at all, but would have run for safe harbour when the wind began to blow.'

'Now *that* would be a fine tale for a broadside, if any printer dared publish it,' said Noell. 'A vampire lady prisoned by a handsome pirate, spirited away to some hot lair in the Canaries, to be wooed or tormented at his whim.'

Of course, no printer could issue such an article legally. The presses in

London operated under the strictest supervision of secular and religious authorities, and the Star Chamber was notoriously sensitive to any direct slander against the aristocracy. Vampires were mentioned by name and by race only in the most favourable terms, even in the plays performed in inn-yards and the lyrics of popular songs – though scurrilous versions of such lyrics were often better known than the true ones. But the eyes of the vampires' agents could not watch every printing press through every hour of every day, and when this rumour reached London, broadsides would appear, as fanciful and as scandalous as their printers cared to make them.

Noell already knew from his years in London how obscene tales of vampires and their human lovers enjoyed wide circulation; he had discovered before coming to Wales that the tale of Edmund Cordery and the Lady Carmilla was becoming well-known, told and told again in the taverns and market-places of Grand Normandy. It had such a glorious end, with Cordery welcoming his own death in order to destroy his lover.

This was one tale of rebellion, though, for which Noell did not care at all, and he would far rather that his father had never been lover to a vampire in the first place, no matter how noble or clever his real intention might have been. Many who had heard the tale were of the opinion that Edmund Cordery had loved the vampire with all his heart and soul, and that his thoughts had turned to murder only after she had rejected him. Even Noell's mother had harboured that suspicion, else she would not have told him, before he set out on his long journey to Cardigan, to disregard completely any such notion.

'Tell me, then,' said Quintus, bringing Noell back from his flight of fancy, 'what you have learned today from Master Scot.'

Noell looked up into the tall monk's gaunt face. Despite its leanness it was not a harsh face. Quintus was one who took the admonitions of St. Benedict very seriously, and lived a genuinely ascetic life, but that had not made him mean. He smiled a good deal, and could be very gentle and patient, though he could also be stern. Lately, he had had more occasions to be stern, as Noell's impatience with his studies had begun to show.

'That he knows very little,' replied Noell, with a slight edge to his voice, 'except that other men know still less.'

Quintus sighed. 'It is a valuable thing,' he said, 'to know where ignorance truly begins. The greatest handicap to the growth of wisdom is not the difficulty of discovering that which we do not know, but the difficulty of forgetting that which we think we know, but is false. Francis Bacon, who was a friend to your father, tells us that there are many idols in the Church of Knowledge, which must be cast down if we are to clear the way to the truth.'

Noell had often sat on Francis Bacon's knee in the days when he was a tiny child. That somehow made it difficult for him to maintain a proper reverence for the philosopher's views.

'The end of scholarship is surely not to debate where it was that vampires first walked upon the earth,' said Noell. 'The true end is to discover a way by which they might be destroyed. If the world is to be made ready for the return of Christ, it must be purged of the minions of Satan.'

Quintus frowned at this reply. He knew that Noell was no Gregorian, nor even a believer, and that his invocation of the name of Christ was entirely for dramatic purposes. Noell realised that he was causing his mentor some pain by trying to use his beliefs to taunt him, but Quintus did not pause for an apology, let alone demand one.

'My son,' he said. 'You cannot properly fight evil unless you first understand evil. That is a truth we have too long neglected. The power of armed might is lessened by ignorance no less than the power of prayer. Satan operates by the permission of God, in order that we may understand what evil is – how could we reject evil and become good if we had no opportunity to understand it?'

'My father said the same,' Noell admitted. 'The vampires rule us first and foremost because they terrify us. We cannot learn to hate them in a level-headed way, unless we know exactly what they are and what they are not. It is good that Scot reduces them, by his argument, to a lesser stature than they have in the fearful imagination. It is no better to think of them as the progeny of Satan than to think of them as the favoured sons of God. Common men they are not, but men they are, and only men – we must learn to hate them as men, and then defeat them.'

Quintus was not entirely happy with this answer, and Noell knew it. He sometimes wondered whether Quintus would have preferred not to hate the vampires at all, remembering Christ's advice that men should love even their enemies. But even Quintus must be at a loss to suggest how the evils of vampire rule might be set aside without the assistance of hate.

'Judgement,' said Quintus, 'must in the end be left to God.'

'Perhaps,' said Noell, 'but for myself, I would rather believe that they who can feel no pain deserve no pity.'

TWO

Noell's bedroom was in the almonry. It had its own separate stair, so that he might come and go without being seen by other lay guests, on the very rare occasions that the abbey played host to such, or by the businessmen who sometimes had dealings there. He did not bother to conceal himself from the poor who came for gifts of food, or from the almoner's boys who helped to dole out such charity, because none among them could possibly know that he was not what he seemed, but he hid from all who might wonder at his presence. For this reason, he was usually alert even while he rested, anxious to catch any noise of hoofbeats on the road, or any commotion in the outer court, and he slept lightly enough that any disturbance of the silence would normally wake him.

In the dark night which followed the night of the great storm, though, Noell was sleeping more soundly than usual, and when he was startled from his slumber he was too confused to know immediately what it was that had disturbed him.

Had there been a cry? Was it one of the almoner's boys whose fearfully raised voice had woken him? Or had it been a dream?

He could not tell; by the time he was fully awake the cry, if cry it was, had been stifled. He lay still for a while, listening, and was almost sure that he had been dreaming when he heard the sudden sound of many footsteps, as though a number of men were hurrying through the precincts of the gatehouse.

Immediately, he sat up in bed. Fearfully, he strained his ears to hear more, and heard steps approaching from the direction of the cloister, which told him that the monks were alert to the presence of strangers. No doubt the abbot would be summoned.

He rose from his pallet, and put on his clothes. The thought uppermost in his mind was that Richard's men had discovered his whereabouts, and had come to capture him. There were, no doubt, a hundred explanations which might account for the noise, but something was wrong. Few guests came to claim their right of shelter at this remote religious house, and they were not inclined to arrive at dead of night.

Noell crept from his room, and began to make his way through the dark corridor to a window, where he could look down into the court, to judge what was afoot.

Before he reached the window, though, he heard a furtive foot upon the outer stair, and knew that someone was coming up as silently as he could. He turned, as quietly as he was able, intending to go to the other stair, but it was too late; he had given himself away. He was seized before he had taken three steps, dragged back from the doorway of his room, and bundled along the passage.

There was light upon the stair, from candles burning low, but it was difficult to turn to look at his captor, because his shirt was held tight at the collar, choking him. His struggles were impotent against his captor's greater strength. He caught a glimpse as he twisted, of a dark and terrifying face, scarred and bearded, which might have been a demon in some nightmarish Dutch painting of Hell. Its most horrible feature was the seeming absence of a nose; there appeared instead to be an ugly patch, like a huge wart.

He was hurried by this monster – who must have been a tall and powerful man to handle him so casually – down the steps, and out into the courtyard.

There was already a great crowd in the open space, some of them hurrying past the brewhouse to the cloister, where laymen did not belong, others guarding the gate, which stood open. There was no doubt that these were laymen, who had no right to go where they were going, but Noell could not tell what might be happening. He was shoved and harried along the pavement, through the arch into the inner precinct. He was not the only one who was subject to such unceremonious treatment, for the three boys who served the almoner were being likewise led, by captors hardly less brutal in appearance than the one which held him, though they were smaller of stature. Their clothes were stained and ragged, and they carried pistols which they clapped to the heads of their prisoners, demanding silence.

Noell found himself set up against the cloister wall, alongside the boys and one of the monks who had come to see what was happening. Then his captor stepped away from him to join others of his band.

Facing the prisoned company was a rank of ruffians who seemed in the half-light as odd and dirty as any Noell had seen in the worst parts of London. All were armed, most with swords and daggers, the great majority of which were drawn. He counted seven, but there had to be more, because they were looking back and forth as if waiting for a fuller gathering, and there was none yet to be seen who took the part of leader. There was a knife-point aimed at Noell's chest from a short distance away, its owner a small, wizened man whose eyes glittered in the near-darkness. The giant who had brought him downstairs had stepped away into the shadows.

More lanterns were brought from the dormitory where the monks slept. The abbot was with them, and Quintus too. Noell's racing heart slowed slightly as these figures of authority approached, though the more the lamplight showed him of the motley crew into whose eager hands he had fallen, the less reassuring he found them. The wizened man was revealed to have an awful toothless grin, and the yellow seams of his face were contorted in an expression of determined fierceness, as though he would dearly love an excuse to use his blade.

It was not until the abbot demanded to know what was going on that Noell saw the leader of the band, which was now revealed to be at least a dozen strong. He was a tall, handsome man with black hair, who carried himself like a gentleman – almost like a vampire – and had not deigned to draw his sword. He seemed much calmer than his fellows, but his expression was grim, his lips seeming tight and bloodless. He was dressed all in black, and his clothes were of good quality, though spoiled by grime and sea-salt.

On either side of this curious captain were his lieutenants, even stranger in kind than he. One of them was the monster who had carried Noell down the stairs, taller than his master, disfigured horribly about the face. It was indeed the case that he had no nose, merely a puckered wound where it had been cut away. His height was emphasized by a coloured turban wound about his head. He was dark-skinned, as Noell imagined a Saracen or a Turk might be; he was certainly no man of Gaul.

On the leader's left-hand side was a figure by no means as fearful, yet all the more unexpected for that. It was a woman in man's clothing, or perhaps a girl, for she looked no older than Noell himself, and a good deal smaller. She was as dark-skinned as the monster, with her long black hair in braids. For a common woman she had exceptionally pure skin, but her brightly-rouged lips were incongruous. She was wielding a pistol in her right hand, a dagger in her left, and raised these weapons in a curiously excited display. Her companions seemed in deadly earnest, but her eyes were alight with excitement, as though this affair were a game which she was fervent to play. And while her companions looked to the approaching monks, she fixed her eyes instead upon Noell, looking him up and down with an eagerness he did not like. This girl was shadowed in her turn by a tiny petticoated servant, surely no more than twelve years old.

When the leader of the invaders began to speak, Noell looked away from the woman, hungry to discover what had brought these ruffians to the abbey.

'We are in urgent need of sanctuary, my lord abbot,' said the tall man, 'and we are hungry enough to think ourselves starving. We have come a long way, and are unused to walking. We beg hospitality, and a measure of kindness.'

'Who are you?' demanded the abbot, fearfully. He had to look up at the invader, being small of stature and rather fat. Noell judged that he lacked the natural authority required to challenge the haughty intruder on equal terms.

'My name,' said the other, with a mock bow, 'is Langoisse.' He was obviously pleased by the audible reaction which this news caused.

'The pirate!' The exclamation came not from the abbot but from several of the brethren.

'A poor sinner,' said Langoisse, languidly, 'forced by injustice to live by thievery, who seeks the charity and protection of Mother Church, and who has brought potential converts to the faith. This' – he indicated the noseless monster – 'is Selim, a Turk, who was a galley-slave with me many years ago; and this' – he pointed to the amazon – 'is Leilah, a Maroc gypsy princess, whose soul stands in desperate need of salvation, though she is gentle of temper and noble in heart.' His ironic tone was lightly contrived, as though he were addressing an audience of ladies in a very different court.

It was Quintus who moved forward now, trying to take control, because he saw that the monks were very frightened, and that the abbot was uncertain what to do.

'There is no need for your men to bare their steel here,' he said. 'Indeed you must have bread, if you are hungry, for it is our Christian duty to provide relief for those in need. No doubt your eventual destination is far away, and you must eat and rest to prepare yourselves.'

Langoisse laughed. He did not immediately reply to Quintus, but sent two of his men across the cloister to the dormitory, telling them to rouse the remaining monks and bring them all to the refectory. Then he sent two others, with orders to search the entire premises bordering the outer court, and then the church, and to bring anyone they found. Then he turned to Quintus and said: 'We are anxious that news of our coming is not carried into the town. No doubt the Englishmen sleep soundly in the castle, and would not like to be disturbed. It may be necessary for us to claim hospitality for several days, and though we have been told that this is a good and safe house, we must be sure that we are secure.'

The pirate turned around, looking back towards the gate. Noell could not see it, but he could hear the wooden bolts being drawn to seal it against the world. Then Langoisse ran his eyes over the line of those stationed against the wall, pausing when he saw Noell, who knew himself to be conspicuous because his dress marked him out as neither monk nor servant.

'Who is this?' he asked, bluntly.

'A lay scholar,' said Quintus, quickly. 'A guest like yourself.'

But another voice spoke up then, and said: 'Master Cordery!'

Noell, astonished to be recognised, turned towards the brewhouse door, where the last of the pirates were now gathering. It was a newcomer who had spoken, and he realised that the intruders had other prisoners. They were bound, and their hands were pinioned behind them, despite the fact that both were skirted. One had her face concealed by a heavy hood, but the other was bare-headed, and it was she who had spoken. She was fair-haired, and seemed just as young as the so-called gypsy princess. Noell recognised her as readily as she had recognised him, and was distressed to see her condition. She was Mary White, the child of a servant in Prince Richard's service, who had grown up in the court at the Tower of London, and had known him there.

Langoisse came quickly to stand in front of him, and now he did draw his sword, to place the point at Noell's throat. 'How does she know you?' he demanded, in an anxious tone.

But before Noell could answer, he saw the pirate's face change, as the name which the girl had spoken touched a chord of familiarity.

'Cordery?' repeated Langoisse. 'Cordery, indeed! A guest here, like myself.' The sword-tip was lowered slightly, and then withdrawn. The pirate put the blade away in its scabbard.

'I am an outlaw,' said Noell, trying with all his might to sound bold, 'like yourself. But the price on my head is a mere thirty guineas, and I think you are held to be worth near seven times as much.'

Langoisse smiled at him. 'As little as that?' he said. 'Richard is too unkind. He knows how much it wounds me when he pretends that my death would be of little interest to him. I think he might remember me better, now, for I have borrowed something from his court which I found aboard the stricken *Wanderer*. The loss of this handmaid's mistress will surely remind the prince what a debt of honour he owes me, and increase the dislike which he has for me.' He took three steps along the pavement, and with a theatrical flourish of his hand he tipped the hood from the face of the second prisoner.

The woman seemed undisturbed by this treatment, and did not flinch from the rough hand. Though the lantern was not near to her, there was no doubting her considerable beauty. Her black hair was very sleek, her features finely-formed. Her polished complexion, utterly without blemish, revealed her for what she was in a world where most common women painted their faces to erase pockmarks and discolourations. Her eyes were almost closed, and it seemed that she was on the brink of collapse, held up by the rough man who gripped her upper arm.

'May I present the vampire lady Cristelle d'Urfé,' said Langoisse. 'Late of the court of Prince Richard, unfortunately interrupted in her journey to Lisbon, by untimely weather and unforeseen circumstance. She is not entirely well.'

The last sentence implied far more than it said. Vampires were rarely made unwell by ordinary sickness or discomfort. Noell guessed that she had been given a drug, perhaps a poison to bring her near to the trance which overtook vampires when they were sorely hurt. That may have been necessary in order to subdue her for what must have been a difficult and dangerous journey.

Noell looked round to see the abbot's reaction. The little man's face seemed quite drained of blood.

'How dare you . . . ?' he began.

Langoisse was quick to interrupt him. 'Bring the devil into a cloister?' he queried. 'But there are no Gregorians here. And if there were, what better place to bring the devil's kin than the Lord's house, where her evil can be countered by your piety? What harm can she do in this holy place?'

Noell realised that this little speech was aimed not so much at the monks, who were all assembling now in the cloister, but at the pirate's own followers. Many of them would be simple men, for whom vampires were the stuff of mystery, possessed of supernatural malefic power. They might well need reassurance that their captain was not leading them to destruction. Yet he might be doing exactly that, for the vampires were ever enthusiastic to punish common men who hurt their own. Langoisse was quite right to say that when Richard found out that a lady of his court had been captured, he would spare no effort to pursue the pirate.

'If you need food,' said Quintus, quickly 'then someone must go to the storehouses, and to the kitchen. Perhaps we should go now to the refectory, where we may talk more comfortably, and let those who must go about their work.'

'Exactly so,' said the pirate. 'But we must make sure that we understand one thing while we are all gathered together, and all must hear what I have to say. If we are betrayed to the Normans, all will die, beginning with the abbot and ending with the least of the boy servants. You know who we are, and you know that we are enough to carry out our threat.'

Noell looked again along the rank of the pirate crew, counting their blades and their pistols. They had no muskets with them, and only one or two carried packs. He guessed that it was by necessity rather than by choice that the band was travelling so light; they must have lost the greater part of their possessions in the gale. Many of the men looked back at him, suspicious or intrigued by the fact that his name was known, and he imagined the kinds of thought that might be stirring in those minds where the name of Cordery had meaning. Outlaw he might be, but he was not like them. He was the son of a vampire-lover who had slaughtered his noble mistress, and tried to welcome a plague to the streets of London. There was no reason why they should like him.

When the whole company began to go indoors, the small man kept the tip of his blade close to Noell's neck. It was as though, in the pirate's reckoning, he required to be watched as carefully and superstitiously as the vampire lady herself. But the gypsy girl carefully fell into step beside him, and he was surprised to see that she regarded him with a more fascinated and kindly eye. It was as though she sought to assure him by her presence that no harm could possibly come to him. She had put her own weapons away.

THREE

W hen morning came, the monastery had already returned to a semblance of normality. The monks were in attendance at matins, consigning themselves to the safety of the Lord's authority with the imperturbable litany of their prayers. The pirates were discreetly quartered, though they kept a watchman at the gate and a lookout in the church tower.

The Lady Cristelle and her servant Mary White had been secured in the cells which were kept, in theory, for the use of penitents. Sometimes, even nowadays, a monk would be ordered to be confined there to expiate some misdemeanour, but the time was long gone when gentlemen who had incurred the wrath of the Church would commission the brothers, in consideration of suitable gifts, to undertake burdensome penances on their behalf. It was a measure of the gradual decline of religious authority that such penances were now very rarely handed down, nor taken altogether seriously when they were. The cells of Cardigan Abbey had seen few occupants these last fifty years, and the monks had been well content to leave them alone. None cried sacrilege, though, when Langoisse decided to redeem the prison from its long disuse.

Everyone had been commanded, by the pirate and the abbot alike, to maintain the appearance of normality. In accordance with this instruction Noell went to the library, but he sat in the larger room, and did not even attempt to work. He wondered whether the visitors knew of the existence of the secret cellar, and concluded that they probably did not. All of a sudden, the documents which had come to seem so tedious regained their aura of mystery and their preciousness. He resolved to protect them, if he needed to and if he could, from the danger of being stolen.

He was not entirely surprised when he was interrupted in his pretence of reading the scriptures by Langoisse, who took a chair nearby.

'I knew of your father, Master Cordery,' he said, in a friendly tone. 'I never met him, but I heard that he was a good and trusted man.' In the daytime, he seemed slightly less handsome; the good light showed up the ageing of his skin, and the oiliness of his hair. He was thirty-five years old or thereabouts, and his cheeks were roughened with old small scars. His eyes, though, were a vivid brown, and very clear. He had a penetrating gaze.

'I am sure that he knew of you,' replied Noell, evenly.

'We have a deal in common, you and I,' said the pirate. 'I spent my own childhood in the Tower, and was similarly exiled. I have some notion of what you must be feeling.'

'We heard that your ship went down off Cape Clear,' Noell told him, not wanting to speak of personal matters. 'Did you know that the *Firedrake* is in Milford Haven?'

'My own ship was long past Carnsore Point before we had to abandon her,' Langoisse replied, 'and the kind wind blew our boat into Cardigan Bay. We came to the bare coast east of here, and made our way across country. It might have been better had we been driven into the Bristol Channel. I could easily gain passage on a ship out of Swansea, but it would be difficult there to avoid an alarm being raised. Now, those who would do me harm need not know that I'm alive until I'm gone, but it may not be so easy to find a shipmaster to take us away.'

'It must be an inconvenience to be a pirate,' observed Noell, 'and yet to have no ship.'

Langoisse laughed, taking no offence. ''Tis not the first time I've lost one,' he said. 'I dare say 'twill not be the last.'

'When they do discover that you're alive, and what you've done, they'll hunt you more ardently than before. The kidnap of a vampire lady is not a crime they'll forgive.'

'Forgive!' Langoisse's voice had more of a snarl than a laugh in it now. 'There is no forgiveness asked. Richard is not forgiven for what he has done to me, nor shall I ever forget what I owe him, and I will not be quieted by fear of the vampires' revenge.'

'But you have placed the good monks in danger by bringing the vampire lady here. They would be blamed enough for sheltering you and your crew, but no one need know about that were you quick enough to leave. The presence of the lady makes this a rather different matter, more difficult to conceal and more likely to invite punishment.'

'I always heard,' said Langoisse, 'that the monks of Cardigan belonged to the True Church. Your presence here would cause them trouble enough, if it were known. I hope to go quietly, and if it should not be so, then the abbot is welcome to tell all questioners that I forced him to help me. I wish no harm to the brothers.'

Noell knew that the monks of Cardigan did indeed think themselves part of the True Church, but whether that was the same True Church that Langoisse meant, he could not tell. For all he knew, Langoisse might be a Gregorian, believing that the vampires were instruments of

Satan, and that the vampire papacy and the Holy Office were parts of the devil's empire. But as he met the pirate's gaze, he thought that he could see the soul of a fellow unbeliever. After all, Langoisse had been high-born among common men, near to becoming a vampire himself.

There was justice, in any case, in what Langoisse said. Noell's presence here was proof enough that the abbot's loyalty was not to the Normans. If he ever were to be found, the abbot would claim, under the spur of necessity, that the monks had not known his true identity. There was little to distinguish the imposition which he made upon the abbey's hospitality from the sanctuary which Langoisse demanded. And yet, to be accessory to the abduction of a vampire lady was a crime of a very high order, even if enacted under threat.

'What would you have me do?' asked the pirate, when Noell did not reply. 'Would you have me let her go, or murder her and burn her body?'

'You should not have brought her here.'

'Now I have her,' replied Langoisse, 'I might take her to hell with me, if I judge it worth my while. If I could get her safe away, I might try to ransom her for another ship, but it might be best to destroy her. I have not made up my mind. Would you like to see her?'

'Why?'

'Are you not a scholar, come here as a member of the Invisible College of England? Is it not your purpose to learn what you can about vampires, in order to fight them? I have heard of this Quintus, too, you see. It is true, is it not, that your father sought to learn the secret of that magic which makes vampires of common men?'

'Aye,' said Noell, quietly.

'And is there aught in your dusty books which promises to lead you to that secret?'

'If it were ever written in a book,' answered Noell, 'it would be no secret. No common man knows yet how vampires might be made. If anyone did know that secret, it would surely be a man like you, who once had every expectation of reaping that reward.' The words were not sincerely spoken; there was a sarcastic edge to them. But Noell, somewhat to his own surprise, was not afraid of the pirate, who seemed for the moment anything but wrathful.

'Perhaps you are right,' said Langoisse. 'Perhaps I could have learned that secret, if I had made the most of my opportunities. But when I expected to become a vampire, there seemed no urgency, and when it became evident that even my kinsman, the Grandmaster of the Hospitallers, considered me so little as to use me as a common brigand, the secret was far out of reach. It was then but a brief step which made me a rebel against their kind. Do you think that the lady might tell us the secret which we crave, if she could be persuaded?'

'What powers of persuasion do we have?' asked Noell. 'The vampires can overcome pain, and need not yield to torture.'

'But they can be threatened with death, can they not? A brave man of honour like Richard would never yield to such a threat, of course, but a gentle creature like the lady is surely made of different stuff. Pain is not the whole of torture, and there is much that might be achieved by fear and horror.'

Noell wondered whether the pirate was trying to test his reaction. Langoisse approached him now as a friend, but had no real reason to trust him. Why should the pirate take it for granted that Noell was his ally? For the greater part of his life, Edmund Cordery had played the part of a loyal servant to the vampire race. The fact that he had died in order to kill his lover was not enough to convince everyone that he had all along been a member of the secret society whose purpose was to free Britain from vampire rule.

'It is said that vampire ladies, and even certain knights, are not permitted to learn the secret by which they are made,' said Noell, cautiously. 'The whole rites are said to be known only to the princes and their magicians, and to be well-guarded. If the threat of death were enough to pry the secret loose from any captive vampire, do you think that it could have been kept for a thousand years and more?'

'Have you heard it said that a common man who drinks a vampire's blood may become a vampire himself?'

'I have heard it said. My father told me that it is a lie.'

Langoisse smiled. 'You do not want to try the experiment, then? You would not like to see what Cristelle d'Urfé might be forced to tell us, or taste what virtue there might be in her blood?'

Noell licked his lips, which seemed very dry. 'I think not,' he said.

'You are a handsome lad,' said the pirate. 'My little Maroc is quite taken with you. She is a pretty thing, you must agree. Would you like to be a pirate, and come with me when I go? I'll make you third mate of my next ship, and you can have the Maroc for your own, if she likes you better than me.'

Noell remembered his yearning for a life of action, but the attractions of piracy seemed to him slighter now than they had then.

'Come, Master Cordery,' said the pirate softly, 'a lusty lad like you was never meant to be a monk.'

Noell looked down at the Bible which he had been pretending to read, but the open page offered no inspiration. 'I do not yet know,' he said, 'what course I would prefer to follow in my life.'

The pirate smiled, mirthlessly. 'The offer will still stand, until we leave. Think on it, I pray you. Now I ask again, would you like to see my lady captive, and hear what she has to say?'

Noell could not help but recall the sight of the vampire's face in the lamplight, and suffered a rush of feeling, which he dared not name. He stood up, and said: 'If you insist.'

The pirate bowed mockingly, urging the boy to precede him. Noell led the pirate from the library, and walked with him through the desolate and labyrinthine corridors to the penitential cells.

The Turk Selim was standing guard in the anteroom which gave access to the cells, though all the doors were securely barred on the outside. When Langoisse took away the bar from the relevant door, and beckoned Noell to follow him inside, the noseless man remained without. Noell heard the sound of the bar sliding back into its bed, and wondered whether he would be allowed to come out again, when the pirate left.

The Lady Cristelle was sitting on a wide wooden bench which had been brought into the room to serve as a bed. Mary White was not with her, and Noell assumed that she had been put in a different cell in order to deprive the vampire of her donation of blood.

When Langoisse came in the lady shrank back against the cold wall, but though she was certainly ill at ease she was by no means terrified. Her face, so pale as to seem almost luminous, was quite still. Her eyes were not so glazed, now; whatever poison they had used to drug her was wearing off.

'I see that you are rested,' said Langoisse. 'I have brought Master Cordery to see you. You must have known him at court.'

Cristelle turned her dark eyes to Noell, and looked at him curiously. 'I knew his father,' she replied. 'But I do not think I ever saw Master Noell. His father was a handsome man, but he should not have destroyed himself that way for love of a lady. It was a silly thing to do.'

The lady's voice was low and musical. She seemed less proud and less assertive than the Lady Carmilla, who had died of the plague which she had drunk in Edmund Cordery's blood, but Noell thought that such humility might simply be the result of her being so far from home. Haughtiness was natural in those who ruled the world when they were safe inside their castles, but she was in a dungeon now.

'He might help me to question you,' said the pirate. 'He is a scholar, and may know better than I what questions we should ask of you.'

'I will not answer your questions,' said the lady, calmly, 'and you know that there is no compulsion by which you may force me to reply.'

Langoisse turned to Noell. 'She means, Master Scholar, that she has no fear of pain. But are we to believe that, without a test? Perhaps it is only a lie, which vampires broadcast for their own protection.'

'All vampires can control pain,' Noell replied, unwilling to play a part. 'It is one of the attributes of their nature. Long life, immunity to disease, the healing of wounds that would kill a man. Common men tell all under torture; vampires reveal nothing.'

'Have you seen that opinion put to the proof, Master Cordery?' asked the pirate.

Noell shook his head. He felt a slight unease in his stomach as Langoisse took a dagger from his belt. 'Where would you like to cut her?' asked the pirate.

Noell would not reach out to take the dagger. It was not because he was frightened of the lady's curse – if such curses worked, then all who sought to do the vampires harm would have been dead long ago – but his awe of common mankind's masters was still sufficient to make the futile gesture repugnant to him.

'You are convinced by what your books have told you, perhaps?' said the pirate, ironically. 'I was once a scholar myself, and I have since found that many assured truths are not so certain as the masters of ancient lore would have us believe. I have heard it said that a man who tastes a vampire's blood, as vampires taste ours, may become a vampire himself, but I may not say it is true, and I may not say it is false, while I have never tried it for myself.'

Noell said nothing, wishing now that he had not come.

Langoisse said: 'Perhaps, on the other hand, it is the Gregorians who are correct. Demons should be exorcised, and we ought not to traffick with them. Should we, then, plunge a stake into her heart, cut off her head, and burn her body, in the fashion prescribed by the last true pope? Authorities proclaim it the most correct and proper method by which a vampire's death can be assured, do they not? Or would you, perhaps, favour the magic which your father used to curse his vampire lover with the plague? He taught you that magic, I trust?'

Noell felt sweat on his brow, though the room was very cool. His heart was beating very quickly. He felt that it was he, and not the Lady Cristelle, who was under attack.

'Let the boy be,' said Cristelle. 'He has not the savage heart for your work. Send him away, and do as you will. It will do no good to spill my blood, and it were better for everyone if its shedding should be on your hands alone.'

The pirate reacted with quick annoyance to her intervention. He lashed out at her without warning, striking at her face with the dagger.

She barely flinched, and it seemed to Noell that she might even have avoided the blow if she had wished. The blade ran across her cheek beneath the right eye, and stopped against the bony part of her nose. It was as if she wanted to come quickly to the business of bloodshed, as though it would be better for her to bring this matter to a head.

Langoisse watched the blood coursing from the wound like a red curtain drawn down to her chin. The flow was sudden and strong, for the cut had gone deep, but it slowed very quickly, and was stemmed within seconds, after the fashion of vampire injuries. The lady drew the fingers of her right hand across her cheek from ear to nose, and then held the hand out to Langoisse, a pendulous drop of blood at the tip of each finger.

'Drink,' she commanded him.

He would not, but Noell could see in his face that it was the fact that she had dared to command him which prevented the act, not any lack of desire. There was a fascination in his eye which suggested that he did not entirely disbelieve the dangerous rumour he had quoted.

Cristelle put her hand to her own lips, then, and licked the blood from the fingers. She made no pantomime of it, and yet Noell found the quickness of the gesture somehow alarming.

'Shall I offer you my heart?' she said, to Langoisse. 'Or my throat, perhaps?' She tilted her head back, though her gaze was unwavering. Noell knew that there was sense in this taunting. If Langoisse were tempted to use the dagger to inflict a deeper wound, then she might slip into the deep coma which all vampires required in order to exercise their extraordinary powers of self-repair. Once in that state she would be beyond the reach of any questioning. Langoisse might kill her, then, but there was nothing else he could do.

The pirate refused to strike again. Instead, he put the dagger back in his belt. He looked at Noell, as if uncertain whether or not to leave him in the cell, but then said: 'Come away, Master Scholar. I would consult with you.' His voice had regained its ironic edge, but there was no lightness in the tone now.

Noell's gaze was trapped by the sight of the vampire lady, and he felt a catch in his throat at the thought of such perfection spoiled by the dagger's careless cut. He knew that she felt no pain, but the tragedy of beauty despoiled seemed none the less for that. When a moment had gone by, though, he tore his gaze away, and followed Langoisse to the door.

As the Turk let them out of the cell, and then replaced the securing bar, Noell heard Mary White sobbing in another cell. He wanted to call out to her, to offer her encouragement and a promise of safety, but he knew only too well that such a promise was beyond his ability to keep.

Poor Mary!, he said to himself, angrily. It was a safer thought to hold in his mind than any idea of sympathy for the vampire.

FOUR

Noell sat upon the three-legged stool before the kitchen fire, staring into the flames. The twin cauldrons suspended over the fire were each host to a pot of simmering meat and herbs, a string bag full of vegetables, and a pudding wrapped in a cloth. This would be the substance of the evening meal, stretched to serve the abbey's unwelcome visitors as well as the brethren. Though he had worked hard earlier, alongside Martin and Innocent, now he had only to watch while the cooking ran its course, rising only occasionally to carry more dry wood to feed the fire, and to pour water from the big ladle into the cauldrons. The food would be served on the wooden trenchers which the monks of Cardigan had used for hundreds of years; they scorned plates, as they scorned forks, precisely because those things were newly fashionable in the mundane world. The followers of St. Benedict were not to be hastily taken up by the currents of change.

Noell had never found his work in the kitchen arduous, because the good brothers took a great pride in their management of the chopping and mixing, while his own role was restricted to lifting and fetching. In spite of the simplicity of the labour, though, Noell often found it oppressive in the hot kitchen, especially in the summer months. He had suggested once to Brother Martin that his work was a sharp reminder of the threat of Hell's fires, but Martin could neither appreciate the jest nor sympathise with the suggestion of blasphemy which it harboured.

On the evening which followed his reluctant excursion with Langoisse to Cristelle D'Urfé's cell Noell was pleased to have a place of retreat, where he could be uncomfortably alone with thoughts and feelings which were prickly with guilt. For once, he did not mind in the least the angry heat of the fire, and relished its pressure, as though it might help to burn away the ferment in his soul, purging him of his fears and his doubts. But he was not to be left alone for long.

He was lost in a dream, eyes bedazzled by the flames which licked the bellies of the cauldrons, when Langoisse's mistress came quietly to his side, and startled him. He would have blushed but his cheeks were already ruddy from the heat.

'I am sorry,' she said. 'I did not mean to alarm thee.'

Noell had read in the grubby broadsides which carried news of pirates and highwaymen even into the precincts of Richard's tower that men like Langoisse had female companions, but had never known whether it was a true report or an embellishment of the literary imagination.

Such tales, their excitement masked by a hypocritical pose of alarm and censure, delighted in painting pictures of scarlet women, temptresses of exotic beauty and uncertain temper. Now he found himself confronted by a legend made corporeal.

Despite Langoisse's description of her as a Maroc gypsy princess, Leilah did not seem quite as exotic or as glorious as a broadside heroine. She seemed to him, now that she came to stand before him, a paradoxical creature. She still wore male attire, and a dagger in her belt, but the excitement which had animated her face the night before was gone now, and she seemed less than intrepid. Her dark eyes were shadowed, and her expression seemed regretful.

When Noell spoke to her, his tone was petulant. 'What do you want with me?' he asked.

'Langoisse has asked me to seek thee out, Master Cordery,' she said. 'He is anxious that he has offended thee, when his wish is to be thy friend.' Her voice was accented, somewhat in the Spanish way. He was surprised that she addressed him in the familiar way, for it seemed to contrast with the pretence of nobility implied by the title 'princess', and by the fact that Langoisse had given her a little servant girl of her own. 'Thee' and 'thou' were not used at court, save by lovers in their intimate moments, or by parents and children. He wondered whether she had learned her English in an archaic fashion, or whether she had chosen to address him in this way, perhaps at Langoisse's instruction.

'I bear him no ill-will,' said Noell, 'but I am a guest here, and I fear for the safety of my hosts. I think he will understand that I would like to see him quickly gone, with least disturbance left behind.'

She stood in front of him, perhaps a little closer than he would have liked. While he was sitting down she was as tall as he, and her dark eyes looked into his own, though he could not see them clearly while her face was silhouetted by the fire. He stood up, and moved away, so that when he turned to look down at her he could see her in a better light. She was good-looking, by common standards, but not *truly* beautiful. She had only the prettiness of common youth, which might be very likeable in its way, but she had nothing, in his eyes, to compare with the pale and opalescent splendour of the vampire ladies of the court, who had set for him the standards of desirability.

She, on the other hand, seemed to be looking at him with a fascination which he found embarrassing. It put him strangely in mind of the speculative gaze with which Carmilla Bourdillon had addressed him on the fatal eve of his flight from London. He had never been much in the company of women, and felt that he could neither properly read nor properly respond to such overtures.

'He would be thy friend,' she told him again. 'A better friend, perhaps, than these monks.'

'His, I think, is the more dangerous vocation,' he replied. 'The brothers are cold friends, but their coldness promises a certain security.'

She did not understand that. 'Wilt thou become a monk thyself?' she asked. 'Art thou made for celibacy and for prayers, instead of adventure and the love of women?'

'Men make of themselves what they can and what they will,' he told her.

She looked around the kitchen, as if to imply that his surroundings told the tale of what he was making of himself. 'Perhaps,' she said, 'but I was a slave until he freed me, and could have made no more of myself, had he not given me the chance. He calls me princess now, but that is only his way. I am free, though, and have killed one or two of that kind of men which once kept and used me.'

'Well,' said Noell, softly, 'I am glad of that. I could not wish that you were a slave, or that you were miserable in what Langoisse has made of you. I beg you to be happy in your fashion, but I truly do not know whether a pirate could be made of me.'

She smiled, then, at the kindness of his words, and he was caught by surprise at the sight of the smile, which gave him a thrill of pleasure. He smiled in return.

Now, it seemed, it was she who became a little shy, and she looked away. 'I like thee,' she said, simply. 'I wish thou wouldst come with us when we go.'

'Perhaps I will,' replied Noell – who felt he could say so honestly enough, so uncertain was he of his fate.

'There was another message too, which I was asked to bring to thee,' she said. 'Wilt thou see that the vampire lady and her maid are fed, but do not leave them together, for my master does not want the lady to have her ration of blood. Take Selim's food too. He is guarding them.'

Noell frowned, and became curt again, saying that he would do as he was asked. Then he sat down on the stool, and made it clear that he wanted her to go. She hesitated, but then Brother Martin came in, vespers having been concluded, and she quickly went away from his censorious glare. The monk looked sharply at Noell, too, but Noell took no heed of the appearance of displeasure. He hardly spared Martin a glance as he went to take up his station, seizing one of the levers with which he and the brother would haul the bags of food out of the cauldrons and away from the fire.

Later, Noell took the food to the cells as he had been asked. He carried two trenchers, while one of the almoner's boys carried a third for the Turk. First, he went in to Mary White, and though the door remained open, denying them any measure of privacy, she flew to him and took him by the shoulders as he laid down her food.

'Oh Master Cordery,' she said. 'You must help us, for they mean to burn my lady, and I dare not think what will happen to me!' She was terrified, and he knew that the presence of the man without a nose could only feed her fears with an extra measure of horror.

He could not bring himself to offer her false comfort, though he knew it might be kinder if he did. He only replied: 'I must see to the lady first, Mary. I will come back in a moment.'

She let him go, and watched him while he closed her door, without setting the bolt back in place. The Turk, who was already shovelling food into his mouth, watched him but did not speak. Noell did not know whether Selim could speak English, or whether he could speak at all, so he said nothing to excuse or explain himself. He had to set the lady's supper down while he removed the bar securing her cell, and he felt the Turk's eyes upon his back as he opened the door and went in.

The Lady Cristelle looked at the meat, not only without enthusiasm, but with suspicion. She was still seated on the bench, exactly as he had seen her earlier in the day. The scar on her face was already fading, and would soon be gone.

'It is only meat, my lady,' he said, interpreting her anxiety. 'There is no poison in it. I saw it prepared, and no hand but mine has touched it.'

She favoured him with a wan smile. 'So they are less afraid of me now,' she said. 'They will let me regain my strength, because they think me helpless in my imprisonment. I think I would rather they persisted, so that I could take refuge in the deep sleep.'

'Can you not?' he asked, genuinely curious.

She looked up at him, her expression unfathomable. 'Have they sent you, then, to question me with cunning? In this case, it hardly matters. I cannot seek the deep sleep; it must seek me. It is not something that we do, but something which happens to us. If I am denied blood, as the pirate seems to intend, then I will eventually fall into the sleep, as I would if he fed me more poison. We are all, in our various fashions, prisoners of our being. But do not wait here, Master Cordery – Mary needs you more than I, and you must do what you can to help her.'

He was suspicious of her apparent concern, not knowing whether it was mere show, intended to impress him. Vampire women were famed for the subtleties of their seductions and the heartlessness of their betrayals. He dared not take what she said at face value. If all he had been told of vampires was true, she could not care at all what happened to a common servant.

He left the cell, and secured the door behind him. He looked at the Turk, who was stabbing the point of his knife into a piece of meat with surprising delicacy and precision. He went back into Mary White's cell.

She had not yet touched her food, and was waiting impatiently for his return. 'What do they mean to do?' she asked, in an agony of fearful anticipation. She did not come to take hold of him again, but stood five feet away, her hands on her shoulders, crossed over her breasts as if she were hugging herself.

'I do not know,' he told her. 'But the monks would not see you harmed, and even a pirate crew has some respect for a house of God. Langoisse is not a rough man, and would not kill you simply for the sake of adding one more murder to his soul's burden of sin.'

'But you will help me, will you not? You will not let them hurt me?'

Why, thought Noell, *she thinks me one of them, an outlaw among outlaws!*

'I will do whatever I can to preserve you from harm,' he told her.

'And my lady too?' Her voice was doubtful, as if she dared not hope for reassurance.

'It is not my wish to see anyone killed, or hurt,' he told her, 'not even the vampire. You must eat, if you can. The food will warm you, and give you strength.'

She nodded, too eagerly, and sat down upon the bed, taking up the trencher from the floor where he had set it down. He went out of the cell, and after a moment's pause, picked up the bar which sealed the door and slotted it in place. Then he looked again at the Turk, who was watching him incuriously while he ate. As Noell went back along the corridor he felt those eyes, made monstrous by their scarred and rutted setting, following the course of his retreat. The boy, who had waited for him, was almost trembling with fear as he walked alongside.

In the refectory, where he was to take his own meal, Noell was called to the high table by the abbot. Langoisse was sitting on the abbot's right hand, where Quintus was normally stationed, and the ancient Brother Innocent was displaced from his station by the pirate's mistress.

'I must ask you to undertake a mission on behalf of the abbey,' said the abbot, in a tone whose evenness could not conceal an underlying anxiety. 'Tomorrow, you must go into the town, to help in arranging a passage to Ireland for our . . . guests. It is undesirable to involve the bailiff or any of the tenant farmers who work the monastery lands, and we are agreed that you are the one most suited to the task. You will be provided with an appropriate letter of authority.'

Noell glanced at Langoisse, who was watching him carefully. It was probable that the pirate had asked for him, though what the abbot said about the inadvisability of involving the bailiff, who normally acted as the intermediary in matters of monastery business, was undoubtedly true. It would be for the best if news of the abbey's invasion could be kept securely within its walls. The reference to the tenant farmers was a veiled plea for circumspection and secrecy, though Noell had his own reasons for discretion whenever he went abroad. He felt that he was being subjected to a new trial, and that his performance would be under strict examination from all concerned.

Why, he asked silently of an invisible witness, *may I not simply be ignored, while all this vile business comes to its conclusion? Why is there no one here who has naught to ask of me?*

He told the abbot, politely, that he would be pleased to do as he was bid. After all, the thought that he might contrive to find a way to rid the abbey of its visitors was welcome. If only they could all be sent on their way, without trace of their sojourn remaining, then his world might regain its steady course.

He went to his place to eat his meal, dreading that every eye in the room was upon him, and that those watchers who were not judging him were scheming instead, to draw him still further into a game of treason as deadly as the one which his father had played.

FIVE

Noell would have preferred to go to Cardigan alone to execute his commission on behalf of the pirates, but Langoisse insisted on accompanying him. The abbot told him which of the ships whose masters had dealings with the abbey were likely to be in the harbour at this time; those masters could be trusted to respond to the appeal for help which Noell carried. The abbey had sometimes lent money to Welsh fishermen and traders, and still had a part-share in a number of vessels – a legacy of more prosperous days. For this reason, Noell thought that the business might perfectly well be carried out quietly and expeditiously, by himself and no other, but it seemed that the pirate did not trust him.

Langoisse was unperturbed by Noell's protest that it would be an altogether unnecessary risk for the pirate to show himself. 'There are few here who would know my face,' he said, 'even if they knew enough to look for it in the crowd. In any case, I ought to see the vessel on which you intend to book my passage; I know these herring-fishers and wherries, and need something seaworthy. I must see her captain, too, to agree with him a place and time at which we might conveniently embark. I mean to get away cleanly if I can, but I cannot march the vampire to the harbour, even by night, and we will need to discover a quiet place where a sizeable ship might come discreetly close to shore.'

So they set off, after prime, together. Langoisse took only a little trouble to hide his features, donning a straw hat such as chapmen often wore, and wearing nondescript clothing.

The Abbey was closer to the sea than the town, and was on the north side of the Teifi, isolated on the crown of a low hill. From the north side of the church one could look across the green-and-yellow fields, and see the way the coast curved away from the river's mouth, the fields gently sloping towards the dunes. Langoisse did not like it. 'Too open,' he said. "Twould be better if there were sheltered bays, as you find in Gower. If it should come to a fight and a chase, I'd wish to find your hedgerows taller, and woods in which to hide.'

The land around the abbey was under intense cultivation, rather because of the need of the people than the greed of the monks. The population of the Welsh towns had grown rapidly these last fifty years or so, and this strip of land close to Cardigan Bay would bear good wheat if kindly treated, while the hilly country which lay inland was fit only for sheep. When Langoisse enquired what lands belonged to the Abbey, Noell explained that the abbot leased almost all of that land to yeomen, collecting rents and heriots through the bailiff; and that the monks nowadays tended only their vegetable plots and chicken-runs, being too old and too few to plough, plant and harvest an entire demesne.

'Perhaps they should take to highway robbery, like the old brigand monks of Valle Crucis,' Langoisse suggested, as they set off on the rough road which forked near to the abbey. The right-hand track would take them to the bridge, which spanned the Teifi two miles upriver of the town.

After a while, the pirate complained that there was a stink in the air the like of which he had never known. Noell told him that it was always the case, whenever rain was followed by hot sunshine. 'We are too far away from the Gower quarries for the farmers to buy cheap lime to fertilise the fields,' he explained. 'They use seaweed from the shore, chopped fine and rotted, for their manuring. Even now, when the crops are high, the scent comes out.'

Soon, when they made the descent towards the bridge, they could see the town arrayed on the distant slope above the harbour, with its castle towering over the cottages like a great Norman carbuncle in frail Welsh flesh. The castle was not much of a fortress, its purpose being to defend its Norman lords against the Welshmen rather than to guard the town against an invasion from the sea. It had never been attacked in earnest, even in the time of Owain Glyn Dwr's rebellion, which had been the last serious attempt in any part of Britain to oppose the vampire empire.

Quintus had told Noell soon after his arrival in Cardigan that what the Welsh resented in Norman rule was not so much the fact that they belonged to an Imperium ruled by Attila's kin, but rather that English landlords and magistrates had been set over them. Had Glyn Dwr been made a vampire, the monk opined, Wales might easily have been made a loyal enclave of the Imperium; as it was, the descendants of Owen Tudor were among the most devout enemies of Richard, and would talk treasonously of themselves as the rightful royal family of the British nation. Some that were loyal to the Tudors called them the scions of Arthur, linking them thereby to a heroic kingdom of legend, but that was mere romancing. But when all the miseries of the Welsh were counted up, still the present holder of Cardigan Castle did not entirely belie his family name, which was Wellbelove, and there was no very fierce resentment of his tenancy, though even landless labourers spoke of him as 'the Norman cuckoo'.

The road into Cardigan was busy. Though it was not market day, there was a continual trickle of oxcarts carrying various goods into the town, and men on horseback. There were dozens of men afoot, humping packs of all shapes and sizes. Noell was not unhappy to find that there were so many others about, because he thought it easier to attract no attention in the midst of a throng of strangers. Langoisse seemed less enthusiastic about the crowd, which he seemed to like as little as the fields.

'How full the world must be of fools!' he exclaimed, as a little cart loaded with leeks, cabbages and onions rattled past, followed by a greater one pulled by two horses, which was loaded with coal. Between them the carts had raised an uncomfortable cloud of dust, which made the travellers on foot guard their faces with their hands.

'How so?' asked Noell. 'But for honest toilers like these, there'd be none to feed a pirate his ration of plunder, or vampires their ration of blood. You should take heart, as Richard would, from the sight of advances in wealth and industry.'

Langoisse gave him a black look on hearing his name coupled with Richard's. Noell could see that the special spite which existed between the two of them was not exaggerated by the stories which told of it.

'Richard would like to see his subjects prosper, no doubt,' answered the pirate sourly, 'for he likes to strut the part of a statesman hero, and is ever annoyed when any fail to honour or to like him. Did you know him, in London?'

Noell laughed. 'Oh no,' he said. 'My father was a mechanician, not a courtier. I kept company with servants like Mary White, not the grand people.'

'The prince was not so proud, in certain moods,' said Langoisse blackly. 'A handsome youth like you might have aspired to be a vampire, had you caught his foul yellow eye.' Richard's eyes were an odd colour, for a vampire, but Noell had not heard them described in quite that way before. It was in his mind to reply that Langoisse might have been a handsome youth himself, once upon a time, but he did not dare. Instead, he said: 'It is no ambition of mine to become a vampire.'

Langoisse laughed, sarcastically. 'A man of the people! No need to be a hypocrite, boy. There's no shame in yearning for eternal youth, even though you hate the noble rabble which has so meanly hoarded the gift to support their tyranny. No one truly seeks to see vampirism exterminated, save a handful of Gregorian fanatics and puritans. Fight against the legion of immortals, by all means, but fight meanwhile for thine own immortality. That's what I'd tell my own son, if son I had.'

'Perhaps Leilah will bear you one,' muttered Noell, turning away with a cough from the dust of another heavy cart.

'I do not think so,' Langoisse replied, calmly. 'She bore a child while still a slave, when she was no more than twelve years old. It nearly killed her, and I do not think she can ever bear another.'

Noell looked at him in astonishment, but said nothing.

'How do you like my little princess?' asked Langoisse, mockingly. 'She is very pretty, is she not?'

'Yes, she is,' answered Noell. 'She told me she had been a slave, and that you set her free.'

'I killed the man that owned her,' agreed Langoisse. 'I cannot say that I did it in any noble spirit, for it was a matter of necessity. But I would not keep her as a slave, and told her she was free. She seemed delighted by the news, though I cannot say that she has learned to act the part. Perhaps you should seduce her, to teach her what freedom really means.'

Noell blushed, which amused the pirate.

'Ah,' said Langoisse, 'I see you have not the passion for it. She is pretty, but not beautiful, like the Lady Cristelle.'

'I am not . . . ' Noell began, but realised that he did not know exactly what he was, or what he was not, and felt miserable in his confusion. But Langoisse relented in his mockery, and went on in a different way.

'The beauty of the vampire ladies is the most cunning instrument of their rule. The officers of their armies are won over by mere ambition, but they have many more loyal servants secured by the passion these ladies inspire. I think it a marvellous cleverness that so many comely girls are inducted into vampirism, and what I know of vampires suggests to me that they cannot take the same pleasure in their ladies as common men would. They are not all like Richard, of course, any more than all Turks are like my faithful Selim, but long life makes them very cold and deadens their desire. They create vampire ladies, I think, not for their own amusement but to bemuse and captivate love-struck boys and passionate men. Admire the likes of Cristelle d'Urfé if you must, but always remember that she is the lure in a deadly trap, and learn to hate rather than to love her. Mark me, Master Cordery, I know whereof I speak.'

'My father had a different account,' said Noell. 'He told me . . . '

Langoisse interrupted, his voice grown harsh again. 'Your father had every reason to offer another account. I do not mean to malign him in your eyes, but he did not see such matters straightly. I know that he killed the lady in the end, but I think that he served the vampires all his life, more honestly and more productively than he knew. Why God gave vampire ladies such charms, I cannot tell, but I know how the vampire lords and princes use those charms, and I tell you again that the wise man learns to hate instead of love. Instruct your heart, Master Cordery, and make it learn the lesson well, else it will betray you, and bring your life to an end on a traitor's scaffold or a heretic's pyre.'

Noell saw well enough the force of the pirate's argument, but he was by no means ready to accept it. 'My father knew the vampires well,' he said. 'He understood better than anyone what manner of being they are, and how their empire of fear is built. The rule of so few over so many is not secured easily, even though the few are so difficult to destroy. They always pretend that they completely control the way by which vampires are made, but my father was not so sure. His opinion was that they would make more if they could, to make certain of their empire. He told me once that the vampires might be as much slaves to superstition as we are, and that even Attila may not fully understand the way by which vampires are made. There may be less design in all of this than you assume.'

'You do not believe in the vampire sabbat, then?' asked Langoisse, in his ironically challenging fashion. 'It is not so that the devil himself is summoned by Prince Richard to the Tower, appearing in the form of a great beast, to offer the privilege of vampirism to those who have done most evil in his service? Was it not argued by some learned school-man that a man need only be fed the flesh of a new-born babe and allowed to plant a blasphemous kiss on Satan's arse, in order to be recruited to the ranks of the undying? And are there are not other versions of the sabbat, too, in which the devil makes men vampires by buggery?'

'Oh yes,' said Noell, 'but those are fevered fantasies, spread in order to rouse the horror of ordinary men against the vampires, if any such rousing were needed. My father used to say that Satan's presence explained far too much, and nothing at all.'

'A riddler, too! What a man of many parts Edmund Cordery became, under the tutelage of his great lady! And yet, I beg to doubt his omniscience, if you will permit.'

Noell had no alternative but to permit it. They were approaching the town gate by now, and the crowd had thickened to the point where they might easily be overheard. It was not wise to discuss vampires where spies might lurk.

They went down the hill once they were in the town, away from the castle and toward the harbour, where the masts of the fishing fleet were clustered.

'We must look in the waterfront inns,' said Noell. 'There we will find the men we are looking for.'

'Aye,' said the pirate. 'And there we might find the truest news, and discover whether any know that I am not dead and drowned.' His voice was suddenly low and bleak; he could not feel safe on land, in a port where he had never been before, not knowing whether those who sought him had given up the chase or not.

Noell led him first to the Mermaid, where two good captains indebted to the abbey usually lodged, but neither was there to be found when he inquired after them. Noell bought beer for them both – better beer than came from the Abbey's brewery, as it chanced – so that they might sit in a shadowed corner, playing the eavesdropper themselves. They heard nothing of import, though, and Langoisse soon told Noell to lead on to another place. They went next to the Three Cups, and there they found the captain of a herring buss: a man named Ralph Heilyn, who stood second on the abbot's list of men who could be trusted to help. He was a rough, grey man of sixty years and more, but stout and strong, and a gentleman of sorts.

Heilyn had never seen Noell, but when Noell showed him the abbot's letter he promptly took the two of them up to the room above a corviser's shop, where he lodged his mistress. He dispatched the slattern about some errand, and bade his guests be seated. He seemed ready enough to discuss business with mysterious strangers, and Noell judged that he was not entirely unused to the carrying of extra cargoes of one kind or another.

Noell explained that discreet passage to Ireland was sought for fifteen men who were friends of the Welsh Church. He did not say so, but attempted to imply that they were heretics in whom the Dominicans had taken an interest. Heilyn looked at Langoisse, though, and Noell saw that he was suspicious. Though the Welshman could not tell a pirate merely by his face and manner, he could surely see that this was a man of action, who had far more likely offended the vampires by his deeds than by his thoughts.

The only complaint which Heilyn immediately made was that fifteen was too many, and Noell was quick to counter that with an assurance that the price paid would be appropriate.

'You can pay in gold?' asked the captain.

Noell hesitated, but Langoisse quickly cut in. 'A little,' he said. 'We do not have much, and need most of what we have in Ireland, but I will gladly give you ten sovereigns, which is a full fifth of what we carry.'

'Too little!' said Heilyn, but there was no force in his refusal, and Noell saw what Langoisse intended by stating that he would be carrying more gold than he was able to give. Heilyn was thinking that he might ask a higher price, once away from the shore, and temptation was distracting his attention from the question of how to make certain that he could collect any fee at all.

'Do not forget, Master Heilyn,' said Noell, 'that the abbey will be in your debt when you have done this, though while we speak it is the abbot who is the creditor.'

Heilyn made a show of looking again at the letter which Noell had brought, but only said: 'It might be dangerous work. I have no wish to offend Wellbelove or the Dominicans. I am an honest man.'

'Master Heilyn,' said Noell, 'it is because of your honesty that we come to you. I have the abbot's authority to implore you. The good monks would be in your debt, and would make good your debts to them.'

'I do not know your name, Master Scholar,' said Heilyn to Noell, 'but I think I know your kind. True Faith you may name your calling, but you'd draw the devil to the heels of such as I. I wish no ill to the brothers, and I stand in their debt, 'tis true, but they must know I'll not thank them for work like this.'

'They will thank *you*, Master Heilyn,' Noell assured him.

'There is a troop of horse from Swansea in the castle,' said the captain, uneasily, 'and marines from the *Firedrake* are on their way here from Milford Haven. I want no trouble with such as these, if they are in any way concerned with you.' His wary eye was now directed at Noell's companion.

'They are not,' lied Langoisse. 'Our business is entirely secret, and need expose you to no risk. You need make no unseemly haste, but should provision the ship as you would for a normal sailing. You need not take us aboard in sight of the town. What is the safest place where we might be fetched from the shore by one of your boats?'

Heilyn hesitated, but answered. 'There is a tiny inlet four miles to the north of the Abbey. It is Evan Rhosier's land. The abbot will know it, and will show you on a chart.'

'You must send a boat to the shore there,' said Langoisse. 'At four in the morning, the day after next.'

'We'll have no fair wind for the Irish shore,' said Heilyn. 'And I cannot do it so soon.'

'Who knows where the wind will lie, after tomorrow?' countered Langoisse. 'And the sooner it is done, the better for us all. I will double the price; it is all that I can do. You have the abbot's good will to add to that.'

'I must know who you are,' Heilyn said. 'I cannot do it otherwise.'

'Do you know Meredydd ap Gawys?' asked Langoisse, before Noell could give any answer. The man named was a Welsh gentleman, currently secured in Swansea jail, awaiting the Great Sessions, when he was likely to be condemned to death for treason. It did not seem likely to Noell that Langoisse knew the man, but Heilyn certainly would.

'You are not one of *his* men,' said Heilyn, carefully.

'I am his friend,' said the pirate.

'But are you not a Norman?' asked the Welshman.

'If I were a Norman,' answered Langoisse, grimly, 'I would not be asking the help of a loyal Welshman. I tell you that I am friend to Meredydd ap Gawys, and you have the abbot's letter. If you refuse to help us, your own countrymen will curse you in time to come. Now, enough of this haggling. I would have this matter settled. How big is your ship?"

Heilyn hesitated, but in the end he answered the question. 'Thirty-five last,' he said.

'How many crew?'

'Sixteen.'

'And what weapons do you have aboard?'

Heilyn frowned at this, and Noell did not like it. The shipmaster tried to stare down the pirate, but could not. 'Five half-pikes and four muskets,' he eventually replied, 'with six pounds of gunpowder and two pounds of leaden bullets. Do you think that we will need them?'

'If you tell no one what you are doing,' said Langoisse, 'we will all be safe in Ireland without so much as the speaking of an angry word. Do not be annoyed because I question you. We are in your hands, now, and at your mercy. I must put my trust in an unknown captain and his ship; you need only trust in the Abbot of Cardigan, whom you know, and in God, who is kind to honest men.'

'I will do it,' said Heilyn, sullenly. 'I am a man who can be trusted, as the abbot knows.'

When they left, having confirmed once again the details of the appointed place and time, Langoisse insisted that they made their way to the wharf where Heilyn's buss was berthed. He said that he must satisfy himself that the ship was sound, though Noell never doubted that she would be. As far as his untutored eye could judge, she was. Langoisse admitted that he could see nothing amiss, but observed that the passage would be lacking in comfort, given the fee which had been agreed.

'She will serve,' said Noell. 'You should not have asked him about his weapons. You might have frightened him off.'

'He is greedy enough not to be easily frightened,' muttered the pirate. 'He knows there is danger in it, and 'twould have been a mistake to be too careful. A man like that must be bullied as well as bribed, if he is to be persuaded.'

'It is your business,' said Noell, with a shrug of the shoulders. 'You are the one who needs the passage . . . though the monks will be very glad to see you gone.'

'Oh yes,' replied Langoisse. 'You lovers of peace want only to see me gone. But I've to think further ahead than that. While your abbot seeks to make an end of his part in my affairs, I've to make a new beginning as well.'

'We have made that beginning,' Noell told him. 'Now we must

hasten back to the Abbey, to wait for the appointed time, and pray that naught disturbs our peace until it comes.'

Langoisse looked down at him from the shadow of his straw hat, and favoured him with a wolfish smile. 'The waiting will not be heavy,' he said. 'We are friends, now, are we not? We shall find ways to amuse ourselves, I do not doubt.'

SIX

That night, Noell slept soundly for the first time since the invasion of the Abbey. He had a sense of everything being in order, because it seemed now that the nightmare might pass, and leave the Abbey and his life there intact and undisturbed. He had come to the point where he wished simply to be let alone, with no one demanding promises which he had to give and could not keep. He thought ill of himself for this craven desire, but that did not stop him desiring it. Sleep came to him as a welcome release: a surrendering of the duty of thought.

But he was not to be allowed to sleep through the night. Some time in the small hours, after the end of the night-office, he was awakened by a touch. Despite his tiredness, the touch was enough to startle him and bring him instantly back from sleep.

By the light of a single candle which she carried he could see the face of the person who had roused him. It was Leilah, the gypsy, her features softened by anxiety and her lips slightly apart. For a moment, his mind was crowded by lust-driven images, but she had not come to climb into his bed. Her expression had more fear in it than lewd intent.

'Master Cordery,' she said, in a voice not much above a whisper, 'I would that thou might do a favour for me.' She reached out to touch his shoulder with her fingertips, imploring his concern.

The words might have been taken as a rude invitation, but for her face. Noell stared at her, unable to guess what it was which had so alarmed her.

'What is it?' he asked. 'Have the soldiers come to take Langoisse?'

'He is with the lady,' she said. 'I beg thee to come. She has said that she would curse him. I heard her tell him, before we came here, that if he hurt her, she would have her revenge.'

Noell realised that Leilah was very much afraid of the vampire lady. She was a Mohammedan, and belonged to a nation where vampires were not tolerated. She could never have seen any other vampire than Cristelle d'Urfé, and all that she knew of vampires must have come from fantastic tales of magic and villainy.

'I do not think that she has any power to hurt him,' Noell said.

'And thou dost not care what he might do to her?'

What lay behind the question he could not tell. Might it be a snare set by the pirate? And what, in any case, was the true answer? 'Why do you care?' he asked, harshly.

She did not reply. Perhaps she was jealous as well as afraid and had called him in order to spoil a rape. But her fear was real. It was the fear of dire magic, of evil incarnate – a superstitious dread of the unleashed power of the devil, in whom Mohammedans believed no less than Christians, though they knew him by a different name.

He could not bring himself to tell her to go away. He dressed himself hastily, not knowing what he intended to do. He owed no debt to the pirate's mistress, and had no reason to think that he had any greater influence with Langoisse than she had herself. Nor did he owe any debt to the vampire sufficient to make him intercede on her behalf with a bitter man who would do her harm, and yet he felt compelled to go. Perhaps it was because of the futile promise which he had given to Mary White.

Leilah took him quickly to the cells. The small man who had once held a knife to Noell's throat was on watch by the outer door. He seemed greatly surprised by their arrival, and moved to stop them, but Leilah moved ahead of Noell, and put her hand upon her dagger. The man hesitated, but he let them go forward.

The door to Mary's cell was shut, and there was no sound from within, but the other door was open wide. Langoisse and the Turk were both inside. They had brought a lantern with them, and a brazier of coals from the kitchen.

They had bound the vampire's wrists with cords, passing them through a ring set in the walls, to which shackles had once been attached. In the ancient days before the Normans had built their castle, the Abbey had been the only secure place which could provide Aberteifi with a jail for its felons.

The lady was uncomfortably stretched, for the ring was set high on the wall; only parts of her feet could touch the floor, and her face was pressed to the cold wall, quite hidden.

One or other of her tormentors had furiously lashed her back with a knotted rope, and the flesh was badly torn. Blood was coursing down her thighs in long streams. There were two knives balanced on the brazier's rim, their blades warming in the coals, and the Turk was blowing air from the kitchen bellows to make them glow more fiercely.

Langoisse was at a pause in his work, waiting for these knives, with which he intended to burn the lady. He did not seem surprised by Noell's arrival, but rather amused, though he looked with some slight displeasure at his mistress.

'Master Scholar!' he said. 'You are most welcome to join us at our play. Perhaps you have a stroke or two of your own that you'd like to pay back, and a question or two that you'd like to put, in the hope that it might be answered.'

The Lady Cristelle was still and silent. She did not turn her head to see who had arrived. Noell could not tell whether or not she had escaped into trance.

'This is a fool's game,' he said to the pirate, trying his best to sound stubbornly reasonable. 'She can control her pain, and will tell you nothing.'

Langoisse laughed. 'How do we know what she feels?' he asked. ''Tis true that she will not scream or beg for mercy, but her body recoils under the lash, and I'll warrant that her flesh shrieks just a little when I burn her. Perhaps she is indifferent, after her fashion, but I am sure that she *does* feel, and knows what it is that is happening to her. She is conscious still, I know. She may yet think it desirable to tell us a little about how she was made a vampire, and what elixir of life it was which gave her the gift of undying.' Langoisse turned his eyes again to Leilah, who cringed from his stare. 'She cannot hurt me, little fool,' he said, scornfully. 'Do you not think that I'm as good a servant of Satan as she could ever be? Why should he let her curse me, or come to her rescue? Do you think, if she'd magic of her own, she'd not have taken wing rather than fall into our hands? I am not tempting fate; it is fate which has made me this present, so that I may collect some debts which I am owed.'

'What debts?' asked Noell.

Langoisse stared at the glowing coals, and the blades of the heated knives. 'I have faced torture and humiliation at the hands of her kind,' he said. 'They sent me to the galleys, despite my station, like some beggarly street-thief. It was not enough that they scourged me while I plied the oar; they had me flogged upon the coursier of that hellish galley with all the Arab slaves and the scum of Marseilles looking on, rejoicing with every cut. Then they sent me to the stinking hospital where my wounds might fester, where men without noses screamed while their faces were consumed by great running sores. And they promised me that if I was not meek, they'd slice my nose from my face, to make me prettier for the day I met the devil.'

Noell could make no reply. The tone of the pirate's voice, both utterly cold and desperately angry, admitted no objection.

'Do you know, Master Cordery,' Langoisse went on, in a lighter way, 'that they cauterise a galleyman's punished flesh with hot pitch? I have none here available, but I think hot blades are a fair substitute. Do you think I healed as easily as she will? I would reclaim the pain which I felt, too, if only I could, and in the fullest measure. And will you say, either of you, that I am not due this settlement?'

'It was not *she* who hurt you,' answered Noell, bluntly, finding courage enough to say so.

Langoisse came close to him, then, and met him eye to eye with an expression full of simmering wrath. 'Was it Carmilla Bourdillon who hurt your father?' he shouted into Noell's face. 'Do you not know that all who share the privilege of tyranny must bear the guilt of its cruelties? Does not Rome's own Inquisition assert, when they burn old crones for witches, that a witch once proven guilty of any *maleficia* is guilty of all the crimes which her kind commit? How can we say less of vampires? Each acts for all, and this lady must stand trial for all. She answers not only for what was done to me, but for all that has been done to Englishmen in the name of the peace and prosperity of the Imperium of Gaul. I'd rather torment lionhearted Richard or some mighty warlord like Vlad the Impaler, that I own, but Cristelle d'Urfé is all I have, and I will not be softened by her fairness, which is a siren mask hiding a wicked soul.'

Noell saw that there was in this man a rage against the vampires which was not yet born in himself, and perhaps never would be, unless he were to suffer one day the kind of pain and degradation which the pirate had known. 'I beg you to stop,' he said, 'for the sake of the good monks. You reminded me today that you must think further ahead than what you will do here. So must we. If, after you have gone, it becomes known that a vampire was tormented within these walls, Wellbelove will have no choice but to tear the abbey down, and the brothers will likely be burned as heretics by that Holy Office of which you spoke. They will be held guilty by association in the exact manner which you have argued.'

Langoisse was in no mood to listen kindly to this plea. 'They belong to the True Faith,' he said. 'In the eyes of the Borgia pope and the Holy Office, they *are* heretics, and seditious too. What is your scholarship, Master Cordery, but pure heresy? Every time you turn a page in one of your forbidden books, you license your own burning, do you not?'

It was true, though it was not a way he liked to think of his work.

'And in the eyes of the True Faith,' Langoisse went on, his voice reduced to a seething hiss, 'is it not the vampires who must burn, to redeem mankind?'

With this he turned away to the brazier. He wrapped a cloth around his hand, for the hilt of the knife which he took up was hot enough to burn him, and he went quickly to the lady, to lay it across her shoulder. There was an awful sound, which seemed to Noell very like the hiss that had been in the pirate's voice, and then a stench of burning, which made the Turk laugh and clap his hands with glee. These were the first sounds which the creature had ever made in Noell's hearing.

Leilah recoiled in dread, and Noell had to catch her in his arms, so that she could hide her eyes in his shoulder.

When Langoisse looked around, he seemed displeased to see them thus, and the look of angry triumph in his eyes wavered, but he smiled crookedly. He dropped the hot knife upon the floor, but unlike the Turk he could not seem delighted with what he had done.

He is human after all, thought Noell.

The Lady Cristelle made no sound, despite what was now a horrid wound upon her back, with the muscle over the shoulder-blade seeming half-molten in its calamity. Her body, though, had shuddered reflexively with the shock, and that made Noell shiver in sympathy.

The lady responded now for the first time, turning her head to look over the afflicted shoulder at her tormentor. The expression in her eyes was difficult to name, but had a certain malevolent contempt which made Noell glad that the gypsy girl could not see it. The Turk, Selim, could see it well enough, but it only made him chuckle the more. He feared no supernatural vengeance for what his master had done.

'Will you burn her, inch by inch?' asked Noell, hoarsely. 'Is that what you intend?'

'Why not?' said Langoisse. 'And injure her in any other way I can. Before she goes to sleep, I have promised the Turk and my loyal servant without that they may take their pleasure with her. Selim prefers boys, like your noble Prince of Grand Normandy, but will favour a female arse if the occasion takes his fancy. He has never had a vampire, and though my lady must have had many a common lover, I'll hazard a guess that there was never one without a nose.'

The gypsy moaned, and gripped Noell's shoulder more tightly.

'For myself,' said Langoisse, 'I take only a measure of blood.'

He ran the fingers of his right hand up her spine, and then held up the bloodied tips much as the lady herself had held up bloodied fingers before, inviting him to taste them. What he would not take from her fingers before, he greedily sucked from his own. He looked again at Noell, and plainly found something objectionable in the boy's stare.

'I would that I could become a vampire,' he said, bitterly. 'For then I'd turn their own wrath back upon them with all due ferocity, and that coward Richard could no longer say, as once he did, that 'twould not be honourable to face me. I'd be as cruel, then, as their fabled Dragulya, and glad to be.' But as he spoke these words, he did not seem so very glad, or so very certain of his own resolve, and he looked at the tips of his fingers thoughtfully. It did not appear to Noell that the blood had been as sweet to the pirate's taste as he had anticipated.

Langoisse went to fetch the other knife. First, he wrapped the cloth around his hand as he had before. As he did so, he cleaned in a furtive manner what was left of the vampire's blood from his fingers. But as he picked up the heated blade, another hand fell on Noell's shoulder, and eased him aside from where he stood in the doorway. Noell looked around, and was glad to see that it was not the abbot, who would likely have fainted with the shock, but Quintus, who was made of sterner stuff.

'Put down the knife, I beg you,' said the monk, his voice soft but clear. The small man who had stood guard had come with him, but plainly had not mustered enough resolve to stop him.

'Go to your dormitory,' said Langoisse. 'This is my own business.'

The pirate moved towards the vampire, but Quintus quickly crossed the space between them, and interposed himself between the torturer and his victim. He put out his hand, almost as if he were inviting Langoisse to place the red-hot dagger in his palm. The implied invitation was as startling to the pirate as to anyone, and he pulled the blade back to his own chest. His face was white, and Noell knew that the hot weapon must be hurting him even through the cloth.

In the end, Langoisse could not bring himself to strike at the monk, and he dropped the blade unused.

'You are a guest here,' said Quintus, steadily, 'and you have no business of your own. What happens in our house, which is God's house also, is our concern and His. In His name, I beg you to desist. Thief and murderer you are, but you are not yet excommunicate from the faith. . . . That is not your desire, I think, and I believe that the name of Christ still means something to you. Can you truly tell me that you long to be damned?'

Noell could not believe that the threat of excommunication meant much to Langoisse, but perhaps the laws of hospitality meant more. In any case, the pirate said and did nothing. Quintus had taken control.

'I thank you for your mercy,' Quintus said to Langoisse. 'If you will take the Maroc lady and your giggling Turk away, I will see to matters here. I will stand watch until matins.'

But that was to ask too much. Langoisse said 'No!'

For a few moments, the monk and the pirate tried to stare one another down. Though Langoisse had outfaced Ralph Heilyn with ease, Quintus proved a much stiffer test of his resolve. It was the monk who dropped his gaze, but he seemed to do it unforced.

Langoisse was pleased with this tiny victory. 'The abbot has been kind to me,' he said. 'I have always been a friend of the True Church, and would not invite its wrath. You may go now; it is over.'

Quintus bowed, deliberately, and said: 'I am content to take your word, sir, that you will not hurt the lady any more.'

'Then have it,' retorted Langoisse, with as much mockery as he could muster. 'But I'll set my own watch upon her, nevertheless. If you want her wounds tended, Master Cordery can do it.'

'Thank you,' said Quintus, glancing briefly at Noell, who nodded.

The gypsy had released her grip on Noell's shoulder, and she thanked him with a look of profound relief, though he knew that he had done nothing – and would have achieved nothing, had not Quintus intervened. He watched Langoisse lead the Turk from the cell. Selim and the little man went meekly enough. Then Noell turned to help Quintus, who was already trying to free the vampire's hands. He felt sick in his stomach, and wanted to go out himself, to hide his eyes and his heart. But he had agreed that he would stay, and so he must, to show the mercy demanded by that Lord in whom he could not quite believe.

Langoisse, however, remained determined to make one last gesture of defiance, and when Quintus had gone, Noell heard the door of the cell close behind him. The bar which secured it fell dully into place, imprisoning him with the injured lady.

SEVEN

Noell helped the Lady Cristelle to lie face-downwards on the bench which served her for a bed. He dared not put a garment on her back, nor look for a blanket, but the flesh of her arms felt cold to him, and he was anxious on her behalf. The brazier was still in the room, however, and he hoped that its heat might soothe her now, instead of offering a means to injure her.

She was still conscious, and seemed racked with discomfort, though the baleful look which she had turned on her torturer was gone. It was plain to Noell that the power which this vampire had over her own pain was not quite absolute, and that the control which she exercised was not without its cost.

Nevertheless, she managed to speak to him. 'Do not be afraid,' she said. 'I will not hurt you.'

He smiled, as if to deny that he was afraid, though he was certainly anxious.

'Is there aught else which you need?' he asked, thinking of water or ointment. He could not fetch ointment, but there was a flask of water by the side of the cot.

'Why, Master Cordery,' she said, faintly and sweetly, 'what I need above all else is a gift of thy blood.'

He recoiled in confusion, thinking at first that she might be teasing, but her dark eyes looked up into his with all seriousness, and he knew that she meant it.

'I do not understand that need,' he whispered. After a moment, he added: 'It does not nourish you.'

'It is need enough,' she said, in a whisper. 'It is a need I feel so sharply that I can hardly bear to debate the point. I would not try to force you, when you have been kind to me, but I swear that you have no cause to be afraid. There is no cost or hazard in such donation.'

He wished that the door were unbarred, and would have left her if he could. To cover his dismay he picked up the first of Langoisse's daggers, which had grown cold now, from the stone floor.

'Don't go, Master Cordery,' she said quickly, not knowing that the door was sealed. 'Do you know what they have done to Mary? I think they might have hurt her.'

'I do not know,' he said. 'I think they have let her alone.' The fact that he did not know made him miserable because of his impotent promise to preserve her. Perhaps the girl *had* been hurt. Suddenly, it seemed alarming that he had heard no noise from the neighbouring cell.

Noell moved the other dagger with his foot, then picked it up, though it was still warm. He threw the two weapons into the corner of the bleak cell. The lantern-light flickered, sending his shadow dancing madly across the wall, as though it were some demonic apparition: a malign incubus, looming above the recumbent body of its intended victim.

'They would not let my Mary come to me,' said the Lady Cristelle, her voice little more than a whisper. 'Langoisse told his man to silence her when she cried out. I fear that she may be dead.'

She came slowly to a sitting position, then, and drew her cloak about her to hide her nakedness. He winced at the thought of the hurt it must cause her ruined back, but then called himself fool for having forgotten that if she could control the pain of the cuts and the burns, the added friction of the woollen cloth could hardly hurt her. Even so, her face seemed very drawn and it was difficult to believe that she had not been agonised by her ordeal.

How do we really know, asked Noell of himself, *what capacity for feeling she has?* He wondered what it might be like to feel pain in its full measure, and yet be forced by duty not to acknowledge it. It could not be done, he concluded. No creature, whatever its nature, could have forborne to scream, had it really felt the full measure of the fire in that red-hot blade. And yet, who but a vampire could say what a vampire felt when its flesh was rent or burned? Still, she was distressed; might Langoisse be right, that she could have been made to tell what she knew, if in truth she knew anything of value?

He stood there looking at her, not knowing what to say.

'You need not be sorry, Master Cordery,' she said. 'You owe me no pity. Richard will treat you as badly as the pirate has treated me, if ever he finds you.'

'Why?' asked Noell, suddenly emboldened. 'Because I am kin to the man who destroyed a lady of his court, or because I know the secret of the making of the microscope?'

She seemed genuinely puzzled by his question. 'What has the toy to do with it?' she asked.

Noell felt that he must be careful, for there was no way of knowing for sure what would become of this lady when Langoisse removed her from the abbey. But he could not pursue his own curiosity without making some play with hers. She did not seem reluctant to talk. Perhaps the distraction was welcome to her, to help her forget her need for blood and the mutilation of her flesh.

'My father thought that the instrument might tell us a great deal about the body and its fluids,' said Noell. 'He knew that Richard planned to have him killed, for fear of what he might discover concerning the nature of human and vampire flesh.'

Her gaze was steady as she looked at him, though her face was still drained of all colour. She had looked less vampire-like in her distress, as though her uncanny flesh were faintly tarnished, but now she had a grip upon herself again, and her composure was almost restored.

'Edmund Cordery would have been arrested for his secret treason,' she said. 'What vanity can have made him believe that he could learn anything to his advantage through that strange spy-glass? Could it see men's souls as well as the texture of their skin? Richard has that skrying-glass which John Dee and Edward Kelley used; I have looked into it, and thought perhaps I caught a glimpse of its host of angels, but even that glass could not instruct Master Kelley as to how he might become immortal.'

'It was not a magic thing,' Noell told her. 'My father did not believe that there is any magic in the making of vampires, but simply a mechanism to be revealed.'

'How like a mechanician,' she said, with a faint attempt at lightness, 'to imagine the world and the flesh as a mere nest of machines. But what was his intention? Did he hope to find a way to destroy vampires, or a way to become one?'

Noell could not be certain of the answer to that, but he answered as if he were. 'He found a way to destroy one vampire,' he said. 'With time, and the microscope to show him the world of seeds and corpuscles, he might have killed you all.'

'He was a very foolish man,' replied Cristelle. 'No vampire save Carmilla Bourdillon has yet been killed, but ordinary men and women are dying in the London streets. The reputation of this disease was ill-deserved. Like all others, it harms humans far more than it harms vampires.'

'And yet Carmilla Bourdillon is dead,' he countered.

'Are you proud of that, Master Cordery? To have put a brutal end to a lovely thing, which might have endured for a thousand years? Do you know how old Carmilla was?'

'Six hundred years and three,' said Noell, too promptly, realising too late that his knowledge would reveal that he had read *The Vampires of Europe*, the forbidden book where the histories of many vampires were recorded.

But she only smiled, and said: 'Perhaps you imagine that you can understand what it is like to live, as my kind does, in the shadow of eternity. Perhaps you think that it is only like your own life, but longer, and no more than that. No doubt you think it a trivial matter, too, that we may live apart from pain, apart from sorrow, and apart from wrath. Yet you cannot imagine how different we truly are. You have no notion of our nature or our heritage, poor little mayfly . . . brief flicker of shadowy life.'

'I understand how cruel you are,' he said. 'I understand how your own immunity from pain makes you casual in inflicting it on others, so that there is no part of the Imperium of Gaul where torture is not a commonplace infliction. I know the tales they tell of Attila, of Dragulya. You Gaulish vampires pretend to be a better breed, maintaining Charlemagne's code of chivalry, pretending mercy and modesty and nobility of spirit. Yet things happen even now within the precincts of the Tower which are a shame upon its builders, and all the gibbets in London are well-supplied with victims. Why should I reckon you, or any other vampire lady, better than Erszabet Bathory, who bathed in the blood of children, because she thought it would make her fair enough of face to be empress of the east? I know the evil that is in you, so do not mistake what I have tried to do for you this night. Perhaps the fault in this is mine, that I have not stronger stomach yet for Langoisse's work.'

She seemed surprised by this outburst of anger. 'We are not wantonly cruel,' she told him, with apparent sincerity. 'Erszabet Bathory was condemned for her crimes, even in Attila's empire. They walled her up in her castle – did you not know?'

'But they could not pay her in her own coin,' said Noell, bitterly. 'They could not make her suffer as she caused suffering in others. Cast alive into the tomb she simply went to sleep, and might wake up at any time in a thousand years, quite ready to resume her life. How long would it take her to die, do you think? Or can she withstand starvation forever?'

'I do not know,' said Cristelle. 'But she is paying for what she did, under the law. There must be law, to keep the world in balance, and if the world were ruled by common men the estates of men would be disordered, and law much harder to sustain. Do the Mohammedans have no torturers? Are they legendary for their gentleness? There would not be one hundredth of the suffering that there is in the world if common men could be content with the estate which God has ordered for them. They are promised a happy immortality of their own, in the kingdom of Heaven, if they will only live as they should.'

'Hypocrisy!' said Noell. 'Vampires are no true followers of Christ, and love cruelty more than merely human beings could ever do. My father told me more than once how you treated Everard Digby for his part in the gunpowder plot. He was dragged through the streets by horses, hung from the gibbet, castrated and quartered. Do you imagine that men could have done so foul a thing had he tried to murder a common princeling? Your lust for human blood and human pain is the most terrible thing on earth, and cannot be ordered by God no matter what your puppet pope may say. Would Christ have given you leave to drink the blood of men?'

She gathered her cloak about her a little more tightly, and dropped her gaze. 'The blood which I have drunk has been given willingly,' she said, in a strangely distant tone. 'Given, for the greater part, with love, or at least with false promises of love. Would you not give willingly of your blood, Master Cordery, for *love*? Your saviour was not ashamed to bleed for love of mankind, and you partake of that blood in holy communion, do you not?'

'It is not the same,' said Noell, insistently.

She looked up at him again, and it seemed to him that she had only looked away in order to prepare that transfixing glance. She had banished the tiredness from her face, and the distress too, and she spoke now in a very different tone of voice.

'If thou wert in love with me, Noell Cordery,' she said, 'wouldst thou not offer to thy lover the gift of thine own sweet blood? Wouldst thou not offer it with joy, as Edmund Cordery offered blood to Carmilla Bourdillon? And in refusing it now, art thou not seeking to torture me, in thine own fashion, as the unkind and furious pirate tried to do?'

He was caught by her stare, as she had plainly intended, and felt himself trapped by the force of his own sight. How could he deny that she was more beautiful than any common girl? How could he help but feel the pressure of his own desire? It was nothing of his choosing; desire moved within him like a supernatural force, a wind from hell. He was, after all, no monk, and if he felt himself more aroused by the vampire than by the so-called gypsy princess or poor Mary White, was it not simply a mirror of the way the world was made? Was Langoisse right, and this beauty of hers a monstrous trap, and she a siren, a Satanic whore? And if not, or even if so, what was a man to think or feel or do?

'I do not love thee,' he replied, his voice much strained, and realised as soon as he had said it how silly his reply must seem, when he had echoed her 'thee' unthinkingly. He made the sign of the cross, not ostentatiously, but covertly and ashamedly, driven by necessity to seek what protection it might give him.

'Carmilla Bourdillon might have loved thee,' she said, 'as she loved thy father before thee. Such comfort might have been found in her white arms as to make thee loathe the life which now must be thine. It was a comfort which Edmund Cordery did not deny himself, even when he thought to murder her in the midst of his loss.'

He backed away from this curious assault, feeling himself more endangered by argument than by any threatening movement she might have made. He found himself backed up against the stone wall, as though pinned there by his consternation.

But she did not laugh to see him so anxious. Instead, she softened her expression again, and looked at him with all the innocence of a child. 'Please, Master Noell,' she said to him, 'for pity's sake, spare me a little blood.'

'No,' he replied, hoarsely. 'I cannot. I will not.' He turned away from her, putting his face to the door, wishing that it might open. It did not.

When he turned round again, at last, she was no longer disposed to pay him the slightest heed. She had gathered up her ankles beneath her thighs, and was curling up as if to sleep. It was as if she were settling herself to sleep for a hundred years, in that mysterious way which vampires had, not to wake again until blood was gently spilled upon her eager lips.

As he watched her long black hair fall across her pale face, he saw that there was now no sign of the scar made by Langoisse's dagger on the earlier occasion when he had tormented her. In time, the wounds on her back would fade away as if they had never been. Langoisse's back, no doubt, still carried its scars and weals, and caused him pain whenever he must use the damaged muscles. Perhaps they had cut so deeply into the frame of his being that they would remain even if he were someday to win that prize which he sought, and become immortal. Some of Richard's knights, converted in maturity, still bore the stigmata of earlier wounds, whose state had passed beyond repair. Langoisse was not concerned with appearances, and would be proud to keep the welts; it was the pain from which he sought his freedom.

Could there ever be an end, Noell wondered, to the toll of blood which the vampires demanded of common men – not just the trickles which were freely and lovingly offered in unnatural passion, but the great floods which were drawn by the torturer's lash and the warrior's blade? All the legacy of vampire rule, it seemed just then, was measured in scars and spoliation; the scars of Langoisse's ruined back; the scars of Edmund Cordery's ill-used breast; the scars of sin on the souls of the undying, who need not hurry to meet their judge and maker.

I want no scars, said Noell to himself, so vehemently that he nearly spoke the words aloud.

Even as he made this declaration, he felt the sin of Adam roiling in his soul, an awful desire whose release could only be bought with blood.

'Oh, Quintus,' he murmured, as he sat himself down in that lonely corner, wedged between wall and door, 'what am I, after all, but a thing of common clay? I dearly wish that I might pray, to ask that God might make me other than I am, though I know full well that He would not do it if He could.'

EIGHT

Noell was awakened from exhausted sleep by the sound of the bar which had imprisoned him, scraping along the stone as it was withdrawn. He came slowly to his feet, picking up the two daggers which he had thrown down. He turned to face the opening door.

It was not Langoisse but Selim who had come to set him free. The Turk looked at him dully, his eyes seeming the only human part of his ruined face as he beckoned, ordering Noell to come out. Noell turned instead to look at the vampire, who was silent and still upon her cot. He picked up the cloak which she had gathered about her, and raised it gently. He was careful because he thought it might stick, caught by the drying blood which had flowed from her wounds, but it did not. He could hardly believe, looking down at her naked skin, that this was the same flesh which had been lacerated only hours before. There was hardly any blood, and where she had been cut by the lash the wounds were already closed. Only where the hot blade had burned her was there clear evidence of the damage which had been done – a great ugly weal, pink and gleaming.

She did not wake up, and Noell guessed from her stillness that she would not wake at all, today or tomorrow. She had escaped into that deeper unconsciousness of which vampires were capable – a coma which might last a year, or a hundred years, from which she might wake briefly at irregular intervals to seek the blood which she still needed. Her wounds would heal, but there remained a hungry void within her, which only common blood could fill.

Noell laid the cloak down again, gently, and then went out of the cell. The Turk pointed to the passage which led from the cells to the cloister, but Noell, having handed over the two knives, told him to wait. While Selim barred the lady's cell, Noell took down the bar from Mary White's door, and went in.

Mary lay on her straw pallet, hands tied and mouth gagged. Her clothes were torn. She moved when she heard him come in, but she could not see who he was, and her movements were inspired by dread.

He quickly went to her, soothing her by calling her name, several times. He took the gag from her mouth, and then began to untie her hands. She whimpered faintly, as though she could not speak, and he fetched her water from the jug. She sipped avidly, but she would not speak, and turned her face away in pain and shame. He realised that she had been raped, and that she was near-delirious with anxiety and lack of sleep. She writhed away from his touch, and he did not know what he ought to do.

He opened his mouth to ask her who it was that had hurt her, but the question died on his lips as she shrank away from him. *After all, he thought, I am only an outlaw among outlaws, who shares their station. Why should she not cower away from me?* He ached with guilt.

'I will send one of the monks,' he told her. 'He will bring a draught to help you sleep.'

She tried to reply, but could not form words. She had looked to him for help, and he had given none. He felt that he had betrayed her. He felt betrayed himself, by his own impotence.

He did not know where to go, but wanted to hide. He did not want to go to the refectory, or to his room, or to the quiet church where, for him, there was only an absence of God. So, when he had told Brother Innocent, as he had promised, about Mary White's distress, he went to the library. He could not have explained precisely why he chose this place above all others, but it was the only place in which he had any sense at all of belonging. For a while he stayed in the upper room, but when the chimes told him that the monks would be at matins, he went down instead into the cellar, there to consult *The Vampires of Europe* on the subject of Lady Cristelle d'Urfé.

Little was said of her in the book, whose many authors had been more interested in the activities and ambitions of the males of her species. The text revealed that she was a relatively young vampire, having been born in Less Normandy about the year 1456, the younger daughter of a cousin of the Marquis de Verney. In 1472 or 1473 she had become the lover of the vampire knight Jean de Castrys, who lived at the time in Rheims, and while in Rheims had become a vampire. It seemed that she had never been to Charlemagne's court at Aachen, and that de Castrys had brought her to Grand Normandy in 1495 – apparently because of some quarrel with Prince Geoffrey. De Castrys, though, had returned to Rheims when he had patched up his quarrel, leaving Cristelle at Richard's court.

The list of Cristelle's common lovers contained only one name which

Noell thought notable: the adventurer Raleigh, who had later married the daughter of Henry Tudor and Nan Bullen before being executed for treason. The crimes listed against her were trivial, and Noell judged that as a stranger in Richard's court, brought there by a foreign knight, she had never been entrusted with any of its labour of intrigue.

When he had replaced the book, and returned to the sunlit room above, he could not bring himself to read. Instead he sat alone with his thoughts, watching the clouds drift in from the sea upon the westerly wind. *I would that it were Elphin's time*, he thought, *when vampires had not yet come to British soil, and the truth might still make a stand against the world, in the voices of honest men.*

Later, Quintus came to him, as he was accustomed to do, almost as if it were an ordinary day. 'I am bitterly sorry,' said the monk, 'for all that happened last night. There is no sanction we can use against the pirate, who has us all in his power. I do not think that he is an evil man, but his blacker moods bring him close to madness. He is fearfully anxious of his situation, though he dare not let his fear show in any honest way. We must pray that naught disturbs him until the hour of his departure.'

'What will happen to Mary White?' asked Noell.

'I will ask that he leave her here, so that we may find a place for her in a convent,' replied the monk, carefully.

'Despite that we do not wish her harm,' said Noell, bitterly, 'she is as much a danger to us as she is to Langoisse. If she were ever to tell what had happened to her here, she could have us all destroyed. And why should she hold her tongue, when the Lord's house offered her no effective sanctuary? Perhaps, good Christians though we be, we should pray that Langoisse might remove her, and take her for a brigand's whore; or that he might kill her, when she has been raped a few times more by the vilest of his crew. She is innocent of any crime, and yet she is a threat to your safety and mine. 'Tis a dire world, which sends us such vexations.'

'I will ask Langoisse to leave her,' Quintus said again, more definitely. 'I will tell him that we shall send her to the nuns at Llanllyr. I pray that he will let her go, and that the nuns can persuade her not to betray to the Normans what happened to her here.'

'And the vampire?' asked Noell. 'Would you send her to a nunnery too?'

Quintus shook his head. 'I do not know what might be done with the vampire, now that she sleeps, but I know that Langoisse will not surrender her.'

'I know nothing,' Noell said, in a voice bitter with pent-up anxiety. 'For all my studies, I know nothing of what I need to know. I do not know the purposes of the Invisible College which took me when my father died. Nor do I know the purposes of these quiet monks, who

keep what they call the True Faith, owing allegiance neither to Alexander nor to Gregory. I do not know what work there is for a common
man to do in this world of lordly vampires and vengeful brigands. I
thought that I did know these things. I thought it a courageous ideal
to preserve an authentic Church of Christ from destruction by a false
pope and his inquisitive friars. I thought I understood, too, why
members of the court might belong to a secret society, plotting against
the vampires even while pretending to support them. I even thought
that I knew what heroic work a pirate might do, trying to claim the
oceans for common men although the land belongs to the vampire
Imperia. Now I see that I know nothing.'

'It is an important discovery to make,' said Quintus, evenly, 'and
one which frightens us all.'

'I am too sick to stomach sophistries,' said Noell, sharply. 'It seems
that the whole of justice, and mercy, and courage, and wisdom, are in
hiding, while in the open part of what we do there is only slyness, and
malice, and fear, and folly. Why is the world so twisted about itself?
Why do not common men simply stand together in great armies, to
face the vampires and cast down their empire, instead of pretending to
submit while secretly weaving sad shadows of defiance?'

'It has been done,' Quintus replied. 'Armies of common men have
faced the vampires a hundred times. But the vampire-led armies have
always won. They are such bold warriors themselves that they terrify
those who would stand against them, and they are very clever in saving
their most precious reward for those men who fight most bravely in
their cause. That is the essence of their power. Another day will come
when good men will go against them, and another and another, but
they will need to bear weapons which hurt vampires more than mere
arrows or musket-balls can. If ever common men are to inherit the
world, they will need the way prepared by such secret societies as you
have mentioned; they will need minds made by the wisdom of the
Invisible College, and they will need souls shaped by the teaching of
the True Faith. Without the first, the world cannot truly be won;
without the second, it would not be worth the winning.'

'But there are those within this very monastery,' Noell told him,
'who believe that the *true* True Faith requires not opposition but patient
forbearance, and that it matters not at all that the material world has
been given to the dominion of evil while we have the more precious
immortality awaiting us in Heaven. Some of your own brethren would
ask us to submit to the temporal power of the vampires while saving
our souls. *Render unto Caesar that which is Caesar's, and unto God that
which is God's.*'

'Is that what you would rather do?' asked the monk.

'How can we know what it is right to do?' asked Noell, his tone
almost pleading. 'How can we even be sure that it is common men and

not the vampires who are the Lord's chosen people? If we accept that they are not the devil's handiwork at all, but were made by God as Adam was, how can we not accept that God placed them over us? How do we know what we must do, to make the world right?'

'God sent his only son to us as a mortal man,' Quintus told him, gently. 'Christ died for us, to show us the pathway to salvation. Only death can redeem us from our sins. It is a hard road, but it is the only road which can lead us to the Kingdom of God. That other immortality is a temptation. I cannot honestly tell whether it is the most clever of all the devil's tricks, or another gift of God which men must one day learn to use in wiser fashion, but I know that the vampires use it ill, and against the interests of man and God alike. It is lawful to oppose their empire, not merely by prayer and by refusal, but by action. As Our Lord cast out the usurers from his father's house, so may we seek to cast out the vampire lords.'

But Noell took up the Bible, which rested on the desk where he had left it two days before, and opened it to the gospel of St. John, quoting: '*Then Jesus said unto them, verily, verily, I say unto you, except ye eat the flesh of the Son of Man, and drink his blood, ye have no life in you. Whoso eateth my flesh and drinketh my blood hath eternal life; and I will raise him up at the Last Day. For my flesh is meat indeed, and my blood is drink indeed.*'

Noell paused after reading, to study his mentor's face, but Quintus said nothing, waiting for Noell to go on. 'May this not be God's commandment to the vampires?' asked Noell. 'Is it not a commandment which they follow most faithfully, after their fashion? Might it then be Richard's kind, and not our own which will enjoy the favour of Christ, when he comes again to judge our world? They do not need our blood as meat, for the ordinary nourishment of their bodies – so what can common blood be to them but the food of the spirit? May not the pathway of salvation be theirs to follow, not ours at all?'

Quintus, recognising the pain of his doubt and distress, did not charge him with blasphemy. Instead, he said: 'The devil is the ape of God, and his task is to twist and pervert the true doctrine by forging a false one. Vampirism is but a mockery of the message of the saviour, whose true meaning is enshrined in the holy communion. Jesus brought his message to human beings, Noell. There were no vampires in Galilee at that time, nor in the whole empire of the Romans which St. Paul set out to convert. I do not hold with Gregory that the vampires are demons in human guise, but I do believe that Satan sent Attila against the Holy Empire when that empire had grown too strong a force for good.'

Noell still could only shake his head in care-worn fashion.

'Tell me the truth,' said his mentor, softly. 'It is not the lessons of scripture and history which trouble thee, but pity for the vampire. Beauty is only glamour, Noell, and it is a most deceitful magic.'

'So Langoisse has told me,' Noell replied, 'and I would that I believed it. But I cannot *feel* it, and when I have seen poor Mary hurt, and heard the laughter of that evil Turk to see Langoisse at his labour of torture, I cannot believe that any Lord looks down upon this house, nor that any scripture can tell us what to be and what to do. We must find our own way, Quintus, and I do not know how to do it.'

'Pray for the maid,' Quintus instructed him. 'And if it soothes thee, pray for the vampire too. Satan's minions were angels once, and it is not beyond doubt that they might yet be redeemed. Above all, perhaps, we should pray for the pirate, for his is the soul in greatest hazard of damnation, which might yet be turned toward salvation.'

But Noell had not the opportunity even to pretend to pray, for the abbot came hurrying at that moment into the library, all flushed with troublesome excitement, to tell them both that armed men were riding toward the abbey. They came not from the town, he said, but along the rough road from Lampeter, and to make things worse, they had black friars riding with them.

'Does the pirate make ready to fight?' asked Quintus, quickly.

'Aye,' replied the abbot. '''Twas his man saw the company from the bell-tower, and now he plans an ambush – though he has but a handful of pistols against their muskets and their pikes.'

'He is a fool!' complained Quintus. 'He must run, if he can.'

Quintus spoke rapidly to Noell, who was stunned, momentarily unable to rise from his seat. 'Do not show yourself,' he commanded. 'Make ready to go to the town, where you must find safe hiding – and stay away from the pirate, if you can.' Then he rushed from the room.

Noell came slowly to his feet, and made as if to follow him, but felt that he was not one whit nearer to knowing the direction in which he ought ultimately to go.

NINE

Noell went to his room, going up by the back stair and intending to make his exit the same way. His plan was to gather up his things, and then return to the church, where he might make an exit on the north side from one of the chapels. He already knew the names of people in the town who would hide him, if only he could reach and cross the river without being seen and chased. Quintus would come to him there, when it became safe for him to do so, but there was little chance of his ever returning to the abbey, if the black friars were coming.

He had barely finished his packing when the door of his room burst open. He turned, half-expecting to see Leilah, but it was only the girl who served the gypsy as a maid. Her dark eyes were wild with fear.

'My mistress sent me to thee, Master Cordery,' she said. 'She asks that thou shouldst hide me, and see me safe through the fighting.'

Noell had had his fill of pleas for help, but this was a little child. Leilah had not told him how she came to have the maid with her, but Noell guessed that she had been a slave in the Arab lands, like Leilah herself. On a sudden impulse, he said: 'Come with me, then, for there is no safety here.'

The child nodded, trustfully, and Noell led her from the room. But in the corridor without, they met Langoisse, who had also come to look for Noell. The pirate was surprised to see the little girl by Noell's side, and paused to smile before he spoke, apparently amused by the coupling.

Noell seized the chance to speak first. 'You must hide, Langoisse,' he said, anxiously. 'The monks will protect you, if you give them the chance.'

'Nay, Master Cordery,' the pirate replied. ''Tis time, I think, to repay the good monks for the hospitality they've shown me. This is only a captain and six men trailing a brace of Dominicans, come on casual business, I don't doubt. I've twice the men and the advantage of surprise; what's more, I need their guns and powder. Where were you planning to go, pray tell? I'd thought that you'd rather guard the lovely vampire than this little chit, or art thou like a child thyself, e'er fickle in thy loyalties?'

'Come with me, Langoisse,' said Noell, urgently. 'I'll guide your men as best I can across the fields. Heilyn will meet us tomorrow, and we can hide until the appointed hour. A fight can only bring disaster on us all.'

But Langoisse shook his head. 'Too little shelter in those fields,' he said, 'and they stink besides. The riders are too close by now, and will see us if we try to flee. You might escape, under cover of the commotion which we will cause, so go if you must, and go safely. But you'd fare better with me, if you've the courage to stay, than in this drear country of the Welsh. You'll only find freedom in a foreign land, or on God's high seas where the vampires fear to go. Stay in this land, skulking in cellars, and someone will surely betray you, for thirty guineas or less. Wales has more than her share of men so poor they'd sell their mothers for half such a wage.'

'You'll bring disaster here,' repeated Noell, as Langoisse turned to go, but he realised as he said it that the pirate had brought disaster with him the moment that he crossed the threshold, and that the taint of his passing could not easily be scraped away. More murders would increase the record of his crimes, but little good could be done now even if Langoisse agreed to stay his hand.

I must go to Quintus, thought Noell, putting aside his former plans. *He must come with me, and we must remove the forbidden books from the library. The Dominicans will come in force if their men are killed, and the monks must flee in their turn, to seek sanctuary for themselves.*

He went to the rear stair, the little girl running behind him for want of anything else to do, so that when he reached the foot of the flight he had to command her to wait by the door. She could not go into the cloister.

In the inner court he quickly found Brother Martin, but before he could open his mouth to speak the monk begged him earnestly to go back and fetch the almoner's boys away from the outer court, to bring them to a gathering in the church.

Noell hesitated, beset by indecision, but guessed from what Martin said that the monks knew full well what Langoisse intended, and had no need of his advice. Still, he turned back towards the brewhouse to do as he was asked, thinking that he would surely find Quintus in the church when the whole population of the abbey was gathered there.

In the brewhouse he found two boys crouched by the barrels inside the door, watching the courtyard in apparent fascination, not in the least concerned to retreat. Noell had to touch them on the shoulders before they even knew that he was there, and they did not show the least inclination to follow him. Before he could begin an argument he heard the clatter of hoofbeats on the road, and saw one of the black friars riding through the open gate, having apparently come on ahead of the rest of his party, perhaps to instruct the abbot what provision should be made for the visitors.

Noell's heart sank; it was too late now to carry forward any plan. He stood as if rooted to the spot, staring out into the courtyard where the tragedy was beginning to unfold.

The horseman looked around, and seemed somewhat vexed to find nobody about. Noell hid himself by the lintel of the brewhouse door, and knew that a dozen others must likewise be hiding, waiting for the rest of the approaching men to come into their trap.

The Dominican let out a loud 'Hallo!' as he turned his horse on the cobblestones.

It was clear that the lack of a response would alarm him as much as the sight of something strange, and Noell judged that it would be necessary to distract the man, or the trap could not be properly sprung.

To his surprise, he saw a man in monk's robes hurry from the gateway to the inner court. For just a moment, Noell thought it was Brother Steven, but then he realised that it was one of the pirates, whose natural baldness made it appear that he wore a tonsure. The imposture was effective enough to let the man go to the standing horse, and take its rein. The scowling Dominican, annoyed but expecting no trouble, began to dismount. The pirate came round to his side, then let go the horse and grabbed the friar around the throat, as if to throttle him as he dragged him away.

The Dominican was no weakling, and clung fast to the horse's rein, trying meanwhile to claw away the arm at his throat. The pirate was still groping beneath his robe for a weapon, and could not immediately free it from the folds of his habit. While the two of them staggered drunkenly about in the courtyard, the second friar rode through the gate. He caught up his reins immediately, seeing what was happening, and promptly set up a clamour of warning.

On the instant, the pirates swarmed from their hidey-holes, those with pistols hastening to the gateway to fire at the men-at-arms. But their ambush had misfired, and only the captain had actually ridden into the open gateway. He was felled by a bullet, but the men in the road outside had leapt from their horses, and in the shelter which the beasts provided were making haste to load their guns. Most of the shots fired at them must have hit the horses, and probably did the cause of the pirates little good, for it made the animals rear and screech in alarm, and kept the attackers from those they sought to slay.

Noell could not see much of what was happening beyond the gate as the pirates hurried out, but the clash of steel told him that the two parties had quickly come too close for firearms to be used. The battle was now commenced with swords and knives. He had heard only one of the muskets fire.

Within the courtyard he saw that Selim had grabbed the second friar by the leg, and was wrestling him down from the saddle. The Turk was too strong by far for the Dominican, who could not resist the tugging, and fell heavily. From the way that he landed Noell guessed that his skull was split.

The Turk then ran to help the pirate who was dressed as a monk. The disguised pirate had at last freed his dagger, and was trying to stab the friar he was holding, but the friar had let go of the horse's rein and was avoiding the blade by pulling his attacker round and around, as though they were infants prancing in some merry game. With the Turk's aid, the pirate had the friar down and mortally hurt in a matter of seconds, and then they turned to join the mêlée beyond the gate.

The two boys, more excited than afraid, rushed forward to see what was happening, and Noell, after a moment's hesitation, hurried after. When he arrived by the gatehouse he saw Langoisse trading blows of his sword with a helmeted soldier, while another of the men-at-arms was holding a group of four at bay, which he was able to do for a while only because none of the four had a blade as long as his own. Two of the soldiers lay seemingly dead and three of the pirates also, with two wounded horses also down, but the other two men-at-arms had already ridden away, with two pirates on captured horses in hot pursuit.

Looking along the road after them, Noell judged, confidently, that the fleeing soldiers would reach the bridge before their pursuers, and he could also see that it would matter little if they did not. The whole affair, taking place on the brow of the hill, had been seen from afar by other travellers on the road, and he knew that a cry of alarm would be carried from voice to voice all the way to Cardigan Castle.

Noell seized one of the gawping boys, and shook him, telling him to go quickly to the church and tell the monks to ring the bells furiously, to summon help. There was no hope now in the pretence of ignorance; the monks must enter the lists in opposition to their unwelcome guests. Which meant, of course, that he must flee, and Quintus too. They dared not go to the town now, but must go north as quickly as they could.

He looked back at the battle, and saw that Langoisse had outfenced his man, and wounded him badly. The four pirates who were at the other soldier had managed to get within his guard, though he had cut one of them badly. The men-at-arms had carried only the lightest armour, and did not seem to be hardened fighting men. The odds were too heavily against them here at the gate, and Noell understood that but for the accident of bad timing, Langoisse's ambush would have been successful. As it was, the killing had achieved no purpose.

Langoisse, the elation of his victory in the duel seeming to override the knowledge that the ambush had failed in its real purpose, shouted to his men to collect up all the spilled guns, and everything else which was of use. He did not spare a moment to attend to his own stricken men, but went to the captain who had been shot in the neck, and began rifling the bloody corpse. Noell watched him from a distance of five yards, unable to tear himself away.

When the bells began to ring out their emergency call, which would bring the whole town to arms, Langoisse looked up as if in alarm, but then he smiled, and caught Noell's eye.

'Here's vampire's mead, then, Master Cordery,' he called, showing Noell a hand all gory with the captain's blood. 'To us, alas, 'tis food for the spirit only.' He paused to look down at a red-stained paper which he had pulled from the captain's pocket. He stared at it for a few seconds, and then began to laugh. He looked again at Noell, and hurled the paper at him. The wind caught it, spilling it at Noell's feet.

''Twas not for me they came at all,' cried the pirate. 'I told you that the world's fair full of men who'd sell their soul for thirty guineas. It's a warrant for you, Master Cordery, for *you*! I believe I've saved your life, though it's damn near cost me my own. A stupid price for a vampire-loving scut, no doubt, but 'tis paid now and the alarum's raised; so flee we must, though the land lies fairer for the hunters than the prey.'

Noell picked up the paper to look at it, and saw that Langoisse was right. The captain had come to arrest him, having set off in the first instance from Monmouth. He must have collected the Dominicans from Brecon, having reported there a denunciation which touched upon the loyalty of the monks of Cardigan. Someone must have given information against him in England, he knew.

A dread thrill of fear went through him as he wondered whether his mother was safe, and Kenelm Digby, and the others who had brought him out of London. There was no way to know, just now, what the true scale of the calamity might be. He looked at Langoisse, who was facing the other way, shouting again to his men.

When the pirate turned back, he saw immediately the expression in Noell's eyes. 'Look to yourself, Master Cordery!' he said, loudly. 'You would not fight for me, and I'll not take you into my charge now. Take the scholar monk, and the little girl if you care enough for her welfare, and make your own way to Heilyn's boat. If Wellbelove can't catch you, you may beg me to take you aboard and save your skin. I'll find out then what stores of mercy are laid up in my heart.'

With this, the pirate ran through the gate. Selim, who had waited for him, grabbed the rein of the horse upon whose back the first friar had ridden intemperately in, and followed.

Noell turned to go about his own belated business, determined that he must find Quintus, and hoping that Quintus would know what to do.

TEN

Quintus was not in the church, though most of the monks were there, seeking the consolation of prayer, apparently with more ardour than conviction. Nor was the scholar monk to be found in the library, although the trapdoor to the cellar was open, and the abbot was in the room below, gathering books into a satchel.

Noell came down into the room where, it seemed to him now, he had spent so little time, not well-enough used.

'Should I take these books?' he asked the abbot, and was startled when that gentle monk rounded on him, red-faced with anger.

'To what safe place would you take them, Master Cordery?' he demanded. 'These things are precious, and will go with Brother John, to Strata Florida, where the Cistercians may care for them. I must forbid you to go with them. I am sorry for that, but I can think only of the safety of the True Church. You must go your own way now, and soon. If they catch you, I beg that you will not tell them you were ever here.'

'And Quintus?' asked Noell. 'Where is Quintus to go?'

'He would not be safe when the Dominicans come,' replied the abbot. 'Whether he may go to another house, I cannot say, but I dare not trust these things to him. I have sheltered him while I might, but all is changed now, and it is best for him to go to Ireland, or further still.'

Noell had never seen the abbot like this, and had fallen into the habit of thinking of Quintus as the true authority here. Now he saw that Quintus was merely at the forefront of certain dealings which the abbey had with the corrupt world outside. The world within the abbey, where the rule of poverty, piety and peace held its own dominion, was and always had been the abbot's, and the abbot was determined to do what he must to preserve from destruction by the black friars.

'Do you know where Quintus is?' asked Noell.

'Look in the dormitory,' the abbot replied. 'And then the kitchen. He will be making ready for his journey, as you must make ready for yours. You have less than an hour now before they come from the castle. You must go to Heilyn, if you can, to warn him that he might yet be caught in this net of ill-fortune.'

Noell went to the dormitory, and then to the kitchen, but nowhere was there anyone who had seen Quintus.

The girl whom Leilah had sent to him was still waiting by the almonry, where he had left his pack, and she looked up hopefully when he came back that way. He had not seen Leilah at all, but could not pause to wonder where she was. It was Quintus he wanted. He remembered one place where he had not looked, and he ran swiftly to the penitentiary cells, where the Lady Cristelle and Mary White were confined.

There, at last, he found his friend. Quintus was in Mary White's cell, standing over her body. Martin and Steven were with him, and all three were murmuring a prayer. The poor girl's throat was cut from ear to ear, and dark blood had cascaded over her dress. There was no sign of her murderer.

Noell remembered that he had said, once, that it might be safer if Langoisse *did* kill her. He turned the twinges of his own guilt into spite against the pirate, and cried *Murderer!* in his mind, though he made no sound to disturb her meagre requiem. Then he went to the other cell, whose door stood ajar. He looked inside, but the vampire lady was gone, carried away while she was lost in her fathomless sleep.

Noell went to touch Quintus on the arm, but Quintus did not look up until he reached the end of his prayer. Even then, he turned first to

Steven, and said: 'You must bury her, and send a letter to London, so that her family might be told.'

'We cannot linger here,' said Noell. 'The abbot begs us to go.' He spoke faintly, his eyes drawn to Mary's bloody corpse, and a sickness of despair in his heart.

Why? he asked himself, silently. *What harm could she do them now?*

Noell and Quintus withdrew together, and as they climbed the stone steps to the cloister Noell told the other that the child was waiting for them, consigned to his care by the Maroc. Quintus was not pleased by the news, but did not propose that they should abandon this charge, so Noell took him to where the girl was patiently waiting.

To his surprise, he found Leilah there too, with a sullen expression upon her face. Before he could ask the question, she said: 'I was told to go with thee. He would not stay to tell me why.'

Noell did not know whether Langoisse had grown bored with the gypsy and sought to abandon her, or whether he was anxious for her safety and honestly thought that she might fare better in the company of the scholar and the monk. There was no time to debate the issue aloud, so they gathered together all that they had, and left the Abbey a company of four.

Langoisse and his men had already gone, as many on horseback as there were mounts to take them, the rest left to catch up as and if they could. They had gone along the eastward road, which had brought the black friars and their escort. Noell guessed that they would try to lay a false trail before turning north, to work their way round to their real objective: the quiet strand where Ralph Heilyn had agreed to collect them, to take them to Ireland.

Quintus, with a pack much larger than Noell's, took them directly to a northward-leading path across the fields, and led them with a sure stride along the hedgerow, between the fields of ripening corn.

When they were more than three miles from the abbey, they stopped to rest in a small copse. Quintus changed his clothes, removing his habit and dressing himself instead as if he were a yeoman farmer, with a cap to hide his tonsure. Noell was astonished by the apparent change in his mentor; in Noell's mind the nature of a monk was so amply signified by the habit that Quintus in ordinary garb seemed a stranger of whom nothing was known. The austere face, which had seemed almost saintly within the cowl, appeared in its new setting as hard as any overseer's, and Noell saw with a shock that here was a man who had at least as much of the appearance of an outlaw as the volatile Langoisse.

This curious new being produced bread from his pack and broke it, distributing it between the four of them.

'Where will we go?' asked Leilah, as she attacked her food. Of all of them, she seemed the lightest in spirit now, and Noell could see in her dark face that same innocent joy in adventure which had so surprised him on the night when the pirate crew came to the abbey. All travel seemed hopeful to her, perhaps because she had so long been a slave that every day which brought a change to her affairs was an affirmation of her freedom.

'We must go to Heilyn,' Noell told her. 'We must go with the fisherman to Ireland. Wellbelove's men will hunt high and low for us here, and there is no safety in the east or south. We need not stay with Langoisse once we are away. The True Church is strong in Ireland, and the Imperium weak. The foreign fishers who dock in Baltimore are almost a nation unto themselves.'

She was reassured by this, and said: 'Langoisse might take me back then, though the vampire will be his mistress now.'

Noell looked at her hard, but there was no doubt that she believed it. 'I think you misread him,' he said.

'Nay,' she replied. 'He beat her like a mistress, and branded her too, and she will curse me because she could not curse him. I will be unhappy, if I stay with him. That is why he sent me to you.' She did not seem to be overly sorry at the thought of being set aside.

'There is no power in her curse,' said Noell, wearily, 'or we'd all be dead by now. Having fed her the blood which she craved, she is asleep, and I do not think Langoisse intends her to wake. He has not taken her to be his mistress, but to destroy her.'

As he said it, he wondered whether he could be entirely sure. Langoisse had advised him against the temptations of vampire beauty, and had claimed to know whereof he spake. Might Leilah be right, and the violence of his treatment of the vampire mask lustful fascination?

'We must find a place to hide until nightfall is nearer,' Quintus said. 'The soldiers will hunt for Langoisse, and will surely find his trail less hard to follow than ours, but whatever they find in the course of their hunt they will take to the castle, and we must not be found. We cannot ask for help from the farmers. In a barn or a hayloft we might lie low for a while, but we'd be safer still in some thicket where no one would go. Then we must make our way by twilight to the place where Heilyn told Langoisse to go, arriving as darkness falls, so that we cannot attract attention to the place.'

They agreed this plan, and moved stealthily from the copse, creeping along the hedgerows with bowed heads, hoping to avoid the labourers in the fields. With the corn in its present state, there were few men about, and they made their way to the bank of a winding stream, which had sparse woods on either side. They found a hollow near-filled with hawthorn and brambles, and found their way into a covert behind the thorny foliage of a spreading tree. There they sat, to wait until Quintus judged that the time was right for their race to the meeting-place on the distant shore.

As the afternoon passed, no one came near them, though Noell could take little comfort from it. No doubt Wellbelove's men had chased along the road in the wake of the pirate; he could not help but wish that they might catch him, so that none would meet Heilyn's buss but his own group of four. Then, and perhaps only then, would their passage to Ireland be certain to be a peaceful one.

What the Normans would do to the pirate, if they took him alive, would be as horrible as they could contrive. They would send him to London, where, Noell presumed, Richard would make a fine exhibition of his death. That would surely serve to complete his legend, and confirm him as a great hero and martyr in the cause of common man's resistance against the empire of the vampires.

The composers of the most scurrilous broadsides would no doubt make much of this last adventure, and their lewd speculations would outdo by far the actual transactions in the Abbey. The Star Chamber would keep a steady eye on the printing presses of London, but somehow, somewhere, the story would be published, then marched around the nation in the ranks of a paper army which bore no standards. Langoisse dead might be a better man by far than Langoisse alive. A legend in print which might inspire men to rebellion could never do such a trivial and unworthy thing as to cut the throat of an innocent girl.

Noell could not make up his mind whether he would rather the vampire were destroyed or rescued. Whenever he sounded her name in his thoughts, what came to his mind, crowding out all else, was the beauty of her image and the purity of her skin. And whether he would or not, the idea of such beauty disarmed his endeavour to count her in the ranks of evil. Had she seemed more callous, or more proud, it would have been easier to hate her, but there was nothing in what she had done or said which he could take as a warrant for revulsion. Even the way in which she had asked for his blood had been a temptation rather than a threat. It might have been easier if he were a monk, and had taken vows of chastity, for then the temptation itself might have seemed a paramount evil, reason enough for violent response. Instead, he knew by his own father's example how comfortably men could be beguiled by vampire ladies.

They did not talk a great deal while they waited. Leilah's excitement had become muted, and her maid, it seemed, loved nothing better than silence. Quintus seemed thoughtful, and when Noell asked him questions he replied in dismissive fashion. They ate another frugal meal while the sun sank low in the west, lighting the cloud from below and turning half the sky into a vast cloak of red and gold. Not until the sun began to set did Quintus usher them from their hidey-hole and bid them hurry to the coast.

The monk's calculations were thrown out by the little girl's slowness, and it became apparent that they would not reach the sea before it grew dark, but they pressed on as hard as they could.

They lit no lantern when the twilight had finally gone, but there was a bright three-quarter moon, hidden only now and again by scooting clouds, and a few bright stars gave what assistance they could. The darkness slowed them down, but Quintus guided them with assurance.

The darker it became, the more Noell found himself alone with his inner thoughts. His unsoothed uncertainties were by no means comfortable company.

And what, he asked himself, *if Langoisse does not die? Will he capture another fighting ship, and go on to greater triumphs of piracy? What legends might remain to be made, if he cares to sail to the mysterious south of Africa, or across the great ocean in search of the ruins of Atlantis, as rumour already urges him to do?*

The real matter at hand, as he could hardly forget, was what would become of Quintus and himself. He was glad to be able to think of the two together, for he was far from ready to be alone in the world. Now Quintus had changed his habit, it was possible to think in other terms than taking refuge in another scholar's hole. Perhaps their future and the pirate's might be further entwined, so that all might seek adventure together. One day, there might be chapbooks of his own exploits, preserving his name for the admiration of future generations.

But there was poor Mary, with her gaping throat, and he could never forgive Langoisse for that.

'What will happen to the monks whom we left behind?' asked Noell of Quintus, completing his catechism of possible futures and drawing his teacher into his game of speculation.

'They will play the victims of tragedy and terror,' replied Quintus, struggling to speak calmly through his laboured breathing, 'as indeed they are. I hope that the Dominicans will prove no heresy against them, and will let them alone. The abbot is not friendless, within or without the Church. To molest the abbey might prove to be impolitic, and if God wills it, the monks will be allowed to go on with their proper business. There will be no sign that you and I were ever there, and the stain of Langoisse's murders will be laved away in prayer and lamentation, as all murders ultimately are. The True Faith is a rock in a troubled sea, which cannot be broken even by the fiercest storms.'

'I hope you are right,' said Noell. 'I truly do.'

By the time they reached the place appointed, to which they had come by a most circuitous route, Noell had lost all track of the minutes and the hours, and was surprised to find himself at any destination, however temporary. They found no sign of anyone, on shore or off, but Quintus reassured them all that the time of the meeting was not yet come, and that they must wait with patience for at least an hour. Then they would see who would come, and who would not.

They rested, too exhausted even to eat, though they drank a little from a waterskin which Quintus carried. They lay down upon the shingle, and waited to recover their strength.

Noell lay on his back, looking up at the starry firmament, half-hidden by the scattered clouds, and half-revealed. It was far easier to suspect the real existence of God when the earth was dark, shadowed from the gaudy sun. The sky seemed almost empty behind the clouds, the few stars which showed were lonely and forlorn. Noell knew that the great majority of men had recently thought the realm of the fixed stars a close and narrow thing. How awesome it was to exercise the imagination upon the truth of things, which was that the darkness was unimaginably vast, and those tiny suns were lost in a wilderness of space.

If we are so very tiny, he asked of the sky, only part in play, *what does it matter whether we live for sixty years, or six hundred, or six thousand? Will not the universe be just the same, untouched and untroubled by our infinitesimal efforts and pains? And if there is, after all, a God who hides His countenance behind that awful vastness, what can he possibly care about the tribulations of such as we?*

The sky, of course, did not answer him. But as he looked up into it, he felt a strange shift of perspective, as though he were looking through some powerful optical instrument, which made the universe seem not so vast and lonely after all. It was as if his sight and consciousness were not contained in such a narrow prison as he had first thought, but free to roam that abyssal infinity where the stars were lost and lonely.

But I am, after all, here, he told himself, *and here is not simply the space inside my head, but everywhere that my senses apprehend, and everywhen that my understanding can encompass. Why, I am as small as I can make myself, or as great, and I have only to look at myself in the right way to magnify myself as greatly as I desire! I have looked into a microscope, and seen the worlds within the world, and now I am staring infinity in the face. If there is a God, He may look me in the face, with His microscopic eyes, and read the very thoughts inside my mind.*

He realised then, with all the shock of revelation, that it was not true what the vampire lady had said to him, that her kind and her kind only lived in the shadow of eternity. In that shadow *all* must live, each kind after its own fashion: those who might not die, and those who must.

He saw that even a common man could not simply say *Here is today and tomorrow, and then naught*; however narrow his allotted span he could not help but be a citizen of the vast empire of All Time. Every common man had ancestors, and most had children too, and whatever a common man did in the world, it was the heritage of all his forebears, and must extend in its consequences across all the generations of mankind, for as long as the world itself would last.

There was something which terrified Noell in the thought that what he was doing at that very moment had as its antecedents the whole history of man and the world, and must extend its effects, however subtly, through all of time to come . . . but it was a cheerful terror, which he was glad to embrace.

He had to swallow a curious lump which had come into his throat, and as he did so was suddenly afraid that he might lose this moment of vision, and forget entirely what it had taught him. But then he saw what a ridiculous fear that was.

It is not simply that we live in the shadow of eternity, he told himself, *but that we are the ones who cast it, human and vampire alike. In the beating of our tiny hearts is the echo of forever.*

ELEVEN

They did not immediately know when Heilyn's buss came to keep her tryst, because she came silently to anchor without showing a light, too far from the shore to be easily seen. The first they knew of her arrival was the splash of oars from a small boat easing its way into the shallows. There was only one man in her, and she could take no more than half a dozen. The fisherman gave out a low whistle, and when Quintus and Noell ran to meet him he called out anxiously to know who they were.

'It is Brother Quintus from the Abbey, and the lay scholar,' the monk replied, as they clambered over smoothed rocks, careful of the slippery weed which grew there, to reach the bare sand where the boat was.

The fisherman seemed relieved to hear this news, but when Quintus and Noell arrived, wading into the shallows, he heard that others were approaching, and said 'How many more?'

'We have two with us,' Quintus told him. 'A woman and a child.'

The fisherman came out of the boat, and helped to pull it further in to shore. 'Is this all?' he asked, the tone of his voice testifying that he would be very glad if it were so.

Even as he spoke, Noell heard the sound of feet upon the wet sand, and knew that there were others here, though they had kept silent until now. He could not see in the darkness who they might be, and thought for a moment that it might be Wellbelove's men come to capture him. He felt himself grabbed by the arms, and though he twisted furiously he could not get free. In the moonlight there were many shadows, and he could not count them. Only when a man spoke, and he recognised Langoisse's voice, was he sure of what was happening.

"Tis a pistol at your head, Master Fisher,' hissed the pirate, in a low tone, 'but 'twill do you no harm as long as you're silent. Brother Quintus, Master Cordery, you must get into the boat, and hide our muskets with your backs when they shine a lantern on you. If you wish to avoid bloodshed, you must convince Master Heilyn that all is well before we board.'

'You mean to steal the ship!' exclaimed Noell. He had enough instinctive wisdom to keep his voice low.

'Of course we must, pretty fool. What did you imagine that I had in mind, when I asked about his crew and their weapons, even at the risk of putting him on his guard?'

It seemed so obvious now. Noell felt himself a pretty fool indeed.

'We can only do as he says,' Quintus told him, his voice resigned. Clearly, Quintus had thought about things more thoroughly than he, and was not overly shocked by this new turn of events.

'Does Heilyn know you?' asked the pirate of the monk.

'He has seen me at the Abbey,' replied Quintus.

'Good. But you must change those clothes which you put on, for they do not suit our present purpose. Do it quickly, I beg of you.'

Quintus complied, while the pirates waited impatiently.

Noell climbed into the boat, and moved to the prow while it was turned about in the shallows. Langoisse gave one oar to Quintus and another to the Turk, while he and two others crouched down, concealing their guns. They rowed out to sea, saying nothing, and Noell strained his eyes, searching the darkness for the shadow of the buss. His heart was pounding again, though he had imagined himself quite composed while they waited on the beach. The journey seemed long, though it could not have been, in terms of the clock.

When he finally caught sight of the waiting ship, he told the rowers to bear to port, and then shouted, at Langoisse's instruction, for a light to be shown.

The sailors on the ship brought a light to her port bow, and Noell could see that four were there, all with muskets ready in their hands.

'Who's aboard?' cried Master Heilyn, as yet unable to see the men in the boat.

'Brother Quintus from the Abbey,' replied the monk. 'And Master Cordery.'

Heilyn lowered the light, and it illuminated the head and shoulders of the monk. The shipmaster grunted with satisfaction, but his fears were not completely allayed.

'What bells were rung at the abbey this afternoon?' he asked, anxiously.

'Dominicans came with men-at-arms,' Quintus told him. 'They came to root out heresy, and succeeded, for here we are as you can see. Put down your guns, Ralph, and help us aboard.'

Heilyn seemed half-satisfied with the reply, and threw down a rope ladder, but told his men to be ready. Noell was the first to climb up to the ship, and Quintus followed him. Then came Langoisse, and as he reached the deck the two men who had been with him in the back of the boat brought up their muskets, aimed and primed.

The Turk had already leapt from the boat, scorning the ladder, and had climbed the side in seconds, pulling a pistol from his belt and a knife from his teeth as soon as his feet were on the deck. Langoisse was brandishing a pistol of his own, pointing it at the head of Ralph Heilyn. The fishermen with muskets hesitated, lost in confusion, and Langoisse told their master to instruct them to drop the guns.

Heilyn looked at Quintus, bitterly, and called him betrayer.

'Alas, Master Heilyn,' said Quintus, "tis better thus. If you carried us to Ireland, and then returned, you'd be in mortal danger. Far better to be rudely dispossessed by the pirate Langoisse than to give him willing succour and carry him safe from his enemies. You must make up a story to explain your loss, and may curse us all as loudly as you like. When all is finished, you may go to the abbot, and remind him what he owes you, if he is still able to pay. I cannot say that you'll not be a loser, but I know that you will not lose your life.'

It seemed that Heilyn could hardly wait to practise his cursing, but once Langoisse was identified to him, he and his crewmen knew better than to start a fight. The fishermen were disarmed, then the Turk and another man ferried half the crew to shore, returning with Leilah and her maid, and some more of their own men, before taking away the rest of the fishers. In the end, they took Heilyn back alone, and left him on the beach to count the cost of his ill luck – railing, no doubt, against the ruthlessness of the wicked fate which had caught him in its net.

When the pirates took up the anchor, and sailed away, Selim took Quintus and Noell down to the mate's cabin, and watched them until Langoisse had taken proper stock of his new possession.

Noell sat on the bunk, and Quintus on the floor, in the tiny cabin, which stank no less of fish than any other part of the buss. The Turk remained patiently in the doorway, his hands folded across his chest. The swinging candle-lamp which lit the cabin sent all the shadows a-swaying when the ship bobbed on the waves, tacking half across the wind. The strange contours of the Turk's scarred face seemed almost alive in the shifting light, as though it was a skull covered in writhing worms, with naught living in it but the gleaming eyes which stared upon them.

Here's a demon, though Noell, *who might easily tend a cauldron in any Hell. But where's the pretty one, the devil's whore?* He had seen no sign of the Lady Cristelle, though he could not be entirely sure that she had not come aboard with the last party brought from shore.

At last, Langoisse came to see them, bearing several packs with him. He pushed the ones which belonged to Noell and Quintus into the cabin, but placed two more outside the door.

'Well, my friends,' he said. 'What am I to do with you? I've half a mind to feed you to the fish, though my pretty gypsy has pleaded most earnestly that I should let you live. You're pirates now, of course, for your part in stealing Master Heilyn's ship, and you will hang at Chatham Dock if ever Richard's navy gets its hands on you. Then again, Richard might plan a more entertaining fate for you on Tower Hill, or at Tyburn, as he surely does for me.'

'We came in search of a passage to Ireland,' said Quintus, evenly. 'Perhaps you might leave us in Baltimore.'

'I'll not make port anywhere that the *Firedrake* might catch up with me,' said Langoisse. 'Master Heilyn did as he was bid, and provisioned for a journey. Without his crew, we've food enough to take us to Tenerife, and I'll feel safer there than in any land within the Imperium of Gaul, if the ship is hale enough to make the voyage. I think she is.'

'And will you be a pirate in a herring-ship?' asked Quintus. 'She'll not deliver much of a broadside, I fear, and you'd be hard-pressed to chase an argosy.'

Langoisse grinned, showing his discoloured teeth. 'I was a pirate in a crippled galley once,' he said. 'When I started in this life, I'd naught but my own strong arms and Selim's friendship. With brave men and muskets there's much that might be accomplished on the Afric shore, and I think I might even make my peace with the vampires of Malta, if I cared to seek sanctuary with the Hospitallers. I might sell you both for slaves, I suppose, but I'm not such a cruel man, as well you know.'

'It was a cruel and vile man which cut poor Mary's throat,' said Noell, coldly, 'and that was not a sin which I could ever forgive. I'll call no such man friend.'

Langoisse laughed drily. 'It was not I,' he said, 'nor did I order it done. And as it happens, the man who did it lies dead outside the gates from which we lately fled. You saw him killed yourself, I think.'

'I do not know that,' said Noell, though Quintus tried to restrain him, 'and I do not believe that you did not order it done.'

A black mood seemed to sweep across the pirate's face in an instant, and he scowled fiercely. 'Never call me a liar, Master Cordery,' he said, 'for I do not take insult very lightly, as you may yet find. I do not care about your silly serving maid, and it pains me not at all that she is dead, but I did not do it, I would not have done it, and I tell you that the man who did is dead. There is an end on't – or do you wish that you and I might come to a settlement in another way?'

Noell felt Quintus's fingers tightening on his arm, urging him to make no reply, and though he was in a mood to be defiant, he dropped his gaze, and said nothing.

'You could have killed us ashore,' said the monk, quietly, 'or left us with Heilyn on the sand. You do not mean to do us harm, I think.'

'You're right,' said Langoisse, though the scowl was slow to fade from his face. 'I would not leave you for the inquisitors and the hangman, not even for the thirty guineas which was Master Cordery's worth before this game began. If he will not clasp my hand, and be my friend, it matters naught to me. But I have dealt fairly with you both, and you have no cause to hate me.'

'I hate no one,' said the monk. 'I pray God's mercy for you as I pray it for all men, and I will thank you with an honest heart if you will take us to a place of safety, in Ireland or elsewhere.'

With that, apparently, the pirate was satisfied, and he withdrew. Noell wanted to speak to him again before he went, to ask what had happened to the vampire lady, but he could see the wisdom of keeping silent, and knew that he would have his answer, if he would only wait a while.

The Turk followed his master, leaving them alone. They picked up their packs, and put them both on the bunk, then sat beside them, looking about at the place to which they had been brought.

'Narrow walls of wood,' said Quintus, 'and a mere shelf on which to sleep. But we are not used to luxury, you and I. It will suffice.'

'It must suffice to be alive, for now,' said Noell, grimly.

'The True Church,' Quintus observed, 'knows no boundaries. Whatever circumstances a good man is brought to, his soul is on the road to Heaven, and he may follow the path of righteousness if he can.'

'The route,' answered Noell, 'seems somewhat round about.'

They prepared themselves for sleep, being as tired as men could be. Noell took the bunk, which was less comfortable a bed than he was used to, and Quintus slept on the bare boards of the floor. Noell did not sleep soundly, but his nightmares could not frighten him awake, and the sun was high when he felt sufficiently recovered to rise again.

When Noell got up, Quintus was not there, and so he found his own way up on to the deck, a little unsteady on his feet. He was hungry, and the stink of fish – which seemed to him far worse than the odour of the fields of which Langoisse had complained – was tormenting him anew.

Everything in his life would be strange, now, until he could shape himself to this new reality of being a passenger among pirates, but he was not entirely disheartened by his situation. He had not one, but two friends, counting the gypsy girl along with Quintus, and the number of his deadly enemies could not be counted higher than before. Three of the pirate's men, who were on deck, watched him as he passed by, but did not speak to him.

The bright light of the warm mid-morning sun felt good when he paused to savour it, and when he went to the bow of the ship to look out at the great unknown, into which they were headed, he felt that he would be able to bear whatever it was that he might see.

What he saw was the ocean, calm and blue beneath a clear and brilliant sky.

It was only when he glanced back again, to look at the mast of the little ship, that he suddenly felt sick again, in his stomach and his heart. For there, suspended by knotted black hair from a driven nail, was the severed head of the Lady Cristelle.

Oddly, the memory that came into his mind was what he had said to the gypsy girl when she told him that Langoisse meant to make a mistress of the lady. *I think you misread him*, he had said. Clearly, he had been correct in his estimation. The pirate had displayed his intention, so that even those who were not schooled in reading could know his mind, and know his valour in the face of the vile temptation of vampire comeliness.

In the days that were to come, Noell Cordery – and he by no means the only one – would cast many a sidelong glance at those dark, empty and accusing eyes. Sometimes, he would fancy that it was Medusa's head which he saw, and he would wonder if its gaze might be slowly turning his soul into adamantine stone.

And in the fullness of time he would observe that although tenacious life had been conclusively banished from the vampire's flesh, the head still resisted, for an astonishing lapse of time, the cruel corruptions of decay.

PART THREE

The Breath of Life

'And the Lord God formed man of the dust of the ground, and breathed into his nostrils the breath of life; and man became a living soul.

'And the Lord God planted a garden eastward in Eden; and there he put the man he had formed.

'And out of the ground made the Lord God to grow every tree that is pleasant to the sight, and good for food; the tree of life also in the midst of the garden, and the tree of knowledge of good and evil.'

(Genesis 2:7–9)

PROLOGUE

The de-ciphered text of a letter received by Sir Kenelm Digby at Gayhurst in the summer of 1643.

Burutu, August 1642

My most loyal friend,

Your letter telling me of my mother's death brings the saddest news that a man can hear, and the reading of it left me desolate for some days. Though it is near nineteen years since last I saw her I think of her often, and I have always treasured her words when you have succeeded in sending them half across the world to my places of exile. Your account of her last days, and of her thoughts of me, is precious to me, though it has called to mind all that I have lost in consequence of leaving my homeland.

It is unfortunate that such news casts a shadow, for in every other respect your letter should have brought me joy. A thousand thanks for the gifts which you have sent to me – all of them invaluable. So much of what we once took for granted in Europe is very difficult of attainment here, and though the trading-post which we have established now plays host to five or six ships a month, there are so many things the captains would never think to include in their cargoes. We thank you for the paper and the inks, and most especially for the books. Among the lenses which you sent, Q has found a pair which correct his ailing sight much better than the old ones, and he is exceeding grateful.

Nothing has so awakened my enthusiasm since I first left England as the microscope and the instruments for the preparation of slides. You say that you are simply discharging a debt, because it was my father's designs which first allowed you to begin experimenting with such devices, but you have improved greatly upon the instrument which he made in London so many years ago. Your ingenuity in using combinations of differently-curved lenses in order to reduce aberration is nothing less than genius. There is so much I might do with this instrument that I know not where to begin.

It is sometimes difficult to remember that our sojourn here has now measured out nine years of our lives. Q seems not a day older than he was when first we quit the Welsh shore, though he is now past sixty. The tropic sun seems to have turned his skin into the bark of some exotic tree – it is golden brown and hard. He invariably wears a white monastic habit and a great white straw hat, and when he strides across the sand by the river's shore he seems to me like a warrior angel of Michael's army, ever-ready to take arms against the fallen. He has the same effect on the natives, who readily accept that he is a holy man, and call him 'the babalawo from the sea'. A babalawo is one of the many kinds of priests which they have here, representing Ifa, the Uruba god of wisdom and divination. Babalawo means 'the father who has the secret'. All native priests of this order wear white cloth, and Q's habit allows him to take an appropriate place within the native scheme of things.

In a curious way, Q seems more at home here than he did in the abbey at Cardigan. He does not always behave in priestly fashion, although he celebrates the sacraments for our tiny Christian community. He does not seek converts among the tribesmen, though he is ever enthusiastic to learn about their beliefs. Nor does he give substantial encouragement to the missionaries who sometimes come here. Sometimes, I wonder whether he is more content to be a babalawo than a servant of the false pope of Rome. He does not consider all of the hundred gods who are worshipped here to be demons, but argues that some of them, like Ifa and Obatala, are aspects of the one true God, called by different names. But he is distressed by the worship commonly offered here to darker gods like Elegba and Olori-merin, whose rituals involve bloody sacrifices.

I, of course, am much changed from the frightened boy who sheltered in your house after the strange death of my father. I have grown as tall as he once was, and I think that I am somewhat like him in appearance, though I would hardly deserve to be called, as he was, the handsomest man in London. I am fortunate in my strength, because few white men flourish in this land of fevers. I have seen persons of great courage and stout constitution so reduced by dengue, dysentery and malaria that they became no more than wrecks of men. Since last I wrote to you we have lost four men, including the worthy Jespersen, and have gained only two – Dutchmen who came aboard the Hengelo. Our colony, if such it might be called, now numbers only fourteen whites, three of them wives, though we have twenty-four black workers living permanently on the station, within the outer stockade.

I have heard it said that what does not kill us makes us stronger, but whoever coined that saw was never in Africa. Every bout of sickness suffered here makes a man weaker, until by degrees he has not the strength to bring him through another crisis. I seem better able than most to withstand such things, but one has to be wary. The river seems to attract sickness, and the handful of white men who have travelled a short distance up-river and returned (many have not returned) say that it is a kind of hell which our race was never intended to endure. The natives put here by God seem hardly designed to endure it themselves. Barely a third of the children born survive the ravages of malaria and smallpox, and those who mature seem always to be suffering from yaws or kra-kra; sleeping sickness and leprosy imperil everyone. We have learned never to go bare-headed or barefoot, to boil all the water that we drink, and to sleep behind veils of fine netting which help to save our skin from the swarms of biting insects. Our exile sometimes seems a kind of purgatory.

We are in the worst part of the rainy season now. These last few weeks it has been raining twice daily, after noon and after dusk. Each storm lasts for three hours and more. The river is perpetually in flood, and this is the season when there is most to fear from crocodiles. The compensating benefit is that it does not get so very hot in the daytime, nor so very cold at night. It is a comfort to be able to take my pen in my hand each day, and though I cannot quite imagine myself back in Grand Normandy, I know that I am addressing myself to my only friend in the land of my birth, and that I am in consequence not entirely separated from the realm to which I hope one day to return.

Trade is slack at this time of year, but ships still come. For the most part they are Gaulish vessels from Britain, Holland and France, but Maroc traders sometimes venture here, despite the fact that the Sultan's soldiers are at war with Songhai in the north. Mohammedan caravanners are attempting to establish a trade-route across the Sahara, but the centuries-old jihad which their masters have waged against the black tribes will probably make it impossible for them to succeed.

Our trading post makes matters infinitely easier for the captains of all these vessels, not one of whom would gladly go back to the days of the Silent Trade, but many seem jealous of our presence here. The Marocs claim that theirs is the true right to trade here, despite the war which has raged since time immemorial. The Portuguese, too, claim that it was they who 'discovered' this entire coast, and that the British have no business here; but the vampire lords of Lisbon and Setubal cut short the naval adventurings of the Portuguese when Henrique fell from favour, and their claims are based entirely in might-have-beens.

I do not like to deal with the Portuguese, because they are more interested in buying black slaves than the goods in which we deal, no matter that slave-keeping is unlawful throughout the Imperium. Because we do not deal in slaves the Oba of Benin sends such goods west to Ikorodu, but that is a much more troubled coast, where the Uruba empire wages war against the Ashanti and the Dahomi peoples. On the other hand, the fact that Ikorodu has become the port of slaves means that we obtain the better part of ivory, pepper, palm-oil and other goods. Benin is by no means as rich in gold as the Ashanti kingdom, but the inland tribes now demand gold for the slaves which they transport to the coast, and much of that gold works its way round to us by way of the Uruba, who rule over the Edau, the Ibau, and other tribes in the interior.

The Uruba have taught their skills of metal-working to the Edau, who are greedy for good English iron – especially guns. No doubt the guns are employed in fighting against the Mohammedans, and also against those tribes which do not pay tribute to the Uruba. When the tribes of this strange empire go to war against one another – as they frequently do, despite their apparent common cause – they use only spears, and though men are often killed or taken as slaves the conflicts seem to be bound by rules which forbid wholesale slaughter.

The part which Q and I have taken in developing this station has made us moderately wealthy. When first we came here there was little more than a group of wooden cabins built by the survivors of the wreck of the Alectryon and deserted by them when they were rescued in 1629. They built on a sandbank in order to be able to defend themselves against the tribesmen, of whom they were much afraid. In fact, though, the Oba was sorry to see them go when they were rescued, for he is fully aware of the importance of trading with Gaul. Now we have built, with the help of native labourers, great storehouses and wooden wharves, and a workshop. There I have made a turning-machine like the one which my father built, in order to make screw-threads.

The two dozen blacks who live on the station with us have virtually established a village here, with vegetable patches and guinea-fowl, though their wives and children still live inland. Q now speaks two local languages fluently, including the Uruba lingua franca. He has some crude knowledge of a few more, but there is such a profusion of tongues in this region that one might take it for the site of Babel. The Oba of Benin has twice visited Burutu, and once sent us workmen to demonstrate for me the techniques of casting bronze in which his people are expert. Our relations with him are not entirely harmonious, though, because of our attempts to be equally friendly with the Ibau who live to the east. They can supply us with many valuable goods because they dominate the banks of the River Kwarra for a hundred miles or more above the delta. Most of our workers are Ibaus, though we have seven Edaus and an orphaned Uruba boy named Ntikima, who has proved to be an especially apt pupil.

It is by river that by far the greater portion of goods like ivory and animal-skins are brought from the grasslands of the north. Ntikima has assured us that our fame has spread into the northlands, though we have not yet ventured more than fifteen or twenty miles inland. The boy assures us that they must know of us in the Hausa cities, and the legendary lands of Bornu and Kwararafa, but there is no way he could know this, and tribesmen are much given to hyperbole, especially when they want to pay a compliment. I doubt whether the boy has ever seen a Hausa trader, and I suspect that Bornu and Kwararafa are as much the stuff of legend to him as they are to us.

Sometimes I fear that our success will be our undoing, and Q has said that it can only be a matter of time before one of the imperial ships brings vampires here. He is anxious that the vampires might decide that there is much to be gained by seeking to establish common cause with the vampires of Africa. Despite all the differences which there are between Gaul and Africa (and none know those contrasts better than we!), both face the hostility of the Mohammedans. It may occur to the lords of the Imperium that if only white men and black could combine forces they might crush the Mohammedans between them, and consolidate their power over their own commoners in the process.

I am not sure that any such alliance could actually be forged. There is no Imperium here, though we speak of a Uruba 'empire'. There are no vampire lords to whom the princes of Europe could send their emissaries. If rumour is to be trusted, the Alafin of the Uruba has a court as grand, in its fashion, as many a court in Europe, but the Alafin and all his chiefs and administrators are common men. Many of the priests and magicians who belong to the Ogbone – the secret society which is the instrument of the black vampires' power – are also common men. Attila's kin might find it less easy to understand a realm where vampires are, yet do not openly rule, than a nation where men still rule because they ruthlessly destroy any vampire who comes among them. I do not find the state of affairs here easy of comprehension, though I have lived here for many years.

I have only thrice set eyes on a black vampire – such persons do not interest themselves in trade. Most of the natives are dark brown in colour, but the vampires have skins like polished jet, sometimes decorated with the faded colour of old tattoos. They are without exception very ancient in appearance, because no common man becomes a vampire until he has proved his worth in a long career as a priest-magician. The Uruba call vampires elemi, which means 'ones who breathe life'. The name also signifies a direct connection with the gods; the sky-god Olorun is often called Olorun Elemi.

The elemi are said to be wise men, yet we are told quite emphatically they have no interest in metal or machinery, or in new things. Their wisdom is an incurious kind, it seems, and is mainly concerned with magic and the properties of medicines. We hear many rumours about the vampires' powers of healing, their ability to mix potions to give men courage or make women fertile. They kill men with curses, too, if we can believe what we are told. The local tribes have no elemi, having lost the few which they had in the great plague twenty years ago. This is a matter of regret and lamentation. If only they had wise men who could live forever, they say, they would be better and more powerful people.

The elemi are to common tribesmen an intimate connection with the distant past, when their ancestors lived. The tribesmen in this region have a great reverence for their ancestors, and seem to believe that although they are dead, their fathers and grandfathers still inhabit their villages, taking an intimate interest in the affairs and fortunes of their descendants. We have been told that in the Uruba heartland, in the great city of Oyo, new monarchs must eat the hearts of their dead predecessors, in order to personify their forebears. The spirits of ancestors are held to have the power to reward and punish, being responsible for much that happens which we would attribute to the will of God or to chance. Their presence is usually unseen, but on certain special days villages are visited by Egungun, the risen dead, who comes to identify those who must be punished for taboo-breaking. Neither Q nor I has seen such a visitation, but the invaluable Ntikima has described it in graphic detail. The part of Egungun is presumably played by a priest dressed in a costume with a great ugly mask, but to the Uruba and their subject tribes such artifacts are sacred, and he who puts them on is the supernatural power which he represents. Egungun's task, it seems, is to judge those whose actions have brought misfortune by offending the ancestors. Mercifully, the blame for misfortunes is not often heaped on innocent people in this way; much evil and mischance is laid at the door of witches, who are said to be the implacable enemies of the Ogbone – that society to which the elemi and common priest-magicians all belong.

The plague which raged here twenty years ago is still remembered as a most horrible tragedy. If our black labourers were told that my father had deliberately infected a vampire with that plague, they would think that he had been horribly mad – not evil, because they could not imagine that anyone would contemplate a crime so bizarre, but certainly deranged. But they would be unable to make sense of the claim that he had loved a vampire lady, because elemi *are always male.* Ogbone *is an exclusively male concern, and though the women may have private societies of their own, such organizations are only concerned with midwifery and with the rituals of female circumcision.*

I find it hard to reconcile the state of affairs here with my father's theories about the nature and creation of vampires. Ntikima, who is a fount of information despite his tender years – I think he is about seventeen – assures us that common men who are to become elemi *must be taken to Adamawara, which is a fabulous country in the interior. There they partake of the heart of the gods in a ceremony which sounds very like certain rituals of human sacrifice which have been mentioned to us. White men are not normally allowed to witness even an ordinary rite of that kind, though Ntikima has described the* ikeyika *rite which was his own initiation into adulthood. This is a kind of circumcision, carried out with a stone knife, often in such brutal fashion that it permanently impairs the functioning of the sexual organ. In his effusive fashion, Ntikima says that the* Ogbone *will surely one day come for the babalawo from the sea, to bring him to Adamawara in order that he might eat the heart of the gods and be given the breath of life, but no such summons has come yet.*

Most of what we know about the elemi *comes from travellers' tales, and it is hard to know how much to believe. The further away a region is, the more extravagant are the tales told about its tribes, and about the power of its* elemi. *There is no way to be sure that such a place as Adamawara exists. Much of what is said about it is reminiscent of the story in the scriptures of the Garden of Eden, where God exhaled the breath of life into Adam. So closely do the* Ogbone *guard their secrets that the creation of vampires is as much a mystery to the common men of Africa as it is to the common men of Gaul. We have the Gregorian accounts of devil-led sabbats; they have stories of their sky-gods descending to earth in Adamawara. My inclination is to treat both with the severest scepticism.*

The elemi *must take blood from common men, as our vampires do, but this has not the same meaning for the donors as it has in Gaul. That which makes the Gaulish vampire seem perverse and monstrous fits much more easily into the African way of thinking. The tribesman is always making sacrifices to his gods, and ritual offerings of all kinds. Whenever flour is ground or palm-oil extracted, a little will be spilled on the earth as an offering to the gods. Whenever a meal is eaten, a little food will be left, likewise as an offering. These things are done unthinkingly, much as a Christian would make the sign of the cross. All such things are called sacrifice, like the sacrifices of animals – and sometimes men – which are offered on holy days. The blood which common men offer gladly to vampires is a sacrifice too, offered as if to* Olorun Elemi *himself. This, to the African, is easy to understand, though he would be unable* to comprehend the communion, where a Christian partakes of the body and blood of Christ.

The tribesmen do not consider themselves to be ruled by the elemi, but there seems little doubt that the real power in this land lies with the Ogbone. The Ogbone supervise all rites, especially the ikeyika, and all trials by ordeal. The Ogbone are the voice of the ancestors, the custodians of oracles and the practitioners of medicine. All chiefs or kings must answer to them, and though the chiefs preside in the courts of law, it is the babalawos who determine guilt or innocence. The chiefs administer punishment, but it is the witchfinders and the 'risen dead' who decide where punishment is to fall. Chiefs declare war, and lead their armies into battle, but their magicians tell them when the time is propitious for them to fight, and against whom.

Q would dearly love to discover what truth there is in the many tales which we are told about the lands of the interior. He has made calculations regarding the provisioning of a journey up-river. I am sure that the year will soon come when he will insist that the time is ripe, and bid me follow him. I have less curiosity about such mythical places as Adamawara, but I would go with him if he decided on a journey of exploration. It would be foolhardy, I know, but I am not by nature or temperament a trader, and I am growing tired of the routines of our life here.

Does L's piratical legend still flourish in Grand Normandy? He still visits us every year. He is no longer as handsome as he was, and has been weakened by disease. Nor is he any longer a pirate, though he proudly wears the glamour of the buccaneer, and swears that there is no greater joy to him than the sound of cannon-fire. The cannon on the station were all his at one time, and he has twice helped to save us from Maroc marauders. His gypsy princess still sails with him, and so does the noseless Turk. It may be the woman's urging which brings him back here again and again. L has no considerable love for me, nor I for him, but the gypsy still carries an affection for me, and I am happy to be her friend. She has grown into a strong and handsome woman, and seems to thrive in the tropics while men of paler hue wither and decay. Jespersen once told me that the only thing which brings her back so frequently is the anguish caused by my celibacy, and that if only I would take her to my bed I might release her from an awful bondage, but I am used to my monkishness. If ever Q dies, I believe I will inherit his robe, and will play the warrior angel myself.

L pretends not to mind that his mistress likes me, but will accuse me, when drunk, of the crime of falling in love with a vampire lady in a cell in wild Wales, and suggests maliciously that I can never love again for thought of her. Though he says it mainly to annoy his mistress, I sometimes wonder in my secret thoughts whether he might be right. Certainly, I find little lustful attraction in the sight of the gypsy, still less in the naked black women of the shore tribes, or the wives of the settlement. I sometimes wonder if there is something in the blood which I inherited from my father which is irredeemably tainted by virtue of the gifts he made to his own true love. To have the microscope beside me now brings back to my mind all the things which happened during those last days in London. I cannot say that I am comfortable with those memories, even now.

I have sometimes wondered whether my father overestimated both the potential of the thing that he had made and the vampires' fear of it; perhaps his suicide was all for nothing, and Richard never intended to have us killed. But now I have your gift beside me, I cannot help remembering that my father thought this a weapon more powerful than any great cannon. I dreamed last night that I was looking down the barrel of the instrument, desperate to see something that my father was urging me to notice, but try as I might I could not do it. Perhaps the tribesmen are right after all, and our ancestors do remain with us, angrily imposing duties that we never quite fulfil. Now that I have the microscope which you have sent me, though, I hope that I might come a little closer to that fulfilment.

I hope that one day I will return to Britain. I feel that it is both my duty and my destiny so to do. It is my most earnest hope that I might strike a blow against the Gaulish regiment of vampires before I die, so that my name might be added to the list of that mortal legion whose endeavours will finally prevail even against the host of the undying. Despite that I languish here, I tell you that I have not deserted that College which you serve, or its cause, and I hope that the day will come when I will take my allotted place on the battlefield which is the land of my birth. On that day, God willing, I will see my friend again, and clasp your hand in testimony to all that our friendship has meant.

I will give this letter to the captain of the Tudor Rose, who is the most trustworthy English seaman I know, and hope for its eventual safe delivery into your hands. I beg you to pray for me; if you can bring yourself to ask God's mercy for an unbeliever.

Fare well.

N

ONE

It was ajo awo, the day of the secret, which was sacred to Ifa. Ntikima knew no more of the day than its name, for the Uruba did not number the days of the month as the white men did.

The white man called Noell Cordery was on the verandah of the large house which lay at the centre of the main stockade. He was peering, as he often did, down the barrel of the brass instrument which had been brought to him by a master of one of the ships which came to trade. He was sketching with his right hand, using a stick of charcoal with quick, delicate strokes. His work had taken on an odd kind of rhythm; he would periodically take his eye away from the instrument, blink to clear his vision, look critically at his work, and add a few more strokes, then apply his eye to the lens yet again. Every now and again he would lay down the charcoal, and nudge the small mirror which caught the sun's light and threw it upwards through the lenses of the microscope, and then he would rock the focusing-wheel gently back and forth, to make sure that he had the best possible sight of whatever was on his slide. Ntikima knew what the device did, because Noell had allowed him to look into it.

The other black men who were watching Noell at work thought of what he was doing as a kind of ritual, so painstakingly were the movements repeated, but Ntikima knew better. Ntikima understood the white men, though the Edaus and the Ibaus could not. Ntikima was Uruba. More than that, he was Ogbone, though of course he was not allowed to admit it. Even the Ibau Ngadze, who had lived here for many years, thought that this strange tall white man was searching for gods inside the creature of brass which lived in a wooden box with an elaborate retinue of tiny iron blades and rectangles of glass. The Ibaus often told their brothers from upriver about the magical devices which the white men had, and about the spirits of awesome power which animated them. Ntikima never joined in with such talk; he was Ogbone, and kept his secrets.

The black men were wary of interrupting the ritual, and so it was not until Noell paused, and turned his gaze their way – though he seemed not to see them, so entranced was he by his vision of the world inside things – that Ntikima called out that a ship was in the channel.

'Is it the *Phoenix*?' asked the white man. The *Phoenix* was expected, and would be welcome. But Ntikima shook his head, and made a sign to say that he did not know.

Noell sighed, and began to pack up the microscope. He did not hurry; he was prepared to take infinite pains to store the instrument correctly, broken down into its component parts. It was very precious to him – far more precious than the telescope which he subsequently took with him to the look-out post atop the seaward wall. Ntikima followed him, dutifully.

The ship was much closer now than when Ntikima had first glimpsed it, and he recognised it immediately, but Noell Cordery's eyes were poorer than his. The white man put the glass to his eye, and kept it there while he watched the vessel approach. The ship was the caravel *Stingray*, its captain Langoisse. Ntikima did not like Langoisse, who was loud and boastful, and he was not displeased to see that the ship was in a poor condition. She lay low in the water, her square sails ragged and her rigging much torn. Ntikima knew nothing of the sea, and could not guess whether she had been in a battle, or whether she had simply been battered by Shango's thunderbolts in a great storm.

Langoisse was finding it difficult to bring the ship to its intended berth, even though the wind was not against him. Burutu was nearly ten miles from the coast, and the ships which sailed here sometimes had to fight hard to reach the wharves, especially in the wet season when the flood-currents were strong. Sometimes native canoes had to tow the merchantmen to the wharves. Though this made things hard for the honest traders, it meant that the stockade at Burutu was defensible not only against native marauders but also against unwelcome visitors from the ocean. This was the direction from which danger had most often come. The six cannon on the station pointed out to sea, not at the inner delta.

The white babalawo, who called himself Quintus, came to the foot of the ladder with Jan de Groot to hear the news, but de Groot turned away again when Ntikima cried 'Stingray!' De Groot did not like Langoisse any better than Ntikima did, and knew that there was little profit to be made from his periodic visits. But Quintus came up to join Noell Cordery and Ntikima, and stood behind them while they watched the ship labouring against the current.

No signal came from the vessel, though Ntikima caught a glimpse of the woman who loved Noell Cordery standing on the bridge and waving. Ntikima could not understand why Noell did not simply buy her from Langoisse, to be his wife, but it was difficult to fathom the attitude to women which these white men had, which seemed out of keeping with their attitude to other property.

'Best kill the fatted calf,' said Quintus, with a sigh. 'The prodigal has come home again.' This was nonsense. There were no cattle in Burutu, and the evening meal would be a brace of fowl, with bread from millet flour and soup made with dazoes and earth-peas. Ntikima knew, however, that Langoisse always brought bottles of exotic wine with him, so that he and his friends could besot themselves in their own manner, instead of sharing the palm-wine and the millet-beer which the black men made.

'Will they need help to dock?' asked Quintus of Noell Cordery.

'They have the tide,' Noell told him. 'It all but cancels out the current, and they have sail enough left to use the breeze.'

Quintus clapped Noell on the shoulder, with enthusiasm that was slightly forced. 'They'll bring tall tales if naught else,' he said, 'and the Phoenix will surely be here within the week, to bring us cargo which we need, and to empty our stores of ivory, palm-oil and rubber.'

Ntikima listened to the exchange carefully. Quintus had shown more than an ordinary interest in the promised arrival of the Phoenix. In the past weeks he had become very intent upon stocktaking and calculating supplies, as if he expected to withstand a siege or to undertake a journey.

Perhaps his powers of foresight were greater than they seemed, and he knew that the Ogbone would send for him soon. Even before Ntikima came the babalawo had begun keeping and breeding donkeys within the outer stockade, and Ntikima had guessed that his purpose was to make a pack-train. Quintus obviously knew that he was destined to make the journey to Adamawara. Ntikima was not surprised; a babalawo must always know something of the future.

While the population of the station turned out to give a lukewarm welcome to Langoisse and his crew, Ntikima watched and listened. The white men rarely paid him much heed, and seemed more pleased than alarmed by his interest in them. He was always near to run errands, always enthusiastic to learn more of the English language, and hear more tales of the lands from which they had come. Noell Cordery and Quintus both liked him, and were pleased to help him learn.

The subtle undercurrents in the relationships of these people were a constant source of fascination. He noted, for instance, that it was Quintus who took the lead in offering a welcome to these visitors, and that Noell Cordery hung back. This was definitely not to the liking of the brown woman Leilah, who looked for a warmer reception from what was perforce the lesser of her two loves. She seemed to live always in the hope that Noell would one day learn to look at her with more desiring eyes. When she leapt to the wharf to greet him, he received her kiss meekly on his cheek, and did not return it. Nor was Noell's reluctance to the liking of Langoisse, who was wounded on his own behalf; Ntikima had noticed previously that the so-called pirate was ever of the optimistic opinion that all men should be delighted with his company. Ntikima was unsurprised that the feast which the traders offered to their visitors that evening, and which he helped to serve, was not entirely enjoyed by any of its participants, though it was clear that the fresh food answered a hunger which Langoisse and all his crew had been nursing for some time.

The one man at the table who frightened and overawed the Uruba boy was the disfigured Turk, Selim, who was ever in a surly mood. Ntikima hated the sight of the man's scarred and twisted face, which made him think of the face of Egungun, the risen dead, or an apparition sent by Shigidi, who disturbed men in their dreams. Langoisse would never turn his most faithful servant away from his table, though there were probably others in the big house who wished that he would command the Turk to eat with the sailors aboard the ship. Ntikima was glad when the meal was finished, and the Turk went away. The woman went too, though she seemed more reluctant to go.

When he was left at table with Quintus and Noell Cordery, Langoisse produced a gift with which he obviously hoped to win the favour of his hosts – a demijohn of Madeira – and then he set out to entertain the company with accounts of the storm through which he had lately sailed, and news of the last few ports in which he had dropped anchor. Ntikima sat on the floor in the corner of the room, shadowed and patient. He understood only a little of what was said, but he was hungry to learn the names of places beyond the sea, and to hear what was said of them.

Every now and again Ntikima would take his canoe and go to the forest, where he would speak to a magician or an akpalo – an itinerant storyteller – to whom he would tell all that he had heard. Even when he did not entirely understand what he was telling, they would nod gravely, and tell him that he had done well. The Ogbone, no doubt, would know what it all signified far better than he.

Tonight, Langoisse's talk was of Maroc and of Spain, and of a land which might exist beyond the great ocean, which he called Atlantis. These names Ntikima had heard before, and he could find nothing new in what was said of them, but he became more attentive when Langoisse asked Quintus whether he had ever heard of a kingdom ruled by a man named Prester John.

'It is a legendary Christian kingdom in Asia,' Quintus said to Langoisse, 'said to lie beyond the Khanate of Walachia, in the desert on the edge of Cathay. The Byzantines sent emissaries to find it, in the hope of finding allies when the Mohammedans drove the vampire armies out of Asia Minor, but they never returned, and Vlad Tepes ultimately recaptured the lost lands without assistance.'

Ntikima's thoughts swirled as he tried to fix these strange names in his memory.

'The vampire lords of Granada are now convinced that the kingdom lies in Africa,' Langoisse said. 'They say that it is identical with a land called Adamawara, of which you have spoken to me before, where the Garden of Eden was in the beginning of the world. It is rumoured that a great river might gives access to that land, the Kwarra is one the three which are suspect. The Spanish will send three ships to the Senegal this winter, if the French will let them, with a company of soldiers and horses. They will set forth in hope, though the French say there is nothing for them to find save deserts and arid mountains. The arabs who know where the Senegal rises laugh at the Spaniards behind their backs. Is it possible, do you think, that it is the Kwarra which leads to this marvellous kingdom?'

'I cannot believe it,' said Quintus. 'I do not believe that any such kingdom as Prester John's exists, and certainly not that it is the country which the Uruba call Adamawara.'

Langoisse shrugged. 'Someone has spread tales of a white king in Adamawara, and it is said to be written somewhere that Christians went there long ago. Perhaps it is the third river mentioned by the legends which is the right one – its mouth is supposedly far to the south.'

'There is a greater river than the Kwarra,' agreed Quintus. 'The Oba of Benin claims that the ships of his ancestor, Ewuare the Great, journeyed there two hundred years ago. Perhaps it is true, though the Beninese vessels are poor things.'

Ntikima knew all the tales of Ewuare the Great. He also knew that there was another great river, far away, beyond the lands which acknowledged the wisdom of the elemi. Nevertheless, the white men had it wrong. The Kwarra was only one of the three rivers which must be followed in order to reach Adamawara, and though there were white people there, they did not rule. Certainly there was no Prester John.

'Do you think the Spaniards will come here?' asked Noell Cordery.

'It is possible,' said the white babalawo. 'Men have travelled further in search of legends than they have ever gone for more practical purposes. The master of the *Tudor Rose* told us of ships setting forth from Bristol in search of Atlantis, determined to sail across the great ocean until they sight land, hopeful of finding a way to Cathay if nothing else. I have sometimes feared that the tales of Adamawara which we have innocently passed on to visiting seafarers might one day bring explorers here, carrying the commission of some curious vampire prince. It is only a matter of time – the world we know is becoming too small to confine the affairs of the Imperium of Gaul.'

'Perhaps the time has come to undertake our own journey of exploration,' Noell Cordery said to him.

'Perhaps it has,' Langoisse agreed. 'The likes of you and I were never meant to be traders. The sea has nearly had enough of my poor *Stingray*, and I might be better employed in journeying up the Kwarra in search of my fortune. I wonder why you are so content to shut yourselves up in a wooden cage like this one, when you hear so much of richer realms in the interior. Why do you not go to Oyo or Ife, or to Adamawara itself? Why must you sit here and barter good iron for the meagre handfuls of gold dust which the savages bring you from their hidden mines, and for the occasional handful of gemstones which they spare from their coffers? I could not be content to deal in ivory and oil and rubber when there are treasures to be had by the men who have the courage to go in search of them, in Prester John's land, or whatever others there are in the centre of the continent. Have you no idea how hungry the world is for gold?'

Noell Cordery seemed not to like this speech, and only replied: 'The interior is dangerous, and has a fuller measure of plague and misery than of gold and glory.'

The white babalawo, however, answered more calmly. 'I do not think the black men mine gold,' he said. 'It is mostly native gold that they use, like the native copper they use in their ornaments, easily refined if not so very easily found. Since first we began to trade for gold and gems, they hunt out all that they can for us, for they reckon iron and tin more precious. They have no secret coffers full to over-flowing. All travellers tell stories of fabulous treasures to be found in lands where they have never been. Beware of believing that because the interior is mysterious, it is also rich. You know as well as we do how many men have gone upriver, and never returned.'

'They had not your knowledge,' said Langoisse. 'If ever there was a man that I would trust to guide me through this heathen land, it is you. I promise you, faithfully, that when you undertake your journey into the interior, I will go with you, not just to seek gold, but to seek the lands where vampires live and do not rule, and the lands from which vampires first came.'

Quintus turned toward Ntikima, and met his eye. 'There is one here,' he said, 'who can tell you about Adamawara.' He beckoned, and Ntikima stood up, and went to stand beside the babalawo, to bear the hostile gaze of the sea-captain.

'He's but a boy,' said Langoisse, dismissively.

'He is Uruba,' said Noell Cordery, quickly. 'And he is a man, for he has undergone the ikeyika rite, and earned his place in the world. He lost his parents to the plague, but he met a god in the forest and was given to magicians to be raised. He is a very clever person, and has learned more English in three years than Ngadze has in ten. Tell, us, Ntikima, what you know of Adamawara.'

'Adamawara is the land of the tigu,' said Ntikima, obediently. 'It is in the country of the Mkumkwe, from which the first elemi came when the world was young. It was made when Shango sent down a great bolt of lightning, so that Olorun might have a place to offer his heart to the wisest of men.'

Langoisse was impatient, but Noell Cordery held up his hand to tell him to wait. 'Tigu', he said, 'means finished. The elemi are tigu because they have undergone a rite of passage; just as ikeyika makes boys into men, so this rite called Ogo-Ejodun makes men into vampires. Ejodun means season of blood, and is the title which the Uruba give to various kinds of blood sacrifice. Is it not so, Ntikima?'

Ntikima nodded in reply.

'In which direction does Adamawara lie?' asked Noell.

'Toward the sunrise,' Ntikima answered, 'But in order to reach it one must follow the rivers – first the Kwarra, then the Benouai, then the Logone. It is a dangerous journey, for those who would become elemi must prove themselves in the lifeless forest, where the silver death strikes them down, and where Egungun comes to judge them.'

'The Uruba heartland is to the west,' added Noell Cordery, 'but the Uruba believe that their ancestors first came to Ife and Oyo from another land, guided by the Ogbone, much as the Children of Israel were brought across the desert in the time of Moses.'

'Is there gold in Adamawara?' asked Langoisse, in a sarcastic voice.

'Oh no,' said Ntikima. 'No gold at all.'

'How do you know these things?'

Ntikima shrugged. He knew because he was Ogbone, but it was not permitted that he should say so.

'How are the elemi made, in Adamawara?' asked Noell Cordery.

'By the Oni-Olorun, which are the wisest of the elders. They prepare the heart of Olorun, so that it may be given to the wisest and the best, who receive the breath of life, to live on while the unworthy die.'

Noell Cordery looked at Langoisse, and made a sign with his hand, as if to say: there you have it.

'Have white men ever been to Adamawara?' growled the pirate. It was a question that neither Quintus nor Noell Cordery had ever asked.

'Oh yes,' said Ntikima. 'Long ago. There are only a few there now.'

All three of his inquisitors looked at him in surprise.

'How long?' asked Noell Cordery, though he should have known better than to ask.

Ntikima shrugged. 'Long ago,' he repeated.

'But there are a few there still?' asked Noell. 'Do you mean that there are white elemi in Adamawara?'

'Oh no,' said Ntikima, patiently. 'They are not elemi, because they are aitigu, but they have lived for a long time. There is a white woman who is older than the elders, though she looks young. There are men, also, and though they will never be tigu, they might never die.'

Ntikima could see that this information caused a certain consternation among his hearers, though they did not seem to know exactly what he meant.

'When you say aitigu, where we might say not finished,' Quintus said, 'you do not mean what we call common men? The elemi are tigu – finished – but there are some who are not tigu, yet live much longer than ordinary men?'

'Oh yes,' Ntikima told them, as if it was obvious.

'Vampires,' said Langoisse. 'You are telling us that there are white vampires in Adamawara?'

Ntikima furrowed his brow, unable to answer.

'Ntikima,' said Quintus, 'Do you know this from the arokin, or from the akpalo?' The arokin were the chroniclers, whose task it was to know the generations of the ancestors, whose tales were believed. The storytelling akpalo who knew the adventures of Anansi the spider and Awon the tortoise, were not to be taken so seriously. Ntikima could not answer this question either. He knew because he was Ogbone, and could not speak of it. He shrugged his shoulders.

Noell Cordery laughed. 'Remember,' he told his companions, 'that this is the boy who was once possessed by the spirit of a dead child, and had it driven from his body by poison – and this is the boy who met a god in the forest, who promised to teach him the secrets of medicine.'

Ntikima knew that the white man quoted these things to show that what he said could not always be be trusted. But when he was very small, and his mother and father had died, he *had* been possessed by an abiku, an evil spirit which had been driven from his body by a magician. And after that, he *had* met Aroni in the forest, and shown such courage that he had not been devoured, but had been given instead to the Ogbone, who would one day teach him the secrets of medicine, so that he might become a white-clad magician, and after that an elemi. What he knew, he knew, and it did not matter what the white men cared to believe.

Quintus intervened then, and told Ntikima that he should go to his bed, and sleep. Ntikima knew that he was being sent away while the white men carried on their discussion in private, but he bowed his head, and went. He did not go to the hut where he slept, however, but kept watch beneath a window of the great house, content to wait although he could not hear a great deal of what was said.

Not until the white men finally went, not soberly, to their curtained beds, did Ntikima finally abandon his vigil, and go to sleep himself. Nothing else had happened, but he did not resent the delay. He was Ogbone, and his time was not his own to use. He knew that he must hurry to tell his masters that the white men were planning an expedition to Adamawara, because he knew that it was part of the Ogbone's plans that they should do exactly that, and the Ogbone would be glad to hear the news. The future was settled, and only needed to unfold, like the measured aspiration of the breath of life.

TWO

The *Phoenix* had come and gone. The rains had slackened, and soon would be seen no more until the spring. Burutu was a hive of activity, because Quintus was busy tallying stores and making calculations regarding the number of donkeys that would be required to carry them. There was much haggling between the monk and Langoisse over the number of men that ought to go on the expedition, and they argued the benefits, measure for measure, of powder and salt, needles and knives, grain and blankets. Quintus interrogated natives from half a dozen tribes about the meanderings of the great river, and the people who lived along it, and the nature of the country through which they might pass on their way to the mysterious land of Adamawara.

Noell had remained on the fringes of this tumult of preparation; he had gone back to his daily ritual with the microscope. The prospect of a journey to this mysterious Adamawara intrigued him, but he could not wholeheartedly believe in an African Eden where a vampire Adam had long ago received the sacred breath of life.

The only person who observed Noell's unenthusiasm was Leilah. She was the only one who felt that she had a right to interrupt him at his secular worship whenever she liked, and though he usually disliked such interruption, the day came when he was glad of it, because his microscopic studies could no longer fully absorb his interest, or distract him from contemplation of what lay ahead.

'Thou hast not been kind to me,' Leilah told him, reproachfully, on the day in question. She meant that he had not talked to her overmuch, especially not in private. In the course of her past visits, he had often been prepared to confide in her, a little, and she had told him her intimate thoughts in exchange. Being a poor sort of Christian, she had no other confessor, nor would she have wanted one, but she liked to think of Noell as a friend even though she could not have him for a lover. She seemed to gain some small glimmering of pleasure from telling him a few of those thoughts which otherwise would have remained secret. During this visit, though, she had not yet succeeded in bringing him to such a confidential mood.

'I am sorry,' he told her. 'I have had much to do, because of the *Phoenix*, and now am repentant because my labour of study has been neglected. There is so much to be seen in the microcosm, and I am a very long way from understanding.'

She sat beside him on the verandah. 'Sad thou art,' she guessed, 'and in bad humour. I know thou dost not like the notion of a journey in the great forest, but I do not think thou wouldst refuse it.'

Her English was better now than it had been when they had first met, and although it was still the case that by far the greater part of her conversation was with Langoisse she knew well enough the conventional uses of thee and thou. But she had continued, obstinately, through all the years of their acquaintance, to use the intimate form of speech with Noell. He never replied in kind.

'You read me right,' he said. 'The forest is a bad place, and there are some there who would do us harm. No raiders have attacked the station for five years now, but that is because the blacks who live nearby benefit more from our continued presence than they ever could from a single looting of our warehouses. They keep their more distant neighbours at bay, more efficiently than the firepower of our cannon. Quintus may have grown too trusting, believing that he can deal with any tribesmen squarely and safely. I am not so sure.

'Then again, there is the fever. Over the years, I have seen Quintus labour to find an effective treatment. He long ago abandoned bleeding as ineffectual, and has lately tried native medicines, but there is no real defence. And there is the heat of the afternoon and the cold of the dead of night. I know that Quintus once walked across half of Europe, and that the emissaries of popes and princes think little of embarking upon journeys of thousands of miles, but in Europe there are roads, and inns, and the climate is much kinder. I know not how far it might be to Adamawara, if there really is such a place, but the journey there and back will not be short, and this quest seems to me to be dicing with the devil, while the dice are loaded to our disadvantage.'

'Then do not go,' she said, simply. 'And I will stay here with thee, to see if our friends return.'

'Can I see Quintus go without me?' he objected. 'Can I bid him hail and farewell, if I think that he goes into danger? Now that my mother is dead, he seems to me the only real kin which I have in all the world, more a father to me than my father ever was. I would not desert him; nor would I trust Langoisse to look after him well enough.'

She did not take offence at his reckoning of those he considered to be his kin; she did not desire to be a sister to him. 'Is that a copy of the device thy father built?' she asked him, pointing at the microscope after a pause in the conversation. 'May I look into it?'

He showed her how to put her right eye to the lens, and close her left, then placed her fingers on the focusing-wheel.

'What is it?' she asked. He explained that the thing at which he had been peering was a tiny seed, which he had divided when it had begun to grow, so that he could examine the shoot and the root which were sprouting from it.

She asked him what he had learned from such examinations, and he told her something of the work that Kenelm Digby had done with microscopes at Gayhurst. He explained that Digby disputed the theory of preformation, which held that all the parts of an animal were present in the egg-cell from which it grew, very small in size, and had only to grow as the embryo developed toward its hatching or its birth. He told her that Digby favoured instead the theory of epigenesis, which held that the parts of the body came into existence by stages, and that the egg was a very simple thing which was dramatically transformed as it developed.

Noell explained how Digby had proved his case by taking a batch of eggs laid by chickens, and breaking them open at different times, to see how differently developed were the embryos inside, and with the aid of the microscope had put his theory successfully to the proof.

He told her that Digby was an atomist, who believed that all things were composed of tiny parts, and thought that all things might be understood if these atoms were to be described, and their transactions and transformations examined. But here, his explanations became too peculiar, and Leilah had difficulty following their course. She begged him to tell her instead what *he* was doing, and why.

'I too am studying the development of seeds and embryos,' Noell explained, 'and I think that the process of unfolding by which tiny things become whole living bodies is a process of multiplication, in which atoms of flesh divide themselves again and again. In the meantime, I believe that they change themselves according to a predetermined plan. I have seen that the flesh of very simple plants is made up of clusters of similar particles, which I think are fleshly atoms. I have seen such atoms in certain kinds of animal flesh too – like the skin, or the liver. Bodily fluids like blood and semen are made up of corpuscles in a liquid serum, and the water of the river is filled with very tiny creatures, some of which resemble the seminal particles.

'I am interested in these atoms because I think they may be the agents of disease: a possibility which my father once debated with Carmilla Bourdillon. We have long been taught to think of sickness as a disturbance of the bodily humours, but our bodies are more complicated machines than that simple notion allows. I think that sickness may be a disturbance of the bodily particles, perhaps because something makes them change in ways other than is proper or good for them. I believe that foreign atoms and corpuscles often get into the body, especially into the blood. It may be that bleeding cures some sicknesses not because it redresses the balance of the bodily humours, but because it lets out of the body some of the particles which have invaded it, but it works imperfectly as a method, because it does not get to grips with the real problem. Effective medicines may be those whose own atoms are poisonous to the atoms of disease, but not to the atoms of our bodies.'

Noell knew that Leilah could not properly follow the logic of the argument, which must seem to her to be rather cryptic, but she would not tell him so, replying to him only with a bland stare. He went on, trying to find words which she might grasp more easily. 'If I am right,' he said, 'then I hope also to begin to understand what vampires are. I cannot believe what the Gregorians say, that they are demons in human guise, or what they say themselves, that the difference is in their souls rather than their flesh. It might be, I think, that the particles which make up the bodies of vampires have undergone some further change, which the fleshly atoms of common men have not. It is clear that the long life which vampires enjoy is not contained in the pattern which God wrote into the seed of humankind, but is put there by a process which only the vampires know. I think that there may be a medicine which brings about this change, and which the vampires of Africa use in the rite they call Ogo-Ejodun just as the vampires of Gaul use it in their so-called sabbats. I do not believe that prayers or incantations, however much the vampires may use them, have any real effect. It is only a transformation of the bodily mechanism, wrought by the addition of some new particle, which makes the atoms of common flesh into atoms of vampire flesh.

'This is what my father may have believed, though he could not give me a full explanation before he died. He may also have believed that the conversion of vampire flesh to common flesh might be reversed – again, perhaps, by some kind of particle introduced into vampire blood. That, I think, is what he might have been trying to prove in the manner of his death. In order to destroy vampires, it may first be necessary to make them human again.'

'Is that what you want?' she asked. 'Not to become a vampire yourself, but rather to destroy the ones there are.'

He shook his head. 'For the moment,' he answered, 'I seek only to understand, to draw aside that curtain of mystery which hides the mechanisms of ordinary life as well as the secrets of vampire flesh. There is more mystery in the growth of plants, or in the lives of creatures too tiny for the naked eye to see, than ever I could have imagined, and I would be glad to win any enlightenment at all. First of all, I must find the truth; then and then only might I begin to see how the truth might be pitted against the evils of the world.'

'And what does Quintus say about your atoms and your corpuscles?' she asked, in all innocence.

Sometimes, Noell wondered whether it was to be his fate that he was to be entirely eclipsed by the shadow of his teacher. Since Quintus had acquired the reputation of being the wisest man in England, the question was always: What does Quintus say? Here, it was no different. Quintus was the babalawo from the sea, to whom the black men listened. Noell was simply the man who stared into the strange device.

Before he could reply, though, Ntikima came running to them, with news filling his mouth so amply that he could hardly spit it out.

'Another ship?' exclaimed Noell, springing to his feet.

But Ntikima shook his head, and pointed not to the channel which led to the sea, but to the forest on the northern shore. He repeated a single word, excitedly: 'Mkumkwe! Mkumkwe!'

'What does he mean?' asked Leilah.

'I don't know,' said Noell, who knew that he had heard the word before, but had forgotten its meaning.

Ntikima said more, the sentences tumbling over one another in his hurry. He spoke in Uruba, but Noell's command of that language was not very good, and he switched to English.

'Men come,' said Ntikima. 'Men of Adamawara. They come with elemi, to seek out the babalawo from the sea. The time has come to go to Adamawara. They come! They come!'

Noell stared at the boy, unable to believe what was being said to him. Only twelve days had passed since Quintus and Langoisse had finally decided that this was the year to outfit the long-planned expedition. How could the elemi possibly know that? When had these mysterious travellers set out from their own land?

'How does he know they are coming?' asked Leilah.

'The forest people can communicate with drums,' said Noell. 'Perhaps he has heard a signal drum. Or perhaps the news has been brought by travellers who have come down the river. The tribes upriver send goods down by canoe, and news travels much faster down the river than overland, especially when its waters are in flood. The African vampires do not often visit the delta – if vampires really are coming, the entire country will be alert to their arrival.'

'Will no one try to kill them?' she asked, ingenuously.

'No one will do them harm,' Noell assured her. 'These vampires are not princes, who rule by tyrannic force, but godlings who weave the tapestries of faith and magic, and are trusted to weave them well.'

Other boys had gathered now, disappointed that they had been outraced in the bringing of the news, but eager to make up now by supplying further detail. There was a clamour of voices, from which it was difficult to divine anything coherent, but it seemed that there was not much else to know. Noell called for quiet, then dismissed them, as soon as he was confident that they had nothing of importance to tell.

'Is this a bad thing?' asked Leilah, uncertainly.

'I cannot tell,' said Noell. 'The elemi are a mystery, and we do not know whether they may mean us harm. If they have come for Quintus, they might as easily mean to destroy him as to help him on his journey.'

'But how did they know that they should come here now?'

'Who knows? Perhaps it is coincidence; or perhaps they do have powers of divination which we cannot understand. But these vampires hold the fate of the station in their hands. If they were to pronounce sentence of death upon us, the tribesmen would readily turn to the business of slaughter. We have seen black vampires once or twice before, but they were utterly indifferent to us, as though we did not even belong to their world. I have always thought that here, as in the Imperium, it is better not to attract the attention of such beings.'

'The *Stingray* is here,' she said, 'and we have many guns to set beside your own if the need should arise.'

He laughed. 'Perhaps we should all go aboard her, and sail away,' he said. 'If the elemi wish us evil, no power will suffice to save us while we are in their land, and we'd far better trust to the mercy of a rotten hull and a tattered sail. But if they really mean to guide us that might be the best hope we have of arriving in Adamawara alive and well.'

Noell watched the boys running to carry the news to Quintus, who was tending his donkeys. He saw the monk take Ntikima by the shoulder, hardly able to confine the boy's excitement. Then Quintus looked across the bright-lit sand, to the verandah where he and Leilah stood, and though he could not see the monk's blue eyes, shadowed by the broad-brimmed hat, he knew that they must be shining with curiosity, and with the warmth of tempting dreams.

THREE

Ntikima watched with avid interest when the party of black warriors arrived in the settlement. Though they came in canoes, and had local tribesman to serve as ferrymen, they were obviously remote in origin. They were tall, and they had round broad heads with almond-shaped eyes set rather far apart. Their thick black hair was arranged in tufts and plaits. Their noses were flat and their lips thick; their cheeks, foreheads and upper arms were scored and the scars pigmented with red and yellow dyes. These were the Mkumkwe.

The Mkumkwe warriors carried themselves in the haughty manner which Ntikima associated with hillmen. Upland herdsmen, who measured a man's worth by the cattle he had, always affected to despise the forest-dwellers, whose only livestock were fowl and few goats, and who therefore lived by uplander reckoning a life of abject poverty. The Mkumkwe carried long spears, with broad iron blades, and they wore plumes of white feathers and ornaments of beaten copper. These warriors announced to Quintus and Noell Cordery, speaking in the Uruba tongue, that a great Oni-Olorun awaited them in a nearby village, to which they were summoned in order that they should hear his words.

It was obvious to Ntikima that Noell Cordery did not like the tone of this summons, but the babalawo told him that he must not mind. Though he must have travelled far to speak with the white men, a priest of Olorun who was an elemi and an elder of Adamawara must insist as a matter of honour that the white men should now come to him.

The white babalawo seemed careful that his own status should be established before he set out to this appointed meeting. He asked the warriors several questions, but they answered him only by echoing his words. Ntikima knew that such men as the Mkumkwe were never willing to direct questions, and he intervened to help Quintus, speculating that the warriors had brought the Oni-Olorun from Adamawara because the elders had heard of the many cures which his medicines had wrought, and wished to learn a little of the wisdom of the tribes beyond the sea. The Mkumkwe admitted that it might be so.

Quintus asked Mburrai and Ngadze – the most imposing of the settlement's black labourers – to take Noell and himself to the northern shore. He did not mention Ntikima, but made no objection when Ntikima also climbed into the canoe. Noell was dressed simply enough, in a white shirt and grey hose, but had fine leather boots. The babalawo wore his white habit, with stout boots beneath, and a big, broad-brimmed hat which only half-hid his glinting eyeglasses. Ntikima, who thought of them as his white men, was proud of their appearance; they seemed to him more than a match for the feathered and tattooed warriors, if only because of their height – they topped the biggest of the proud hillmen by an easy handspan.

The walk through the forest was an easy one, along a well-worn track, though Ntikima would have advised the white men to go on donkey-back had he been asked. Usually, when Ntikima went this way in the hazy morning light, the forest was nearly silent and there was no one about, but today there were Ibau men and boys out in force, to see the Mkumkwe, and to gossip about the meaning of their arrival. Ntikima was glad of this attention, pleased to be seen in this exotic company, and strode along with the self-possession which was fitting in an Uruba warrior among men of subject tribes.

By the time they arrived at the village the sun was getting high. Ntikima could see that Quintus and Noell hoped that the meeting would not be a long one. Once noon was past, the heat of day grew intense, and with the rainy season ending there were no longer any clouds to soak up the light of the sun. The walk back, if they had to come in mid-afternoon, would be an uncomfortable one for the white men.

The Ibau village was built close to the shore of the lake, though it had a palisade on that side as well on the others, to guard against crocodiles. The huts were tall, shaped after the fashion of squat clay bottles, their steeply-sloping conical roofs thick-thatched to withstand the lashing of the wet-season rains. The doorway of each hut faced south-west so as to be shielded from the harmattan: the dry season wind which often carried a fine, cloying dust, even as far south as this.

The Oni-Olorun was waiting in the square before the chief's hut, and Ntikima looked at him as curiously as the white men. By comparison with his gaudy escort he seemed a dull bird, neither bedecked with feathers nor so lavishly decorated with coloured scars. It seemed, though, that he had once been tattooed in the same way, for there were traces of coloured lines still visible beneath his furrowed skin – lighter patterns set against the deep black. The Oni-Olorun was a small man, no more than five feet in height. Nevertheless, he had a

commanding presence of his own, which demanded the kind of obeis-
ance which the Ibau were only too delighted to show to him.

The Oni-Olorun was very old. There was no way to judge from
mere appearance how long he had walked upon the earth, for that
would depend on the age which he had reached before he became an
elemi. It meant little that he had wispy, grizzled hair, and that his face
was etched with lines, the places around his eyes much creased, or that
his arms were very thin. His muscles looked wasted, as though they
had shrivelled from their former substance, but there was something
in the way he stood, and in the way he studied his visitors, which
spoke to Ntikima of great age and great wisdom. This was a man who
stood higher in the ranks of Ogbone than any other he had seen, near
to Ekeji Orisha, the eldest among the elders.

The Oni-Olorun bowed, in dignified fashion, to the white men.
Quintus bowed in return, and Noell Cordery too, while Ntikima,
Ngadze and Mburrai all stood back. Then the Oni-Olorun sat down,
indicating with his claw-like hand that Quintus should do likewise.
The Oni-Olorun seemed hardly to notice Noell Cordery, but he sat
too, cross-legged like them, slightly behind the monk as well as to the
side of him.

The Oni-Olorun spoke in Uruba, just as the warriors had, having
obviously been told that this was a tongue that the white babalawo
understood. He began by expressing his hope that the white tribe which
had come to live on the great river was flourishing within the great
brotherhood of tribes. He was undoubtedly aware that frequent attacks
had been made on the settlement in its early days, but the tribes of the
great brotherhood were constantly at one another's throats; it was part
of the pattern of life. Ntikima was not surprised to hear Quintus
assuring the elemi that the white tribe thrived, grateful for the amity
of its neighbours.

'It is decided,' the Oni-Olorun remarked, 'that you will soon journey
to the north, beyond the great forest.'

At this, Noell Cordery showed some sign of surprise, though
Ntikima had already told him that the Oni-Olorun knew of their plans.
Though the white man did not know how far the elemi had come, he
knew full well that the journey must have taken many months. He
must be wondering whether the elemi of Adamawara had some miracu-
lous gift of prescience which had told them about the white babalawo's
intentions before they were even formed in his own mind. Ntikima
had no such cause for surprise; he was the chief source of the Ogbone's
knowledge of the white men's schemes and desires.

'That is so,' Quintus replied, in a calm fashion. 'We have heard much
about the tribes of the interior, and of Adamawara itself. There is much
that we would like to learn about the lands of the great River Kwarra,
and the Benouai, and the Logone.'

The Oni-Olorun showed no surprise when Quintus named the three
rivers which marked the way to Adamawara, but simply said that the
white babalawo was known even in Adamawara as a wise man and a
healer, and that the Ekeji Orisha made such as he most welcome in
that land.

Quintus seemed to understand what was meant by Ekeji Orisha,
though Ntikima had never spoken of that person; he would understand
the Uruba words, which meant 'next to the gods', and had obviously
inferred that in this case the phrase was used as a title.

The Oni-Olorun went on to tell Quintus that the journey to Adamawara would be very difficult, and that even the brave Mkumkwe did
not like to travel certain parts of the way, which were inhabited by
savage tribes, and haunted by demons and strange creatures. Quintus
replied that tales of such wonders were all the more reason why a
curious man should want to go there, and that he had brave companions
of his own, who would dare to go anywhere in search of wisdom.

The Oni-Olorun complimented Quintus on the bravery of his
companions, but told him that one such as he could not successfully
cross the lifeless forest, and survive the silver death, except with the
assistance of an elemi who had strong medicines and amulets to guard
against witches and their supernatural evil.

Ntikima could see that the white babalawo hesitated here, knowing
himself to be on perilous ground, and being afraid of giving offence.
Finally, the white man replied: 'We would consider ourselves the most
fortunate of men, were we to find such a guide and protector'.

The Oni-Olorun replied, with condescension, that Ekeji Orisha
would gladly extend his protection to a man as wise and good as the
babalawo from the sea, and had appointed the elemi Ghendwa, a wise
Oni-Osanhin and a wearer of the white cloth, to bring the white men
to Adamawara.

Ntikima knew that the white men did not fully understand the business of offering and accepting gifts, which was was more complicated
than the business of honest barter. The making of gifts was very much
a trading in obligations, which could regulate the relations between
different tribes, or spoil them almost beyond redemption. If a man
wanted to live long in this part of the world, he must needs be careful
in accepting gifts, and twice as careful in giving them. In either case he
could set in train a pattern of implied promises which, if broken –
however unwittingly – could provoke violence. He found himself
holding his breath, hoping that the white babalawo would accept this
offering with all due gratitude. He sighed with relief to hear Quintus
expressing profuse thanks, acknowledging the great debt that he was
incurring. Again, though, Ntikima looked at Noell Cordery, and saw
his obvious anxiety. The white men did not like to be reminded of

their dependence on the good will of the black tribes to whose land they had come.

The Oni-Olorun clapped his ancient hands together, and from the dark interior of the chief's house there came another elemi, and with him an unfinished man, an Ibau magician. This elemi did not seem so ancient as the Oni-Olorun, though he was similarly wrinkled and thin. He was wearing a white robe, secured at the shoulder, and he carried leathern pouches of medicines.

'I am Ghendwa,' said the elemi.

'I am Msuri,' said the Ibau, who had the medicines which marked him an adept in healing magic. Ntikima guessed that Msuri was also to be taken to Adamawara, to be judged and, if found worthy, to be trained for eternal life.

'These will be your guides,' said the Oni-Olorun to Quintus. 'They will bring you safe to Adamawara. The Mkumkwe must go with me, to the city of Benin, but I think you have your own warriors, who will guard you from savage men.' He got to his feet when he had finished speaking, to signal that the interview was ended.

Quintus got to his feet also, and bowed. Noell Cordery scrambled up and did likewise. The Oni-Olorun went into the chief's hut, leaving Ghendwa and Msuri behind.

'I will come to you,' said Ghendwa, 'when the last of the rain has come and gone. You must prepare for a great journey, because we cannot return until the dry season comes again.' Having completed this speech, the elemi bowed in his turn, and returned with Msuri to his hut.

Dismissed, Quintus and Noell turned away to where Ntikima, Ngadze and Mburrai waited for them. The Mkumkwe had gone away, to seat themselves in a close huddle near to the palisade, where they were still stared at by a group of the village boys.

'What do you make of it all?' asked Noell of Quintus, as they left the village.

'It might be a Godsend,' Quintus told him, unsmilingly, 'or a most subtle trick of Satan. Time will tell.'

Ntikima rejoiced at the apparent wisdom of his white babalawo, who knew that the Oni-Olorun was indeed the emissary of the god which he served, but who seemed also to understand that in the course of their journey they must have some intercourse with Shigidi, who had power over men while they slept – for surely it was Shigidi that white men called 'Satan'.

Time would indeed tell, thought Ntikima, how these strangers from beyond the sea would be judged by the elders of Adamawara, and by Egungun, who was the voice of their ancestors.

FOUR

The elemi Ghendwa came to Burutu two days later. Noell watched while he was received with much ceremony by the native tribesmen, who made their own arrangements to accommodate him. He had little to say to the white men, and they – not altogether at ease – did not try to press him. They were instead content to watch him closely as he made his way about the settlement, inspecting the buildings and their contents. Whenever there was activity in the houses or about Langoisse's ship, Ghendwa would be there, observing from a distance, usually with Msuri and Ntikima by his side. But wherever the elemi went there would also be many pairs of eyes observing him, with equal or greater fascination.

'He has come to us not only to guide us, but to discover what we are like,' Quintus declared to Noell and Langoisse as they supped that evening. 'He is instructed to find out what we are, so that his Ogbone masters may decide what is to be done with us.'

'And while his spying is done,' said Langoisse acidly, 'we may go with him to his home, and deliver ourselves into the hands of those vampire masters, as if to await their verdict meekly. But we have our guns, at any rate.'

'This spying is a blade that cuts both ways,' Noell pointed out. 'We want to visit his land, and he will take us there. It is plain that we have more to gain from his protective presence than he from ours, and we may learn from him while he studies us.'

'I believe we have the right to be anxious,' Quintus said, in a vexed tone. 'When I proposed that we set out to find this fabulous land, I did not think that it would promptly send emissaries to us to welcome our approach. This smacks just a little of the spider and the fly.'

'These Ogbone know altogether too much of our affairs,' said Langoisse, looking moodily into his empty cup.

'We cannot tell how much they know,' Quintus told him. 'It is only natural that they are curious about us, and sent a spy to investigate this station, but I do not think the old vampire set out on his journey only to seek us out. I surmise that he discovered our intention to visit his land only when he arrived here, and instantly built it into his own schemes. If the Ogbone meant us harm, they could destroy us very easily without bringing us to their own country. Should the elemi command it, all Benin would rise against us. If the Oni-Osanhin says that he will take us to Adamawara, I suppose he will take us there.'

'But they have not said that they will let us out again,' observed the pirate. 'I had rather trust to my guns and powder for our best protection.'

'Guns can only give us part of the protection that we need,' said Noell. 'I do not know what virtue there is in the medicines which these men have, but we will need all the help we can find if we are to survive the fevers which await us. What other perils there may be in this lifeless forest which Ntikima has mentioned, with its silver death, we cannot tell. Ghendwa is the one who knows these things, and we will need his knowledge as much as we need your guns.'

'It is folly to trust a vampire,' said Langoisse, uneasily.

'We are in a land where vampires are trusted above ordinary men,' Quintus reminded him, 'and where they have no reputation for cruelty. It would be folly to oppose the elemi here as we once opposed the masters of Gaul. This is another world, where we live on the sufferance of the black men, who might all too easily turn against us.'

There was a brief silence, before Noell spoke again. 'How different things would be in Europe,' he said, 'if the vampires there took the same part in the world's affairs as the vampires here. Yet this Adamawara, we are told, is the land from which the vampires of our empires first came. How is it, I wonder, that the vampires of Africa are so very different from their bastard kin?'

'Perhaps because they were differently received by men,' said Quintus. 'The black men have welcomed and revered the vampires, but the Arabs cast them out, and destroyed them whenever they could, with whatever fierce effort that required. Perhaps the vampires had no choice – if they were to cross the great desert at all, perhaps they could only do so by adopting new ways, and imposing the rule of force.'

'More likely they are different vampires,' said Langoisse. 'I never did hear of a black vampire in Europe or the East, and there were no great ships in ancient times to carry men of our sort to this ugly coast.'

'I am not certain of that,' Quintus told him. 'It has been written down that Christians and other white men reached the nations of the black vampires in ancient times, by more routes than one. I have read of a Greek captain who sailed around the foot of Africa, and the Phoenicians were fine sailors too. Christian missionaries from Syria went into the Ethiop lands in the third and fourth centuries – Ezana, the King of Axum, was converted by Frumentius and made Ethnarch of Ethiopia by St. Athanasius. Other missionaries doubtless went further to the south and west, and it is conceivable that because they were holy and learned men the vampires of Africa met them as equals.

'Some historians suggest that certain of these would-be saints may have been converted, returning to Asia Minor as missionaries of a different kind, there to inspire the Black Huns with their dreams of conquest. Some say those Syrians still live, still invisible behind the thrones of Attila's chain of empires; others contend that Attila, once made vampire, was greedy enough to destroy those who had brought him the gift, and conceal their part in his adventures.'

'And is that the doctrine of the True Faith?' asked the pirate.

'No,' said the monk, with equanimity. 'It is the inference of the true historian.'

Noell had often heard Langoisse and Quintus dispute on matters of history and theology. Langoisse the great sinner was ever ready to find heresies in the ideas of Quintus the saintly.

'If what you say is true,' said Noell to Quintus, 'what attitude might the vampires of Adamawara have toward their errant descendants? Perhaps it is to have news of them that they want us brought to their homeland. We must be very careful, I think, to conceal our true attitude to the vampires of Gaul and Walachia.'

'It may be too late for that,' said Quintus, contemplatively, 'for I have noticed that the elemi spends a great deal of time with Ntikima, who has ever been anxious to learn what he can of our thoughts and ways. It is too late to keep secrets of that kind. But we do not know that the elemi of Adamawara would be any better pleased with their descendants the huns than were the common men they conquered.'

'We know all too little,' Langoisse lamented, 'in spite of your long years of education.'

This remark annoyed Noell, but Quintus simply shrugged his shoulders. 'It is because we know so little,' he pointed out, 'that we must be enthusiastic to travel in these alien lands. We seek not gold but understanding, which in my eyes is worth the greater risk. You have the *Stingray*, and may put to sea if you have changed your mind; but if you stay, then you must accept this Ghendwa as our guide, and submit to his advice.'

'I am set on the adventure,' Langoisse insisted. 'The presence of this vampire and his minion will only make me more careful to guard us all from treachery and harm. If what you say is true, there are no guns in Adamawara, and I will defend you there, and bring you out if the need arises.'

'Ours will be a journey of many months,' said the monk, 'and in that time, much may happen to test us. We will surely need your guns, but we must not place too much faith in their power.'

'I have faith enough for all of us,' Langoisse assured him.

Here Noell intervened again. 'I have watched this black vampire carefully,' he said. 'I know that he is far from being a fool. He is very curious about us, and has asked many questions of the Ibaus and the Edaus on the station. He has come to me while I was using my microscope, and watched so very carefully that I had to invite him to look into it. He said nothing, and I do not know what he thought, but he is learning all the while about us. We must try our best to match him.

If we meet his questions with questions of our own, as so many of the tribesmen seem to do, we might win knowledge by the kind of barter in which we have become expert these last ten years. As we have exchanged needles and knives for gold and ivory, so we might exchange the wisdom of Gaul for the wisdom of Africa. No matter how much faith we have in our guns, let us arm ourselves as best we can in every other way.'

They had finished eating by now, and Quintus had pushed his chair back from the table. The monk nodded his head, soberly, to signify his agreement with all that Noell had said. Langoisse shoved his own chair back to give him space to stand, and shrugged his shoulders.

When the others went away, Noell did not immediately rise, but waited instead for Ntikima to come to clear the table. He watched the boy at his work, occasionally looking away to stare through the window at the darkening night.

'Are you afraid, Ntikima, to come with us to Adamawara?' he asked, eventually.

'Oh no,' replied the boy. 'When I met Aroni in the forest, many years ago, he told me that one day I must make this journey. I am not afraid, not even of the silver death.'

'And will you come back with us, when we return? Or will you stay with the Mkumkwe, and hope to inherit the breath of life yourself?' Noell watched carefully as the boy looked back at him, his big dark eyes apparently innocent of any confusion or intent to deceive.

'I do not know,' Ntikima said. 'I will do as I am told.'

Not until the boy had disappeared did Noell realise that Ntikima had not specified whose instructions it was that he would obey.

Noell retired early to his bed, so that he might rise before dawn. He knew that while they travelled they must begin each day's trek at first light, and stop soon after noon, if they were to conserve their strength. The sun could not be defied, and when its fiercest heat established its dominion, it was best for men to hide and wait. He slept very lightly, as he was always wont to do when new things were impending, and in his dreams he saw demons – not the Satanic demons of his own faith, but the stranger spirits of Africa, whose names and natures he had but recently learned. These phantoms of the night taunted him with the promise that their power to hurt him could only increase, the deeper into their realm he allowed himself to be led.

In spite of all this, the early hours of the next day found him already hard at work, arranging for the donkeys and their goods to be ferried across the river to the northern shore, from which the journey was to begin. He had decided that if they were to go, then they must go with determination, and that he, the strongest of them all, must be prepared to act the part of leader.

The expedition had twenty-two donkeys, all but three to be used as pack-animals, and the others only to be ridden if members of the party became too sick to walk. The expedition numbered sixteen in all, of which seven were whites. Langoisse had determined that Leilah and Selim must come with him, and those two of his sailors who were the most expert in the use of muskets. These were Englishmen named Eyre and Cory, the one small and wiry and the other a big man who had once been a marine soldier. Noell had questioned the pirate's decision to include the woman, but Langoisse would not be without her, and swore that she was as clever as any man in all the work that would face them. There was certainly no doubt that she would far rather come with them than be left with the *Stingray*'s sailors, and Noell had not pressed his complaint.

The seven settlement blacks who were to come with them were led by Ngadze, who had lived in the station longer than any, and who had learned English to complement his knowledge of half a dozen local languages; Mburrai and Ntikima were in this group. Ngadze's authority was purely nominal, for Ghendwa easily assumed a hegemony over the blacks from the station which superseded that of the white men. They were willing to defer to Msuri too, which left Ngadze, tacitly, in the situation of third-in-command. It was clear to Noell that in any conflict of instruction that might arise, only Ngadze could be reckoned likely to hesitate, and even he would probably choose to obey the elemi.

The donkey-train eventually moved off three hours after dawn, with Quintus and the elemi marching at its head. Noell followed, leading the first donkey, which carried the monk's and his own personal effects, including the box where the parts of the microscope were stowed. Langoisse and his men had charge of those animals which were carrying guns and powder, while the blacks brought up the rear, leading trains of two or three donkeys apiece, carrying supplies and trading goods which could be used to purchase food from native villages when the need arose.

Thus was the journey into the interior begun, and Noell found, looking back at the station which had been his home for many years, that he was not at all sorry to be going from it, even though he could not tell what future lay before him. Now that he was adrift on the sea of destiny, he felt calm and patient, ready to find whatever this strange continent had in store for him at its deepest heart. He felt, in fact, that this was the great adventure of his life, by which he might ever after be measured, in his own eyes and the estimation of other men.

FIVE

In the early days of the journey the progress which the expedition made seemed to Ntikima to be painfully slow. The difficulties involved in moving heavily-laden donkeys through the forest were great, and the frequent delays gave rise to much frustration. Noell Cordery and the white babalawo had known what it would be like, and were patient, but Langoisse and his sailors were free with their curses and complaints, and the boy soon learned to steer clear of them whenever he could.

They moved away from the shore of the watercourse on which Burutu stood, heading north-east toward the main stream of the Kwarra, but had to cross many rivulets and tributaries. These creeks were neither deep nor fast-flowing, but the crossings were hazardous because crocodiles were often to be found in the shallows, and had to be driven off with spears or guns. The land between these rivulets was marshy, swarming with biting insects. There were black leeches everywhere, and though the white men were relatively safe in their clothing the seamen became anxious to avoid them. Ntikima knew how to dislodge such creatures from his legs quickly and easily, but he was irritated nevertheless by the itchy sores which they left.

Once they were above the delta the way became easier for a while, but the path soon gave way to untracked coarse grass, which made a thick undergrowth between the palms. Walking was often difficult here, and their route was by necessity far from direct. There were many swamps and slowly-drying mud-flats which were even more troublesome. The larger swamps were dismal and noisome, and the travellers could not stop to make camp. On more than one occasion they had to keep up their march far longer than they wished, with the sun beating down relentlessly.

Apart from the crocodiles, the larger animals of the forest posed little threat, though when they came across pythons lolling from the branches the white men gave them a wide berth. They learned to ignore the monkeys and chimpanzees which chattered at them from the treetops. The tiny creatures were infinitely more troublesome. Ntikima had always ignored them, having grown used to their attentions, but Quintus had urged him to believe that they were, in their way, more dangerous than crocodiles. The babalawo had given his fellow whites thin veils to wear, to keep the biting insects from their faces, and insisted that they slept amid festoons of netting. Ghendwa told them that they had nothing to fear, and that the medicines which he and

Msuri carried would protect them all, but the white men preferred to take their own precautions and Ntikima had sufficient respect for the white babalawo's healing abilities to listen with one ear to each of his advisers. Quintus had told him to drink no water which was not boiled, because boiling drove diseaseful spirits from the water, and this he did. He looked forward with interest to the time when Quintus's skills might be pitted against Msuri's, to put their different methods to the test.

Langoisse had initially protested against the veils, but allowed himself to be persuaded. Even Selim disliked tiny insects and seemed to fear their stings far more than he hated or feared anything against which he could defend himself with his sword. For this reason he was quite ready to go veiled – which had the advantage, from the point of view of his fellow-travellers, of concealing his wrecked features.

Whether or not it was in consequence of these measures Ntikima could not tell, but the white men suffered no serious fevers while they trekked through the forest. They had problems with stomach-aches and diarrhoea in spite of driving the evil spirits from their drinking-water and making sure that they cooked their food most thoroughly. Several of the donkeys sickened, but they carried their packs regardless, and only one died. The only other loss which the expedition suffered at this stage was two of the Ibaus, who disappeared in the night, presumably finding the lure of their own villages more of a temptation than the prospect of a journey into unknown lands.

Now that the dry season had begun the waters of the great river were in gradual recession, and the avenues of mud and sand which appeared on either side of the Kwarra became gradually more accommodating to their passage. There were many villages beside the banks, which now had fertile fields planted where the waters had receded, and food was abundant because the river supported many fishermen. Most of these villages were pleased to welcome the Oni-Osanhin, and though he sometimes had to linger to assist in secret ceremonies it was a great boon to the expedition that local priests and magicians were magnanimous in their attempts to claim him for a friend. Most were equally enthusiastic to be generous in their treatment of Msuri, who might one day return to this land as an Ibau elemi.

The shore was by no means so densely wooded when they went further beyond the delta, even where the banks were high and sheer. A cooling breeze blew along the river, easing the discomfort of the march and clearing away some few of the biting insects which clustered so thickly in the swamplands. The constant companions of the expedition in this region were the birds of the river – the cranes and the egrets which fed from its waters, and the vultures which picked the carrion left by crocodiles. The donkey-train was covering a good distance between each daybreak and noon; the hot afternoons could usually be spent in comfortable idleness, with friendly neighbours and plentiful food.

At night, when it became cold, the white men pitched their tents on open ground, preferring to do so even when a native village was near, where they might be allowed the use of wattled huts. On such nights, Ntikima would go with Ghendwa and Msuri to their meetings with the Ogbone, who were always aware of their approach. Sometimes the other blacks would go to the villages – except for Ngadze, who always stayed with the white men – but only Ntikima came to the secret conferences. He was disappointed, though, with what happened there, because very little magic was made.

The white men were wary of accepting the hospitality of the villages, save for obtaining supplies of food, and they never failed to post guards. Ntikima could see the wisdom in this; what their donkeys carried would be reckoned a substantial treasure by any chief. He doubted that their guns would have been adequate if the white men had not been under the protection of the Ogbone; no one would scruple to murder them in order to take possession of their goods, and many might be prepared to risk their guns. The villages here were a law unto themselves, and had far more respect for the person of Ghendwa and what he represented than they had for any distant authority such as the Oba of Benin.

As the days went by, and no hostile hand was raised against them, the white men became more confident of their safety. Noell no longer carried a musket, and became more adventurously curious about the places which they visited, and about the movements of the elemi. Quintus began to study Ghendwa closely, though covertly. When the elemi took blood, usually from Msuri but sometimes from Ntikima or one of the others, the sacrifice would often be discreetly observed. When Ghendwa, Msuri and Ntikima brought back plants from the forest which they had gathered to make medicines, Quintus would often ask Ntikima to tell him what was being made, and how. When Ghendwa offered sacrifices, or made magic, or simply sat by himself and chanted the measures of his wisdom, Quintus would usually be watching and listening. Ghendwa did not seem to mind this curiosity, and never forbade Ntikima to answer questions, though his own answers were always evasive.

When the elemi took blood from Ntikima he used a bronze-bladed knife to open a vein, and sucked patiently for a few minutes before dressing the wound with some kind of paste which he made from ingredients taken from his pouch. Ntikima had never made such a sacrifice before Ghendwa required it of him, but the sense of importance which it gave him soon wore off. None of the wounds made by the elemi ever became infected, and the elemi would sometimes dress ordinary abrasions on the bodies of the tribesmen in identical fashion, helping the wounds to heal.

Ghendwa never asked to take blood from any of the white men, and left the tending of stings and scratches suffered by the whites entirely to Quintus. Ntikima noticed, however, that just as the white men kept account of the results of the vampire's medication, so Ghendwa would take some notice of the progress made by wounds which Quintus had treated. Ntikima wished that he knew more about the white men's ways, in order to be useful to the elemi, and he began asking Quintus about the reasoning which supported his methods, struggling conscientiously to understand the replies which he obtained.

Langoisse and his musketeers could not hunt in the forest, and in any case were anxious to conserve their shot. Nor were the Ibaus, for all that they were forest men, skilled hunters with bow and arrow. Such meat as the travellers had came either from their own dwindling supplies, or from the local natives, who kept domestic fowl. Fish was in much better supply but the basis of the travellers' diet was millet, in porridge or cakes, and soup made from sesame oil and earth-peas. The Ibaus were much better foragers than hunters, and they found fruits of various kinds, including bananas, paw-paws and yams, and also dazoes and ground-nuts. These were not abundant, but plentiful enough to make sure that the company was adequately fed when no village was near. Ngadze predicted dolefully, however, that such foraging would become much more difficult in the upland country.

When the forest thinned further the north-east wind began to carry a thin blue haze of dust; this was their first taste of the harmattan, which would blow throughout the season, making the air dry and thick. It painted the sunsets gloriously, but it made the days less comfortable, for the travellers often had to head directly into it, with the dust forever in their faces, hurting their eyes and their throats. Ntikima did not like this any more than the white men, but Ghendwa told him that this problem would only get worse; the further north they went, and the higher they went into the hills, the drier and dustier would the harmattan become.

There were rounded hills close to the shore of the river, with brown grass on their crests and ridges, while palms grew densely in the green valleys in between. In the mornings, the peaks of mountains could be seen in the north-west, but by midday the haze of the harmattan curtained them. From the hilltops at night the fires of dozens of villages could be seen scattered across the land, and once they saw the red glow of a great bush-fire in the west – the first of many which would devastate huge tracts of land in the coming months. Often they passed through regions where the trees were blackened and gnarled from the fires of former years.

Eventually they came out of the forest and into the plain which was the territory of the Nupai, who were cattle-keepers like the Mkumkwe. The Nupai men did not dress as extravagantly as the Mkumkwe warriors who had escorted the Oni-Olorun, and decorated themselves with ornaments rather than coloured scars. Noell Cordery seemed to regard the land of the Nupai as a less strange and hostile place than the forest but Ntikima was forest-born and forest-bred, and the open lands of the herdsmen were to him foreign and alien. He tried to give no sign of this, though, because he was Ogbone, and to the Ogbone, no land in this great continent should be alien.

Two of the blacks from the settlement were suffering from the disease which Quintus called yaws, which was common in these parts, especially among children; Ghendwa gave them medicine. Ntikima knew that most sufferers eventually recovered without treatment – even small children rarely died from the disease – but he also knew that it could be a sore trial, and often left men disfigured. He was not surprised when these two decided that they had had enough and deserted. This left only Ngadze, Mburrai and Ntikima of the tribesmen who had come from Burutu. Noell Cordery was annoyed by the loss, but not unduly dismayed. The donkeys were much easier to handle now that they were in open terrain.

Mburrai was slightly incapacitated too, his right arm affected by what he claimed to be a worm which had been growing inside it for some years. Quintus did not believe this at first, but in the course of their journey through the villages near to the river Ntikima was able to show him other men and women suffering from the same ailment. One of these had taken advantage of the fact that the worm's end had become briefly exposed in a sore near the wrist, and had begun to wind the creature inch by inch on to a stick. Ntikima assured Quintus that by this means the man would ultimately be able to dislodge the parasite, though it was a tortuous business. Mburrai asked whether the worm which afflicted him could somehow be drawn from his arm, but neither Quintus nor Ghendwa could offer an effective means of achieving that end.

With these exceptions, the worst problems the black men had suffered on the journey were caused by chigoes – burrowing insects which both Ghendwa and Quintus were equally adept at digging out with the point of a needle. There was thus no opportunity yet to test the black magician's powers against the white's.

The white men's boots kept them safe from chigoes, but they had to be careful to shake the boots thoroughly before putting them on each morning, lest scorpions had crept into them. On one occasion the small man Eyre shouted out in blind panic because a huge fruit-spider had dropped on his back, but Ntikima was able to reassure him that such creatures were harmless. Ntikima had no fear of spiders, and would let them walk over him, rejoicing in the fact that even the noseless Turk considered this evidence of unusual courage and fortitude.

On the plain where the herdsmen lived Ntikima saw many animals which were as unusual and astonishing to him as they were to the white men. He was no less amazed than Noell Cordery when they first saw giraffes feeding from the foliage of tall trees. Strangely, some of these creatures which he had never seen were not new to Noell, who told Ntikima that he had seen lions and leopards, and even an elephant, in captivity in a place where he had once lived. Noell seemed to expect such creatures to be much in evidence now that he was in their native territory, and was disappointed that the big cats were too shy to be easily seen, though their cries could often be heard. Noell actually described lions to Ntikima before Ntikima had the opportunity to glimpse one, but the hyaenas and jackals which could often be seen scavenging among the rubbish outside the village compounds were as unfamiliar to the white man as to himself.

Noell seemed very startled by some of the things which he saw. He seized Ntikima and interrogated him about the habit which some nomadic groups of cattle-keepers had of bleeding their cattle as well as milking them. These herdsmen would make incisions on the necks of their beasts, and would mix blood and milk together into a frothy concoction. When this was offered to the travellers Ntikima found it quite palatable, but he saw that the white men were strangely reluctant to taste it, and seemed perturbed by the custom. Ntikima concluded that the white men subjected themselves to strange and strict taboos regarding the use of blood, which were not unconnected with their attitude to the elemi. But when he told Ghendwa of this discovery, the Oni-Osanhin was unimpressed.

Travel across the plain was so easy that by the end of their second day upon it they were within sight of the place where they must cross the Kwarra and follow the Benouai, whose confluence with the greater river was near. There was no possibility of wading across the river, and they had to persuade the fishermen of one of the larger riverside towns to ferry them across. Even without Ghendwa to help them, this would have posed no great difficulty, for these tribesmen were well-experienced in the river trade. Many spoke Uruba, and some of them eagerly claimed that they had visited Burutu. They were not in the least astonished or frightened by the sight of the white men, unlike the forest tribesmen, many of whom had not liked to have them near. The headman of this village received the travellers far more hospitably than any of the chiefs of the forest-dwellers.

Beyond the confluence of the rivers there was only a narrow strip of land between the Benouai and the hills, and along this strip they marched eastwards, following well-worn paths in common use by local traders. There were few cattle kept permanently in this strip; Ghendwa told him that this was because of the prevalence of the falling sickness. Only a few miles away on higher ground, however, cattle could graze with impunity, and the travellers occasionally driven down to the bank of the Benouai from the hill-country, which was becoming parched. The hillmen who came with their cattle on such occasions were feared and hated by the local people, for they often raided the riverside villages when they came, and even Ghendwa seemed wary of them. On more than one occasion they passed the ruined ditches and stockades of former villages, which had been utterly wiped out by such marauders.

Two groups of Hausa traders from the west tagged along behind the donkey-train for three days, apparently trusting in Langoisse's guns to deter any would-be attackers. Like the villagers at the confluence of the rivers these Hausas had seen white men before, and considered them no more alien than the local people. Normally, the Hausa traders would have continued to travel during the afternoon, but in the circumstances they were content to stop when the white men sought shelter from the sun. They would lodge their goods in the forking branches of trees, and come to sit with Ngadze and Mburrai, exchanging jokes and anecdotes. Ntikima kept his distance, preferring to be near the elemi. Ghendwa ignored these hangers-on. The Hausas went their own way when Ghendwa led the donkeys away from the river, heading north again through the hills, following the course of a small stream.

When the journey came at last to seem tiresomely endless, Ntikima was inspired with the courage to ask how many days more their trek would take them – a question which Noell Cordery had already asked. But Ghendwa only told the boy, as he had told the white man, that they had barely begun, and that the fertile land of Adamawara was not easily to be reached by the kind of men which his travelling companions were.

SIX

Noell was roused from the relaxed state which preceded sleep by a distant whining sound, which cut cleanly through the still air of the tropic night. He raised his head immediately from the rough pillow which he had made from spare clothing, but then recognised the sound and knew that there was no cause for alarm. He rolled over on to his back and opened his eyes but made no attempt to rise. He knew that the noise would cease, in time, and then he could go back to sleep.

Quintus, with whom he shared his tent, was similarly undisturbed – but he did sit up, pushing aside the hanging folds of his mosquito net, and pulling on his boots. His face was eerily lit by the tiny night-light which burned on the ground between their beds.

'It is Oro,' said Noell. 'No concern of ours.'

THE BREATH OF LIFE

'Langoisse will not know that,' the monk replied. 'He and his men must be warned to stay in their tents. The last thing we want is for a man with a musket to go running into the night in search of a wild beast. If there are to be dead men displayed in the morning, I would rather they were Hausa thieves or delinquent Urubas.'

'Of course,' Noell answered. 'Shall I come too?'

'There is no need. I will do what is required.'

The monk straightened his white habit, and fought his way free of the meshes which confined his bed. As he left the tent he closed the flap behind him, but it did not long remain closed. Leilah came in, and scrambled under Noell's net. He was startled by the invasion, but perversely relieved to see that she was dressed; the nights were cold now, and her night attire was fuller than the light clothes she wore in the fiery afternoons.

'What makes the noise?' she asked, nervously. She sat upon his bed, trying to appear calm, but was obviously alarmed.

'It is Oro,' he told her. 'The word means fury, or perhaps fierceness. The tribesmen say that he is a kind of demon, who comes to punish the guilty, but the noise is made by a slotted piece of wood whirled around a priest's head on a thong. He is probably not unlike Egungun, who appears at other feasts. He is summoned by the Ogbone to exact revenge on witches and other offenders against unwritten law. When they hear his voice all women must shut themselves up in their huts, for his business is only to do with men. The criminals who are given to him are often never seen again, but sometimes their twisted bodies are found in the branches of tall trees, where the demon is said to have thrown them away. Their blood is taken, though, and drunk by ordinary men and elemi alike, and smeared upon the big drums which they call *gbedu*, as a form of sacrifice.

'Sometimes, when Oro comes, there are also sacrifices of slaves taken in war, or children, but that depends what feast it is. If it is the feast of Olori-merin, who is the god which guards towns, a new-born babe must be sacrificed. The day falls four times a year, but even if this is an affair of that kind it is no threat to us.'

'It is not our coming which has roused them?' she asked.

'No. Our passing by is of no significance to these people. They may be glad to have the vampire Ghendwa at their ceremonies, and might put on a special show for him. He is an important person in the ranks of the Ogbone. But he is a priest of Osanhin, who is a kindly god of healing – his hand will not be turned to any murder.'

'This is a horrid land,' she complained, 'where all are vampires whether they live long or no. The gods these black men fear demand the spilling of blood, and even the milk which their infants drink is stained by the blood of beasts. It is vile.'

'These forests run no redder than the streets of any city in Gaul,' he told her, cynically 'and I doubt that the arab lands are any cleaner. Neither Christians nor Mohammedans show overmuch scruple in dealing with their enemies, and we all claim the sanction of our particular gods in what we do to them. Olori-merin is a dark god, to be sure, but there's a kind of honesty in offering cruel deeds to the service of cruel gods whereas the pope's inquisitors torture in the service the good and kindly God who is said to love and cherish us all.'

Outside, in the distance, Oro's voice faltered, and died slowly away.

'Is that the end?' asked the gypsy.

'Oh no,' said Noell. 'There will be drums now – but we are some way from the town, and they will not seem so loud. We are safe, and we must try to sleep.'

'If I could stay with thee,' she said, 'I would sleep sounder.'

'Langoisse would miss thee,' he replied, trying as best he could not to sound unkind.

She would have replied, and bitterly too, but Quintus came back then, and looked at the two of them, sitting uncomfortably apart in the folds of the protective netting. Leilah had an anxious reverence for Quintus, though he was never stern with her, and she drew further away from Noell because embarrassment was added to her annoyance.

'Do not be afraid,' said Quintus. 'The camp is safe. Ngadze will watch. Ghendwa and Msuri are gone – Ntikima also. Perhaps it is only that he is Uruba.'

Noell nodded, thoughtfully. Neither he nor Quintus believed that Ntikima had gone only because he was Uruba. They had come to the conclusion that he was Ogbone, and that he had from the very beginning been appointed to watch the traders of Burutu, and report to his masters their actions and their plans. They did not resent this as much as they might have done, for they both liked the boy, but it made them more careful in their dealings with him.

'I will go to Langoisse,' said Leilah, 'though he does not need me any more. If he learns the secret which these black vampires have, it need give him no pause to wonder whether he might lose too much in the using of it.' With that, she left the tent to go back to her own. Noell stared after her, momentarily puzzled.

'What did she mean?' he asked the monk.

Quintus returned carefully to the shelter of his own bed, and pulled off his boots. 'I think,' he said, 'she is trying to tell you that Langoisse is impotent, or nearly so. He has hinted as much in trying, delicately, to inquire about my healing talents.'

Noell still stared at the monk, uncertainly, still not able to make sense of what the Maroc woman had said. 'What has that to do with the secret of the black vampires?' he asked.

'Have you not seen beneath the elemi's pouches?' asked Quintus.

Ghendwa was rarely without his pouches, or the cloth which he wore about his loins. He did not often bathe. Noell had not seen what was beneath; he always looked away when any man or woman stood naked.

'His prick is mutilated,' Quintus told him. 'I thought when first I glimpsed it that he had been the victim of a bad circumcision, or an accident, which had happened so long before he was made a vampire that he could not be made whole again, but it may have been deliberately done. If *ikeyika* is the rite by which a boy is made into a man, there may be a similar ritual when a man becomes elemi, and this might be what is meant by Ogo-Ejodun. The elemi are revered for having risen above ordinary pleasures and ordinary temptations, and we know that the coloured scars which such tribes as the Mkumkwe inflict upon themselves do not entirely heal when their wearers become elemi. It is possible that the head of Ghendwa's prick was cut off and anointed to prevent it growing again when he became a vampire.'

Noell was surprised by the wrench which his stomach felt. For a moment, he thought that he might actually be sick. He had seen Edaus who had been injured by careless cutting during the ceremonies of initiation into their tribes, and he found the sight of an inflamed and suppurating penis uniquely disturbing. The idea that the process of elevation to the status of elemi involved a more radical castration was somehow more horrible than the thought of what might be happening only a mile or so away, where the blood of a tiny child might even now be draining into a calabash, to be placed on the earthen mound where the sliced flesh of the infant would later be buried.

'It cannot be so,' he said, in a harsh voice not much louder than a whisper. 'It is some kind of buggery which creates vampires, or so my father believed.'

'So others have believed,' admitted Quintus, 'though the Gregorians have always said that 'twas the devil who performed the act. I am sorely curious to see the private parts of other elemi, to see what might be missing.'

With that, the monk lay down to sleep, and though the gbedu drums were already beating in the town not far away, he seemed to slip readily enough into the arms of Morpheus. Noell, by contrast, found his thoughts stirred up so violently by what he had been told that he tossed and turned for hours, and was still awake when the drums had stopped. In the morning, his eyes were red and tired, and he was unusually sluggish in his work, drawing vexed glances from Langoisse. The pirate never mentioned what had happened in the night, but plainly retained a certain curiosity as to what had passed between Noell and his mistress – who was, it seemed, no longer a mistress in the full sense of the word.

The lowlands which the expedition had been crossing for some time were lush and prosperous, and the villagers' herds were thriving, as were their patches of millet, cassava and yams. But the road now became stony and eventually petered out. The land and its inhabitants grew progressively poorer. The course of a day's march took them from a land apparently flowing with milk and honey to a harsh country where the grass was withered, the trees sparse, and the tribesmen sullen. The sun went down that night with a strange lurid glow, the harmattan obscuring the purple horizon where the ridge of a plateau loomed over the plain like a monstrous cliff, stretching as far as the eye could see in either direction.

Ngadze told Noell and Quintus that the Hausa traders who had travelled with them for a while had called this the Bauchi plateau, and had warned him against it because its people, the Kibun, were savages and cannibals. The Kibun men, the Hausas had told Ngadze, were red of skin, and their women had tails. These red men rode like demons across the dusty uplands, upon their lean ponies. Worse still, they were no lovers of elemi. Not only did they have none of their own, but they did not live in hope that one day the wise men would come to them. Instead, they gave thanks to their savage gods that the Ogbone had no power over them. Ngadze repeated tales which the traders had told him of vampires killed and devoured by these monstrous people, but when Quintus asked Ghendwa whether the people of the plateau posed a threat to them, the elemi seemed not in the least perturbed.

As Ghendwa guided them across the last miles of the boulder-strewn plain toward the precipitous granite cliffs, Noell saw that they were heading for a gap in the rock-face, where there was a path beside a fast-running stream. This steep path took them up no less than eighteen hundred feet, and was very hard for the donkeys. The packs had to be taken from the animals during much of the ascent, and carried by the men, sometimes broken up into smaller parcels. But the climb was completed before the sun was at its worst, and the white men were able to pitch their tents at the summit while the others completed the transfer of goods from the foot of the cliff.

On the following day they saw the first of the Kibun villages near which they must pass. It had no wooden wall or ditch, as the villages of the Nupai and their neighbours had, but instead was surrounded by a tall hedge of prickly cactus. The huts were small, and the compounds partitioned by lesser hedges, about the height of a man. Millet was growing inside the compound, and the fowls and ponies which were the Kibun's livestock were penned up.

Kibun men watched from the safety of their stronghold as the travellers passed by, but made no move to come out to attack them. Noell saw that they really were red in colour, but that this was because they smeared their naked bodies with some kind of dye. Their spears were light, not nearly as long as those the Mkumkwe warriors had carried. No women could be seen, and it was impossible to judge whether the

Hausas were right to say that they had tails. At the closest point of passage, Ghendwa turned to the watching Kibun, raised his right hand high, and shouted at them: 'Sho-sho! Sho-sho!' To this greeting they replied in kind, raising their arms and crying out in unison: 'Sho-sho, aboki!'

Beyond this village there was a plain, on which few trees grew, and these wind-worn and stunted. The grass was short, yellowing, and sometimes blackened by fire. When they set camp that evening the only conspicuous green which Noell could see was the cactus hedge of the village, still visible on the southern horizon behind them.

They made good headway when they went on, the bare ground offering little or no hindrance. The sun glared down at them from a cloudless sky, and the harmattan blew all day, but they were high enough now for the heat to seem less burdensome. The plateau seemed sparsely populated by comparison with the lowlands, and when they passed the cactus fortresses which surrounded the Kibun villages the natives would usually hide in their compounds, responding in kind to the vampire's greetings but never venturing forth to meet the travellers or to offer gifts of food. As Ngadze had predicted, the foraging was very poor, and there was little game to shoot. Without food from the villages, the supplies which the expedition carried had to be rationed, and they soon found themselves hungry. Sometimes they saw groups of Kibun hunters, mounted bare-back on their lean ponies, and Ngadze would try to signal them in the hope of trading knives and needles for fresh meat, but they would not approach.

At night a cold wind would blow, which felt quite unlike the dusty harmattan as it played upon Noell's skin and teased his hair; it made them all huddle in their blankets. There was little fuel to be found, and such fires as they were able to keep burned meanly, giving little heat. Ngadze and Mburrai slept sitting up, with their knees drawn up beneath their chins and blankets wrapped tight around their shoulders. Often they cradled their spears in their arms, with the blades pointing at the sky behind their shoulders, but they always refused the shelter of the tents. Ghendwa fought the cold – or so it seemed – with magical incantations; he would sway from side to side, reciting songs which often dissolved into long choruses in which a single phrase would be repeated countless times: 'A-da-ma! A-da-ma!'

Despite the clothes which Noell persuaded them to wear, the Ibau men shivered in the cool mornings, and when the donkey train started on its way they would jog and dance until the warmth was back in their bones. Ntikima seemed less bothered by the cold wind than his elders were, but eventually caught a chill, which the elemi's medicines could not altogether ease; he had to ride instead of walking.

The plain began to rise again in gentle undulations as their direction changed and they headed more to the east, skirting the cones of three ancient volcanoes. At one point they had to cross a deep gorge by way of a poor bridge made of rope and spars of wood which caused great distress to the donkeys, who had to be coaxed across it most carefully by Quintus and Ngadze. The territory was becoming very rough, with numerous rocky outcrops jutting from the parched soil, and rocky ridges winding in strange convolutions over the hills.

The tribesmen who populated this land were Jawara, who built larger settlements than the Kibun, sprawling over hilltops or clustering around shallow fertile valleys. Like the Kibun, the Jawara were reluctant to approach the travellers, and responded with reluctance to the vampire's greetings until one day they came to an unusually large settlement in a wooded valley, where Ghendwa was greeted with enthusiasm. Noell realised why this was when they were conducted to a hut in a clearing, where dwelt the wise men of this tribe. They were elemi, three in number, all very ancient in appearance.

Here the expedition was able to renew its supplies, and partake in a feast prepared in honour of Ghendwa's visit. Long into the night, Ghendwa and Msuri conferred with the Jawaran elemi, while the men, women and children of the tribe came to stare at the white men, whose like none of them had ever seen. No one had ever told them tales of the pale people whose ships were gradually extending links with the peoples of the African coast.

To Noell the Jawara seemed more civilized than most of the forest tribes. Though they did not work bronze in the clever manner of the craftsmen of Benin they washed tinstone from the sands of the semi-desert, smelting it in clay furnaces, and moulding it into wire and ornaments. Their fires and kilns, their hammers and workshops, aroused in Noell a curious sense of nostalgia. Here were men who were mechanicians of a sort, whose arts connected them with him in mysterious intellectual kinship.

But he did not spend much time watching the native workmen plying their trades. He was drawn instead to the huts of the elemi, to play the peeper in the hope of catching a glimpse of the loins of the Jawaran vampires. He had seen Ghendwa's mutilated organ now, and was as anxious as Quintus to see whether these other elemi were likewise incomplete, wondering what really might be signified by the kind of finishing called tigu. This curiosity, and its exercise, made him feel a little contemptuous of himself, but he could not resist the temptation. Alas, he could find no opportunity see what he wanted to see.

The expedition had by now crossed the summit of the great plateau, and their route descended again from its heights. Eventually they came to the northern shore of a river which was obviously a major water-course in the wet season, but which was now running low in its bed. Ghendwa called it the Gongola. They moved along a thinly-wooded margin between the flood-plain of the river and drier grasslands. This fertile margin was intensively grazed by the cattle of a nomadic people who called themselves Fulbai. The Fulbai were equally different from the forest blacks and the plateau-dwellers, their skin being coppery brown and their hair long and straight. Many were bearded, in contrast to the forest tribesmen, who plucked out the meagre hair which grew on their chins. These nomads and their compounds screened with zana matting dominated the region.

The Fulbai seemed to be on bad terms with their crop-growing neighbours, and the travellers found two villages which had been deserted and wrecked in the recent past, the gleaming bones of dead warriors scattered by vultures and jackals. Ghendwa would not go near the herds of the Fulbai, and Noell was advised by Ntikima that this was a time when Langoisse's men must have their muskets ready for use. Even the elemi, it seemed, feared men as wild as these. Noell asked Ntikima whether the Fulbai had elemi of their own; he said that they did not.

The region was haunted by peculiar odours, apparently caused by the decay of vegetation left exposed to the sun's cruel glare by the dwindling of the river. The stink reminded Noell of the fields around Aberteifi, and their seaweed manure. Here, for the first time, Noell saw considerable herds of antelope, though the greater part of the land was utterly dominated by the domestic herds of the tribesmen.

They followed the Gongola until it passed through a broad, flat-bottomed valley between two escarpments, after which its course swerved south, while Ghendwa headed east, taking them up to another plateau. This tableland was not as high as the summit of the Bauchi plateau, and was more wooded. The bush was thicker here, and the walls of the permanent towns – maintained by a people called the Tera – were strongly fortified against raids by the Fulbai. These towns had elemi, and Ghendwa was welcome there, so that the travellers suffered none of the hardships which they had lately been forced to endure. The white men pitched their tents inside the fortified compounds, to share the benefit of their defence, but after spending two nights inside such compounds they moved into barer territory.

Here they were quickly attacked by Fulbai marauders, who clearly did not understand how well-protected the expedition was. The first raiders to come at them rushed from a thicket to the side of the trail which the donkey-train was following. They had let the greater part of the train pass by before emerging, hurling their spears at the men walking beside the last three donkeys. Cory and Langoisse were carrying their muskets, and soon had them unslung, while Eyre, Selim and Noell came back as quickly as they could with their own guns. When the guns were fired two of the bearded raiders were felled, one by Langoisse, who had fired at close range, and one by Eyre, who hit a man as he threw back his arm to launch his spear.

The other raiders immediately turned and ran for the thicket, but one spear had hit a donkey in the flank, sending it mad with pain. Three animals, released by Cory and Langoisse, broke loose and ran, two of them into the thorn-scrub into which the Fulbai had vanished. Cory made as if to follow them, but Noell restrained him, urging him instead to get the remaining donkeys closer together. The expedition had too few members now to risk any in pursuit.

The raiders struck again that evening. This time, thirty or forty men charged from the bushes, howling and casting spears, and Langoisse was forced to form his men quickly into a rank, consisting of himself, Cory, Eyre and Selim, to fire a volley, while Noell, Quintus, Leilah and Ngadze waited behind, ready to take their place.

Though the distance which the attackers had to cover was more than seventy yards, only three fell quickly, and it seemed that the fighting must come to a hand-to-hand affair. But when the Fulbai came closer to the guns their charge slackened and their fear showed. They yelled their war-cries, but paused in their approach. The Turk Selim yelled back at them, more blood-curdlingly than they, and his companions were allowed one reloading more than they might have had, which they used to good effect. While the spears cascaded around them, they fired again, killing or wounding five more men. Eyre took a spear in his side, and two more donkeys were wounded, but again the raiders turned and ran.

At first, Noell thought that this was a lucky escape, but Eyre died in the night of his belly-wound, and when they tried to assemble the donkey-train they had to abandon the wounded animals, and parts of the packs which they had carried. Ghendwa, more anxious than they had ever seen him, urged them to make what hurry they could to escape this dangerous place, and Noell was inclined to agree with his judgement. It was a depleted expedition, therefore, which set out the next day, and Noell felt that luck had turned against them. It seemed that the perils which had so far stood back were now descending upon them in full force and fury.

And so it proved; for this was was the beginning of a bad time, when many things went wrong.

SEVEN

Ntikima was badly frightened by the Fulbai raids, not least because Ghendwa – whose infallibility he had not previously doubted – had been impotent to anticipate or deal with them. He could see that had it not been for Langoisse's guns the expedition would have lost everything. He was glad that the gun which Eyre had carried was now given to him, at Noell Cordery's insistence, and that Langoisse consented to give him lessons in the loading and firing of the weapon; though it proved that the lessons in question were indefinitely postponed.

Until they left the scrubland where the Fulbai had attacked them they moved quickly and nervously, but when several days had passed without incident Ntikima began to believe that the worst was past; the Fulbai were not seen again, and it seemed that they were content with what they had captured.

The travellers came now into a curiously varied territory, in which islands of forest interrupted a plain of high grass which was both difficult to traverse and dangerous. The grasses often grew to twice the height of a man, having sprouted lushly during the rainy season, and now that the heads of the stems were dry they were prone to catch fire. The blackened areas where fires had come and gone were easier to cross, though they were foul places thick with ashen dust, but those areas not yet burned were traps which placed the expedition in obvious hazard.

When they were four days into this territory, and had seen no other human for three of those four, they found themselves in the path of a fire blown towards them from the north, and had to run aslant, hoping to escape before it could catch them. There was no hope of stopping to avoid the sun's worst heat, and the further they went, with the smoke billowing behind them and its acrid odour in the air, the more terrified their remaining pack-animals became. They kept going under the stars, as best they could, until they had crossed a wide and shallow stream into greener vegetation, where they were sure that they were safe.

By this time, the expedition had only seven donkeys remaining, virtually no food in stock, and all save the elemi were suffering from a frightful exhaustion. Ntikima had a hacking cough from the smoke which he had inhaled, and his chest hurt. Most of the tents were gone, and the protective netting which the white men used to keep insects away was lost – though there were far fewer insects about now than there had been in the forest. The greater part of their stock of blankets had been taken by the raiders, and the nights were still cold. He was afraid that his cough would get worse, but as things turned out he was rarely required to sleep without cover. Noell Cordery and the white babalawo were content with their clothing while he was ill.

The morning after the fire, Langoisse and Cory were showing signs of sunstroke. They made poor progress that day, and on the following morning, Langoisse developed a fever. Because they had so few pack animals left even the white men were carrying packs, so he could not ride, but an hour's walking left him staggering and nearly helpless. Quintus rigged a stretcher, which Selim and Noell carried until noon. In the afternoon the black men went foraging for earth-peas and roots, and though they found food enough to make a good meal the entire party was in direly low spirits that evening.

On the next day, Cory too had the fever, and though Langoisse was a little better, Leilah was in more than a little distress. Ntikima had by now recovered from his cough, and surrendered his blanket to those in direr need. Quintus was tired and weak, though not ill, and it was obvious to Ntikima that Noell and Selim could not continue indefinitely to bear the burdens which were now falling to their lot. Now, it seemed to Ntikima, Ghendwa must prove the worth of his medicines, else his guidance would not suffice to bring them to Adamawara.

Ghendwa tended Langoisse and Cory with great patience while they waited throughout a long and painful day. He chanted prayers, and gave them medicines from his impoverished pouch, and then went away to sit by himself through the long darkness, squatting on the ground with his heels tucked together, singing softly: '*A-da-ma! A-da-ma!*' This incantation he repeated, as was his habit, for hours on end, apparently having passed into some kind of trance. Ntikima watched curiously, and saw that Msuri was equally curious.

Despite these attentions the sick white men showed no sign of making an early recovery. Rather than deplete their equipment further the white men slowed their progress to a snail's pace, and made only a few miles before pitching another camp. At dusk Ghendwa sent Ntikima to Noell and Quintus with an unprecedented summons, and they were taken to confront the elemi in a formal fashion which he had never permitted before.

'There is no help nearby,' said Ghendwa, speaking the Uruba tongue in a flat tone which sounded remote and strange to Ntikima. 'It is dangerous to linger long, for there may be more fires, and if there are not, there is still the fever. We must travel quickly tomorrow – the men who are sick must walk. I will give them a new medicine, which will make them think they are strong, but there is danger in it. They might walk until they drop, and never get up again. I can do nothing else.'

'How much further must we go,' asked Quintus, 'before we reach our destination?'

The elemi had never yet given a precise answer to the question of how far away Adamawara lay, but now he made a concession of sorts. 'Between twelve days and twenty,' he said. 'Better twelve, but what my kind can do, yours cannot. Msuri is strong, but your companions are weak. It is for you to decide how much you will carry. It is for you to decide what the sick men will do. I will give medicine to all of you, but I warn you that when we reach the lifeless forest, there will be more sickness. The silver death is worse than these fevers, and the way will be difficult.'

'If you are telling us that we might leave our friends,' said Quintus quietly, 'we cannot do it.'

Ntikima looked on as the elemi's dark and ancient eyes stared into the face of the white magician. He could not tell what either man was thinking, but felt that some kind of battle was being fought as they tested one another's gaze.

'I will bring you to Adamawara,' said the elemi, finally, 'as I was told to do.'

'We will measure our supplies most carefully,' promised the monk, 'but Langoisse will not abandon his guns and powder, and I would not have him do so. We will carry all that we can, and we will pray that your medicines will bring us alive to Adamawara.'

'It shall be done,' answered Ghendwa. 'I do not ask you to throw away your weapons, nor the eye which sees into things. I only warn you that the journey will be hard, and that some may die though I do all that I can.'

'Thank you,' said the white babalawo to the elemi, bowing his head slightly. When he and Noell Cordery walked away, Ntikima went with them, and Noell drew him aside to question him.

'I remember that you told us of the lifeless forest and the silver death,' said the white man. 'I wish you would tell me now any more that you know, for what the elemi says has troubled me.'

Ntikima looked up at the tall, bearded white man. 'I know only what I have heard,' he said. 'The land about Adamawara is dark, and no birds sing there. Men are consumed by the silver death, which takes the feeling from their bodies.'

Noell Cordery frowned. 'Like leprosy?' he asked, but Ntikima could only shrug his shoulders.

'Shigidi comes,' Ntikima added, after a moment's pause. 'In the sleep of the silver death, Shigidi comes.'

Ntikima had spoken before about Shigidi, who had power when men slept, and was a bringer of terror. He could not tell whether the white men truly understood him.

'Ntikima,' said Noell, 'Will you tell me why the Ogbone have ordered that we be taken to Adamawara?'

Ntikima made as if to shrug his shoulders, but hesitated. The white men knew now that he was Ogbone, although they had never said so. They had known it for some time, and had not sought to conceal themselves from his curious eyes, or to refuse to answer his questions. He wished that he could give an answer, or the reassurance which was what Noell probably desired. But he could not. 'You will be safe,' he said, though he did not know for sure that it was true. 'Adamawara was made by Shango, with a thunderbolt, but it is the Oni-Olorun who rule there now, and they are gentle. They do no harm. There is no evil in Adamawara, where the heart of Olorun is the food of man, and the breath of life preserves the finished, so that they need not go quickly to Ipo-oku.'

Noell Cordery shook his head. 'It is all riddles, Ntikima,' he told him. 'All words, empty of meaning. Do you hope that one day you will become a babalawo, and join the elemi, so that you too will be finished, and need not go to Ipo-oku?'

Ipo-oku was the land of the dead, to which even the finished went in the end. Ntikima did not want to go there sooner than he must. 'Aroni, when I met him in the forest,' he answered, 'promised that I would learn the secrets of the plants, and wear the white cloth as the babalawos do. One day, I will have the heart of Olorun and receive the breath of life, and I will try to be the wisest of the wise.'

'And will you undergo the greater ikeyika, as Ghendwa has?'

'I will be tigu,' Ntikima told him, and then he went away, to help Ngadze cook food for the evening meal.

After the meal, Ntikima sat by himself, a little way from the fire, and watched to see what the others did. The cold of the night was not yet come, and it was too hot to huddle by the fire, so the white men dispersed. Langoisse and Cory were allotted the remaining tent, and went directly to lie down there. Quintus took Ngadze aside and entered into an intense conversation with him. The Turk Selim sat with his back to the bole of a tree, whittling at a piece of dry wood with a broad-bladed knife. Noell Cordery and the woman sat together, looking westward at the waving grasses and the ragged trees. Ntikima followed the direction of their gaze, and looked for a moment or two into the dust-clad face of the half-set sun, which shone blood red in a purple sky. It was quickly descending into a cleft between two hills on the horizon.

'This is a terrible place,' he heard Leilah say. 'I had not imagined the heart of Africa to be like this. The travellers who told us tales spoke of steaming jungles and wild beasts, not yellow grass and black-burnt trees. Even the insects do not like it here, save for the scorpions.'

'It is an unfortunate season,' Noell agreed. 'But in the wet season we could never have come through the forest, nor crossed the flood-plain of the Gongola. I believe we have faced the least of the possible evils, though they have been bad enough.'

'We have found no treasures,' she said, bitterly, 'such as Langoisse came to seek.'

'We have not reached the fabulous kingdom yet,' said Noell, though the dryness of his voice told Ntikima that he did not honestly expect to find what Langoisse called treasure even in Adamawara. 'He should not have brought you on such a quest as this.'

'I did not come for him, but to follow thee,' she told him, in a whisper. 'He did not bring me. I brought myself.'

'You have the fever,' Noell said, almost as if it were an accusation. 'You will not find it easy, tomorrow or the next day. More of us may die before we reach our destination.'

'But thou wilt live,' she told him, 'for thou art a man as near in strength and cunning to a vampire as ever there could be.'

Ntikima did not understand that, because Noell Cordery did not seem to him to bear any resemblance at all to an elemi. He could imagine that the white babalawo might one day join the ranks of the elders of Adamawara, but not Noell Cordery, who seemed more warrior than priest.

'I am blest with a strong constitution,' said Noell to the woman, 'but my father was stronger, yet died of a plague from the Afric coast.'

'Mayhap thou art the more fortunate man,' she told him.

'Nay,' he answered. 'He was a great man, and could not entirely trust me. I am the lesser, and dare not trust myself.'

Langoisse cried out for water then, and the woman rose to her feet to go to him, but Noell Cordery turned and saw Ntikima sitting there. He bade her be still, and signalled an instruction to Ntikima, who looked around for water to take to the sick man.

There was a kettle boiling on the fire, and some water which had already been taken from it had been put in a gourd to cool, but that was very warm when Ntikima tested it. He took it, nevertheless, to Noell, who drank a little and made a complaining face, but nodded. Ntikima took the gourd into the tent, and gave the pirate some to sip. Langoisse took some, but complained bitterly that it had no relief for him.

'Wait for the night,' murmured Ntikima. 'You will have cold enough, when the darkness comes.'

Langoisse was bathed by an unnatural sweat. His eyes were wide, a rim of white being visible all around each iris, as though the eyeballs were swollen and painful.

'Go away, black boy,' he said, bitterly.

Ntikima shrugged. Langoisse did not like him, nor he Langoisse. He would not be sorry if Langoisse died, though he would rather see the noseless Turk in dire straits, for there was a dislike even more profound between himself and the monster.

'Ghendwa will bring medicine,' said Ntikima. 'Trust in the elemi.'

'Trust in the devil!' retorted Langoisse, in a wild voice. 'Oh aye, the devil owes me favour, for such work as I have done on his behalf! Mark me, black imp, there's an honoured place in hell for the likes of me. The faith says to us that the wages of sin is death, and I feel hell's fires within me now, burning through my guts. But I fear not your like, though you have poor Eyre's gun, and Cory's too. I have sent demons back to hell, as thou canst testify before the throne of God, if I should call thee to my witness, little black one.'

Ntikima, unperturbed, held the gourd to the sick man's lips, so that he could sip again. Then he turned to Cory, who was too sick to rise, and splashed a little on to his lips.

Langoisse tried to shake his head violently then, as though to bring himself wholly to his senses, but the movement hurt him and made him cry out. Ntikima put out a hand to soothe him, but the white man seemed resentful of his touch. Ntikima guessed that Shigidi had come already to Langoisse, and would torment him more than a little even before the silver death could open up a passage to his heart.

'Sleep,' said the boy.

'Get out!' whispered the pirate. 'Send me Selim. He must watch over me, and keep black devils away. Away!'

Ntikima went. He returned to Noell Cordery, and told him that the pirate was very ill. Noell only shook his head, because he already knew it. 'We will go on when we can,' he said. 'We have come so far, and the land we seek is close at hand. The elemi's medicines may help us.'

'Shigidi is coming,' said Ntikima. 'The man Langoisse feels his nearness, though he does not know his name.'

'Delirium and nightmare are the names by which we call your god of terror,' Noell told him. 'And there is not one of us who does not know of his approach. Go to your own rest, Ntikima, and keep Shigidi at bay, if you can.'

Ntikima did as he was told; and Shigidi did not trouble him that night. But there was in the silence of his slumbers an undercurrent of unease which told him that one day soon, Shigidi would come to him, not in any merciful mood, but rejoicing in the fearsome fury of his malevolence.

EIGHT

Noell woke next day in a poor temper, not ill but racked by aches and discomforts, feeling a mere shadow of the man who had set out from Burutu. At dawn they breakfasted, poorly, on millet porridge with cassava and earth-peas. Ghendwa gave Quintus a dark powder which was to be added to the bowls of the sick men. Though the powder was not bitter, and its particular taste was concealed by the food, it was not easy to persuade Langoisse, Cory and Leilah to consume a full measure. They had slept restlessly, and though their awakening had brought them back to sanity they had little appetite.

They were all three very thirsty, however, and Quintus persuaded them to eat by requiring them to take mouthfuls of the porridge between gulps of hot coffee.

When they began the march again, Noell could see little improvement in the three, who seemed dazed and unready, but once they were under way their strides became more purposeful and it was as though they had slipped into a kind of trance.

It was so difficult to make a path through the tall grass that in the hours between dawn and noon they covered little more than ten miles, but they continued into the afternoon until the combination of heat and exhaustion became too much for them. Langoisse, Cory and Leilah fell into a deep sleep as soon as they were allowed to stop, and Noell erected the tent to hide them from the sun's glare.

Ngadze came to Noell to tell him that he planned to go into the grass to forage for food. He asked that Noell should bring a gun, so that they might also hunt for meat, but Noell shook his head, knowing himself to be too poor a shot. He asked Selim to go in his stead, and the Turk readily agreed. Ngadze, Mburrai and Selim went off together, promising to return well before dark.

When sunset came, though, there was no sign of them.

Noell and Ntikima gathered great sheaves of the tall grass to make a big fire, which would serve as a beacon to guide the hunters back, though they should not need any such crude signal. Noell knew that some misfortune must have overtaken them.

Quintus could not wake the sleepers to share the evening meal, and told Noell that he feared for their lives, especially Cory's. Ghendwa, when he was told that the three seemed weaker, simply replied that their chances of survival would be less if they were forced to wait too long in the sea of grass, instead of pressing on.

Two hours after dark, Ngadze and the Turk returned, the latter wounded in the head and raving with the pain. A glancing blow from a spear had torn away the top of his left ear and a long slice of flesh from his skull, adding yet further to his fearsome repertoire of scars. The flintlock which he had taken was gone. Ngadze had managed to gather a few things which were edible, but not enough to save their stores from further depletion.

Ngadze explained that while they were stalking game they had been ambushed by a group of Fulbai youths, who must have been following the expedition for several days, ever since the last attack. Selim had been felled almost immediately, because the attackers' first object had been to seize the gun, and the Ibaus had thus been forced to fight with their own weapons. They had cried out for help, but had wandered too far to be heard in the camp. Mburrai had been struck dead before the marauders made off with the gun, and only one of the attackers had been killed.

'They will not turn back yet,' said Ngadze. 'They will surely try to steal more from us, though they may be too few to attack the camp.'

Quintus bandaged Selim's wounds, while the Turk muttered half-formed curses in his grotesque fashion. Ghendwa made him chew a root which, he said, would help to reduce the pain, but any effect which the medicine had was not readily evident.

'The Fulbai will not follow us beyond the grass,' said the elemi. 'When we reach the hills where the Logone rises, we will be safe from attack, but we must make what haste we can.'

It proved possible now to wake the exhausted sleepers, so that they could take a little food along with Ngadze and Selim, but after they had eaten only Cory went easily to sleep, and that did not seem to Noell to be a fortunate omen. Langoisse and Leilah tossed and turned in the grip of their sickness, sometimes raving with delirium. Noell sat with them both, and tried to calm them. In consequence, he slept little, and when dawn came he felt the need of Ghendwa's powder himself, though he dared not take any. He told himself that he was only tired, and that he must not let fever get a grip on him.

Cory was roused, with difficulty, and persuaded to take some drugged food, but he seemed worse than before. Noell was distressed by the sight of him, because he was so thin and haggard; his tallness only accentuated his leanness. Langoisse and Leilah were not so bad, and had not suffered the same deterioration, but Langoisse had carried from the beginning the disadvantage of his greater age.

By noon, they had covered twelve miles, but Langoisse and Leilah seemed to be nearly as sick as Cory, who could no longer walk without support. Ghendwa wanted to continue, but Quintus insisted that they stop. The monk hoped that Langoisse and Leilah might improve sufficiently overnight to make the next day's prospects better. Ngadze, Ntikima, Quintus and Noell each took a turn to stay awake with a gun across his thigh, fearing that the Fulbai would recognise their weakness and take the chance to attack.

The next morning was very little different. Cory was roused, but Noell could not believe that he could last another twenty-four hours, and though Langoisse and Leilah were not so feverish, the march soon sapped their hoarded strength. As they tramped across the grasslands the harmattan blew heartily and carried the smell of smoke along with its gritty dust, urging them to greater efforts. In the far north, by eleven o'clock, they could see great plumes of smoke from the fire, but it was a long way off, and even the harmattan could not drive it very fast. Nevertheless, it was necessary to keep walking beneath the afternoon sun, with only the briefest of rests at the end of each hour.

During the scorching hours of that afternoon Noell's spirits were as low as they had ever been, for the grassland now seemed endless and inescapable. Thirst and hunger were plaguing him, and he felt that he must soon succumb to the same fever which beset his companions. He longed to throw himself down on the ground and give way to exhaustion, but he watched Ghendwa and Msuri marching ahead of him, the Oni-Osanhin's ancient legs moving like clockwork despite the fact that his muscles seemed mere strings stretched across the bones. Msuri, who likewise old in years, and not even a vampire, matched the elemi's stride without any obvious sign of strain. Noell was much bigger than either of them, and powerfully built, so he told himself furiously that what they could do, he must surely be able to do also. He scolded himself for the frailty of his pallid flesh. This determination was ultimately rewarded, though the fire came closer to them for several tense hours before they effected their escape from its path.

Later, Noell wondered whether the fire had been a blessing rather than a curse, not only because it had forced the donkey-train to keep moving, but also because it may have persuaded the Fulbai to give up their chase and turn back. By the time the sun was setting behind them, the grass was thinning noticeably, and the wooded islets were becoming common again. They had no difficulty in finding a more open patch of bush, where they could make camp, and even while they walked Ngadze and Ntikima found it possible to gather a little food. When they had stopped, Msuri brought down a bird with an arrow, to provide meat for the meal. This made it seem to Noell that the worst must be over.

After dark, Noell and Quintus watched the distant glow of the bush-fire, and saw that the flames were being blown to the west of their route, where it would destroy land which they had already crossed. Ntikima came to join them, and told them that they need not worry now about the supplies of food, for there was a belt of good land before they entered the lifeless forest, where villages could be found, and elemi who would help them. In order to prove his point he drew them to the other side of the camp. In the east, where they were now headed, they could see the distant gleam of other fires.

Ntikima said that these were the fires of the Sahra tribesmen, who were near kin to the Mkumkwe. They would give food to the travellers, and their elemi would renew Ghendwa's stock of medicines. Beyond the land of the Sahra, he promised, was Adamawara itself. The Uruba boy seemed more excited by this prospect than Msuri or Ghendwa, and Noell could not find the energy to reflect the boy's enthusiasm.

Langoisse and Leilah slept more easily that night, and Noell judged that they were getting better, but Cory's sleep was of a different kind. He was beyond the reach of nightmares, but Noell feared that when morning came he might also be beyond the reach of wakefulness. So it proved; Cory died during the night, and though Quintus said a prayer for him they left his body for the scavengers, for they had not time to dig a grave with the crude tools which they had. Langoisse and Leilah were a little better, though Ghendwa insisted that they took more of his medicine in order to keep up with the required pace.

They came to the first of the Sahra villages shortly before noon, and were taken in as guests. It was a small village spread around a well, and each conical hut had a small portion of land marked out by screens of matting. The village granaries were made of straw, shaped like beehives, and erected on wooden stilts to keep them safe from insects. The women of the tribe wore discs inserted in their lips, stretching them considerably, and giving them the appearance, Noell thought, of wide-billed birds. The men tattooed themselves in a fashion not unlike the Mkumkwe warriors. The village was abuzz with countless noxious flies, which went some way to spoiling the quality of its hospitality, but the travellers were so very grateful for the fresh food that the flies seemed a trivial nuisance.

The village had four elemi in residence, a contingent larger than any comparable village which they had visited before. The elemi had a hut beside the headman's, outside which they sat in a row, each and every one of them seeming to Noell to be more ancient than any person he had ever seen. They were more wrinkled than the Oni-Olorun who had come to Benin, their hair almost gone and their eyes seemingly sunk back into their skulls. He could not guess how old they were, but would not have been surprised had someone said that they had lived here for a thousand years. They wore no pouches at their waists, and had only thin thongs instead of loincloths, so that he was able to see that they had been treated as Ghendwa had. Each man's penis was reduced to a ragged stump, as ugly and unnatural as poor Selim's nose. Their scrotal sacs, however, were still intact, so that they were not entirely castrated.

After a very formal meal, in which Langoisse and Leilah were barely able to join, the Sahra gave their visitors araki, a spirit made from millet which was much stronger than ordinary millet beer. Quintus hardly touched it, and Noell drank very moderately, but Langoisse, Ngadze and Ntikima became rather drunk, and Leilah drank enough to render her insensible. These excesses seemed not to please Ghendwa, whose anxiety about the prospect of delivering his charges safely to their destination was still very clearly manifest, and Noell was also anxious lest the bout of drunkenness lead to a relapse into more serious fever.

Noell watched carefully how Ghendwa behaved in this village, and the way he was treated. In the west, his arrogant remoteness had been complete, and even when he met elemi he had expected to be treated with reverence, as a person of importance. Here, his status seemed markedly different. These elemi treated him as an equal. Noell guessed that though the tribesmen they lived with were neither wealthy nor powerful, they had more prestige among their own kind than any others he had seen.

That night they slept within the compound of the Sahra village, posting no guards, and slept better than they had for many days, though Noell felt that he had not entirely shaken off his petty maladies.

The next night, too, they spent in a Sahra village, and by the time they set forth from there Langoisse and Leilah had recovered sufficiently to need no more of Ghendwa's medicine. Though they had both become thin, and Langoisse looked very careworn, they declared that the worst was over. One more donkey had died, leaving them only six, and Selim's wound continued to be troublesome enough to require attentive treatment from the elemi, but their stocks of food had been renewed and Ngadze and Ntikima were in good spirits.

But the Sahra territory was a narrow region of fertile land. They came again to rising slopes which were heavily forested. Ghendwa led them with a confidence which suggested that he had been this way before, but the heat was intense and the insects very troublesome. Noell and Quintus wore their veils continuously, and Quintus forced Langoisse to wear his, even under protest, but no one dared try persuasion on the anguished Turk. The people who suffered most from the bites and stings were the blacks, and Ghendwa was busy that evening applying ointments to their backs and faces.

The trees in this region were like none that Noell had ever seen. There were a few familiar species, including the ubiquitous palms and owalas, and some of the dika trees on which wild mangoes grew, but these were larger than usual, often having twisted trunks, as if some giant had long ago seized them and wrung them between his hands. There were others, black-barked and festooned with creepers, which grew in lonely majesty, shading the ground for many yards around them, and they grew crookedly too, as if their boles were made of gourds haphazardly transfixed on long spears. The undergrowth was sparse, and many of the bushes which commonly grew in the open areas where tree-canopies did not meet overhead seemed sickly and diseased.

Ngadze and Ntikima went foraging for fruit that evening, but when they returned to the camp Ghendwa insisted on sorting through their haul. They had brought back a number of unfamiliar fruits, some of which Ghendwa hurled away, telling the travellers not to touch their like.

Higher up in these hills, they found the course of another river, which Ghendwa called the Logone, but it was virtually dry, with only a stretch of moist and sticky mud in its bed. Beyond the river, the forest became stranger still. Its undergrowth thinned out almost to nothing, and the layered canopies were so high that it was easy to walk on the forest floor; but in spite of the ease of their passage this was not a pleasant place to be. There were very few birds, and they saw no monkeys at all. There were numerous insects, but there were few scented flowers to attract their notice. Indeed, the most colourful things lit by the sunbeams which filtered through the layers of the canopy were ledge-fungi growing in the clefts formed by the twisting of the tree-trunks, which were often orange or yellow, and sometimes white streaked with purple or blue. Such fungi often clustered on the leafless hulks of dead trees, and the further they went into this region the more it seemed to Noell that every familiar species of tree was represented only by twisted and decaying lumps of dead wood.

They crossed a number of small streams which fed the Logone during the rainy season, and a few had water in them, but they were entirely free of what Noell had come to think of as universal inhabitants of African waters – crocodiles and leeches. Nor were there any water birds, and as far as he could tell, no fish either.

They went north-eastwards after crossing the Logone, tramping through the ugly forest for many miles, but discovered no native villages. They camped twice beside the turbid waters of tiny streams, and found the nights eerily silent. Langoisse suffered a relapse into deeper fever, making Noell frightened for his life, but Leilah had gradually shaken off her own sickness.

'Is this the lifeless forest of which you spoke?' asked Noell of Ntikima, when they camped in an open space on a mountain-side. 'It seems an unearthly region, and one which men would not readily visit. An unlikelier place to find the Garden of Eden I could not imagine.'

Ntikima confirmed that this was indeed the great forest which surrounded Adamawara: a bad place, where no one lived. It was not entirely lifeless, for there were insects here as well as trees, and there were great black bats which found some kind of fruit in the treetops. There were chimpanzees, too, and Ntikima reported that among these chimpanzees there were ancient beasts which lived long past their natural time, taking blood from females and children as the elemi did among humans. Noell was not sure whether or not to believe this.

In due course they came to a ridge – a black, rocky cliff perhaps three-quarters of a mile across. Here there would be a waterfall in the wet season, perhaps forty or fifty yards across, though five times broken by jutting teeth of rock, but now the stream was dry there was no water at all trickling down the face. There was a long ledge, which must, when the rains fell, be behind the fall; but it was easy to cross over now. The face of the cliff alongside which they walked was pitted with caves and coverts. It was not so easy for the donkeys, being not wide enough to make them comfortable, and they had to be led across the cracked and muddied bed beneath.

Beyond the cliff was another steep ascent which was more difficult for the animals than the slope which had taken them up to the Bauchi plateau. They had to be unburdened, and even so one slipped and broke a leg, and had to be butchered for meat. Everyone, by this time, had a pack to carry, and everyone had now to carry even more, except Langoisse, who found it difficult even to carry himself. Ghendwa would not let them leave anything edible, implying that the foraging would become more difficult as they went on, and Noell became anxious about their water-supplies.

Their path now wound its way up into rockier terrain. The trees were far fewer here, but the way much more difficult, for they were climbing very steeply into a mountainous region. They were exposed for much longer periods to the glare of the sun, but the air was not so humid, and the more altitude they gained the less oppressive the heat seemed. Their veils became unnecessary, as they came into a region which was as devoid of insects as the lower forest had been empty of birds.

Selim's head would not heal, despite Ghendwa's best efforts. The festering wound must have been extremely painful, for the Turk, who was an unusually stoical man, jabbered continually and angrily in his private language of squeaks and groans. Noell imagined this babbling to be a lonely, acrimonious argument with the vengeful deity which had cruelly afflicted him. Beside the wound a strange stain had begun to spread beneath the Turk's skin, extending down from his neck on to his shoulder and arm. It was as though something were growing in the layer of the flesh below the skin. Quintus had never seen its like before, but the Oni-Osanhin looked at it with great anxiety. To Noell the stain seemed to be coloured black or dark grey, and it did not immediately occur to him to connect it with the silver death of which Ntikima had spoken, but the boy told him that this was what it was.

'Shigidi is coming,' said Ntikima dolefully, by no means for the first time.

Msuri and Ngadze were having problems with much smaller wounds which they had sustained, and which would not heal, growing worse with every hour's passing. The abrasions themselves were trivial, but it was not long before Noell could see the tell-tale signs of something spreading through the flesh. Against their ebon skin the stain seemed much lighter and greyer, and he saw why black men called it the silver death. Though Ghendwa fed medicines to all three of the afflicted men, there was no apparent improvement in their condition, and the elemi seemed not to expect any, though he evaded questions about the likely development of the disease.

When they made camp that night, in the highest place they had yet reached, Noell went in search of wood for the fire, and found a group of corpses nestling in a small cave in a rock face, clustered around the ashes of a long-dead fire. Dried and shrivelled by the sun, the bodies were little more than skin stretched upon bone, but it was easy to see that the remaining skin was not brown or black, but had an ashen hue like the stains on the bodies of his companions. Quintus was quick to point out to Noell the fact that these bodies, though they must have lain here for many years, had never been molested by scavengers. No leopard, jackal or vulture had come to strip the flesh from the bones, nor even leisurely maggots to devour the putrefying remains.

Noell was disturbed by this discovery, though he was sure that by now they must be at the very threshold of Adamawara. It seemed that Langoisse might not be able to cling on to life long enough to reach their destination, and the silver death could easily claim the Turk before another day was through. Noell wondered whether even he could survive until the fateful meeting which still lay, frustratingly, ahead of them, and he searched his flesh by the light of the fire for the signs of the sickness which seemed to him more fearful than any fever. He saw Quintus doing likewise, anxious about every scrape or bruise.

Later, Noell walked away from the fire in company with Quintus, and confessed these fears to the monk, as though seeking absolution from his anxieties. Quintus calmed him, seeming himself to be quite invulnerable to any terror. 'Ghendwa says that one more day might take us to the gateway of Adamawara,' said the man of God. 'At the most, it will be two. We have come so far, and endured so much, that the Lord will surely deliver us now. Even Langoisse, who is a great sinner and a sick man, has so far been preserved from the silver death. Trust in providence, Noell, for I believe that the angels still watch over us.'

Noell touched the older man on the shoulder by way of thanks. They sat down together on a great boulder, and looked up at the star-filled sky above them. The air was very clear here, far beyond the reach of the harmattan's incisions dust, and Noell thought that he had never in all his life seen the stars so bright and sharp.

'Their cold light makes our warmth seem feeble,' said Noell. 'Sometimes, the stars make me feel terribly tiny, as though I were beneath a microscope, lost in an infinite wilderness.'

'It is your unbelief which makes you tiny,' Quintus told him. 'Without faith, all men are lost.'

'No doubt,' answered Noell, 'but I wonder whether you have cause and effect the right way around. I think it is the consciousness of being so tiny – and so lost – which forbids me to believe. And yet . . .'

He paused, and Quintus said: 'Go on.'

'Sometimes . . . if I stare at the sky for long enough . . . the sensation changes. I begin to feel huge instead of tiny, as though the stars were within me as well as without . . . as though something of me is in them and something of them in me. And then I feel *stretched*, as though my body were the cosmos, and every moment an eternity, and I do not know the difference between everything and nothing.'

Quintus opened his mouth to reply, but then turned, having heard the noise of someone approaching. Noell grew tense for a moment, but then relaxed when he saw that it was Leilah and Ntikima, come to find them.

'Is something wrong?' asked the gypsy.

'No,' said Quintus. 'We are only measuring the size of the universe, and the greatness of the human soul.'

'The stars are the grain from the mill which Olorun grinds,' said Ntikima, 'while he walks around the world with the sun in his heart.'

'I do not think so,' Leilah told him, taking him by the shoulder in a curiously maternal fashion. 'Langoisse has told me that it is the earth which turns, and stars which are still. Is it so, Father Quintus?'

'It is the round earth which spins,' Quintus confirmed, 'and the cycle of the seasons marks its progress around the sun. The fixed stars may turn around some other centre, a very great way from here, but we cannot see the central sun of Creation with our limited vision, any more than we can see the hand of God at work in its mechanism.'

Ntikima did not seem to believe it.

The gypsy sat beside Noell. 'And the stars are very far away – more miles than you or I could ever count, if we began now and continued until we died. Are they not as far as that, Father?'

'The planets are millions of miles away,' answered Quintus, 'and the stars so far beyond them that I doubt we shall ever measure their remoteness. They are suns with worlds of their own, where there are seas and forests, men and beasts. On some other earth, invisible in the firmament, other travellers are coming near to their own Adamawara, in search of the breath of life and the light of wisdom.'

Ntikima looked up, then, as if suddenly seized by the wonder of the notion, and Noell wished that there was light enough to see the expression on his dark face.

'Are there then a million worlds,' asked the boy, 'where Shango casts his thunderbolts? Is the heart of Olorun to be found in every world, to make the best of men strong and wise, and chain Shigidi in the darker corners of sleep, calming his anger?'

'A million worlds and more,' Quintus told him. 'And the heart of God within every one of them, nourishing the souls of men, and guiding to the kingdom of heaven those who have the will to go.'

NINE

Ntikima and Ngadze had to huddle together within a single blanket that night. They sat close to their meagre fire, because the darkness was bitterly cold. Noell Cordery, Quintus and Leilah had all crammed themselves into the single tent with the stricken Langoisse, leaving Msuri to borrow what warmth he could from Ghendwa, and Selim to lie alone, with a blanket which no one cared to share. No one but Langoisse could bear to be close to Selim at the best of times, and now he was made madly restless by his unhealing wound he was set even further apart from his fellows.

'I do not like this strange land of Adamawara,' said Ngadze to Ntikima. 'Its lifelessness is frightening. I had thought that the world was everywhere alive, but these ugly trees have poisoned the land, and I would be glad to see a scorpion or a snake.'

Ntikima was himself oddly disturbed by the unnatural forest. The forest where he had lived his early life, and where he had met Aroni, was very different – not without its dangers, but in essence hospitable. The gods one might meet in a region such as this were more sinister even than Aroni, who was himself a destroyer of those he did not favour. This was surely, as he had been told, the true home of Egungun; this was the domain of the risen dead, and he had no doubt that he would soon be face to face with one who spoke for his ancestors, who would judge him on their behalf, as he had been judged before in the Uruba villages where he had spent his childhood.

Ntikima had warned his companions that Shigidi would come to them now, first in the delirium of their fevers, then in the deeper and darker sleep of the silver death. Ghendwa had warned him of this. He could not help but ask himself whether Shigidi might have a greater power here than in the lands from which they had come. Did Elegba live here too? he wondered. Elegba, a god of wild maleness and angry lust, had surely been banished from Adamawara, where the tigu had nothing of him, but perhaps that was all the more reason for him to prowl these desolate spaces which surrounded the space which Shango had made for the breathers of life.

Ntikima would have asked these questions of Ghendwa, but the elemi had become anxious and uncommunicative. Perhaps too many had died, and he was anxious lest he fail in his mission to bring the white babalawo to Iletigu, the place of the finished. Perhaps even an elemi could be weakened by such a journey as they had taken – Ntikima could not tell.

Ntikima was frightened of the silver death, which had already made its mark on Msuri and Ngadze. He had no doubt that it would come in its own time to claim him too, for he had been promised a meeting with Shigidi which would test his courage, but he had no real understanding of the summons which had brought him here with the white men. Ghendwa had said nothing to *explain* what was being done, and Ntikima had begun to wonder whether the Oni-Osanhin himself had been told. Perhaps only Ekeji Orisha, who was next to the gods themselves, knew what was wanted of the white healer and his friend; perhaps only the gods knew, and Obatala, the lord of the white cloth, would descend to earth himself to confer with the disciple who called him by another name. That would be an opportunity for eavesdroppers! Having met Aroni, Ntikima was enthusiastic to see more of his gods walking on the earth – and where else but Adamawara would Obatala set his foot upon the soil, or Shango Jakuta come to see what his stone from heaven had wrought?

Something moved out in the night, and Ntikima shuddered suddenly, made nervous by his runaway thoughts. But it was only the man without a face, tossing and turning in his sleep. Ntikima could hear him murmuring impassionedly. He knew that Selim could not pronounce real words, even in his own mysterious language, because his tongue had been cut, yet the babble which he made to voice his suffering sounded so full of meaning, like the talk of some soft and spirited drum, or the chatter of a messenger bird.

In time, Ntikima slipped into a shallow sleep, despite the coldness in his feet and in his haunches. He waited for Shigidi, but Shigidi did not come, and time passed, in its dissembling fashion.

He knew not what hour it was when he was abruptly shocked awake by the sound of a terrible scream, and sat bolt upright in the pitch darkness. Ngadze came suddenly awake too, and leapt to his feet, carrying the blanket with him, and exposing Ntikima's flesh to the cold strike of the night air.

At first, the character of the scream suggested that the voice was Leilah's, for it was a thin and panicked thing, and not a masculine roar. Then he realised that the cry had come not from the tent, but from the place where Msuri and Ghendwa had been sleeping.

For one dreadful instant, he thought that it was the elemi who had screamed, and the idea that there was anything in the world which could wring such a cry from a breather of life was a terror such as he had never before imagined. He scrambled blindly to his feet.

He could hear the man Langoisse groaning with the fever, and cursing foully; even he had been awakened. Then he caught a glimpse of Noell

Cordery's silhouette as he hurried to leave the tent, and the pale gleam of the white babalawo's habit.

Above, the stars still shone brightly in a cloudless sky, but there was no moon, and only the merest hint of pre-dawn light near the eastern horizon. There were tall trees to either side of the campsite, which cast long starshadows, and the fire had burned down to mere embers, giving no light even though Ngadze was now trying to stir up the ashes and light a torch which had been placed there, ready for an emergency. Ntikima looked about him wildly, the cry still echoing in his mind.

The silence was split again by a second cry, and now he had to whirl about to face its source. Something hurtled at him out of the darkness, and he crouched, suddenly angry that he had no weapon at all with which to meet the charge. But then he threw himself sideways, and whatever monster it was blundered past in the dark, bowling Ngadze over and scattering the remains of the fire as it went. It bounded down the slope and into the trees, gone as quickly as it had come.

At that moment, the rim of the sun breached the horizon, and sent a sliver of light flashing across the forest canopy.

Noell Cordery took Ntikima by the arm and tried to draw him upright, but Ntikima shook off the helping hand, scrambled to his feet without aid and ran to where Ghendwa and Msuri had huddled together against the cold, near to the place where the four remaining donkeys were tethered.

Ghendwa was still there, but in the gathering light Ntikima saw that blood was leaking, with unnatural slowness, from a great wound in his chest. There were slashes about his arms and head. His eyes were wide and staring, the whites catching the glimmer of the nascent sunlight.

Beside Ghendwa, with his arms enfolded around the elemi's waist in a futile gesture of protection, was Msuri, bleeding much more copiously from wounds to the head which had surely battered all the life out of him. Msuri tried to look up, but could not; he must have died in the space of that very moment.

There was a third howl, not so much a scream of anguish this time as a cry of pure animal wildness with as much exultation as fear in it. Ntikima looked up in time to see a fan-like array of sunbeams, separated by the dark boughs, touch the bounding figure of the Turk Selim as he ran downhill through a clearing which interrupted the twisted trees. His sword was waving giddily in the air, yet somehow it stubbornly refused to catch and reflect the light. The capering figure was in view for one brief second, and was gone. Noell Cordery took three strides in that direction, then stopped, and looked back at Ntikima, who could see that he understood well enough what had happened.

Noell came to Ntikima's side. He looked down at the elemi and Msuri, at their hacked-about heads. He knelt to touch Ghendwa's throat, which was torn almost completely across, though it was Msuri's blood which was running over the black rock and mossy earth in a great spreading lake.

Quintus had followed Noell from the tent, and the monk came quickly to kneel beside the vampire, pushing Ntikima aside. Ntikima gladly surrendered all initiative and authority to the white babalawo.

'We should not have left him alone,' whispered Noell, as Ntikima reached out to take hold of his sleeve. 'Poor mad thing! We should have done what we could to care for him. Langoisse would not have let us abandon him to rave alone, if he had been well.'

'He has done a terrible thing,' said Ntikima bitterly.

'Nay,' said Noell, in a sorry tone. 'I have done it. The fault is mine, that I could not stand to be near him.'

Quintus turned to look up at him.

'Will he die?' asked Noell.

'Msuri is dead,' replied the monk. 'But Ghendwa is a vampire. He cannot die of such wounds as these.'

Ntikima looked down at the stricken elemi, whose eyes were wide open, though they seemed not to see. Despite the gaping flesh, Ghendwa had lost very little blood by comparison with poor Msuri. He watched Quintus place his hands gently to either side of one of the gashes in Ghendwa's flesh, and ease the edges of the cut together. The babalawo had to hold the wound for a few moments, but the flesh did knit.

The great wound in the chest was not so easily persuaded to close, and the monk worked at it with his fingers, pressing and coaxing with what seemed like practised efficiency, though Ntikima could not imagine that Quintus had ever tended a stricken elemi before. But Ntikima was not unduly surprised. Whatever god or magician had taught the white babalawo his craft must have entrusted him with such secrets as this, in readiness for the day when they would be required.

Ngadze was weeping, and shivering with distress, but Ntikima could not tell whether it was sympathy for the elemi that made him cry, or fear of what reprisals might be taken against those who were party to the maiming of an elder of Adamawara on the very threshold of that sacred place.

When he had done what he could to help Ghendwa's cuts, Quintus reached up to draw down the vampire's eyelids, covering the staring eyes.

'Is he entranced?' asked Noell.

'I think so,' Quintus replied. 'The stab-wound in his chest may have pierced a lung, or even touched his heart. I cannot tell how long it might take to mend, but I am certain that he will sleep for a long time. Perhaps months.'

Noell looked around, and Ntikima followed the roaming of his gaze. The place where they were seemed as still and darkly safe as it ever had, with no birds calling or flying insects humming. For Ntikima, though, and perhaps also for Noell, it had taken on the quality of a limitless tomb. It was as though they were outside the world, on the way to Ipo-oku, where their spirits would now be sure of a stern reception.

Shigidi is coming, Ntikima said to himself, silently; but even as he said it he realised that Shigidi had already come, and had claimed the monstrous Turk for his own, setting free all the foul hatred which had long been seething in his soul.

Leilah stood outside the tent now, looking back and forth between the place where Quintus knelt and the place where the mad Turk had vanished. Ntikima watched her for a little while, to measure her reaction, but then turned to look at the donkeys, which were oddly calm in spite of the manner of their awakening. Perhaps they had been so long in the service of men that there was nothing in the quality of a merely human scream which could alarm them.

Noell went to Leilah, to explain what had happened. 'It was Selim who screamed,' he told her. 'He murdered Msuri and attacked the vampire. The festering of his wound has taken away his senses.'

'Will the vampire die?' she asked. It was odd, thought, Ntikima, that the question always sprang so readily to mind, though everyone knew that to kill an elemi was difficult in the extreme.

'He will live,' said Noell. 'But a vampire sore wounded must slip into a deep kind of sleep while his body is repaired.'

Her face was almost devoid of expression. 'Why?' she asked.

'My father's friend William Harvey,' said Noell, unnaturally calm in this moment of crisis, 'mapped the circulation of the blood in its vessels. He said that if the blood became still, the mind must lapse into unconsciousness. He proposed that vampires can tolerate the stilling of the blood, and even induce it, while their active flesh heals itself.' After a pause, he added: 'Ghendwa will live, and unlike the Turk, will show no scars to tell the story of his ordeal. But I do not know whether it will need days or months to make him whole again. In the meantime, we have no guide. Nor do we know how to use his medicines, which have been helping to keep us alive.'

'We are lost in this dire place,' she said, seizing upon the worst of it, 'and might wander here until we die. And if we are found, how will they punish us, when we have allowed a vampire to be attacked in Adamawara itself?'

They turned, together, to look at Ntikima, who realised that the eyes of the white babalawo were also on him. They did not look at Ngadze, but at him, because he was Ogbone.

'I do not know,' he said to them. He made as if to shrug his shoulders, but the gesture suddenly seemed inadequate. Instead, he said: 'I cannot tell which way Adamawara lies. But we must take Ghendwa there, if we can, so that he may rest in Iletigu.'

He could not entirely understand why the Turk, moved by Shigidi or no, should turn against Ghendwa in this fashion. The white babalawo had told him once that the elemi of Gaul were cruel and harsh, and would kill those who offended them, but he had thought of that as he thought of Oro, as the working of a law, not as something which might inspire hatred and lust for revenge. He had not entirely trusted the tale, either, even though the arokin told their own stories of the desert lands where the men were demon-led sorcerers who would butcher and burn elemi, and spurned their healing gifts. He had seen that the white men feared and mistrusted Ghendwa, even when he gave them medicine, but he had not imagined that anything like this could happen. His thoughts were swirling in confusion.

The white babalawo stood up, and said to Ntikima: 'Perhaps you are right. We certainly cannot go back, so we must go on to Adamawara. But how will they receive us there, when we bring Ghendwa to them in this fashion? Will they not be angry?'

'I do not know,' Ntikima replied. 'Perhaps they will. Perhaps they will punish us all.'

'What shall we do?' asked Leilah, anxiously.

'There is nothing we can do,' Noell Cordery told her. 'There is nowhere we can go but Adamawara. We are here, and the elemi is hurt, and we must take whatever consequences come. How could we hide?'

'We must go forward,' said Ntikima. 'We know the direction from which we have come. We must go on, up into the mountains. We know that Adamawara is near.'

'He is right,' said Quintus. 'We must eat, and then we must go on. We must carry the elemi – and Langoisse too, if he is too ill to walk.'

Ngadze was ready enough to obey instructions now, and to begin preparing food. Ntikima helped him, preoccupied with the questions which Quintus had asked. How would they be received in Adamawara now? What would the Ogbone expect of their servant Ntikima? Would they punish the white men? Would they punish *him*? These questions had to be put aside. Msuri was dead, the Turk was gone, and Ghendwa was now a burden to be carried, not a carrier. There was no more food to be found in the forest, so they had to carry all that they had, and their pots and water-bottles too. They dared not leave the tent or the blankets, with the nights so cold. The white men would not leave their guns and powder either, nor what remained of their tools and instruments for making fire. They had precious little left, and it was very difficult to name anything which they could leave behind to lighten their load.

'Ngadze and I can carry the vampire,' said Noell to Ntikima, when they made their plans, 'and we must all carry packs besides. We must load the donkeys as heavily as we can, and hope that they can answer our need. Do you agree?'

Ntikima looked at the white man gravely, unused to consultation. He was surprised that he had been so easily conceded this authority. Yet he did not feel strange in accepting the responsibility. After all, he was Ogbone.

'I agree,' said Ntikima. 'I will carry as much as I can bear. I think we have not far to go'

'We must surely be very near to our goal,' answered Noell, 'unless this dreadful land in boundless.'

'The gods will guide us,' Ntikima told him, 'if we cannot guide ourselves. They know that we are here, and are waiting for us to come to them.'

Noell Cordery managed a wan smile, and said: 'I hope their appetites are blunt, and they have had their fill this season of the sacrifice of blood.'

'In Adamawara,' Ntikima assured him, 'the gods, and those who share the heart of Olorun, have all the blood they need.'

TEN

When they began the march, Noell took the lead, despite the fact that he was helping to bear Ghendwa's makeshift stretcher, with Ngadze behind him. The way was not easy; they trod such uneven ground that they seemed always to be going uphill or down, and had often to skirt great outcrops of rock. Noell was careful to keep the morning sun always before him, steering directly into its garish light.

Every time they came to the crest of a ridge Noell hoped that some evidence of civilisation would come into view: a rocky fortress or a planted field, or a trail where the imprint of human feet could be seen. But there was no such sign, and he saw nothing moving in the forest save for a flattened beetle with a polished carapace which stirred beneath his boot, and a few other crawling things of indeterminate character. Once, they heard a distant cry as of a predatory beast, but when they looked at one another, Noell could see that they all knew what it must be. Selim still lived, lost in the hell of his own delirium.

Quintus took Ngadze's place after an hour, and then Ntikima took a short spell before the Ibau man resumed the burden. Noell would not let anyone take his own place, though his arms ached terribly and the makeshift straps securing his pack chafed the skin of his back even

through his shirt, scraping his shoulder-blades every time he looked up
to measure their course. The sweat that he shed made him thirsty,
though their supplies of boiled water were low and they had not found
a spring or stream for a long time. He knew that it was now the
middle of the dry season, and remembered almost with a shock that the
beginning of the new year could only be a day or two away, though
Quintus, who was surely keeping track of the calendar, had not
reminded them of it.

At noon they stopped, shadowed by a tall, broad column of black
rock, which hid the afternoon sun. They ate ground-nuts, and pasty
balls of millet-flour, all dry because they had very little water, and what
they had they used to make coffee.

Ghendwa remained quite still, breathing very shallowly. Quintus
could detect only a very weak and slow heartbeat, but pronounced
himself satisfied that the vampire was well and might soon recover. He
was not so satisfied with Langoisse, who was now without the aid of
Ghendwa's medicine, and seemed both desiccated and exhausted. When
the sun was low, in a sky barely tinted at its distant edge by the haze
of the harmattan, the monk told Noell that they could not possibly
continue for more than one day, and that might easily kill the pirate.
Thirst would then rob them all of their last reserves of strength. Leilah
tried to ease Noell's aching muscles with the pressure of her hands, but
his skin was raw in too many places, and he had to ask her to desist.

Before the sun set, Noell found a way to climb the jutting crag, and
drove himself to make the ascent, hoping that the last red rays of sunset
would light for him some builded wall or tower, to show him that the
journey was near enough done. But when he stood atop the bare mount,
and looked about him, he could see nothing but the grim canopy of
dark green, rippling like a turbid ocean about its grey islands of rock
and scree, roiled by the slow, cooling wind. It seemed infinitely more
empty and soulless than any other country he had ever looked upon.

There is no city of the vampires, he told himself, sourly. *Ghendwa
brought us here only to abandon us to desolation. Had he not been hurt, he
would have vanished by now, to go down and not up, back to the welcoming
waters of the Logone and its streams.* He did not believe it.

He wondered whether this wilderness could possibly be worse than
the desert across which Moses had led the Children of Israel, and
whether it was on a mountain such as this that the prophet was given
the Ten Commandments. But when he looked up into the darkening
sky he could find no sign of the merciful presence of God.

Can this be Eden? he asked. *Where are those trees pleasant to the sight
which God planted there? Where are the fruits good to eat? Where is the fabled
tree of life? Where is the tree of the knowledge of good and evil, of which Eve
was tempted recklessly to eat? Where is the breath of life, which God put into
Adam's clay, that he might be an emperor over all the birds and the beasts*

which God had made? Are these God's trees, or are they Satan's, rooted in Hell itself, whose shrivelled fruits bear the bitter knowledge of failure and damnation? If Adamawara ever was the Eden to which our scriptures refer, then God has surely abandoned it; and even the serpent which betrayed mankind no longer keeps its vigil in this wilderness.

He reached up to brush a lock of hair from his eye, and caught sight of his sore hands. On his right palm there was a burst and bloodied blister, and around it in his pale flesh was a dark halo.

A thrill of horror went through him when he saw it, and he was suddenly very conscious of all the aches of his body. Quickly, he opened his shirt and looked down at his breast. There was no sign of the blackness there, but on his right shoulder, where the strap of his pack had chafed, there was a thin black rivulet, like a black snake creeping patiently towards his throat.

In that moment of despair, these marks were to him a symbol of impending death. He did not curse God, or ill fortune, or the curiosity which had brought him to this pass; he was too lonely for curses. Nor did he pray for deliverance, for his desolation was not sufficient to light the flame of faith in his unbeliever's soul. He went down again, because the bottom of the sun's disc was already beneath the jagged horizon, and he did not want to make the descent in darkness.

When he reached the base of the rock-face, he found Quintus pulling his white robe from his shoulder, and he saw that the monk's back had two black stains spreading from the shoulder. He went to his friend, and traced the imprints of the silver death with his forefinger, so that Quintus could feel their extent across his shoulder-blades.

'I have spoken to Ntikima,' said the monk. 'He says that the sickness is called silver, though its stains are not silvery in hue, and despite that it is called by the name of death, it rarely kills. He warns me, though, that Shigidi will come to me when I sleep.'

'Thou art armed against nightmares,' Noell told him. 'Better armed than I, no doubt.'

His next thought was that he must look for the gypsy, and discover whether her body too was prey to this monstrous pollution, but as he turned away his eye was caught by a strange light in the darkening forest. He stared at the spot, and again the glimmer came into view for a moment, between the distant boles, like a will-o'-the-wisp. Then another flame flickered, and a third, and he realised that men with torches were coming through the trees towards the black rock.

Men, or monsters.

Quintus had seen the torches too, and he quickly gathered his habit about him, as though fearful of the shame of being seen bare-shouldered, with the devil's stigmata about his body. The monk took a step forward, as though to go to meet these visitors, but he stopped when he too realised that they had not the appearance of men.

The figures which bore the torches were very tall, dressed in long grass robes, with giant faces which were hideous caricatures of human features. They had great red-painted mouths jagged with sharpened teeth, and vast staring eyes with huge pupils, black as pitch.

Noell looked swiftly around.

Leilah was not to be seen, and must be in the tent with the stricken Langoisse. Ngadze and Ntikima had been busy with the fire, but now they knew something was amiss, and they stood up, each to his full height, waiting to see what would happen.

It was Ntikima who came to Noell's side, and said: 'Egungun!'

Noell had never seen Egungun, though Ntikima had told him what it was. Like Oro, Egungun had his appointed days, when he would come to a village and dance through the streets, supposedly having returned from Ipo-oku, the land of the dead, to interrogate the living on behalf of their ancestors. To touch him was death, and to be accused by him was a terrible denunciation, marking those who must be punished for giving offence to the parents of their tribe. But in the Uruba villages Egungun always came alone. Here there was a whole troop of Egungun, nine in number: a veritable regiment of the living dead, come to discover them.

They are only men in costumes, Noell instructed himself, but he knew that there was more than a comedy of masks to this affair. When Ntikima had met the god Aroni in the forest, he had met him in the person of a priest or magician wearing regalia such as this, but in the eyes of the Uruba boy, the magician had not been in any way pretending to be the god; he was the god. These approaching figures were not pretending to be the risen dead; they *were* the risen dead. In the Uruba way of thought, they did not have to be one thing or the other; they could be both. They were costumed men – Mkumkwe warriors or elemi – but they were also the risen dead, come to settle their accounts with the living.

The torch-bearers came closer, until they had come right to the edge of the camp, where they gathered to stand in a semicircle, peering at the invaders. They stood silently, and Noell wondered whether any language he knew would be adequate to offer a greeting to the strange figures who faced him. Leilah came from the tent, knowing that something was happening, and hurried to his side. Though she clung to him in fear, she did not cry out, and he was proud of her fortitude.

'They will not hurt us,' he whispered to her. 'They mean us no harm.' But he turned to Ntikima, and said: 'Tell me what to do, I beg of you. You must be our guide, now, for we have neither the elemi nor Msuri to act on our behalf.'

Ntikima reached out, and took Noell by the wrist. 'The woman must stay back,' murmured the boy. 'This is not woman's business.'

Leilah understood. She released her hold upon Noell, and let Ntikima take him forward, towards the company of the living dead. The boy looked round and beckoned urgently to Quintus, so that the monk fell into step with them. The three together, with Ntikima in the middle, went into the focal point of the semicircle which the Egungun had formed.

Ntikima raised his arms, and greeted the vampires in the Uruba tongue, bidding them welcome and asking, in ritual fashion, what they had come to say.

When one of them made reply, he did so in words which Noell did not know, though he presumed they must be Uruba. It was impossible to judge to which of them this spokesman addressed himself, but Noell could only wait in silence.

Ntikima spoke again, bowing his head and gesticulating. Noell heard him use the word 'Ogbone' several times, and 'elemi', and 'Oni-olorun', and some others that he knew, but he was unable to follow the precise details of the explanation which the boy was giving for their presence. When Ntikima pointed to the place where Ghendwa lay, the Egungun were perturbed. Only six were carrying torches; three of these were also carrying short spears; the three who had no torches carried ceremonial drums. Some also carried feathered wands of a kind which Noell had seen in temples, which he knew to be associated with Elegba and Olori-merin, and hence with the most powerful kinds of necromantic magic. When Ntikima pointed to Ghendwa, spears and wands alike were raised as if in threat or accusation, and Noell did not know which of them he should fear the more.

One of the Egungun separated himself from the group, and went to Ghendwa, to bend over him and see what his condition was. When he stood again, and turned his awful painted face towards the torchlight, he cried out in anger, and levelled the wand which he carried, seemingly aiming at Ntikima's heart.

Ntikima screamed some kind of denial, but recoiled from the staff as if he had been struck.

Noell had no doubt at all that the boy was in mortal danger, no matter how harmless the gesture seemed, for these were the risen dead, come to face the living with the burden of their guilt. Whatever the real properties of that wand – however feeble it might be as a mere physical object – it could destroy Ntikima more surely and more absolutely than any spear or cannon.

Almost without thinking, Noell stepped in front of Ntikima, to shield him. He thrust the boy behind him, and took a single pace forward, towards the accusing wand.

'The boy did nothing,' he said, in Uruba. 'He is not to blame. He has served the elemi and the Ogbone as loyally as he could.'

'*Be careful!*' hissed Quintus.

Noell did not need the warning. He knew well enough that the tribesmen did not recognise Gaulish ideas of blame and responsibility. When things went wrong, they looked for scapegoats, who would bear the burden of guilt for their tribe, even though they might by reasonable reckoning be innocent of any wrong action or idea.

'It was one of us who struck the elemi,' said Noell, speaking very slowly because his command of Uruba was not adequate to let him speak fluently. 'It was one made mad by the silver death. Shigidi came to him!' He struck the side of his head with the heel of his hand, to emphasise his words with a sign.

'Shigidi!' replied the Egungun, and took a step toward Noell, still holding the wand parallel to the ground, pointing it now at Noell's racing heart.

When Noell said nothing else, the lone Egungun took another step, and now it was Ntikima who whispered, urgently, in English: 'If it touches you, you will die.'

'We have come to Adamawara,' said Noell, in Uruba, 'because we are summoned by Ekeji Orisha. We are not to be destroyed. We are not to be accused. You must take us . . . every one . . . to Iletigu. Olorun commands it.'

The Egungun took another step, still pointing his staff of death.

'Olorun commands it,' repeated Noell.

He did not dare to turn his eyes away from the grotesquely-exaggerated stare of the huge mask. Absurdly, he began to feel, in his chest, the pressure of the wand upon his beating heart, as though his life had been caught in a deathly trap, which would squeeze him until the blood burst from his body and his soul shrivelled like a moth in a candle-flame.

He knew that what he faced was a man in a mask, and that the thing which pointed at his heart was not a weapon, but only a symbol which had no meaning in the context of his own beliefs. Even so, he felt that if the wand touched him then he would surely die, as Ntikima said. One way or another, the Egungun would ensure it.

All of a sudden, as he faced the wand, Noell found himself uncomfortably aware of a fever brewing in his body. Neither the place on his hand nor the place on his shoulder, where the black blight had begun to grow, was painful – indeed, both places seemed numb – but he was nevertheless nauseous and dizzy. The effort of this strange conflict threatened to leave him without resource, and he knew without a shadow of a doubt that if the wand touched him, he would fall.

Though he could not see Quintus, he could see the others of his party, behind and to either side of the solitary Egungun. Leilah was rigid with the tension, unable to understand what was happening, but terrified by the knowledge that something vital to their survival was taking place. Ngadze was equally afraid, the whites of his staring eyes catching the torchlight. The Ibau had as much reason to fear Egungun as any Uruba, for Egungun was one of the devices by which the Ogbone exerted their hegemony over their subject tribes.

And then, with a slight cold shock, Noell saw Langoisse.

The pirate had come to the maw of the tent in which he had been placed, sick and very tired, to sleep away the worst effects of the morning's exertions. He had slept, to be sure, but he did not now seem in any way refreshed. His face was gaunt, his dark hair and ill-cut beard in dusty tangles, his eyes by some trick of the torchlight shining as if enflamed by the fever burning in his flesh. He was kneeling, and on his left thigh he was resting an elbow which supported the musket along whose barrel he was carefully sighting.

To Noell, there seemed curiously little difference between the chimerical masked man, levelling his wand of doom in which was concentrated the wrath of all his dark and heathen gods, and the maddened pirate, stranger in this vile and mortified land, aiming his lead-spitting firearm.

'Langoisse!' he shouted. 'For the love of heaven, no!'

Perhaps the love of heaven was the wrong appeal to make. Perhaps he should not have exclaimed at all in a language which the magician inside the death-mask could not understand.

The Egungun cried out, wordlessly, and thrust himself forward, stabbing with the wand, striking at Noell's breast.

Langoisse fired.

The Egungun was suddenly snatched aside. The path of the bullet was angled some thirty degrees to the line of the masked man's thrust. The wand missed Noell's breast by a matter of inches, and struck no one as the Egungun fell to the ground upon it.

There was no sound at all from the eight figures who still stood in their semicircle. They stood and watched, paralysed by surprise.

The stricken figure lay still for a moment, and then moved, jerkily, thrusting upwards and coming apart. The great false face cracked and splintered, rent asunder by the urgent movements of the head which had been inside it. Noell realised, as the tattooed face of a Mkumkwe priest was raised from the wreckage, that Langoisse's shot had smashed the mask but had missed the skull of the man who wore it. He was shocked and frightened, but otherwise unhurt. He rose to his feet – a living man, born out of the carcase of the risen dead, in remarkable inversion of the natural and supernatural orders of things.

'We are summoned by Olorun,' said Noell, now looking into the real eyes of a living man. 'We are not to be harmed.'

The magician did not attempt to pick up the wand. He was not Egungun now. He met Noell's gaze for the briefest of moments, then looked beyond him, at the arc of risen dead men, whose task it still was to accuse or to denounce, to judge on behalf of all the generations of ancestors whose lives had traced the lineage of the black tribes from their own dark Adam.

Those who had wands did not raise their instruments of judgement. Those who had spears made no motion with their weapons. There was to be no execution, now. One spoke, in rapid Uruba which Noell could not follow, save that the name of Shango, god of storms, was spoken.

'Shango protects you,' whispered Ntikima, by his side. 'You have brought us safe to Adamawara.'

'They would have killed us,' whispered Noell. 'Ghendwa brought us across half a continent, and yet they would have killed us all.'

'Oh no,' said Ntikima. 'They would not have hurt the babalawo. One life, or perhaps a handful, is all they would have required. They would not have hurt you, except that you put yourself in my place. It is a man's right to choose, to offer himself in such a fashion, though I do not know how you knew it. I owe you debt of life now, Noell Cordery, and the time will come when I shall pay.'

Noell felt his legs go suddenly weak, and Quintus had to take his arm to prop him up. 'It should have been me,' said the monk, in a low tone, as intense as any which Noell had ever heard him use.

'Nay,' said Noell, weakly, as he put his blackened palm to his head, wondering why the dizziness was now increasing, though the danger was entirely past. 'Yours is the mind and mine the strength . . . .mine the strength . . . '

He knew even as he said it that the strength had at last run out.

The last image which his eyes took in was the face of his mentor, the man of God, who tried his best to hold him up, though the burden was too heavy for the old man's weakened arms. The bright eyes seemed to be staring at him, beckoning him, like pools of godless darkness.

As he lost his hold on consciousness, he felt quite apart from the aches and pains of his body, as though his soul was floating free; and for the first time in his life he felt that the idea of that providence in which Quintus had asked him to trust was not entirely absurd.

PART FOUR

The Season of Blood

'The empire of fear hath the greatest of all despots set at its head, whose name is Death, and his consort is named Pain; this emperor sends warlords against the hosts of mankind, whose names are War, and Plague, and Famine; and bids them worship the eidola which hide from them true knowledge of the divine and mundane worlds.

'Common men are deluded if they believe that the vampires are their enemies; for the true enemies of mankind belong to that greater empire, which is the empire of fear and ignorance, and not to the petty empires of Attila and his kin, which must one day fall after the fashion of their kind.

'It will not save mankind from grief to fell the petty empire while the greater still remains, and I beg you to remember that it is those other eidola which must in the end be broken, if right is truly to be done.'

(Francis Bacon, in a letter to Edmund Cordery, May 1622)

PROLOGUE

T*he followers of Gregory the Great say that before vampires go to their Sabbat they anoint themselves upon their bodies with an unguent made from filthy ingredients, chiefly from murdered children. At their meeting-place they light a foul and horrid fire. Satan presides over their assembly, in the shape of a goat with batlike wings, sitting upon a throne of black stone. The vampires approach him to offer their adoration, as suppliants on bended knee. They offer him gifts, of black candles or infants' navel cords; and they kiss him upon his hairy hand in sign of homage. Then they give him account of what cruel deeds they have performed since last they stood before him; of the tortures which they have afflicted on common men, and of the misery they have spread about the world.*

The devil provides his worshippers with food, which is vile and worm-ridden, but which is to the vampires no more evil to the taste than bread and sugar, for there is much in it of human blood and the flesh of children, which they love to consume. The devil gives them also a black wine served in a great drinking-horn, which is compounded of urine, spices and blood, and which the vampires drink with much relish.

It is then the custom of the vampires to dance to the sound of pipes and tabors, which they do wildly, whirling about in a way to make their senses reel. In this dance they are frequently joined by the imps of hell, who love to dance upon the land that was made for men, polluting it with the trampling of their clawed feet, and spoiling it with their excretions.

Only at the last are the vampires allowed to approach their master, to receive his dreadful communion, and then they must go on all fours, moving backwards to his throne, offering their hindquarters to his pleasure. His member, which is like the member of a horse, and cold as ice, is thrust into their bowels, and there ejaculates a semen black as night, which feeds the demon spirits imprisoned in their flesh. Then the vampires rend their own flesh, and offer their dripping blood to the monstrous tongue of their master, who drinks it most greedily, for it is the pure spirit of evil.

These wounds which the vampires inflict upon themselves heal quickly, and whether or no their master drains them dry, and gnaws upon their bones, which he sometimes does in the grip of his insatiable hungers, they rise again at cockcrow, whole and hearty, to visit more evil upon the world, which God made for man, and not for their kind.

These things have been seen, by those sent to bear witness for the race of men, to know what a horror is come among them. The risk in this is great, for when a man is detected in such spying, he is brought to the place before the throne, and a pointed stake thrust into him, in place of the devil's member, and the stake is set into the ground, and made a maypole for the vampires' dance, and the ground where the imps and their minions cavort is oft soaked with the blood of martyrs.

The vampires have set themselves up over common men to be their masters, by means of the powers given to them by Satan. They have done this in order to obliterate that path to salvation which God laid down for common men. While the vampires rule the earth, the souls of men remain in dire peril, and many who succumb to the temptations of temporal power will sacrifice the Kingdom of Heaven for the pleasure of long life and freedom from pain. But it is promised to men that Christ will come again, to judge the living and the dead, and they who have not departed His path shall live forever in the Kingdom of Heaven. Attila is the Anti-Christ whose advent was prophesied by St. John of the Apocalypse; and the false pope, Alexander, is his minion. Christ will one day cast them down, and all Hell's legion with them, to purify the earth. They who would not suffer on earth will burn eternally; while they who bow to the will of God, accepting the pain and death which he gave to the fallen sons of Adam, will see God and know the truth of his mercy.

(From the *Compendium Maleficarum* of Francesco Guazzo, 1608)

ONE

He awoke from a dream whose memory vanished within an instant, though it left him with the vague knowledge that it had been remarkably unpleasant, and that he had been desperately glad to leave it. Before he opened his eyes he struggled to remember where he had gone to sleep, and where he might be now, but he could not guess.

He blinked, but could not bear the light, and shut his eyes.

For a moment, he could not quite remember his own name, and when he struggled for recall the first syllables which came to his parched lips were not his name, but were instead: *Shigidi.*

Then, with a flood of relief, he knew that he was Noell Cordery, saved from the wrath of the risen dead by providence . . . or by a bolt from heaven, hurled by the Uruba god Shango . . . or by a bullet fired from a musket by the pirate Langoisse.

There was a red glow upon his closed eyelids which told him that the sun was up, and that its rays were shining directly upon his face. He knew, therefore, that he must shade his eyes with his hand before opening them again, and this he tried to do. He found, on trying to raise his right arm that he could not do it, and that no feeling was discernible in that limb. He quickly clenched the fingers of his left hand, and used it to shade his eyes when he opened them.

The sun was shining through a wide rectangular window, perhaps ten feet across and four deep, sharply cut from a wall of rock. He tried to sit up, but found difficulty in doing so. He had to turn his head away from the glare and use his left hand to propel himself upwards. A blanket, which had covered him, slid from his upper body and he was able to look down at himself, exclaiming in horror as he saw that his right arm and shoulder, and the right side of his body from armpit to hip, was mottled with black and ashen grey, as though his flesh was rotting beneath the skin.

The effort of sitting up made his senses reel, and he felt as though drugged with opium or strong liquor. He was very thirsty, his mouth and throat burning with an angry dryness.

The bed on which he lay was a pallet of dried vegetation, perhaps ferns, loosely bound by a length of cloth into a covered mattress. There was a wooden table beside the bed, being a section cut from a huge tree-trunk, on which there stood a stone jug filled with water. Noell yearned to seize the jug, but it was on his right hand side, and he could not make that hand reach out. He had to prop himself up, resting his breast on updrawn knees, then turn by degrees until he could reach the jug with his other hand. Despite his thirst he peered anxiously at the water within, unsure of its purity. He sipped, and could find no fault with its taste, so he took a larger gulp, and let the water linger in his mouth before swallowing, to soothe his cracked tongue.

When he put down the jug his attention was caught by the rings on the polished tabletop – thousands of them, curiously skewed so that they were not concentric. He had been told that each ring seen in the sectioned trunk of a tree represented one year's growth, and he knew that this table must have been cut from a tree which was growing before Christ was born. He blinked tears from his eyes as his senses were confused by the rings, which seemed to sway and rotate.

He looked about him, though his head seemed very heavy as he moved it. He saw that he was in a room some ten feet by eleven, with walls made from blocks of solid stone. There was no furniture but the rough bed and the table beside it, though there was a rush mat covering three-quarters of the floor. There was a door opposite the window, made of a wood so dark as to be almost black, with rusted iron hinges. There was an alcove opposite the bed, with a ledge a few inches from the ground, bearing a wooden cover. He was alone, and naked, though there was a pile of clothes at the foot of the bed, and resting beside the heap were his boots and his straw hat.

He drank again from the jug, then tried unsteadily to replace it on the table. So poor was his control over his body that it crashed to the stone floor as he released it. It smashed, and hurled water in all directions. With a great effort, he forced himself from the bed. Though his senses reeled, and sweat seemed to flood from his pores, he managed to crawl across the room on hands and knees, and crossed to the alcove. He felt as though half his body was dead, and only half alive, so that part of him was struggling to drag the dead weight of the rest.

He lifted the wooden cover to expose a hole of indeterminate depth. The odour was sufficient to assure him of its purpose, and he was able, with difficulty, to use it. He then sat slumped in the alcove, utterly exhausted, and near to fainting. The clarity of mind which had come to him upon his awakening had now all but deserted him, and he had a sense of detachment which made him wonder if he might be dreaming. But there was something about the cold roughness of the stone against his skin which was too real to be doubted.

After a minute's rest, he felt better. He wondered whether he could put his clothes on, but decided that it was out of the question while he could only command the obedience of half his upper body. He knew that he could not even get his boots on but was determined to get to his feet if he could. He dragged himself over to the window, and tried to heave himself up, but there was no purchase or leverage to be gained from his helpless right arm, and he could not stand up. He only managed to bring himself up to the point where he could look over the ledge at what lay beyond. The sight which met his eyes was unexpected, and he caught his breath in amazement.

He was looking down from a great height upon a huge valley hemmed in by a distant fringe of cliffs and granite slopes. Away to the east he could see the sunlight glinting upon a lake. He reckoned that the valley must be twenty miles or more across, and it seemed to be circular in shape, rimmed by worn grey rocks. The whole floor of the valley was planted with crops, those nearest to the cliff being a mixture of orchards and fields of green root-crops, everything arrayed in careful lines.

When he looked along the curving wall of the cliff he could see other windows, and there were buildings perched on ledges both to the sides and below, built into the face of the cliff, clinging in defiance of common sense to an unreasonably steep slope. This, he knew at once, was the *real* Adamawara, and the strange lifeless land through which they had travelled was only the barrier separating it from the greater world, preserving it from invasion.

He could see workers moving in the fields, tiny and insect-like. They were clothed in white. Noell tried to lean out to look down, but was seized by an awful giddiness which sent him reeling back into the room, his limbs sprawling as if he were a rag doll dropped by a careless child. He fell on his right side, and felt the impact dully, though it was not what he would normally have called pain. Even so, tears came to his eyes, and his thoughts became confused. The door opened behind him, and he turned his head sharply in surprise, but his sensibility was so disturbed that he could hardly take in the events which followed.

The first person to enter was a black woman dressed in a loose-fitting white robe. Her face was so smooth, he thought at first that she might be elemi, but the way she moved aside told him almost immediately that she was a servant, and therefore common. The man who followed her had to be a vampire, though he was like no person of any kind that Noell had ever seen.

He was not black, but pale brown, with light brown eyes which matched his skin. He was nearly as tall as Noell, which was unusual in the extreme for the people of these climes, and his hair was hidden by a turban. His face was not wrinkled like the faces of the ancient black vampires Noell had seen, but in spite of that he somehow gave the impression of being very old indeed. His limbs were slender, but by no means as devoid of flesh as Ghendwa's, and he moved with a smooth slowness. He was dressed in a long chemise of white cloth, which hung to his knees; his calves were bare and he wore light sandals upon his feet.

When he saw that Noell was out of bed, and that he had fallen, he hurried forward to help. As the man tried to lift him, Noell felt sure that he was going to faint, and the sense of being in a dream returned to him very forcibly. His vision was blurred, and so he could not at first make out the features of the other person who came to help him. It was not until the two of them had placed him on the bed that her face suddenly came into focus.

She was, to judge by the lustre of her skin, a vampire, but she was light in colour – lighter than Leilah, though not as pale as a Gaulish vampire lady – and her hair was russet brown, not black. Her eyes were strange, more grey than brown, the left lighter in colour than the right. Her face was rather angular, with straight cheek-bones and a square chin. She seemed to him then the most beautiful woman he had seen since he left the waters of Cardigan Bay half a lifetime before.

The man spoke to the servant-woman in a language which Noell did not know, and she began picking up the shards of the water-jug. Then he turned to look down at Noell, pausing before he spoke as though he were not entirely sure that Noell could hear or understand.

'Do you understand Latin?' asked the visitor, in that language. To Noell, trying to collect himself, it seemed utterly absurd. He had expected to be addressed in Uruba, and might have been less surprised to hear English. But to hear instead the language of the church!

He felt unable to speak, but he nodded.

'May I speak to you in that language? I will use Uruba, if you prefer.'

Again, Noell nodded, hoping that his meaning was clear. His head was aching.

'Then it falls to me to bid you welcome,' said the visitor, softly. He

looked toward the window, having obviously guessed that Noell had
looked out of it before his fall. 'This is our home,' he said. 'It is
Adamawara.' He glanced briefly at the servant, who was now making
her way out of the open door, carrying the bits of the broken jug. Then
he signalled briefly to the vampire lady, who also left, without having
spoken a word

'My name is Kantibh,' he went on, in a tone that was clearly meant
to be soothing and friendly. 'The lady is Berenike. You are in her
house, in what we call the place of the aitigu. You know, I think, that
the word means unfinished. I must tell you that the disease you have
is still progressing, and that its worst effects are yet to come. You must
have heard it called the silver death, but it rarely kills, and the elemi
have medicines which will sustain you. You will feel very helpless – a
prisoner in your body – and your mind will wander in strange regions
of impossibility. You may feel that you are gone to Ipo-oku, or burning
in the fires of your Christian Hell, but you will come safely through
the ordeal, I promise it. Can you reply now?'

Noell licked his lips, and managed to say: 'Yes. I understand,' though
he had to grope for the Latin words, which did not come readily to his
tongue. He added an attempted question: 'My companions?'

'All alive,' answered Kantibh. 'The one called Quintus has told us
your names. He too has the sickness, but not so badly yet. It is the
same with the woman. The one called Langoisse is the worst; he is
greatly weakened by the fever, though the silver death has not yet
claimed him. The Ibau Ngadze is sick now but will recover soon, and
the Uruba boy Ntikima should suffer least of all.'

'Ghendwa?' asked Noell, faintly.

'He will live. As for the one who hurt him – he will die in the forest,
I think. The Mkumkwe will not search for him.'

Noell relaxed a little, content with this information. He looked up
at the shadowed features of the man. 'Are you elemi?' he asked.

Kantibh shook his head. 'Aitigu,' he said. 'Unfinished. But I am
what you would call a vampire. I came here like yourself, as a traveller,
some hundreds of years ago. I came to the city of Meroë in the land
of Kush with ambassadors from my own people, who lived in Persia.
I was a learned man, and had visited Rome and India. I journeyed with
a caravan across the great desert to Bornu, where I first heard of
Adamawara. It was long in my mind to seek out this first nation of the
world, and when the time came for me to begin my journey, an elemi
came to me, to be my guide. The first Christians had already come
here, and returned into the world. The first white men here had been
Greeks from Alexander's time, but there were brown men from Sumer
and Egypt before that. Berenike has been here nearly two thousand
years. The vampires of Adamawara cast a wide net, to catch the wisdom

of the world, but they are patient in its casting. It is long since they caught a man like you.'

Noell was not quite sure what the other intended to signify by the words 'a man like you', but he did not think the reference was simply to the colour of his skin.

'Caught?' he repeated.

He felt that he had to speak now, if he could. He thought he should introduce himself, but he had to cough, and could not immediately stop. The other laid a cool hand upon his shoulder, as though to draw the spasm out of him.

'You are very ill,' said Kantibh. 'I think you will be better for a little while, when you have rested, but then the silver death will carry your senses away. We will try to talk again, I promise you, but it would be better for you to sleep now. I will come again.'

Kantibh was still watching him, apparently greatly concerned for his welfare. Noell nodded, giving permission for the other to go, if permission were required.

Kantibh smiled at him. 'You will be hungry,' he said. 'Berenike will send food, and will have your possessions brought to you. She may send servants with water, in which you may be bathed, if you are strong enough. I must return to Quintus now.'

As Kantibh left, and drew the door shut behind him, Noell closed his eyes again. He felt angry with himself for his helplessness, for his incomprehension. He knew there were a thousand questions which needed to be asked, but he knew that time must pass before he would be able to take up the mission which had brought him here: the mission of understanding what Adamawara was, and the nature of the breath of life.

He was determined to prove the truth of Kantibh's words, and live, no matter how Shigidi might torture him in the days to come. If he did not, all his sacrifices would be in vain, and he had come too far for all his efforts to be cancelled and made void.

'I am Noell Cordery,' he whispered. 'Edmund Cordery's son.'

TWO

His season of dreams did not begin immediately. He was able to watch black men – presumably Mkumkwe, though not decorated like the warriors he had previously seen – carry jars of water into his room, pouring them into a bath made from polished wood. He was weak, but awake, when they came to move him, though he could barely feel their hands upon his body when they lifted him. The water was not hot, but it had been warmed, and perfumed. The serving-men washed him carefully and tenderly, using soap – not the greasy soap made from shea butter or crabwood, which he had perforce become used to, but something more solid. It too was perfumed.

While they bathed him bread and fruit were set on the table, but they were in no hurry to make him eat. They left him alone for a little while, to soak the dirt from his body at his leisure, returning after an interval to wash his long, lank hair. One man took the clothes which were piled at the foot of the bed, and washed them, hanging them over the window-sill to dry in the rays of the noon sun. One of the servants brought a razor, and spread soap over his whiskers, then set about shaving off the shaggy beard which he had grown since the expedition set out.

His clothes dried quickly, and when they helped him from the bath they put a shirt on for him, and trousers also, so that he could attend to his meal with such dignity as it was still possible for him to achieve in his reduced condition. He ate little, and with great difficulty. He could raise himself to a half-sitting position, but his movements were awkward, and he still could not use his right arm at all.

Afterwards he collapsed back on the bed, unable to muster the energy to move his good hand or stir his legs. He seemed to lie there for a very long time, quite still. When a shaven-skulled elemi came in, wearing the red and white beads which marked him an Oni-Shango, Noell no longer knew whether he was awake or dreaming. He had begun a second journey, which was, in its fashion, as long and arduous as the one which had brought him to Adamawara; it was to lead him through the unknown labyrinths of his soul.

Perhaps the Oni-Shango gave him medicine, or touched him with a feathered wand more benign than the one with which the Egungun had nearly struck him dead. He could not remember. But when that elemi came to him, he was somehow taken across a threshold of experience, into another dimension of his being.

All his life, Noell Cordery had dreamed, but for the most part – as with all men – his dreams were lost to him. They happened, and were gone, usually so completely that when he woke, he often did not know they had happened at all. In this season of dreams, however, the order of things was turned about, and it seemed to him that while he journeyed with Shigidi he moved through the realms of all the dreams he had ever dreamed, which now were present in his memory and jostling for attention in a way they never had before. It was his waking self which now was forgotten, and his dream-self that was set free, to take command of his consciousness.

It was as though everything that he had ever dreamed in all his life could now be dreamed again, and everything that he had ever enacted in the safe haven of sleep – secure from the judgement of man and God alike, concealed by the stillness of his body – was now to be subject to the twin burdens of examination and conscience.

At first, his journey with Shigidi took the form of a long interrogation, a questioning of his innermost soul, in which all the instruments of inquisition could be brought to bear.

His waking self had never gone into the torture chambers which lay beneath the prisons of the Tower of London, though his ears had sometimes caught the distant echo of screams. But his dreaming self, in the days when he was a child, had often wandered those dark corridors, spurred by curiosity and fascination, and watched the prince's men at work. He had lain upon the rack himself and fearfully faced the threat of heated irons. He lay shackled on the rack again, now, and watched the play of red-fired metal dancing in the dark air, while sepulchral voices demanded acquaintance with his secrets.

Paradoxically, he felt no pain, yet felt a stern obligation to pretend at all costs that he *did*, so as to give the appearance of terror and despair to his interlocutors, to conceal from them his immunity to their tricks.

Why must he pretend agony? He could not tell. He did not know what further threat it was which they held over him, which made him play the part of a man so hurt and terrorized as to be incapable of lie or concealment; he only felt that he must do it, to justify to himself and to those he betrayed the inevitability of his revelations. Perhaps it was not they who threatened him at all, but he who was over-anxious to betray himself, eager to confess in order to unburden his soul. He was threatened with death, again and again – of that he was sure. Was it really his torturers who threatened him? Was it his own perversity? Was it that merciless deity Shigidi, in whose creation he was forced to dwell? He could not tell.

It was not all interrogation and inquisition; there was a universe to be explored, enlightenment to be sought in so many matters which had sorely confused his older self whose coherency was tied to wakefulness. His waking self knew nothing of the vampire sabbat and the mysterious magic by which vampires made themselves, but his dream-self had discovered such conventicles, and had seen what happened there. He had seen Satan at his work, receiving homage from the vampires, watching them dance with his imps, savouring his unnatural intercourse with them, tormenting their flesh secure in the knowledge that it would heal again. Now, he was free to make such visits at his leisure, and understand what he saw.

He saw Richard the Norman at the sabbat: copper-eyed *Coeur-de-lion*, laughing with his flattering friend Blondel de Nesle. He saw Carmilla Bourdillon at the sabbat, red-eyed with fever, her fingers like talons dripping blood. He saw Ghendwa at the sabbat, parading his virtuous spoilt prick, demonstrating to pale ladies how he could piss blood despite his condition, and leak black semen in a sticky stream.

He saw men who were not yet vampires come to claim their heritage from the Prince of Hell, saw them swear their horrid oaths, and heard the chanting of the spells which were intoned when Satan ran his icy phallus into their guts. He strained his ears to hear those spells, determined to remember them, but each time he repeated a phrase to himself the rest were lost, and it was all in a language which he did not know. When the sabbat ended, he still did not know what magic was required for the making of a vampire; but he had recognised some of those who swore the oath and offered their hind-quarters to be ravaged.

He saw Langoisse at the sabbat, carrying the severed head of the Lady Cristelle, whose lips were trying to speak. He saw Ntikima at the sabbat, masked as Egungun, carrying a feathered wand. He saw Edmund Cordery at the sabbat, wearing a different mask, which marked him as a member of the Invisible College of England.

Noell wanted to cry out to these three, to plead with them that they must not sell their souls, and to trust instead in providence, to heed the message of the saintly Quintus, but he dared not give himself away lest the vampires find him spying on their rites, and impale him on a sharpened stake to see him squirm.

There were other mysteries to explore, each as fascinating in its way as the sabbat.

His waking self had never been to Tyburn, to see the poor wretches brought to the three-legged mare, crowded in carts. He had never seen a man noosed and left to dangle, kicking and shitting his soul away. But his dream-self had been there. He had been there with Shigidi, and forgotten and forgotten and forgotten . . . but now he need not forget, and could engrave such sights upon the surface of his soul.

His waking self had never been to an African village on a day of sacrifice, to see a child's throat cut for Olori-merin; to see its flesh dissected, its blood trapped and tasted. He had never seen the priests of Ogun take out the heart of an ennobled slave, to be pounded with medicines and eaten. But his dream-self had been there, more often than he ever could have guessed until he came to Adamawara, and came to know more of these secrets than he had ever sought to have revealed to him.

His waking self had never been to Hell, and knew nothing of its fiery pits and frozen wastes, its lakes of blood and iron spits . . . but his dream-self knew that realm, with an intimacy he would not have dared to suspect, and he had seen men there whose damnation he would rather not have known. His dream-self knew that Edmund Cordery burned in Hell, and that a place was set aside in company with him for his ingrate son . . . and his dream-self wished devoutly not to know it, but to no avail.

In a world such as this, with Shigidi gibbering inside of him, there could be no question of secrecy, no question of concealment. He looked into the underworld beneath the waking self which he had always thought to be the real Noell Cordery, and wondered what he was.

He was asked many questions, and gave account of himself, without mercy to himself or others. But the worst questions were those which he asked of himself, and he received such answers which made him doubt that there could be any forgiveness anywhere. He saw within and beneath his soul that which he could never forgive in himself, and that for which he could never ask forgiveness from anyone who loved him; he understood why the mercy of God must be infinite, else it could not begin to contend with the secret dreams of men.

Sometimes he caught glimpses of his questioners, but the voices came as often from a formless darkness which might have been a baleful God, or the shadow of some monster too terrible to behold.

Kantibh was one who asked questions of him; Quintus was another; Edmund Cordery was a third. One of them told him he would burn as a heretic, but he could not tell which. One of them promised him martyrdom, but which of them it was that could be so reckless, he did not know. One of them told him that he was still so far from his ultimate reckoning that that his dreams had an unimaginable wealth of wonders yet to reveal to him, but who might utter a promise so direly ambitious he could not guess.

Everything he told them of himself he relived, not as as his waking self had seen and felt it, but as his dream-self knew and understood it. He talked of childhood, of the Tower, of his father and mother. He talked about Grand Normandy, and the Imperium of Gaul. He spoke wildly of the arts of the mechanician, saying a great deal about the kinds of machines which were used in Europe now, and the myriad ways in which they changed and channelled the lives of men. He gave elaborate discourse upon the various doctrines of Christian belief, of the heresies of Gregory, the corruption of Rome, the parties of the clergy, the follies of faith.

When he told them about the world, he spoke with the authority of being the world, as though it were all encompassed – great round earth and endless history – by the bounds of his own small soul; as though it were constituted by his thoughts, his learning, his attitudes and his feelings. He spoke of Africa as though there were naught in Africa but that which spilled from his fecund imagination: comical beasts and monstrous godlings and sweating forests all alike in the great river of his thoughts, mere waves and eddies upon the surface of his being.

Long afterwards, when he came to the conclusion that some of his questioners had been really present at his bedside, and that a fraction of what his dream-self babbled out was really heard by them, he tried

to remember what he might actually have said to his phantom interrogators. It was an impossible task.

Of what had he accused himself? What confessions had exposed his
soul? He could not tell.

There was more.

His dream-self, while his dream-soul was confined to the dream-
flesh, was injured in other ways than by the tortures and punishments
of his interrogation. On numberless occasions he felt himself buggered,
though his waking self had never suffered any such indignity. Having
no real experience on which to base the illusion of penetration, there
were conjured up for him all manner of absurd sensations.

At one time, the organ which forced him open felt cold and slimy,
at another hot and sharp. At one time the unseen prick would be huge,
its copious ejaculation filling him up and making him choke in his belly
and his throat alike; at another it was comfortable and smooth, but its
semen tore him like shot, shattering his bones. At one time, such a
rape was committed by a figure resembling Quintus, at another it was
Langoisse's Turk, who stuffed him while he was pinned in a pillory
which gripped his wrists with iron hands.

His dream-self was no more beyond the reach of shame than it was
beyond the reach of misery, and he suffered these assaults, without the
saving hope that one of them might plant within his flesh the seed of
immortality. The Satan of the Gregorians was never one of those who
hurt him thus, nor was Richard Lionheart or any of his kin.

But if all these chapters in the season of his dreams were only different
circles of a Dantean Hell, he had also glimpses of Paradise.

His waking self had journeyed further across the face of the world
than was ordinary, and yet had seen very little of the vast Creation
engineered by the hand of God; that waking self had often looked raptly
to the sky, failing to count the stars or compass the wanderings of the
planets. But his dream-self, unfettered, had often dragged his sentient
soul far away from the prison of flesh, to fly aloft with all Creation at
its mercy, leaping free into the sky to bathe in the rays of the sun or
blaze a comet-course among the stars, lonely in the great darkness yet
proud in its power.

Alas, the taste of heaven within these dreams was a faint one, for in
the abyssal reaches of the void he could feel a special remoteness which
was as hellish, in its way, as the labyrinthine prisons of solidity to
which nightmare sometimes confined him. He felt, when his soul
strayed too far from the comfort of the sun, which became as tiny as
any other star, that like Odysseus he had incurred the wrath of fate,
and would be tortured by postponement of his homecoming. Such
flights of the soul seemed never to reach any final climax or conclusion.

But there was another demi-paradise, which he shared with the
women of the vampire race, who used him far more kindly than his

interrogators, or those to whom he played the catamite. He thought when he later tried to appraise this season that perhaps he had been saved from the extremity of despair only by the vampire ladies.

Or, at least, *one* vampire lady.

His waking self had never lain with common woman or vampire. He had never made love, even to the gypsy who had liked him since she was a girl. Shy and shamed, made ever more cowardly by the long extension of restraint, his waking self had put erotic feelings aside, tight-binding them with personal taboos.

But his dream-self . . .!

Neither shyness nor shame had shadowed that phantom being which moved within him, and no bonds forged by consciousness could possibly contain the impulses which rose unbidden in the sleeping body to command the service of the dreamlocked soul.

In his dreams, he had never lacked for yielding flesh, lustrous and undying, for the bloody kisses of immortals. There Cristelle still lived, no severed head sent screaming into Hell but whole and free, couched and clad in any wise he might imagine, always open to him, always anxious to caress. Carmilla Bourdillon was also there, not bloated by the plague which had turned her blood to bile, but warm and white and everlasting, ever-gentle, ever-lovely, ever-thirsty.

In his dreams, there were a thousand vampires, often faceless, always perfect; often nameless, always soft. In his dreams, which knew no limit to fear and fury, monstrousness and malevolence, no bounds were set either on beauty and bewitchment, ecstasy and ease. But there were no common lovers even in his dreams, for his dream-self knew no necessity to favour frailer flesh, to prefer the flawed to the immaculate, the rotten to the sempiternal.

In his long season of dreams, his demon lovers did not desert him, but were instead expanded in their number, by one who came with subtle touches, one who served him languidly and well. This one was like no other, not because she transformed the nature of his lust, but because she whispered to him while she lay beside him; as though she too were lost in a season of dreams, condemned to pour out her heart to invisible inquisitors which teased her pain-free flesh with arrows of delirium.

The name this phantom vampire gave herself was Berenike, and his dream-self learned that she had been born in Alexandria, in the declining days of Alexander's empire, while Rome was in its cradle. She was sold as a slave to adventurers, who crossed the desert in search of Solomon's Ophir. The desert was less cruel in those long-gone days, and Alexander had sent several expeditions into the heart of Africa, some of which returned. Her masters, hearing of Adamawara, believed that it must be Ophir, and they had come to search for Elysium on earth.

The lifeless forest, unlike the desert, had been crueller then, and the survivors of the party which brought Berenike the slave into its shade fell direly sick with the silver death, and all had seemed sure to die. She lay in fevered terror for many days, lost in nightmare, consumed by anguish. That Berenike would have died, but the elemi found a medicine which saved her, and which made her almost like themselves, but aitigu: unfinished.

In the centuries which followed, other men came to Adamawara, from the arab lands and those empires which rose and fell in the Mediterranean cradle of civilization. For a while, the elemi used their medicines to drive away the silver death, and made of them undying aitigu, and Berenike was not alone. But the elemi had become angry, offended by things which the aitigu had done, and they used that medicine no more. One by one, the aitigu died, or went away, and Berenike had long ago become lonely. Her seasons of dreams, she said, took her away to the folds of paradise, where she need not be afraid of time, but she would sometimes return to less fortunate spaces, if there was a reason. He was the reason, it seemed, for her present descent from paradise.

Making love to her, in his season of dreams, was like being touched by an angel. His encounters with her were confused, and often he did not know whether it was Berenike who came to him or one of those myriad others, but there was always joy.

Sometimes, it was Cristelle who gave him ease. Sometimes, it was Carmilla. Sometimes, it was the nameless one, whose face he had yet to see. One of them told him that he was the handsomest man in England now that he had killed his father, but he did not know which it was. One of them said that the breath of a better life was in him, and that his children would renew the widowed world, but he could not tell which one. One of them told him that she would always remember him, through all the seasons of dreams which were yet to come, and would find him again and again and again in every face which she touched and every drop of blood she drank, but he could not recognise her voice, and knew her only by the name which was everpresent in his dreams, and attached itself to everything: *Shigidi*.

THREE

Wakefulness intruded into his season of dreams by slow degrees.

At first he forgot the events of wakefulness as soon as he returned to sleep, but as time went by his fugitive consciousness regained and tightened its grip upon the world without, and he dragged himself from that infernal pit into which the silver death and its Uruba demon had dragged him.

His memory of actual events was recovered in a fashion which was at first confused and fragmentary. Remembered sensations of cramming food into his mouth, and drinking from a cup, were mingled with a cacophony of broken conversations. He knew that Kantibh had often been with him, sometimes with an ancient black vampire, Aiyeda: an Oni-Shango who spoke to him in Uruba. He knew that he had spent much time in sore discomfort, and had sometimes been madly feverish. Sometimes, he thought, he had raved and babbled in response to interrogation, driven by some deep inner impulse to get certain thoughts and ideas out of his system. He had tried to expel them with his voice as though they were poisons in his being, stored there through all the long years when, as a non-believer, he had refused the confession and communion required by religious observance.

He knew, too, that he had sometimes looked at his naked body, with open and waking eyes, to see it almost completely covered in a black stain which gave his body the semblance of a huge bruise. Remembering this, when his thoughts became coherent once again, he wondered what kind of burning it was which had left him so ashen, as if Hell's fires had reduced him to a mere calx. Was this, he asked himself, what the condition was to be throughout eternity of sinners and unbelievers? Had he seen a vision of the soul's corruptions evidenced in the flesh? Was this why God allowed Shigidi and his kin their limited domain within the human soul?

His waking self became again the emperor of his senses and his memory, but it was a victory not easily won, and not without its setbacks. In ruthless fashion his newly-hatched consciousness set out to suppress and plough under all but a tiny fraction of that which his dreams had liberated, but he could not conceal from himself the truth that he was a changed man. Whether he was the better or the worse for it, he was not sure.

From all the flotsam and jetsam of his delirium there was one sequence of happenings that his soul did take care to salvage, and which his memory preserved as best it could, anchored by the image of a face: the face of the woman Berenike. He knew, when sanity returned to him, that the lovemaking of his dreams had made a bridge with reality. Berenike had actually come to him, as his interrogators had actually come, and she had lain with him.

How many times this had happened in fact, and how many in mere fancy, he could not tell, but he knew that in the matter of his lust and tenderness there was little partition between illusion and reality. Perhaps, he thought, it was always so. Perhaps passion was the true meeting of the inner and outer worlds, powerful enough to forge a weld between dream and reality, dark and light, Hell and Heaven, sterility and potency, vampire and common man.

He reflected that Berenike must have had lovers seventeen hundred years before he was born, and that her affections reached him now across the great expanse of human history. Thus she connected him more intimately to all the intricate pattern of human cause and consequence which lay within the shadow of eternity. He felt, the first time he made love to her in a wholly conscious way, that he was embracing the Heart Divine, and taking his allotted share of the breath of life, even though it was too poor a portion to rescue him from pain and death.

He supposed that she must have talked to him a good deal despite his delirium, telling him about her early life, and about the centuries which she had passed in Adamawara. Perhaps she had spoken out of a need to unburden herself which was not too different from his own. When he was whole again, and fully conscious of their meetings, she became shy and seemed reluctant to talk to him, and this made him shy also.

He knew that Berenike had drunk his blood while she made love to him in his delirium, and this disturbed him. Perversely, he had not been anxious for himself, that he should have become vampire's prey, but anxious for her, because he thought harm might come to her if she drank the foul black blood from his diseased veins. More than once, he thought, he had cried out in wordless protest when she bent over him, and he thought that he remembered seeing her withdraw in confusion, not knowing what had alarmed him.

He did dream, at least once, that she slit his throat with a knife, and licked the blood which gushed out with lustful avidity, but when he was sane again he knew that it had been a dream. When Berenike took blood from him, she took it from his breast and not his neck, and he felt nothing but a languourous acceptance of what was being done to him.

There was no single moment when he knew himself to be returned from the morass of fragmentary memory to full and proper consciousness, but there was one moment which he was later to recall as the true resumption of problematic life. It happened at night, when he became conscious, with frightening clarity, of the fact that some sound had brought him back from sleep.

He was immediately conscious that he was lying down in his bed, on his left-hand side – which, he knew, faced the blank stone wall of his cell. He could feel the roughness of the blanket where it warmly lay upon his body, and the texture of the mattress on which he lay. The flesh of his neck caught a draught of cold air, which stirred the hairs on his nape. Behind him, in the room, something was moving.

He did not immediately turn, but lay there listening. The sounds continued, as though of a body being dragged across the floor while someone breathed, heavily and raggedly.

He made one effort, and failed, before finally forcing himself to turn over. He said, though it surprised him a little to find that he had a voice: 'Who is it?'

There was a small cry of alarm, quickly strangled. 'Cordery? Master Cordery? Is it thee, in truth?'

The voice was not easily recognisable, but the words told more than the quality of the sound.

'Langoisse?' he said, trying to sit up. He realised that he could feel all of his own body again, the right-hand side as well as the left, and that he had command of his every muscle.

'Thank God!' exclaimed the pirate, almost sobbing. 'Master Cordery, I have been in Hell! I have burned, friend Noell, and how the devils have tormented me!'

'Aye,' said Noell, still more concerned with the fact of his self-awareness than the nearness of his visitor. 'I have been there myself, and am only now certain that I am not there still.' He peered into the darkness, trying hard to see something of the pirate's face. The night was clear, and there were stars visible in the rectangle which was cut out of the wall by the window. Their light was feeble, but the room was not utterly gloomy. When a hand reached out, groping at Noell's face and then moving down to discover and grip his arm, he could see a vague shadow. The head was lower than his own, and the arm had reached upward, so he knew that Langoisse had indeed dragged himself across the floor, presumably unable to walk, or even to crawl.

'Help me,' begged Langoisse. 'For the love of God, help me!'

Noell could not imagine what help he could give, but as Langoisse gripped his right arm, so he reached over with his own left hand to grip the pirate's wrist, to steady it with his clutch.

'Be still, man,' he said 'Thou'rt returned, now, from that Hell to which thy dreams have taken thee. This is the world again, and the silver death is quitting thy tired flesh. We'll be bleached as white as bone before we know it.'

'If I am not in Hell now,' said the pirate, 'then I have surely but recently returned, and will go there again if I fall asleep.' He did not seem to believe that Noell knew whereof he spoke in uttering his reassurances.

'This Hell is inside us all,' Noell told him. 'We have been ill, man, and that is all. The silver death has given us a taste of the hereafter which we fear.' He remembered, while he spoke, that Langoisse had been sick even before the dark discolouration had appeared in his own flesh. Langoisse had walked all through that long last day, sweating and near-delirious, showing an excess of strength and courage in his resistance to exhaustion and collapse. He realised that Langoisse probably did not remember that the Egungun had come to meet them, or that he had tried to kill the risen dead. Langoisse might not know that they had been brought to Adamawara.

'Did they question you?' he asked.

'The imps of Hell tormented me,' Langoisse complained, 'in a cursed tongue I have all but forgot.' Langoisse had been an educated man in his youth, and must have learned Latin then, but that had been a long time ago. The pirate knew no more than a handful of Uruba words. Whatever information the elemi had gathered from Quintus and himself, they must have had to be content with a leaner ration from Langoisse.

'Where is this place?' whispered the pirate.

'A citadel in Adamawara,' Noell told him. 'A palace of vampires. Have you not seen a Persian who calls himself Kantibh, or the woman Berenike whose house this is?'

'Master Cordery,' Langoisse replied, in a throaty whisper, 'I do not know what I have seen, or what has been done to me. Until I found thee, I would have sworn that I had been in Beëlzebub's palace in the City of Dis, where his Satanic majesty made vicious play with my flesh and my soul, and I'd have sworn, too, that I repented all that I have ever done, and made confession of all my sins. 'Sblood, I would have begged forgiveness of Richard himself, had he come like the noble knight he pretends to be, to release me from that misery!'

'Hush,' said Noell, gently. 'If Quintus were here, he'd accept your repentance and hear your confession, but I am only Noell Cordery, who holds sins to your credit he cannot quite forgive, and who would not ask you to repent your enmity for Richard Lionheart and the tyranny of Gaul. I wish there was a lamp nearby – or a candle and a way to light it.'

'Oh no,' said Langoisse, with a sob. 'I am not what I was, and you would not like to see me. If I am not dead, Master Cordery, I am certainly clad in foul black leprosy, and more hideous to the eye than faithful Selim ever was.'

'I think not,' said Noell, still trying to make his voice as soothing as could be. 'I too was stained, and as I have told thee, cleanness is returning to our flesh, though it might never return to our immortal souls. Hell cannot have us yet awhile, and we may one day make our bid for the breath of life.'

'My God,' moaned Langoisse. 'Thou dost not . . . thou canst . . . oh, what truck hath the likes of me with the vengeful Lord? Curse God and all his work! But *thou* must forgive me, Master Cordery, forgive me for all that I. . . .'

Noell knew that he did not want to hear much more, and did not altogether like it that Langoisse should first curse God and then ask him instead for that forgiveness he desired. But Langoisse was unable to finish his plea in any case. His voice decayed to racking coughs, and then he slumped upon the floor.

Then came more sounds, and Noell knew that others were entering the room. Langoisse released him, gradually, from his insistent hold, and Noell let go of the pirate's wrist.

The flicker of candle-light reflected from the stone walls, and two men loomed as great black shadows above the bed. Then the flame itself appeared, and behind it the face of the Persian, Kantibh.

Langoisse raised his head from the floor, with difficulty, and turned his face towards the light. He seemed for an instant no more than a ghastly caricature of a man, his face still blotched with fading grey, his lips limned with black and his eyes wild with lunacy. It seemed to Noell that he had taken on the aspect of the risen dead, and become a painted mask, in expiation of his act of violence against Egungun.

'It is Satan!' sobbed Langoisse. 'Oh Master Cordery. . .!' He turned to Noell, to stare him straight in the eye.

Noell looked at the pirate's terrified expression, and the echo of Egungun which he had seen there faded away. The features, mottled with grey though they were, lost their symbolism of the unearthly world, and became instead mere signs of fear and misery. It was as though Langoisse was filthy with streaks of soil, but not deep-stained by sin, as he seemed to imagine. Noell saw that the flesh of the pirate's hand and arm had also been blackened by the silver death, but was returning to its normal state. The sickness within him had now the aspect of a retreating shadow, instead of an all-consuming blight.

'It is not the devil,' said Noell, not so gently, because he was trying to force the pirate to hear him. 'It is only a man. A vampire, but a man.'

He had never before seen Langoisse in such a state, stripped of all anger, all cruelty, and all haughtiness. But Langoisse was a man, after all, and a man of great courage in spite of this and other fallibilities. Though he did not speak aloud, Noell forgave Langoisse those things for which he had once hated him.

Langoisse seemed somehow to see that it was so, for his agonised face relaxed, and he tried instead to smile. 'Why, Master Cordery,' he whispered. ''Tis only thee. I have been dreaming, friend Noell . . . dreaming . . . '

The black servitors raised the pirate gently, and Noell could see that he did his best to help them.

'Langoisse,' he said, 'we are in Adamawara. Whether we are guests or prisoners, I cannot tell, but they do not mean to let us die yet. Go with them, and I will come to you when I can.'

After he had said it, he wondered whether he was free to make such a promise. How could he know what Kantibh's intentions might be, now that the elders of Adamawara must know the greater part of what

Quintus and Noell could tell them? What would happen tomorrow? Was he a welcome guest or a fruit wrung dry, to be discarded?

"Tis a sickness,' said Langoisse, as though trying to fix the news within his memory. Then he laughed. It was a weak, thin laugh, but a laugh nevertheless. 'Are there microscopes in Hell?' he asked, and seemed to collapse into himself again, slumping unconscious in the arms of the white-clad men who held him. They picked him up – without much difficulty, for he had become very thin – and carried him away.

Kantibh followed, but did not close the door. Berenike came in, carrying a candle of her own, and looked down at Noell. She did not say anything, and there was a strange expression in her eyes, as though her thoughts were very distant, trapped in the world of dreams, unable to find proper release.

It was not the first time he had looked at her with conscious eyes, measuring her beauty with wakeful attention, but when he had done so before he had been under the spell of his affection, and had seen her only as an object of desire. Now, there was a distance between them. She was not one whit less beautiful, with her perfect skin, her full lips drawn back a little from her neat white teeth, and her bright coppery hair, whose like he had never seen. She was so beautiful, in fact, that his breath caught in his throat as he looked at her. But he saw now what he had not seen before – that *she* looked at *him* in a very different way, which held no tenderness and no admiration, but only a kind of greed.

He put his hand to his head, as though to test his fever. His mind was clouded now, as though the effort of helping Langoisse had driven him too far.

'Leave me, I beg of you,' he said. 'Let me sleep . . . let me sleep.'

She bowed, politely, and withdrew, but he called out after her then, and asked her to leave the candle in his room. She returned, and placed it on the table made from the bole of a tree, which rested solidly beside the place where he laid his head.

'I will be better soon,' he promised. 'Very soon.'

But when she had gone, and he slept again, he dreamed that she had surreptitiously returned, and was with him in his bed, and that she cut him about the throat, and sucked his blood while they tossed and rolled together, until a pain grew in him and drove his soul from his body to haunt endless corridors where it swam like a silvery eel through empty air, thrusting itself on and ever on, without prospect of an end or memory of a beginning.

While he dreamed this dream, it seemed real enough, but when he woke again in daylight it evaporated as all dreams should, and let him look with steady eyes at the grey walls of his little cell, and the great blue canopy of the sky beyond the window.

FOUR

The sun was already high in the sky, and Noell rejoiced in a feeling of well-being such as he had not experienced for a very long time.

He sat up, thrusting aside his blanket in order to inspect his body. He was not naked, being dressed in some kind of light chemise, but his arms were bare, and he saw that the discolouration beneath his skin was very faded there, and that the ordinary colour was nearly returned, though paler for the lack of recent exposure to the sun. When he pulled the hem of the nightshirt up to his waist he was able to see that his legs were still somewhat darker, and there was not the ordinary degree of feeling in his calves or his feet. His legs were much thinner than he remembered them, and the flesh on his arms was reduced, as though the muscles had wasted.

He found that he could stand up, with a little difficulty, and managed to limp across the room to the alcove. Then he looked for his clothes, in order to dress himself, but while his other possessions, including the microscope in its box, were still at the foot of the bed, his clothes had been taken away. He sat down again, greatly enfeebled by comparison with his former state.

Later, he was able to sit up to eat a breakfast of cool porridge and fruit, and he asked one of the black men who brought the food if he could have his clothes again. The servant did not understand the words he used, but gestures helped supply the meaning, and his clothes were brought, along with water to wash himself.

As the sun reached its zenith he was visited by Kantibh. Berenike was not with him, but there were two ancient vampires, who were introduced by the Persian as Aiyeda and Nyanya. Aiyeda was the Oni-Shango that Noell had seen several times before, though he could not entirely recall the occasions or the circumstances.

'Are you well enough to talk with us?' asked Kantibh, in Latin.

Noell reflected that they had tried him with as many questions as they could even when he was not well enough to provide coherent answers, and told them that.

'It is true,' admitted Kantibh, squatting on the mat with the elemi to either side of him. 'We have found out much of what the elders asked us to discover. But there are many things which you could not communicate in your former state. We would like to hear more reasoned arguments, which can only come from a calm mind.'

'Are we prisoners here?' asked Noell, abruptly.

'You are prisoners of circumstance, certainly,' replied Kantibh, smoothly. 'When the Logone and the Gongola are in flood, the journey to the headwaters of the Kwarra is very difficult. You could not reach Bauchi before the wet season is at its worst.'

Noell stared at the man suspiciously. 'The wet season! The wet season will not begin until April.'

'By your calendar,' said Kantibh, serenely, 'it is the month of May. You have been in Adamawara one hundred and forty days.'

Noell tried to hide his astonishment, but Kantibh must have known what effect the revelation would have. He added: 'The silver death brings a special sleep – a sleep not unlike the sleep into which the elemi must go when the breath of life is weak within them. You have been very ill.'

Noell recalled the way that the Mkumkwe had picked up Langoisse when he collapsed, and looked again at his slender arms. It was not the wasting of days, but he had not thought it the wasting of months, either. In his season of dreams, he had lost all contact with ordinary time, in body as well as in spirit.

'Why did you bring us here?' asked Noell, quietly.

'It was your intention to come,' Kantibh pointed out. 'Without Ghendwa, you would have perished on the way. The elemi helped you because they were curious as to what manner of man the greater world is breeding now. Quintus, whom the tribesmen called the white baba-lawo, was represented to the elders as a man who could instruct us in the world's wisdom as well as its history, and Ekeji Orisha directed that his way should be made easy.'

'And what will happen to us now?' Noell persisted. 'Are we free to go where we will in Adamawara? Are we free to leave it, when we wish to do so?'

'In Adamawara, all are free,' Kantibh replied, levelly. 'Here, the gods are close to earth, and the undying walk with the risen dead. Few leave Adamawara, for there is no other place on the face of the earth where a man should prefer to be.'

'But some have gone from here, have they not?' asked Noell, speaking sharply because he felt resentful of the way that they had questioned him while he was delirious. 'The aitigu who brought the breath of life to Walachia and Gaul were not content to walk with the risen dead and the gods of the Uruba and the Mkumkwe.'

Kantibh smiled. 'They were intemperate men,' he said. 'They had not the gift of patience, nor the happiness of true wisdom.'

Noell looked at Aiyeda, whose black eyes were fixed upon his face, watching very carefully, as though to calculate what measure of patience and wisdom might remain in Noell's heart, now that he was returned from the void into which the silver death had cast him. Noell knew how difficult it was to obtain an honest answer to a direct question, if an African did not want to give it. They would not tell him what they intended to do with him. For all that he knew, he was still under the sentence of death which the Egungun had tried to pass before Langoisse had earned him his reprieve. He decided that he must find a different kind of question, which would bring him the reward for which he had come here: an understanding of Adamawara, and the breath of life.

'So Adamawara is really the Eden where the vampire race began,' he said. 'Whence came the Adam of the vampires? How and when did the conquest of pain and death begin?'

'The arokin tell us that there were men in these hills before there were elemi,' said Kantibh, speaking in Uruba now. 'Those were the ancestors of the Mkumkwe and the Sahra, the Uruba and the Jawara, the Ibau and the Edau, and countless other tribes. Olorun commanded Shango to strike the earth with a great thunderbolt, and sent Shigidi and other messengers to trouble the dreams of men until the priests knew what sacrifice was required of them. Then Olorun gave the priests his own heart to share, so that the breath of life entered into them, and they were elemi. The elemi began Ogbone, the community of men, and sent them into the forests and the plains, to be guardians of the tribes.'

Noell watched the Persian while he spoke. It was exactly the kind of story Ntikima would have told, recited flatly, as though every phrase had been handed down from time immemorial, perfectly shaped and never to be altered, so that the story became a thing in itself, separate from any teller.

'How long ago did all this happen?' he asked.

'In the beginning,' replied the man with the turban.

'And how are common men made elemi?' asked Noell, determined that he ought to ask, though he could not expect to be told. 'How are they made aitigu?'

'The forging of the heart of Olorun is the greatest of the secrets,' Kantibh told him. 'It is not to be told, even to the elemi, until they join Ekeji Orisha in Iletigu. But in Adamawara, all are free, and may see the gods. It is permitted that men of all the tribes may take part in Ogo-Ejodun, to bear witness to the worthiness of the elemi, and the tribes of white men are not excepted. If it is your desire, you may go to Iletigu when the next day comes; that is the law. But you may not know the secret of the heart of Olorun; that is forever forbidden to you.'

Noell did not have to ask the meaning of Ogo-Ejodun, of which he had heard before. Ejodun, which meant season of blood, was the title which the Uruba gave to all their most important sacrifices. Ogo was ordinarily used to refer either to a knobbed club or to the penis. Noell had seen the mutilated genitals of Ghendwa and the Sahra elemi, and had already deduced part of the rite by which men became elemi. Ogo-

Ejodun was the further *ikeyika*; the African vampire sabbat. That much he already knew. However important it might be in the eyes of the elders, Noell suspected that it had little to do with the more fundamental aspect of the transformation of man into vampire. Though he had never seen Kantibh naked, Noell surmised that that sense in which he was unfinished – aitigu – was that his prick was unmutilated. He had not undergone Ogo-Ejodun, and yet he was preserved from pain and death. Clearly, therefore, it was the heart of Olorun which freed men from pain and postponed the moment of death.

'What of the medicine which made the aitigu?' asked Noell. 'You no longer make it, I assume, to save those in direst need from the silver death?'

For the first time he had the satisfaction of seeing Kantibh startled, and even the solemn black vampires who silently flanked him gave some slight suggestion of surprise – but then Kantibh glanced briefly at the door, and Noell knew that he had remembered Berenike.

'That secret was buried, long ago,' Kantibh told him. 'The aitigu who were ancestors to your Attila betrayed the trust that was placed in them. They had not wisdom, because they were not finished. Ekeji Orisha commanded that the secret be forgotten, and the arokin among the elders have erased it from their minds.'

'It does not seem to be forgotten in Europe,' observed Noell, drily.

'It is buried,' repeated Kantibh, 'and gone forever from the world.'

By this crude insistence, the Persian told Noell the most valuable thing, in his estimation, that he had so far learned. It told him that it was possible – even likely – that the vampires of Europe were not made in the same way that their ancestors had been made in Adamawara. If that were true, he thought, then not all the ways in which vampires might be made were known in Europe. Perhaps – was it possible? – the way in which Attila had made vampires was not fully understood by the elders of Adamawara.

'Perhaps it is better so,' said Noell, with soft and silky insincerity. 'But when the armies with their cannon come to conquer Adamawara, they will surely want to dig it up.' He knew as he said it that it might be a foolish thing to say, but he could not resist the temptation. For more than a hundred days, it seemed, these men had put him to the question when he was helpless to resist, and heaven alone knew what he might have told them. He wanted to say things to them now which might cause them a little discomfort, if he could.

Again, all three of the squatting men reacted, but not with any exaggerated alarm.

'What army do you mean?' asked Kantibh, coldly.

'I do not know,' Noell told him, boldly. 'But you must know from what Quintus and I have told you that it can only be a matter of time. It may be the Fulbai, or other black tribesmen, or it may be the

Mohammedans from the Arab nations, or it may be white men from Gaul; but in the end, they will come. So many others have come, have they not? One day, conquerors will come, with machines of death more powerful than any that the tribesmen have. You already know, I think, how hungry the Ashanti and the Edau are for guns. How long will it be, do you suppose, before the Oba of Benin and his soldiers decide that they need bend no longer to the will of the Ogbone?'

'Where the Ogbone are,' said the elemi called Aiyeda, speaking in a voice like rustling leaves, 'the will of Olorun is. The Mohammedans may cross the desert, but they cannot cross the forest lands, which belong to Egungun. No one can. Ours is the heart of Olorun, and the breath of life. If you doubt it, you have not wisdom.'

'The silver death is no threat to vampires,' Noell told him. 'Perhaps the Fulbai and the Mohammedans are helpless to cross the forest, but a legion of vampire knights would be an army of a different kind. One day, an army of the aitigu will come.'

'An army of the aitigu cannot march without blood,' said Kantibh, as though it settled the matter, but Aiyeda held up a hand to command him to be silent.

'In your land,' said the Oni-Shango, 'Common men and aitigu are locked in enmity. You have told us this. You have told us that the common men of Gaul will rise against the aitigu and destroy them all. Which is your true prophecy? The one which you voice now, in cunning wakefulness, or the one which Shigidi brought from your mouth?'

'I am not, alas, a prophet,' Noell told him. 'The future holds many possibilities.'

But Aiyeda turned his head slightly, to signify his rejection of this statement. For him, there was only one future, whose shape was determined by his dark gods. To Aiyeda, a prophecy derived from god-guided dreams was worth infinitely more than any saying of a waking man, and he must have listened very carefully to what Noell had said while babbling in his dreams. Suddenly, Noell felt a small stab of contempt for the elemi, who did not know the true worth of reason. Perhaps it was a matter yet to be settled, who truly had the happiness of wisdom, and who did not.

In fact, as Noell was quick to notice, it seemed from the way that Kantibh then took up the conversation again that future possibilities and probabilities were of some concern to the people of Adamawara, and that the elemi were not entirely content to rely on the messages of dreams, whether his or their own.

'With every year that passes,' said Kantibh, reverting again to Latin. 'Gaulish ships come further south. It is said that some have already sailed around Africa to reach India. Why is this happening? Is it because your emperor hopes to extend his rule across this continent?'

'I think not,' said Noell. 'The vampires do not like the sea. They never like to travel in small numbers, and seem uneasy with the thought that if they are pitched into the sea they will sink to the bottom in their strange deep sleep, there to be devoured alive by the grateful fish. A few vampires in charge of a loyal army do not fear mutiny, because everyone knows what a punishment would be visited upon mutinous soldiers, but the crew of a ship might always sail away to some safe haven. The ocean is vast, it seems, and there are too many islands upon it. The vampires who rule Gaul rarely trust themselves to the ocean, and they are content to leave the captaincy of ships to common men.'

'Is it only common men, then, who have brought their ships to the Afric shores?' asked Kantibh.

'Oh yes,' Noell told him. 'The bravest of them love to sail the oceans because it frees them a little from vampire rule. It is common men who have learned how to make their vessels bigger and more clever, by combining the square and triangular sails. It is common men who are ambitious to enrich themselves by trading, and ambitious to discover new lands. The vampires have sometimes tried to stop voyages of discovery, but they are not entirely united in that purpose. Even the Spanish and the Portugese, whose adventures were severely inhibited in my father's time, now venture forth freely, to compete with the British and the Dutch. But British ironwork is the best in the world, and the Dutch make the best ships, so it is the northern nations of Gaul which accomplish the greatest things upon the sea.

'Some sea captains dream of finding another great continent on the surface of the globe, where Christian men might establish an empire of their own, to be defended against vampire invaders in the way that the Mohammedans defend their desert wilderness. Perhaps the vampires, under force of necessity, will take to the sea, in time, but the ships whose journeys are measuring the full extent of your shores are extending the interests of common men for now. It is of little concern to Ogbone.'

'All which exists is the concern of Ogbone,' said Kantibh, coolly. 'Ogbone is the great guardian of the world, which makes it a fit and lawful place, and secures the well-being of the brotherhood of tribes.'

'We have different ideas of well-being, I think,' said Noell, still trying to find a vent for his spite against these men, who had abused him while he was helpless. He knew that his words were reckless, but for the moment he did not care.

Aiyeda reached out a claw-like hand to touch Kantibh's arm before the Persian could reply, and spoke again, in Uruba. 'The gods have given us Ogbone,' he said, 'to make order in the world. There is a brotherhood of tribes, though there are many tribes in the world who do not know it. One day, all the tribes will accept Ogbone, and all men will know the will of Olorun. The aitigu who betrayed Ogbone will be called to account by the risen dead, and Oro will destroy the guilty. We are the breathers of life, and without us the tribes are beset by shame and strife. You do not know it, but Shigidi has helped you tell us the truth of the future. There will be war, in all the parts of the world where the will of the Ogbone is not there to contain it; that war will destroy the tribes which have set themselves outside the brother-hood, and those which remain will accept the guidance of the elemi.' He looked directly at Noell, his staring eyes as black and bright as a bird's. 'Do you know no ancestors of your own?' he asked, softly. 'Have you no babalawos, no arokin, to describe the shape of the future and the past?'

Noell was surprised by the question. 'We have a holy book,' he said, 'which tells us that we are descended from Adam and Eve, who lived in Eden, but were expelled for a sin they committed, whose stain upon the soul of mankind saddened the God which made us. The same book tells us that God sent his son to redeem us, and show us the way to Heaven, and it is promised that the son of God will return to earth again, to put an end to our troubles.'

'We know the book,' said Aiyeda. 'But you do not believe it?'

'No,' said Noell, reluctantly, though he did not know why he should be reluctant. 'I do not. Quintus is a believer, who trusts God and Jesus. I cannot. For me, past and future are alike unknown; the latter yet to be made by the hopes and desires of men.'

'And the vampires of Gaul?' asked Kantibh. 'What do they believe?'

'That,' said Noell, 'I cannot tell you. They have set their own pope upon the throne of St. Peter, and rule the Church as they rule all else in Gaul and Walachia, but their beliefs are not the same as the beliefs of common men. They keep the secret of their own beliefs because it includes the secret of their nature. The early vampire lords were not Christians, but pagans. Later, a few encouraged the Christian belief that vampires were demons, because it helped to make men fear them. Nowadays, they pretend instead to belong entirely to the Christian world. The new Churchmen preach the doctrine that men and vampires each have their place in God's scheme, and that God has ordered the estate of each kind. But I cannot tell you what the Borgia pope really believes, and can only say that his is not the True Faith, but a masquerade.'

'The truth is in Adamawara,' said Aiyeda. 'Without that wisdom, and the guidance of their ancestors, a tribe has no finished men, but only wayward children, who do not know how to live.'

'What tribute do you extract from the tribes outside this valley, to whom you send vampires to serve as wise men?' asked Noell.

'None by force or obligation,' said Kantibh. 'They send many gifts, but it is neither asked nor expected. The wise ones return to the tribes as of right, for they are the ancestors of those tribes, and to them they belong in part, though they belong also to Adamawara.'

'Do you produce everything that you need, here in the valley?'

'Everything that we *need*,' said Kantibh.

'Do you smelt iron?'

'No. We have little need of iron, for we do not make cannon, or any of the other follies of your world, but we have iron tools, sent to us by the Uruba, and tin from the Jawara.'

'You know of the iron of Gaul, and the things which we make with it? Weapons and machines are not counted among the things which you need?'

'They are not,' replied Kantibh, dismissively. 'It is the frailty of common flesh which gives you such regard for the products of your ingenuity. If your vampires love iron and the things which it makes, it is because they fear the common men whom they rule. Here, there is no fear, and no need of iron.'

Noell looked again at the black vampire Aiyeda, who was still watching him intently. He knew full well, as he looked at those birdlike eyes which measured him, that he was telling them as much with his questions as with his answers, but it was a blade which cut both ways. Now that he was awake and aware, there was a great deal that he might discover, simply in finding out what they wanted to say to him. He still did not know what they thought of him, or what they intended to do with him. He was not even certain, now that he saw what they were like, what he ought to want of them, or what he might obtain if he was clever enough. But he would see Ogo-Ejodun; that much at least was promised. As for the making of heart of Olorun, which none was permitted to know, and the medicine which had been forgotten, he must wait to see what might be learned.

'I am tired,' he said, truthfully. 'No more questions now. You will return, I suppose?'

'Oh yes,' said the Persian, smoothly. 'We will return.'

FIVE

Noell sat tiredly upon his rough bed, regretting now its roughness. With the return of consciousness and sanity had come the return of petty discomforts and annoyances – small aches and pains. But it was not the things which he could feel which caused him most anxiety; it was the parts of his body to which feeling had not yet returned.

The silver death had almost lost its grip on his flesh, but the stain still lingered in his lower legs and in his feet, whose numbness made it difficult for him to walk. He was eager to leave this grey cell and

begin the work of exploring the house into which he had been taken –
and after that the valley of Adamawara – but his body's work of self-
repair had not yet run its full course.

When he pulled his right ankle up on to his left thigh, where he
could conveniently massage it, he looked anxiously at the ashen
mottling, which was in some places under the sole only beginning to
fade. There were places on his left foot where the stain was still very
black, and when he jabbed such places with his fingernails, which had
grown long during his illness, there was no sensation of sharpness and
no pain. He could feel the pressure, but only as a dull presence.

Was this, he wondered, what vampires felt instead of pain, when
they were so minded?

His eye was caught then by the bundle of his possessions which had
been placed in the room, at the foot of the bed. In an open pack, on
top of other things, was the box which contained the microscope and
its various accessories. It lay on top, he presumed, because it had been
investigated carefully by his hosts.

He pulled the box towards him, and found within it a small knife,
whose blade was as sharp as a razor, and which he used for slicing thin
sections of plant and animal tissue. Carefully, he placed the blade beside
the darkest area of his foot which he could find, and he began to draw
it across, scraping a thin sliver of flesh. He could feel the cut distinctly
enough, but it was not painful.

The first piece which he removed was only skin, almost translucent,
and only slightly stained with black. The greatest concentration of
abnormal colour was deeper, and he had to take a second cut before he
produced a thin layer of flesh which was almost jet black in hue. The
cut bled sluggishly, the blood discoloured purple, but it did not hurt.

He placed each of the two slivers on glass slides, and then dipped his
finger in the water-jug beside his bed. He dabbed a tiny drop of water
on to each slide, with practised delicacy, and then laid other slides on
top, so that the thin pieces of flesh were trapped.

Quickly, he set up the microscope on the wide stone sill of the
window, assembling the pieces rapidly but carefully. The light was
well-nigh perfect, the sky bright and clear with the sun high above. It
was easy to catch sufficient light with the concave mirror beneath the
stage to let him see what there was to see.

At first, he was disappointed. The first slide was very like many
other pieces of skin which he had examined, with just a little diffuse
colour. Even the second was less interesting than he had hoped, but he
could see that the black colour was not evenly distributed within the
flesh; it belonged, in fact, to structures which looked oddly like
spiderwebs. He had seen their like before, when investigating certain
moulds. So the silver death was something which invaded the body,
and grew within it. It was a living thing, a kind of mould. What, then,

of the changes which came into the body with it? What determined the loss of feeling in the affected parts? How was it responsible for that long, strange sleep, like and yet unlike the sleep into which vampires went when they were hurt?

His mind went back to the explanation of his ideas which he had tried to give to Leilah in Burutu. Was it possible that the silver death changed the atoms of human flesh in some way, to make them more like the atoms of vampire flesh?

He looked at the microscope quizzically, wondering whether it would show him more, if only he knew exactly what to look at. But it could not tell him what flesh was made of, or how one kind of flesh differed from another. It could show him the different appearances of skin and bone, muscle and blood, but not the difference between commoner and vampire.

Was it possible, he wondered, that the heart of Olorun was nothing more than another kind of mould – found, like the silver death, in Adamawara and nowhere else? He could not believe it. It was not so simple. And yet the making of vampires was not so simple a matter as his father had thought, either, for however the elemi gave the heart of Olorun to the wise ones who earned it, it was not by common buggery or any other form of sexual intercourse. Nevertheless, it was not Satan, or any Uruba counterpart, who came from outside the earth to import his demons into the flesh of men; of that he was certain. Whatever took the place of the black semen of Satan, about which Guazzo wrote with such relish, it was something of this world, not of any supernatural realm.

The truth, he told himself, *was supposed by Francis Bacon to be manifest, if only we could cast down the idols of false belief, which prevent our seeing it. My father thought that he had cast down those idols, and that what remained was naught but buggery, but he was wrong. There is one more idol yet to be broken, but I do not know its name.*

And then, as an afterthought, he added: *Shigidi. Perhaps its name is Shigidi.*

He had never taken Guazzo's account of the vampire sabbat seriously. His father had laughed at it, and Quintus too. It was a nightmare, conjured up from fear and dread, and dressed with any repulsive detail which the writer could discover. Of course the devil's semen would be black, just as his prick must be as cold as ice and as big as a horse's member. It was for a similar reason the sabbat must also involve the sacrifice of babies and the eating of their flesh. Nothing could be spared if it would make the image of the occasion more frightful.

But was not Edmund Cordery's account of the making of vampires a nightmare too? Was it not the case that it still wore the same dress of repulsiveness and horror? And as for Ogo-Ejodun . . . why, the name itself promised an abundance of nightmare elements. Babies really were sacrificed, it seemed, in that season of blood which belonged to Olori-merin; could there be any doubt that pricks were cut off in Ogo-Ejodun – a violation which many would consider more nightmarish than buggery?

It was all nightmares. Shigidi had a hand in all of it.

Noell sat back in his chair and stared out of the open window at the sky, looking into infinity. The source of vampirism was here in Adamawara. The silver death was here too, and nowhere else. Was that yet another idol of confusion, part of the smokescreen of falsehoods in which the truth was concealed?

In Africa, vampire women were not commonly seen. Berenike might be, for all he knew, the sole exception. But the elemi, unlike the aitigu, could not penetrate a woman – or a man either, for that matter – because of the mutilation that was done to them. Could they still make and discharge semen? Perhaps. But still, the elemi lay with no one. When they made vampires, it was not by means of any sexual intercourse. How had the forgotten medicine been administered which saved those likely to die from the silver death? Was it fed to the sufferers in their food, or like most African medicines smeared upon the body? Did it carry the seed of vampirism to fight the seed of the silver death? Was the seed of vampirism a similar thing to the silver death? Vampires were not stained silver, but their skin was certainly changed, in colour and in texture, and their hair was almost always altered too. Was vampirism no more than a benign mould, which preserved instead of spoiling, and was the silver death merely its malign counterpart, a breath of Satanic hell instead of Heavenly immortality?

Noell put his head in his hands, wishing that he could see a way through the cloud of questions. *Oh father!* he said, silently. *Would that I had thy counsel to help me now.*

The Lady Carmilla, he remembered, had asked Edmund Cordery if he had looked through his marvellous device at human blood. Did that mean that she thought the secret was to be found in blood? Or had she simply been too cautious to mention semen? Had she been encouraging her mechanician-lover to go in the wrong direction, or had the vampires' fascination with blood become the focus of their own superstitions? And if Edmund Cordery were right, and Gaulish vampires at least were made by some kind of transfigured semen, then where did the blood fit in? What kind of nourishment did the blood provide?

Noell had looked at blood beneath the microscope, and had seen that its redness, like the blackness of this disease, was carried in rounded corpuscles, and that there were other shadowy forms abroad in the straw-coloured fluid which coursed in the veins. Might the vampires need some shadowy thing which was only found in common blood?

There were too many questions, and too many possible answers. He could not find a way through the wilderness of ifs. But he felt a paradoxical sense of confidence, because he felt that he was nearer to the answer than he had ever been before. He had returned from Shigidi's realm of nightmares and was as clear-sighted now as a man could be. He felt that his eyes and his mind were ready to break idols, to see through smokescreens.

The vampires of Adamawara, he thought, *have no need of iron, no need of machines. They can do what they need to do, and think that they need not look beyond. But I think they do not know what they are. Though their elders may have lived here three thousand years, their eyes are blinded by countless idols. Ogo-Ejodun is a nightmare, but somewhere within it is a very different dream, which I intend to see if I can.*

He dismantled the microscope, then, and put his slides away. He did not destroy the slides which he had made from his own flesh, but he knew that when they dried out they would begin to decay.

He lay upon his bed, but he did not sleep. His mind was racing, and it was almost as if the mental efforts he had made were bringing back his delirium. When servants brought food to him, as the sun was setting, he still had not slept, but he was rested. The food was most welcome, his appetite having returned in full measure, and when he had eaten his fill his thoughts became calmer again. The heaviness of the meal in his belly had a soporific effect, and though he lit a candle by his bed he went quickly into a deep sleep.

He was awakened by a gentle pressure on his shoulder, which eased him back from somewhere very remote, where there were no dreams to trouble him.

It was Berenike who had woken him. She was sitting on the mattress beside him, her white robe falling away from her shoulders, though the night was cold, almost exposing the nipples of her breasts. Her bare arms reached out to him, so that her hands cupped his face.

Her fingers seemed very cold.

He remembered that stories of nocturnal visits by vampires to suck the blood of unsuspecting victims always said that the touch of a vampire was cold, and now, of all times, he realised how obvious it was that it should be so. Common men hugged their clothes and blankets about them, to shield them from the cold, but vampires did not need to do that. All a vampire had to do was forget the hurt of the cold. And so, by night, vampires became cold, unless they took care not to.

He knew, by the way she touched him, that she had not come to him now to offer him comfort, and console him in his distress. She had come to answer her own need. And yet she seemed so distant, so apart from things, as though she walked perpetually between waking and dreaming.

Is she mad? he wondered. *Have the centuries through which she has lived taken toll of her senses and her mind?*

He did not feel the same powerful attraction toward Berenike that he had felt towards Cristelle. It was not that her beauty was the less, but rather that beauty had somehow changed the meaning which it had for him. In earlier days, he had felt helpless in the grip of desires which seized him as though from without, and he had struggled against them. Now, his desires seemed much more a part of himself, and he did not feel that he was held captive by the beauty of her appearance. He knew that he had the choice, to offer his blood to her, to accept her caresses.

He took her in his arms, and kissed her. And then, because she was careless of the coldness of her body, he drew her under his blankets, to warm her, so that he could more easily bear her touch.

She had brought her own sharp-pointed instrument, with which to open his vein, and though it hurt far more when she used it than the knife which he had earlier used to cut himself, he found that the pain was not entirely unpleasant, and that what he received in compensation was worth more than he had imagined.

This day, he told himself, without shame or accusation, *I am become my father's son.*

Afterwards, she clung to him without affection, as though completely lost in thought. He had anticipated coolness, but found this exaggeration of her remoteness annoying. She was not aware of him as a person, as Noell Cordery, but merely as an item of flesh, to serve her hungers. He knew that she must have taken blood almost every day of her life, but he did not know how often she had combined her blood-letting with love-making. For all that he knew, he might be the first man she had lain with for centuries.

As he brushed her face with his hand, he felt a cold tear at the corner of her eye. Strangely, that affected him more than anything else which had happened between them.

He touched her eye again, wonderingly, and though he spoke no question, she began to talk, as she must have talked when she came to him in his season of dreams. Shigidi was with her, and perhaps was always with her, releasing the secret thoughts which were poisons in her soul. He had come back from Shigidi's realm, and now was cleansed. She never had.

'All lovers die,' she said, in Latin. 'They change and die, or they change and never die, but when they change so that they never die, they can be lovers no more. Sometimes, I wish that I might die, but never enough to contrive it. Love is not so important as life, and that is why I weep. I often weep – once or twice in every hundred years.'

The words, spoken in a tongue which was neither her first language nor his, sounded quite devoid of emotion. There seemed to Noell to be a barrier raised between them, which prevented them from sharing any real unity, even in their physical intimacy.

But it might have been different with Cristelle, he thought.

Then he changed his mind. *It would not*, he told himself. *It would not.*

'I can love,' she assured him, though he could not believe her. 'I have lived so long in this unchanging place that I can only love things which come from without, but I can love. I love you all the more, because you are so near in looks to my own kind, and because you suffered so with the sickness. It seemed at one time as though you might die, and I weep for that thought. I weep often.'

Perhaps, if she had been speaking English, she would have addressed him as 'thou'. In his mind he could have translated the Latin words in order to produce that sense of intimacy, but he did not. Latin was the language of scholars and of the Church, and it had no intimacy in it. It was entirely right that they should be speaking in that tongue.

'I am glad,' he told her, 'that you chose me above Langoisse.' But Langoisse, he remembered, was old now, and not the handsome figure he had seemed when first Noell knew him.

'And now,' she said, continuing with the thread of her own thought without attending to his interpolation, 'they will let you die, because they have begun to think that all the world, outside Adamawara, is unworthy of their gift of law. They will let you die, and ask that all the world dies with you, save only Adamawara.'

Does she know whereof she speaks? Noell wondered. *Or is it merely the wandering of her mind?*

'Do you never long to leave here?' he asked her. 'To return to the world from which you came?'

'No,' she answered. 'This is the only world where I have been happy. The world from which I came used me cruelly, and I shall never return.'

'You would not lack for lovers there,' he told her.

'When death is always near,' she said, 'it matters more what kind of life you live. When death is far away, life is precious in itself, and the years are their own reward. I can love, but first of all is life. I will live forever, if I can.'

'You will not come with me, then, when I go away?' The question was much to tease as to test her, for he already had her answer, and he sought only to draw out of her some exclamation of regret at the thought of his departure. But that was not what happened, for she picked her head up from where it lay upon his shoulder, and looked him in the eye for the first time since they had made love together.

'When you go,' she said, her voice seeming more strange than it had been before, 'it will be to your grave. I cannot follow you there. But I will shed a tear. I will shed a tear, for the love I lost.'

This reassurance did not cheer him Indeed, he felt as if the blood were running cold within his veins, for she had spoken to him across the centuries, whose passing – if she could be believed – he was not destined to share.

SIX

The next day, when Kantibh came to him Noell asked to see Quintus and his other companions. Kantibh agreed immediately, and for the first time Noell left the room where he had been confined during his illness. The route by which he was taken led him through cloisters and passages such as one might find in the monasteries or prisons of the outer world. The doors through which they passed were made of wood, and all seemed very old. In one room which they passed he saw Ngadze, apparently well, but he did not linger there, being impatient to see Quintus. The monk was lodged in a room very like his own, no more than forty yards away.

Quintus was still in his bed, too feeble to rise from it even though there was no trace of blackness beneath his skin. Kantibh had told Noell that Langoisse was in a like condition, and would find it very difficult to talk coherently, but Quintus was conscious and quite clear-headed. He was delighted to see Noell enter the room, and pleased to see him strong enough to move about, albeit limpingly.

At first, Kantibh seemed inclined to linger, but as soon as Noell asked that he might be left alone with his friend the Persian withdrew. Noell squatted down upon the mat beside the bed, feeling quite comfortable; he had grown used to places where there were no chairs during his long exile.

'How are the others?' Quintus asked him.

'I have spoken only to Langoisse,' answered Noell, 'and he is in a very distressed state. He is still sick. I have seen Ngadze, though, and I am told that Leilah and Ntikima are recovering well. I will try to see them both. Kantibh seems anxious still to bother me with questions, though I suspect that between the two of us, we have told them a great deal of what they sought to discover.'

'Perhaps,' said the monk. 'I am not certain that they know exactly what it is that they seek to know. What have they said to you?'

The two exchanged details of their interrogations.

'What do you suppose they will do with us?' asked Noell, when the monk had finished his account.

'They will keep us, and be kind to us, while we are docile. I do not think that they will harm us if we do not offend them, and Aiyeda has said that the elemi will be glad to learn all that I care to teach them of the wisdom of the world. They treat me as though I were a babalawo of some distant tribe, as the Edau and the Uruba came to reckon me.'

'Will you tell them all that they want to know?'

'Certainly,' said the monk. 'God made me a teacher of truths, and I will teach them to any who care to know. Adamawara is not the enemy of other nations. We came here out of curiosity, and its people have the right to be curious about us.'

'And if we should desire to leave when the rains end, to carry what we have learned back to the world from which we came. Will they help us to do that?'

Quintus shook his head. 'I do not know. We have not yet been fully examined, and I do not think they will decide so soon what they want to do with us. Without a vampire guide to intercede with the tribesmen and help us with his medicines, without pack animals, without guns, we would have little chance of returning to Burutu. I do not think they intend to give us these things. It is no part of their plan that we should carry news of Adamawara back to Europe; it is possible that they would kill us rather than let us try. On the other hand, they might give us leave to go, and bid us a sorrowful farewell, secure in the conviction that we would die in the attempt.'

'And what if we stay?'

'It is too early to judge, but they seem determined that we should not become aitigu, and despite that they call me a babalawo and are ever ready to speak of the great brotherhood of tribes, I do not think that they intend to make me one of them.'

'I am sure,' said Noell, drily, 'that they have no intention of welcoming me to their ranks. In any case, I do not think I would like to play the sacrifice at Ogo-Ejodun. I wonder if they have really forgotten the secret of making aitigu, but I suppose they would never reveal it to us if they had it still. I have the feeling that what we have told them of our world has troubled them, and I may have taken too little care to spare their anxieties. I fear that they will not readily let us go.'

'They have little to fear,' said Quintus. 'They are walled about by stone cliffs, evil forests and deadly disease. No army could hope to conquer this citadel while the silver death remains its moat. They seem sincerely to believe that the empires of the aitigu will come to naught, and have taken our enmity against the vampires of Gaul as evidence supporting that conclusion. But you are right, I think; they are troubled by what we have told them, and what Ntikima has told them, and what they have found in the possessions which we brought. I suppose they have taken Langoisse's guns?'

'I do not know,' admitted Noell, 'But I would not be surprised. Is it their aim, do you think, to extend the rule of Ogbone throughout what they are pleased to call the brotherhood of tribes, even to the cold Siberian wastes, the Indies and far Cathay? Might Adamawara be a vision of the world as it must one day become?'

THE SEASON OF BLOOD 221

'How can I tell?' replied the monk. 'Perhaps the common men of Europe and Asia will be reconciled to vampire rule one day, and be willing to play the part of cattle, as the Mkumkwe here seem content to do. Perhaps this is the only kind of paradise which the earth has to offer, and perhaps it is only a paradise of fools, who have convinced themselves that they are all-wise because they have lived so long with a foolish faith.'

'I am not sure that these vampires are united among themselves,' said Noell. 'Kantibh and Berenike are not like Aiyeda and the other elemi they brought to see me. I do not find it difficult to imagine how those other young ones, who went as ambassadors to the world to serve the cause of Adamawara, came to betray that cause. The elemi who live with the further tribes have lives of their own, and within a secret society like Ogbone, there may flourish societies more secret still. I am not convinced that the rule of the elders can be eternal.'

'Perhaps not,' said the monk.

'I see that there is a balance here, which there is not in Europe,' said Noell. 'In Africa, the elemi have made their condition less enviable, and they exploit the natural deference these tribesmen have for magicians, for the old, and for their ancestors. I suspect that they die almost as quickly as they are created, so that the order of things changes very slowly. In Gaul, what was once a handful of vampires has gradually become a legion, and that increase offers both a temptation and a threat to common men. If we seek to see the shape of the future, it is easier to imagine the triumph of the aitigu, who will multiply themselves until they are enough to secure any goal. Even if common men can bring about the fall of Attila's empires, I doubt that vampirism would disappear from the world, as the Mohammedans would wish; once its secret is set free in our world, then every man and woman born will want to be a vampire.'

'Where, in a world of many vampires, would vampires find the blood to feed themselves?' asked Quintus, softly. It was the old riddle, asked even by children, offered as a proof that vampires must always be sparing with their gift, that there must always be common men to serve the drinkers of blood.

'If what makes a common man a vampire is a kind of creature,' said Noell, reflectively, 'and if what there is in human blood which vampires need is also a kind of creature, then we might hope to find a way of liberating the one creature from the semen of vampires, and the other from the blood of men. If we could do that, then vampires would not need common men to nourish them, and common men would not need vampires to convert them. Then there might be a world of immortal men.'

'A world without children,' Quintus reminded him, softly.

'Women might have their children first,' Noell pointed out, 'and be converted later. A world of immortals would not need so very many children.'

'What kind of a world might that be?' asked Quintus. ' A world like Adamawara, without the servants. A world of people who became older and older, ancient whatever their appearance, settling more securely into their habits, not only careless of divine mercy but uninterested in change, unable to find anything new. A paradise, do you think?'

Noell thought of Berenike, cold through and through, all but lost to the world of thought and feeling. But that was not the path of thought which he was trying to explore.

'What of a world of men who really did become wiser and wiser, without limit or end?' he asked. 'What of a world of men intent on discovery, from whom nothing could ultimately be hid? Not uninterested in change, or unable to find anything new. Perhaps it is only fear which confines the undying within ironclad tradition, committed to changelessness. The immortals who live now cling to what they have, but perhaps it is not necessarily so. When all danger is gone, when all fear is finished, then exploration of the new might be all joy, all pleasure. Might it not?'

Quintus bowed his head, wearily. 'I cannot tell,' he said. 'I think no one can. I think that I would rather trust in the life which God has made for me.'

The monk was too tired to continue the discussion, so Noell bade him farewell, and promised to come again. He went to the door, and asked a passing servant to summon Kantibh, and when the Persian came he asked where he could find Leilah.

She was further away, in another corridor down a precipitate stair. She was well enough to be up and about, though he thought it must be the first time she had dressed herself, ready to return to the world at large. When she saw him, she leapt to her feet with obvious delight.

'I tried to come to thee,' she told him, 'but I could not find thee, and could not make myself understood. They have been kind to me, most especially this man Kantibh, who has taught me some words of his language, and managed to tell me that thou wert well.'

Noell turned to Kantibh, and thanked him for that kindness. The Persian bowed, and withdrew again to leave them to talk.

'Have you been very ill?' asked Noell.

'I thought that I would die,' she told him. 'I was lost in awful nightmares, and more than once I thought that my soul was consigned to your Christian Hell.'

'Be thankful they could not speak to you,' he told her, 'else they would have questioned you even in thy dreams. But it must have been hard, with no one to speak to. I saw Langoisse, who was much disturbed, but I think that he is getting well now, and Kantibh does not think that he will die.'

'And Quintus?'

'I have come from his bedside. He is well. I saw Ngadze too, but not Ntikima.'

'I have looked out at this kingdom from my window. It seems to me a poor place, made all of stone, with no golden treasures to astound us after all. What shall we carry home, to make us rich?'

'We must see what we can find,' he told her, 'when we are well enough to travel across the valley. Perhaps the lake is shored with diamonds, and the hills are hewn from philosopher's stone, which will turn base lead to gold. But if it is only soil and stone, as it seems to be, at least we have come where few men have come before us, and none in nearly a thousand years.'

'And will I be a vampire now, to be thy noble courtesan?' She laughed, as she had always laughed, with the same forthrightness she had always had. He remembered her laughing like that when she and he had been little more than children.

'Your own people would stone you and burn your body,' he told her, without matching her laugh.

'Ha!' she said. 'I am an unbeliever, like thee, and do not care what those who once owned me would believe. I would that these were my people, they seem so nice and good. We will not go to Araby, my love, but to the grand courts of Gaul, where we will be vampires both, and have the best which all the world can offer.'

'But then we could not be lovers,' he reminded her.

She frowned at him, and said: 'But we are not lovers as we are, so where would be the loss? I think thou might love me better, though, if I were a vampire lady. Hast thou seen the one called Berenike?'

'I have,' said Noell.

'And has she come to thee, to drink thy blood?'

She laughed as she said it, but she was standing before him, looking up into his eyes, and before he could move to interrupt her she had reached up playfully, to pull the folds of his shirt apart, to look at his chest, where the marks of a vampire's knife would be.

It was only a game, a silly tease born of the high spirits which the sight of him had brought her to. But the shirt came away from his breast, and there were the punctures made by the vampire's awl, still livid near his nipple, and she saw what she had been morally certain that she would not see.

The colour drained away from her face, and her eyes grew hard as marble. When she raised her gaze again, to look him in the face, the high spirits were gone.

'You are not a monk,' she said, 'after all.'

He tried to remember whether there had ever been a moment when she had forgotten herself, and called him 'you' instead of 'thou'. If there had been such occasions, he had not noticed them.

'Leilah . . . ' he said.

She turned away. 'Oh no,' she said. 'I am the pirate's mistress, and your sisterly friend. It matters not to me whether you are a monk, or a common man. I am your friend, and that is all. *Thy* friend. Choose thy lovers where thou wilt.'

'Yes,' he said, softly. 'Thou art my friend, and the best I have.'

She went to her window, and he followed her. They looked out at the great valley, which seemed very peaceful, and very orderly. The fields were bright beneath the golden light of the morning sun, and it was not too hard to think of this as a kind of Eden: a little garden-world cut off by high walls from a cruel and ugly vastness without.

There was a haze of dust in the air, though there was no wind blowing, which drew a veil across the lower slopes of the mountains. There was a single snow-capped peak in the great distance, which rose above the haze, like a crocodile's tooth pointing into the blue sky.

'Was it worth the hardship we had in coming here?' she asked, soberly.

'Perhaps,' he said. 'It is for Quintus and Langoisse to say, for it was they who brought us.'

'Will they make Langoisse the gift of eternal life?'

'It has been made clear to me that they do not think us altogether worthy. But if Langoisse can prove himself to the satisfaction of the elemi, who can tell?'

She smiled at that, but only briefly and sarcastically. 'You think my love can conduct himself like the noble Ghendwa, more monk than your friend the monk? I think his dream is to be a vampire like Cesare Borgia or the legendary Roland, not a withered sage like one of these. He dreams of becoming strong again, so that he might challenge Richard Lionheart to fight with him, as once he did before, and in his dreams he slays the wicked prince, time and time again. I suppose he cannot hope that they will give him what he wants. And what might I do to prove my own self worthy? What is it that I might become, to earn the station of yon Berenike? Perhaps I am too old, with crow's feet about my eyes and mouth, and ragged hair, and bruises in my flesh. When I was younger, though, I still had not the beauty of a vampire lady. What must I become, to live forever? Thou wilt tell me, I know, that I must give up the hope, that I must be content to wither away, and let the flesh decay upon my bones. We will grow old together, will we not, and grow apart?'

He took her in his arms, as he had on many an occasion before, to comfort her when she was sad or sick, or to bid her farewell when Langoisse was taking her away. 'Do not be afraid,' he told her. 'I do not think that anyone here means us any greater harm than to let us die in God's good time. If we do not offend them, they will not hurt us.'

This speech did nothing to soothe her ire, ignoring as it did the real cause of her distress.

'And that is our treasure?' she said, sharply. 'That is the victory which we have won in crossing half the world and coming near to death? If we are good, and take care not to offend, they will let us live! I beg you tell that to my friend Langoisse, and see what he will reckon to the privilege of dying here!'

He wilted under her scolding, demoralised. There was no answer he could give. It would do no good to declare that they had set out from Burutu a tiny army, but arrived in Adamawara in a very different condition, in no shape to attempt a conquest. It was not that helplessness, in any case, which had disturbed her

When he said goodbye, she would not let him kiss her on the lips, though she put her cheek upon his wounded breast, as if to listen to the beating of his wayward heart.

SEVEN

The place of the unfinished was a good deal larger than Noell had thought at first, but much of it was empty and derelict. If one looked at the windows, ledges and balconies which overlooked the valley there seemed to be only a few dozen dwellings, but let into the rock were dozens of winding corridors and tunnels, which gave access to many more chambers.

Noell discovered that the small and underpopulated realm of the aitigu did not easily offer access either to the plain far below or to the forest without. Clearly, there must be a way up from the Mkumkwe's fields, by which food was daily brought, but Noell realised that it must be as much within the mountain as without, and though he asked Kantibh where it was he could not get an exact answer. He was assured that when the time came, he would be taken to the valley floor, and across the plain to Iletigu, the place of the finished, which, he concluded, must be set in the opposite wall of the remarkable circlet of stony ramparts.

He found himself free to come and go as he pleased between Berenike's house and Kantibh's, where all his companions save Ntikima were lodged. He was let alone to explore the corridors and ledges as he pleased. Despite its title, there were many elemi in the place of the aitigu, which seemed in essence to be a place of instruction and learning.

There were many more instructors than pupils, and many of the elemi seemed to be engaged in some esoteric business of self-instruction. He soon became used to seeing crabbed and decrepit black men, squatting alone, murmuring to themselves in sing-song fashion as though entranced.

At first he thought that these meditators were communing with their gods, or sending themselves forth upon odysseys in the dreamlands of their private selves, but he soon realised that this was only a part of the story. In Adamawara there was neither paper nor parchment nor papyrus. Though the elemi knew the skills of inscription they used them in the most sparing fashion, cutting words in softer stones with tools which were mostly stone themselves. They had no books to store what they knew, but they had a great supply of memories which could extend over centuries, and so could keep that information which they deemed necessary in the heads of men which were carefully trained to bear it.

Noell had previously thought of the elemi as men trained in mock-practical arts – in medicine and magic, in the properties of plants and the dispositions of deities and demons. Perhaps that was so, among the tribesmen, but here in Adamawara the accumulation of wisdom which was counted most significant was the careful stocking of the memory with layer upon layer of information. As each long-lived generation passed away, these carefully-ordered edifices of words were handed on from one elemi to another, fixed by endless rhythmic repetition; every time that new things were added to the store, new elemi were appointed to make it part of the commonwealth of wisdom which was Adamawara.

When he first realised this, Noell's imagination was seized by the awesome weight of this tradition extending over thousands of years. He marvelled at the vastness of the stores which must be spun into the souls of these ancient arokin. But then he began to doubt. The real implications of it became clearer to him when the elemi began in earnest the business of taking from him that which he had to add to their store. He was by no means unenthusiastic to instruct them, and thought that he might have many things of value to impart. He was, after all, his father's son; a mechanician whose like the heart of Africa had never known. He was zealous to reveal to his hosts the secrets of pumps and turning-machines, of clockwork and gears, of drills and furnaces, bold in his intention to be a prophet of iron and of glass, and of all the means of manufacture which had created the world into which he was born.

Alas, that was not what Nyanya – the elemi appointed to be his master pupil – desired to know. What Nyanya wanted, first and foremost, was to learn the English language, and then the beliefs which the men who spoke that language had about the natural and supernatural worlds. What Nyanya wanted was the names of things, as if there were a special magic in naming whereby it was enough to know what a thing was called, rather than what it could be made to do. Nyanya wanted to know *what*, but never to know *how*. He wanted words in vast strings, to be spun around some invisible mental spool, creating a tight-wound thread which he might unravel at will. Nyanya's memory was, in its way, prodigious, but as Noell saw his own wealth of knowledge transformed as it passed from his own tongue to Nyanya's ear, he began to reappraise the wisdom of the elemi, and came to a different view of what they were.

Noell saw that the elemi were not so much masters of their knowledge as prisoners of it. He realised for the first time that a good memory, in the Gaulish way of thinking, was one which was not merely expert in remembering, but adept in forgetting too. The work of the mind which he was used to doing had often seemed to be cursed by doubt, generating questions far more prolifically than answers, but now he saw that this was no curse at all. The elemi did not deal in doubt, and permitted a traffic in questions so narrowly delimited that their mental universe was very different from his own.

Nyanya borrowed all the words that Noell could find for him, with an appetite insatiable, but Noell quickly grew tired of instructing him, not because he sought jealously to keep secrets from those who had made him captive, but because the sieve through which his given knowledge was strained upon receipt became a barrier which cut him off, and made the words he spoke into little more than empty noise.

Another barrier, no less confining to Noell's spirit, grew by degrees between himself and his vampire lover. He continued to live in her house, but it seemed to him that the moment he became properly conscious of her visits to his bed the weight of feeling invested in such occasions began a long decline.

Berenike had been the perfect lover when she was far more a creature of his dreams than a real being. Her beauty was no longer enough to satisfy him, now that he had become aware of her own dreaminess – her simplicity of mind, the emptiness of her life. He quickly found out that he was to Berenike no more than an instrument of self-stimulation, attractive by virtue of his colour and form, which seemed pretty to her, but not as a living and thinking being. He was conscious of the fact that as he became more familiar to her, she grew bored with him, and that she would eventually be finished with him, ready to put him away and commit him to some cobwebbed corner of her dreaming mind.

He might have transferred his awakened affection to Leilah, mortal as she was and lacking all the crystal beauty of a vampire, but Leilah's eagerness to be near him had gone now – evanished, it seemed, with the knowledge that he was vampire's prey. She avoided his company, and spoke to him coolly when they met. If he cornered her, she protested that she was his friend, and yet she had become unapproachable.

It was the other way round with Langoisse, who now deemed Noell a better friend than he ever had before, though he never spoke of that night when he had crawled into Noell's room, desperate with an anguish more hellish than the one which had given him his name. But Langoisse had not fully recovered from the silver death, or perhaps from the fevers which had preceded it – he remained very weak in body, and tired in spirit. He spent most of his days in his bed, and Leilah had often to be his nurse, for he did not like the Mkumkwe servants who attended him. No elemi took instruction from Langoisse, and it was clear to everyone that the pirate could not, in his present condition, contemplate a journey away from the haven of rest to which fate had brought him.

The only one who dissented from this opinion was Langoisse himself, and that as loudly as one who protests too much his innocence. Of them all, Langoisse spoke most often of the return, of the sea, of things which yet remained for him to do. How could he linger here, he asked his friends, when he still had accounts to settle in his own country? How quickly must the destined day be approaching when he would meet Richard the Norman, as once he had tried to do, on the field of honour? These rhapsodies of the imagination seemed to Noell to be a kind of delirium, and it was plain that the bed-ridden pirate had not completely returned from the dream-state into which the silver death had taken him.

Langoisse's friends humoured him in his fantasies and speculations, the sober Quintus as much as any.

It was, of course, to Quintus that Noell turned for solace and a sense of purpose. It was with Quintus that he discussed the passing of every day; what he had learned and what he hoped to know. But it was Quintus who was most excessively plagued and pestered by the vampires of Adamawara, who never supped his blood but sought instead to drain him of every thought his mind possessed. He, much more than Noell, was the one whose words they valued, the one whose memory they respected. Though he was not as sick as Langoisse, the journey had taken a heavy toll of Quintus too. The monk did not like to make an exhibition of his distress, but Noell was often reminded of the fact that this was an old man, nearly run to the end of his due threescore-years-and-ten, and that exhaustion of body and spirit was so near that only courage and endurance were keeping it at bay.

Noell asked himself whether any of them could even begin to contemplate a return to Burutu, let alone to Gaul. Appearance argued that they were condemned to measure out their years in this strangest of all the world's prisons. Noell recognised that in spite of his relative youth and considerable physical resources he was only half the man he once had been, and that there could be no guarantee that he would recover his own strength and wholeness. As the days went by, routine stifled initiative, and Noell grew use to his captivity. He gave no offence to his hosts, and lost sight of the thought that there might be any further advantage to be gained by what he was doing. Even when Kantibh first named the day of Ogo-Ejodun, it seemed far off, and no great cause for anticipation and excitement, but the interval passed smoothly, uninhibited by any impatience, and the hour eventually came when Noell and Quintus were invited to cross the valley for the first time. Langoisse was too weak to make the journey, and Leilah stayed to watch over him, but Ngadze was brought into the party, as one whose place in the Adamawaran scheme was yet to be determined. Of Ntikima there was no sign; he was nowhere to be found in the place of the aitigu

They began the descent to the great valley of Adamawara shortly after dawn, on winding stone staircases inside the mountain. Eventually, they emerged into the morning light, on an inclined path. Wherever the way was uncomfortably steep, steps had been cut to ease their passage. When the path turned on itself, as it did every hundred yards or so, the turning had been worked by stonemasons, and boulders were usually left on the rim, so that anyone sliding down the slope would not slip over the edge of the platform without having a chance to arrest his fall.

The closer they came to the floor of the valley the vaster it seemed. The further mountain ridges seemed to retreat, and this illusion was enhanced by the purple haze which cloaked them. The valley itself, by contrast, seemed the more full of life the closer they approached. Its fields of green and yellow came into sharper focus, so that they could see the crowns of the trees in the orchards, and the rows of dazoes, bean-plants, ground-nuts and egg-plant bushes.

Though he had passed before through African lands under intensive cultivation, near to the city of Benin, Noell had seen nothing remotely resembling the fields of Adamawara. Throughout the lands of the Kwarra delta the tribesmen lived in relatively small towns and villages, each cultivating only a few acres; the climate would not permit any other way of doing things. The tropic soil was exhausted very quickly, and the depredations of pests and weeds were difficult to resist. Fields and orchards like those of Adamawara would normally require the full-time attention of dozens of workers apiece. Here, if Noell's count of the white-clad toilers could be trusted, one man or woman could do the labour that would elsewhere require five or six. If the land all around was poisoned, why was the soil *within* the crater so good? Had the giant gnarled trees once extended their gloomy dominion over this land too, gradually cleared away by the labour of generations of tribesmen? He had to remind himself yet again that men and vampires had lived here for thousands of years, uninterrupted by invasions from without and, so far as he knew, undisturbed by strife and dissent within.

When they reached the foot of the cliff they found small horses waiting for them. Though the animals were bridled with rope they had no saddles or stirrups, and it was clear that they would move at a sedate pace. Kantibh rode at the head of their column, with the vampire who had brought the summons from the elders beside him. Quintus and Noell came next, with Ngadze behind them and two servants in the rear.

The villages of the people who lived on the valley floor were not stockaded or walled about in any way at all. Their huts were rounded, their conical roofs very squat. The villagers carried no weapons, and the men and women worked alongside one another in the fields. Wherever the horsemen went the villagers would stop to watch them pass, and small children would often follow them for a mile or more, running alongside the horses, calling out in their own tongue. Occasionally, Kantibh or one of his rearguard would shoo them away with shouts, but not roughly.

The heat was not oppressive at this altitude, and they had their straw hats to keep the sun from their faces, so the journey was not uncomfortable. They ate a midday meal in one of the villages, which was near the shore of the lake. Noell was glad to find that the lake had a large population of wading birds: the first birds he had seen in many a month. Their presence made the valley seem a little less alien. He concluded that the waters of the lake were rich in fish, though there were no boats on the water, and he saw no sign of fishing-nets in the village where they rested.

Beyond the lake the land changed its character, being no longer under such intensive cultivation. There were villages, but not so many, and the people seemed not to be involved in growing their own food, but rather in following other crafts, including the preparation of palm products, the making of pots, the carving of wood and a certain amount of metal-working. Long before the sun had descended to the rim of the western ridge they began the approach to Iletigu, the place of the elders. The eastern ridge of the valley was by no means so sheer or so high as the western one, and was rather different in character, there being many shale slopes and rocky screes, with loose boulders aggregating in clefts where poor soil supported meagre thorn-bushes and patches of parched grass. They followed a road, of sorts, worn by the passage of countless hooves and feet, with occasional cuttings which testified to the labours of men in times long past. Eventually, this road brought them to the so-called place of the finished.

This was certainly a much larger collection of dwellings than the place from which they had come. The city seemed vast as it sprawled over the haphazard undulations of half a dozen ridges, but though it was very large Noell was immediately struck by the idea that it seemed dramatically underpopulated. There were very few people – elemi or servants – to be seen in the streets. The buildings were made of stone rather than mud and clay, but they seemed very crude by comparison with the houses of Gaul.

The travellers did not go far through the city streets before they surrendered their horses to be stabled, and were taken into a narrow doorway into what seemed quite a small dwelling. It was not until they were inside, and had been taken some way along lamplit corridors, that Noell realised that this city, like the one from which they had come, was as much inside the crags as outside, and that the builders of the city, over the millennia, had taken full advantage of the many natural lacunae in the bedrock, as well as patiently quarrying new caves with their crude tools.

The stone corridors were very cold after the heat of the afternoon sun, and they were taken to a room with no furniture but mats upon the floor, where there were pitchers of water and platters of fruit and bread. Kantibh told them that he would send for coats, to keep them warm. He told them to eat what they would, and rest after their journey, because they would not be going to their beds for many hours. What they had come to see, he told them, they would see when the sun had set.

Noell ate sparingly, being more tired than hungry, and finding the gloom of the stony chamber not at all to his liking. The waiting was not easy, and their rest was not as comfortable as they might have hoped. Even when Kantibh brought them coats made from some kind of spun cotton cloth they still felt the cold, which made them shiver. They were glad indeed when the Persian told them that it was time to go, and led them away into the corridors, where they turned to left and right so many times that Noell completely lost his sense of direction.

In the end, they came out into the open again, into a place where the starlit sky was above them, albeit ringed by very high walls. They were in a kind of amphitheatre, with a series of circular steps surrounding an open space where four fires were burning, in the middle of which was a stone dais. There were candles on the dais, but none in the outer parts of the theatre, so that it was difficult to see the crowd which gathered there, seated in silence. Even so, Noell caught his breath in astonishment, for he had never seen such a crowd before.

He had grown used by now to the aged appearance of the vampires of Africa, and to the meanness of the flesh upon their bones. He had seen men who had put him in mind of walking skeletons, their cheeks drawn tight about their skull, and their hair reduced to fragile wisps of white. But he had seen such creatures one or two at a time, never in thousands, and never so strange as this. The lustrous, polished skin which was the mark of the vampire reflected light well, and the firelight was thrown back from a thousand faces, in such a way that the eyes were twin pools of shadow in every visage. This made the heads look like skulls indeed, and the elemi sat so still that it would have been easy to think of them as carved statues.

The faces all turned towards the newcomers as they emerged from the tunnel, so that the shadowed eyes might examine these strangers from another world. Noell understood this curiosity, but could not escape the feeling that those myriad eyes were looking at him with avid malevolence, transfixed by his pale and alien features, his frail and luscious flesh. He stopped, and Kantibh had to take his arm and pull at him insistently, drawing him away to the left. Noell allowed himself to be drawn, but he did not look where he was being taken; his eyes still scanned the serried ranks of the elders of Adamawara, who seemed more like a company of the living dead than a congregation of immortals. It was as if this was a court of corpses: a thousand maskless Egungun, lifted from their coffins to preside over a trial of living men.

Why he thought, *is this Hell after all? Is this a conventicle of sad souls brought to utter misery by the wiles of Satan?*

But the thought made him want to laugh, for it seemed in some idiotic way to be comical, and not terrifying at all. And he nearly did laugh, as Kantibh turned him and pushed him down, so that he sat upon a cold stone ledge, facing a gap between two of the fierce-burning fires.

Then, though it did not proceed according to the scheme laid down by Guazzo, the vampire sabbat began.

EIGHT

Some of the elemi near to the central stage, who held drums between their clenched knees, began to beat them with their hands. The sound was not loud, but the raps were sharp and clear in the still night air. There was a basic rhythm of three beats, carefully spaced and then repeated. Even before the voices joined in, Noell knew where he had heard it before, endlessly intoned by Ghendwa during the long nights of their epic journey.

A-a-a-a . . . da-a-a-a . . . ma!
A-a-a-a . . . da-a-a-a . . . ma!
A-a-a-a . . . da-a-a-a . . . ma!

Here, the meaningless phrase was carried by a thousand voices, each one no louder than a stage whisper, so that in sum the chant was like a restless seething tide, not loud but somehow filling the air. It possessed the attention of the listeners as completely as it absorbed the voices of the chanters.

A-a-a-a . . . da-a-a-a . . . ma!
A-a-a-a . . . da-a-a-a . . . ma!

Noell looked about him curiously. The elemi seated immediately behind him were now quite oblivious to his presence. Their eyes, like the eyes of all the others, were staring up into the sky, open but seemingly unfocused.

A-a-a-a . . . da-a-a-a . . . ma!
A-a-a-a . . . da-a-a-a . . . ma!

Kantibh was not chanting. Here, he was as much an outsider as those he had received into his house. Ngadze was silent too, and his face was masked with fear. Despite the fact that Kantibh did not join in the chant, it seemed to Noell that the Persian was willing prey to its hypnotic rhythm, and Ngadze too. While he watched Kantibh's face he thought that he could see all thought drain away, displaced by the reverberations of the rhythm; the Persian and the Ibau man were alike entranced, sucked into a magical vortex of some kind, as though transported into a dream. Noell had little difficulty in reacting against such absorption; he would not willingly surrender his thoughts to the dominion of Shigidi.

Noell scanned the firelit faces, which seemed identical and inter-changeable, though he supposed these men had been born into dozens of different tribes. Vampirism had transformed them all into the same thing. Adamawara belonged to all the tribes, and all the tribes belonged to Adamawara, for this was a place outside the common order of things.

A-a-a-a . . . da-a-a-a . . . ma!
A-a-a-a . . . da-a-a-a . . . ma!

This is no Sabbat, thought Noell, as the pulse-beat went through and through him. *It is not an act of worship, holy or unholy. What we have been brought here to witness is a transformation, a rite of passage. This is how the Africans see vampirism: it is a pathway to another kind of adulthood, to the membership of a tribe beyond all tribes.*

While the chant continued, several individuals came into the space marked out by the four fires. Noell saw them only as men in costume but he knew that the elemi did not see them thus. They came from shadows, as though materialising out of nothing, and they wore the raiment of gods and demons. He was not surprised to see Egungun: a whole troop of the risen dead, like that which had come to find them in the Tartarean forest. But there were others dressed in more striking masks, their bodies painted in garish colours. By likening their appear-ance to statues, carvings and symbols which he had seen in those Ibau and Edau villages which acknowledged the Uruba gods, he recognised these deities. He knew Shango by the streaks like lightning which ran across the shiny black flesh, and by the round stones which he held. He knew Elegba by the red and purple patterns on his skin, and by the phallic club which he wielded. By similar tokens he knew Obatala, Ogun and Ifa, and the goddesses Orisha Oko and Ododua. Nor was there any mistaking Olori-merin, the four-handed one, whose limbs were the directions of the compass, and whose body was entwined with snakes.

Four others came with them, naked and painted but not masked: men with bowed heads and loose-hung limbs. These, Noell guessed, were the wise ones sent by their tribes to be candidates for acceptance into the society of vampires – priests and magicians, shorn now of their regalia and made small of importance, before they might eat the heart of Olorun and take his breath of life.

Poor Msuri! lamented Noell. *He should be here, to take his place in this company, before this altar which is no altar at all.*

Noell watched the gods as they began a slow dance to the rhythm of the drums. How much it meant to the assembled elemi he could not guess, but to him, who could barely recognise which gods they were, it was difficult to fathom. He watched Shango enact the storm which was his appearance in the world, and hurl thunderbolts to the ground. He watched Elegba and Orisha Oko mime some mysterious communion which had to do with fecundity and replenishment, which also involved Obatala and Ododua his wife. He watched the dancing figures move as though to allow the passage of one invisible among them, and he guessed that Olorun too was there, unseen. The arena was too crowded, though, with the Egungun and the gods, and too poorly lit by the great fires whose play of brightness and shadow was full of confusion. The moving figures became blurred in Noell's sight as he tried to map the intricacies of their transactions.

A-a-a-a . . . da-a-a-a . . . ma!
A-a-a-a . . . da-a-a-a . . . ma!

There were other drums beating now, producing complex rhythms to regulate the dancing of the gods, but the underlying rhythm remained, and the hypnotic chanting to which it gave birth.

Bowls were brought by the Egungun and set upon the dais, and the gods took turns in picking powders from pouches contained within their costumes, sprinkling them in the bowls from above, slowly enough that all could see what was being done yet with no delay. Against the background of the chant other voices were raised now, each one declaiming according to a kind of rhythm, but not in unison, so that the songs were muddled and mingled, in an order so intricate that it seemed always to be teetering on the brink of cacophony. The candidates joined in for a little while, crying to the sky as though possessed by some emotion that Noell could not name.

The would-be elemi became quiet again when a god, who might have been Osanhin or Aroni, gave them medicine to take into their mouths. Noell watched their jaws move steadily from side to side in an oddly rhythmic chewing motion which he had sometimes seen Ghendwa use. The men – there were four – now seemed slightly unsteady on their feet, and their eyes were glazed. It was not only the chant which was possessing them; Noell judged that they were drugged. Everything seemed to be happening more slowly now. The gods . . . the masked men, Noell reminded himself . . . seemed tortuously deliberate in their motions as they concluded their work in preparing the bowls. What elaborate concoction had been made therein? wondered Noell.

We are supposed to be deeply impressed by this, he thought. *We are to marvel at the wonder of it, and become aware of our own smallness of mind. But I know what a futile masque this is, and what a smokescreen of mystification surrounds a tiny kernel of authentic power. We are watching the gods, visible and invisible, mixing an awesome elixir of life. No doubt the vampires of Gaul have a rite of their own which is no less elaborate and no less strange, yet the difference must be in the costumes and the empty, powerless words. What is essential here is but a little fraction of the whole, so little that I think it might seem absurd without such extravagant efforts to elaborate it.*

Noell wondered whether there had ever been a man here before who could look at this rite with eyes unclouded by the mysteries of masks and words. Had anyone ever seen it as it really was, with eyes not bewildered by Shigidi, with a mind which found idols transparent? It suddenly struck him what poor fools these were who danced in their masks and would soon begin to cut with their savage knives in cruel and stupid celebration. And was the sabbat of the Gaulish vampires any different, in essence? Would there not be masks and idols there, in equal profusion, and cruelties to answer the demands of Shigidi?

Why, he thought, *these men might really rule the world, if only they had ever paused to consider coldly the elements of what they do, if only they had ever experimented with the means which they use, to separate out the vital from the irrelevant. They achieve their end in a ridiculous, perverted fashion, without knowing what it is they do, or how they do it. And it is the same with the vampires Attila made, who are likewise blinded by their own ignorance and superstition!*

Now it fell to a number of the Egungun to grind and mix the contents of the bowls, and they did so with stout pestles, the rhythm of their movements quite taken over by the rhythm of the continuing chant, while Noell watched, grateful that he was secure in his waking self, and that the season of his dreams had been brought to such an absolute end.

He glanced sideways at Ngadze, and saw the Ibau man sweating despite the cold, in the grip of a fever of anxiety: a man in the company of his gods, appropriately cowed. He looked then at Quintus, and saw that the monk was sweating too, albeit more lightly, and that his eyes too had become a little glazed. Shigidi had not conquered Quintus, but Quintus was not entirely free of the magic spell of nightmare-vision.

A-a-a-a . . . da-a-a-a . . . ma!
A-a-a-a . . . da-a-a-a . . . ma!

Noell had lost all track of time, but it seemed to him that nearly an hour had passed, with the ceremony proceeding first at one tempo, then at another, but always with the fundamental rhythm of the drums beneath it. The gods moved aside from their preparatory rituals, and the first of the candidates stepped forward to a shaped wooden block, which had been brought to stand before the stone dais. Although Noell had guessed what was to happen, his throat constricted and his gorge rose when he saw one of those who played the part of the risen dead produce a dull-bladed knife.

Ngadze clearly had not worked out in thought what was to happen, for he gasped very audibly when he saw the first of the candidates place his penis – already circumcised after the rough fashion of his people – upon the saddle of the block, ready for semi-castration. As the blade of the knife was drawn along the penis, to slit it open like a pea–pod, Ngadze let slip a little scream. Noell, glancing sideways, saw that even Quintus had buried his head in his hands, unable to look, while Kantibh, somewhat to his surprise, was staring avidly, apparently unable to tear his jealous gaze away.

A-a-a-a . . . da-a-a-a . . . ma!
A-a-a-a . . . da-a-a-a . . . ma!

The gush of blood which spouted from the wound was neatly intercepted by another of the ceremony's officiators, caught in one of the two great bowls which had been prepared to receive it. Noell bit his lower lip in anxiety as he watched the flowing blood collected, wondering whether many men might bleed to death before their dreadful initiation was complete. But three others of the risen dead were ready with another gourd, and as the first was carried away they came quickly into place to take some moist mixture from within it, caking it upon the wounded member with some liberality, pressing it into and around the long slit. The blood-flow ceased, and the naked man moved back from the block, having made no sound, nor shown by any expression in his face what an ordeal he had undergone.

The second man stepped forward, and suffered the same incision. Again the gushing blood was taken into the collecting bowl, the opened member being left to bleed for nearly a minute before the gourd was brought forwards again, and its poultice applied. Again, the blood-flow was stanched, and the man was able to step back, no less in control of himself than when he had entered the arena.

But this is not a means of healing, Noell reminded himself. *It is a means to stop healing, for when this man becomes a vampire, most of the wounds he has recently received will heal. He is unmanned for all eternity, by the design of these petty gods and foolish wise men.*

He watched this part of the ceremony repeated twice more, and now he was no longer sickened by the flow of blood, though he wondered why they caught it so carefully in that greater bowl. He had lost track, somehow, of the number of the bowls and gourds which were upon and around the dais, and what had been done to each one to prepare it for its role in the affair, but he believed that the mixture of substances which the gods had made – and to which the invisible Olorun might be assumed to have added his heart – had not yet played its part. He turned again, briefly, to look back at the sea of faces, ecstatically turned to the heavens, chanting relentlessly with a rhythm which was now gradually but perceptibly speeding up.

A-a-a-a . . . da-a-a-a . . . ma!
A-a-a-a . . . da-a-a-a . . . ma!

The drugged and mutilated men, surely brought to the threshold of death by age and loss of blood, were poised now between the life they had finished and the life which was to begin. They stood in line, waiting, while the gods moved past and around them, speaking now in murmurous tones. Their winding procession distracted Noell's attention from the Egungun, but they were about to step back into the principal role, and now they had new vessels in their arms, which surely were the ones into which the gods had poured their offerings. The blood which had been taken from the candidates was poured liberally into them. Again there was mixing and stirring, but Noell could only imagine what a loathsome mess was thus produced.

But then came the knives again, and the risen dead came back to taunt the living, drawing long wounds across the breasts and heads of the would-be elemi, who did not flinch. Then, the mixture of blood and the offerings of the gods was pressed upon the bleeding breasts, and poured upon their heads, much as the ointment from the gourds had been plastered on the stumps of the severed pricks. But Noell knew, as he watched, that this was no ointment, to heal or to save from healing. This was the elixir of life itself, nurtured in blood and set now upon bleeding wounds, which it must invade in order to make these men immortal.

Like the silver death! he thought.

All the elemi in the amphitheatre were standing now, gathering into a great procession which spiralled around and around the space beneath the sky. The procession moved forward as the vampires of Adamawara came in single file to take their own part in this ceremony of initiation, this terrible season of blood whose sacrifice was the price of eternal life. The black vampires, their polished skin shining in the firelight, moved between the fires and between the silent figures of their gods, past the motionless Egungun, in a smoothly-flowing river of life whose measured passage must have been practised a thousand times and more.

The voices never ceased their chant.

A-a-a-a . . . da-a-a-a . . . ma!

A-a-a-a . . . da-a-a-a . . . ma!

The procession seemed to go on forever, and yet it moved with uncanny smoothness, each member striding as though impelled by a machine along a pre-planned path, with no collisions or interruptions, no pauses or hesitations. The chant had now changed its timbre as well as its tempo. Noell could see that Kantibh, though he uttered no sound, was mouthing the phrases, completely lost in the rhythm. But Ngadze had recoiled, and had turned his face away.

'For the love of God!' murmured Quintus, in distress. His voice was too low for anyone else but Noell to hear.

'Dost thou mean the God which fathered Christ?' asked Noell, and would have added: *Or the gods which Shigidi serves so well*; but thought more kindly of it.

The ceremony was not finished yet, and Noell held his position patiently while the great procession wound on and on to its inevitable end.

A-a-a-a . . . da-a-a-a . . . ma!

A-a-a-a . . . da-a-a-a . . . ma!

The four candidates still stood side by side, waiting. Their jaws still moved as they chewed whatever narcotic pulp had been given them, and their split members dangled raggedly beneath them, smeared and caulked after the fashion of amputated limbs cauterized with molten pitch. Their heads and bodies were covered in gore, and in that blood were the agents which would give them eternal life, if death did not come to claim them first.

Many must die, thought Noell. *This is not an easy road to take, for men as old as these.*

When they had first come into this place, Noell's mind had been filled with memories of Guazzo's description of the vampire sabbat. He had half-expected to see some ritual of serial buggery, after the manner of the pillory escapades in London's Tower. Now, he realised that it probably would not matter overmuch which orifice of the body or laceration of the flesh received the brew contained in the devil's cauldron. He could not guess how necessary to the elixir the blood might be, nor whether any of the unseen powders and pulps which had been put into the bowl when the rite began made any contribution at all, but he was convinced that he knew one element of it, and that he had known it for a long time. He had no doubt at all that Edmund Cordery had guessed, and guessed true, what kind of heart or ejaculate it was which Olorun or Satan gave to his chosen people. Noell was sure that

he knew what had happened here, and what was the hidden core of the
secret concealed in all this mummery.

I think that I might now begin to make an elixir of life, he thought, *and
by experiment bring it to perfection. But where might I look for the heart of
it? What elemi would ever give to me a measure of that semen which he must
labour so very long to produce, and leak with such awful difficulty?*

The thought that he did know, and that he had seen this ceremony
with penetrating gaze, made him feel that he had won such a triumph
as his father must have envied him.

A-a-a-a . . . da-a-a-a . . . ma!

A-a-a-a . . . da-a-a-a . . . ma!

He watched the candidates spit out the stuff which they were
chewing, and saw them slowly fall to the ground, where the Egungun
wrapped them up in coloured mats, and carried them, one by one, into
the shadows. Noell knew that they had fallen into a deep sleep, from
which they would awaken elemi, or not at all.

A-a-a-a . . . da-a-a-a . . . ma!

A-a-a-a . . . da-a-a-a . . . ma!

It came to him with a slight shock of revelation that the vampires of
Adamawara could not have known what a silly thing they did when
they brought him to see this ceremony. They had intended to show
him a great display of godly power and magical extravagance, to
demonstrate what an awesome, solemn and horrible thing it was to
contemplate becoming a vampire, so that he would be thoroughly
deluded. In much the same way, those credulous witnesses to the
sabbats held by Attila's kin, whose tales had been reported by the
Gregorians, must have seen something which seemed to them terrible
and unnatural, and had found only anguish instead of knowledge. But
he, who had sat upon the knee of Francis Bacon, and carried in his
flesh and spirit alike the heritage of Edmund Cordery, had seen neither
gods nor devils, nor any superhuman magic, nor anything at all to
humble the soul of a common man with fear and dread. He had seen
only opportunity – the birth of a confident understanding which made
him feel that he was no longer a bondsman in the empire of fear, but
a free citizen of the republic of enlightenment.

He knew then what treasure had been in Adamawara, waiting to be
discovered, and he believed that he had found it, though he could not
yet imagine how he might attempt to carry it away with him.

NINE

Returned to the place of the aitigu, Noell and Quintus quit the houses where they had been lodged, and took over for their own purposes another dwelling at the southern edge of the town. Ngadze came with them, and when they had it ready they brought the sick Langoisse, and Leilah to look after him. The elemi with whom they worked made no objection to this, but tried to smooth the way for them by offering four Mkumkwe servants, whose attachment to the household Noell was reluctantly persuaded to accept. He asked Kantibh whether they might instead have Ntikima to help them, but the Persian said that Ntikima was in Iletigu. Kantibh deflected further questions by telling them that the house which they had chosen had been the home of other Christians fourteen hundred years before: those Syrians following Frumentius who had tried to carry news of Christ's sojourn on the earth into the very heart of Africa.

Noell took more trouble now to pursue his own researches. By patient exploration he discovered the way from the place of the aitigu to the lifeless forest, and went there to collect parts of the strange trees, samples of soil, and specimens of the few insects and worms to be found there. He compared these things with what he knew of the living things in the Kwarra delta, and with samples which he collected inside the crater. He tried hard to make sense of it all, but enlightenment evaded him and he grew gradually frustrated by his inability to under-stand why the forest was so antipathetic to the living things which existed in profusion elsewhere.

He returned, on occasion, to Berenike's house, and sometimes she came to seek him out, but he knew that their love affair – if thus it might be called – was really over. There seemed to be little pleasure for either of them in their couplings, which became much less frequent as time went by.

In the meantime, Quintus began to learn the use of the elemi's medicines – or such, at least, as they were willing to teach him in return for the Gaulish lore which he imparted to them. Noell watched his friend grow visibly weaker and more tired as the days passed, and was sorry for him. It was not the physical debility of the man which seemed most unfortunate, but the decline in his sharpness of mind. He remained, in Noell's eyes, the wisest of men, yet he seemed to have absorbed as if by infection something of the ways of his inquisitors. He was often to be heard murmuring lists, as though trying to fix them in a memory reluctant to hold them, and often cursed the fact that there was neither paper nor ink to be had in Adamawara. Quintus also spent much time in prayer, renewing a habit which he had allowed to weaken in recent years. It seemed that some argument which he conducted with his maker, once settled by truce, was now made urgent again. Noell could not guess why this was so, and did not like to ask.

Langoisse, who had no interest in learning the lore of Adamawara, nor in Noell's patient collecting, lost himself in tedium, and in doing so gave way a little more to the sickness which was devouring his spirit. Periodically, he seemed to realise that he had become his own enemy, and would rouse himself to the business of planning for the future, romancing freely of quests to come, sailing the reconstructed *Stingray* across the western ocean in search of Atlantis, or taking her up the Thames to bombard the Tower of London and begin the over-throw of the Norman tyranny. All too often these excitements would run away with him, and end with curious bouts of intoxication. In the grip of such light-headedness he would often shout at the frightened servants, cursing them for the inadequacy of their understanding, and abuse poor Leilah if she tried to keep him calm.

At other times, the pirate became morose and morbid, bewailing the absence of meat and – in heartfelt fashion – the weakness and foul taste of the millet beer which was Adamawara's only means of inducing drunkenness. He seemed to forget that his eagerness had played a part in launching the expedition, and began to blame Noell and Quintus for bringing him to such an evil place to die. Leilah stayed close to Lango-isse through all these moods, and he drew her, it seemed, much closer to him than before, as though she must now take the place of the lost Turk.

Leilah's attitude to Noell remained politely distant. Her behaviour towards him was studied, when in the past it had always been spon-taneous. He did not think it entirely fair of her. Had she not been Langoisse's mistress through all the time he had known her? What complaint could she legitimately offer now merely because he had had a mistress of his own? But she did not see things the same way and though she would not name his association with Berenike a betrayal, it was plain that she felt it to be so, in her heart. Noell was confused enough in his own thoughts to wonder whether she was right. Unlike Edmund Cordery, who had used his affair with Carmilla Bourdillon to political advantage, he had given himself to a vampire in answer to desire – a desire which was not even returned, in any sincere fashion. Berenike had long since banished herself from the world of ordinary emotion and desire, and was more like an automaton than a thinking person.

Berenike was the one subject which Noell would never discuss with Quintus. He always felt, though Quintus never said so, that he had suffered much in the monk's estimation in becoming the vampire's lover. He imagined that Quintus must secretly despise him for it, or at least despair of his weakness. Why he felt this, he was not entirely sure. Quintus had never asked him to become a monk, or suggested that it was a vocation to which he was fitted. But Quintus was so unassailable in his own celibacy as to set a most intimidating example, and there was no denying that Quintus had made a powerful imprint upon the form and voice of Noell's conscience. Noell had always felt that in making Leilah his friend instead of his lover he had been true to an important aspect of Quintus's ideals, and now he had alienated himself from that approval.

The impossibility of discussing Berenike, however, meant that Noell could not confide to Quintus certain ideas about vampires in general which he extrapolated from his growing understanding of his lover. He began to wonder whether her condition provided an insight into the state of being of the elemi.

Noell knew, of course, that it was dangerous to assume that living for millennia would have the same effect on all who did so. Kantibh, who was only a little younger than Berenike, took such an active role in the affairs of Adamawara that he rarely seemed to be lost in a trance, living entirely by habit. Aiyeda, who must be nearly as old as the mysterious Ekeji Orisha, was equally capable of interesting himself in the daily flow of events, and had his wits very much about him. But the elders who lived in Iletigu, under the direction of those supposedly next to the gods, were not involved in such projects as the preparation of candidates and the learning of new things. If hearsay was to be credited, they spent their time in meditation and ritual, and in giving forth pronunciations as to what must be done in the world, and what must become of the world.

Noell thought it significant that Kantibh spoke with a kind of awed reverence of the time when Ekeji Orisha – presumably a predecessor of him who held the title now – had decreed that they must send no more unfinished envoys into the greater world, because such envoys were known to have betrayed the cause of Adamawara. Was that, wondered Noell, the last time the elders had said anything new? Was it the last time that they had changed anything at all? Were the elders he had seen in that strange arena in Iletigu any different in their way of being from the disconnected, dreamlike state into which Berenike had lapsed? Were they convinced that what they knew was all that needed to be known, so that they had ceased to think, in any meaningful sense of the word? These questions could not be answered, but the asking of them made it very easy for Noell to entertain the notion that Adamawara, far from being the home of all wisdom, as its reputation claimed, was actually in a state of dire decay.

And if this empire of vampires was built on such a poor foundation, he thought, what then of the Imperium of Gaul, and the Khanates of Walachia, India and Cathay? Were the elders of those empires – Attila and Charlemagne, and the legendary Temujin – slaves to their own great age, having lost their grip on the fabric of everyday life? He remembered that Attila was said to be living in seclusion, in his citadel, having delegated the business of ruling to such favoured heirs as Vlad Tepes, and that Charlemagne was rarely seen in his own court. Had a kind of decay – a mould like the silver death – begun to extend its invisible corruption through all the world where vampires were?

Edmund Cordery had pointed out to his son, long ago, that common men were innovators, while vampires remained slaves to tradition. Noell had understood then, in a vague fashion, how that might be connected with the fact that vampires lived much longer than common men. Now, he understood better what drawbacks vampire life might have, to make it less than the unqualified boon it seemed. The confidence which had come to Noell during the rite in Iletigu grew firmer by degrees, as he began to believe that common men might be in some ways superior to vampires, and that the cleverness of the short-lived must ultimately give them the means to throw off the tyranny of the undying.

The elders of Adamawara saw no need to learn the use of iron, or the use of parchment and paper, or the use of machines, because they were complacent in their belief that whatever they did not already know was not worth the knowing. Noell knew that there was a power not only in particular devices like the cannon and the musket, but in the general process of unfolding discovery, which could change the world more thoroughly than the elders of Adamawara could ever imagine. He suspected that the stubborn blindness of the elemi would never allow them to realise it.

He saw, once he had reached this conclusion, that the most significant evidence of the fallibility of the elders which had ever come to Adamawara was himself. He and his companions were already an uncomfortable thorn in the side of those who were trying to absorb what they had to teach – and trying, as they absorbed it, to render it harmless, devoid of its real significance. In time, Noell knew, Kantibh and Aiyeda were all too likely to reach the decision that there was something intolerable and unclean about him, which must be obliterated to preserve their peace of mind. Not only was he not worthy to be an elemi, but he was not worthy to live in Adamawara at all.

Every time he went into the lifeless forest he would climb to some vantage point where he could look out across the oceanic canopy and wonder whether, now that he was safe from the silver death, he might attempt to cross that wilderness. Every time he returned to the shelter of the twisted trees he would look about uneasily, expecting to see a band of the living dead among them, come to direct their wands at his evil heart, to condemn him to death.

And all the while he kept returning his thoughts to the one particular practical problem whose solution might save all their lives, and give them the means to cross the forest and the plain beyond, careless of all the dangers of those treacherous lands.

How, he asked himself, over and over again, *might I obtain a supply of vampire semen, with which to experiment, in order to discover the elixir of life?*

TEN

W hen the season of rains approached its end, Noell and Quintus knew that it was time to plan their leave-taking, if they did indeed intend to leave Adamawara. They had time to prepare, because the streams feeding the Logone would remain a barrier to their progress at least until the end of October, but once the rains had stopped, they could no longer postpone the time of decision.

They both knew that the vampires did not expect them to leave, and they had often raised discreet questions in order to discover whether the elders or any of their subjects would actually try to prevent them going. There had never been any hint that force might be used to keep them here, but Noell hesitated to draw any conclusion from that. The black vampires were convinced that it would be foolish for their guests to contemplate a return journey, partly because they could not see that the outer world had anything to offer which could stand comparison with the safety and tranquillity of Adamawara, but principally because they considered the journey itself so fraught with hazards as to be well-nigh impossible.

Quintus told Noell that he had investigated the possibility of recruiting an Adamawaran vampire to their party, but had found that even the unfinished vampires, who lived on the margins of Adamawaran society, dismissed out of hand any suggestion that the world beyond the lifeless forest might be worth investigation. Kantibh had not the slightest desire to see the land of his birth again, or any other like it. Quintus had made inquiries, therefore, to determine whether any vampire would be returning to the Kwarra delta – or any nearby region – in order to rejoin his tribe following his initiation.

That vampires did indeed leave Adamawara every year on just such expeditions, accompanied by groups of Mkumkwe fighting men, could not be doubted, but Quintus's suggestion that he and Noell might be allowed to join such a party was curtly dismissed. The Oni-Olorun who had visited Benin had found reports of the white men sufficiently interesting to send Ghendwa to ease their path to Adamawara, but the Adamawaran notions of courtesy and hospitality did not extend so far as easing their way in the other direction. Like the Mkumkwe, who could become stubbornly silent in the face of direct questions, the vampires of Adamawara could become stubbornly unhelpful in the face of direct requests. Quintus more than once declared, bitterly, that the task seemed hopeless and that he could see no reasonable alternative to spending his remaining years in Adamawara.

At first, Quintus and Noell did not involve Langoisse in their scheming. The reason for this exclusion was that they were certain that even if they had the strength to make the journey, Langoisse had not. They did not doubt his desire to leave the place where he was, but there seemed to be no possibility of getting him to another. He was simply too ill. Eventually, though, Langoisse demanded his own part in their discussion and decision-making and Noell was not surprised to find that the pirate had a different point of view to offer. Langoisse, determined as he was that he did not want to spend another year in this oppressive place, could see quite clearly that there was only one way he could be made ready for the journey.

'The answer lies in your hands,' he told Noell, 'for have you not spent these last few months poring over your spy-glass, dabbling with potions and applying your alchemy to the wisdom of blood? Do you take me for a fool, not to know that you are hotly bent on discovering the secret which you saw in action in that foul rite which they allowed you to witness? Why, I have been waiting for you all this time, to find a way to make us all into vampires? Then we will cross the whole world, eldritch forest and all, unscathed and at our ease. Man, we must be our own guardians, and can entertain no other thought. We want no vampire guides; we must become vampires ourselves!'

Noell was at first over-cautious, explaining to the pirate how difficult it would be to determine precisely what was necessary to make a vampire of a man, but he soon realised that the stricken man would tolerate no prevarication.

'Why else did we come to this foul land, but to snatch the secret from their grip?' Langoisse demanded. 'Do you tell me now that for all your patient scratching, you really know no more than you did in Cardigan, so many years ago? Have you not seen the vampire sabbat? Have you not your microscope and your scholar's cunning? I have risked much to bring you here, Master Cordery, and we are all of one company now, however much you have not liked me in the past. Do you think of betraying me?'

'I do not,' said Noell. 'Truth to tell, no one can be sure that he has the secret of making an elixir of life until he has done it, and has seen its effect. I know what ingredients I would like to have, in order to begin an experiment, but I have not thought of a way of obtaining the more precious of them.'

'What kind of fool are you, to keep it to yourself?' demanded Langoisse. 'Had you told us all, we could all be on the trail of it.'

'I am not certain that mere numbers will increase our chance,' Noell told him, 'but I have no ideas of my own, and will be grateful for any which you can provide. From what I have seen and previously heard I think that two ingredients only might suffice. One is common blood, of which we have no shortage . . . the other, I fear, is the semen of a vampire. I am not sure that these will be entirely adequate to the purpose, but without the more important, I cannot put the proposition to the proof.'

'Are you sure that they used vampires' semen in the rite which you saw?' asked Langoisse, 'How can such creatures as these produce seed? Did you not see how their pricks were destroyed in their vile ceremony?'

'I saw,' said Noell. 'But it is the testicles which produce the seed, and they are not removed. I think they may discharge their seed only with difficulty, and I suspect that vampire men produce seed in much lesser quantities than commoners, but produce it they must. It seems to me that it may need some nourishment by blood before it is introduced into the body. I am not sure that it matters how it is taken in, though it might not work if drunk. It is probably best to try the method which they use here, and put it upon an open wound. The problem, however, is to obtain the semen. Can you imagine what answer I would get if I asked Aiyeda for such a gift as that?'

Langoisse lay upon his bed, staring up at the ceiling.

'It is part and parcel of the vampires' hardihood that they produce their sperms so slowly,' Noell went on. 'I believe that our bodies are made up of a great many tiny particles, or atoms, which are in a state of constant exchange. Just as our hair and fingernails grow, so the outer layer of our skin is always being shed, as new skin is born beneath. When we eat and drink, some of the atoms in our food become atoms of our body, and this is how we are nourished – but at the same time we cast off atoms that were once part of us, in our excretions. In the same way, atoms of ourselves are shaped into the sperms that will reproduce us, continually gathered in a tiny vesicle, ready to be ejected toward their destined soil in a woman's womb.

'In the vampires, this process of exchange must be very much slowed down. Their long life may be explained by the fact that their atoms are much hardier, cast off and replaced at a much reduced pace. Though the vampires of Europe eat as we do, they can go without food for much longer periods, as the vampires of Adamawara always do, and this proves that they take less nourishment from their food than we. I believe that they lose far fewer atoms of their bodies, day by day, than we do, and that in parallel with this reduced loss, there is a great reduction in the production of the special atoms of reproduction. Thus, their sperms are much more slowly accumulated in the vesicle which holds them, and they feel far less pressure to let it out.

'You know what pressure a common man may feel in his loins when he has not lain with a woman in some days, and you know that a common man may sometimes ejaculate in his sleep, while dreaming of a woman. That is because the atoms of reproduction need to be let out, just as we need to let out other excreta. The vampire men feel that need far less than you or I, and this explains much about their attitude to women, and the nature of their relationships with them. The initiation rites which I have seen take this reduced need as a virtue, and they exaggerate its reduction, insisting that a finished vampire has transcended any need to lie with women, and making it impossible for him to do so. Even an elemi still produces sperms, though, and must still discharge them, though what power of the imagination they need to control their release I cannot tell. Nor am I sure of what they do with the semen, though I am convinced that they use it in their rite, just as the vampires of Gaul do, after a different fashion.'

'Say you so?' said Langoisse, softly. 'Say you so.'

'This does not mean that I know beyond the shadow of a doubt how to formulate a magic potion that could make any man a vampire,' Noell warned him. 'It is by no means certain that all the other things which they put in their mixture, save for the blood, are unnecessary.'

Langoisse, fascinated, considered the matter for some time, serious enough in his contemplation to ask for several points of clarification regarding Noell's theorising about the nature of vampire flesh. Inevitably, he came eventually to the most puzzling question.

'Why blood, Master Cordery? Why do they need the blood?'

'I do not know,' Noell confessed. 'But I have an idea. I think that just as the body makes sperms continually, so it also makes blood. That is why a man who loses blood from a wound, though he may be pale and weak for a while, will ultimately recover his colour and his health; and that is why common men can feed vampires continually, without themselves being totally drained. It cannot be doubted that the vampires can make new blood, perhaps in great quantity, even though their wounds do not bleed as profusely as those of common men. If they could not make new blood, I do not think the vampires could recover from injuries which would cause death in humans. This means that we cannot draw a direct analogy between the blood and the sperms; the manufacture of blood cannot simply be slowed down as I suppose the production of sperms to be. But there must be something unique about the process of manufacture – which we must suppose to be unnaturally rapid in vampire terms – that requires an intake of appropriate atoms from the flesh of common men. In all other matters, the flesh of vampires can sustain itself with a slower exchange of atoms than we are victim to, but in this one respect the vampires must prey on those whose nature is to produce new atoms more quickly. That is why vampires need men – and why there may never be a world in which all men are vampires.'

'I think you are a wise man, Noell Cordery,' said Langoisse. 'Does the monk concur with all these judgements?'

'He agrees with many of my chains of reasoning,' he replied, evasively, 'but we can neither of us be sure that I am right, until the matter is put to the test. I have not posed the question of how we might obtain a vampire's semen; I did not think it . . . seemly.'

'Seemly! We are speaking of eternal life and painful death, and you do not think it *seemly* to raise such questions aloud. Oh, Master Cordery, thou art a strange creature. Why didst not come to me a long time ago, if 'twas only the courage that you lacked?'

'What do you mean?' asked Noell, a little sharply.

'Why man, we are in a world of vampires. If they have the semen inside them, we need not wait for them to bring it out for us. Vampires they may be, but they are old men, many living quiet lives, virtually alone, in this ancient city.'

'You think we should secure what we need by murder!' Despite the pretence of shock, this was a thought which had occurred to Noell before, though he had always shied away from it.

Langoisse laughed. 'Murder?' he said. 'Nay, Master Cordery, you know better than that. No murder, nor even permanent harm. The gentle sleep into which friend Ghendwa fell. That which we take will surely grow anew! And if it works – why then, we'll set such a rumour abroad in Gaul that every man of mettle will have no higher goal than to castrate a vampire knight to steal eternal life from his balls.'

Noell looked around at the walls of Langoisse's house, as the idea that they might be overheard took sudden possession of him. 'And what will the vampires of Adamawara do if they convict us of such a crime?' he murmured. 'They have been tolerant of our presence, and seemingly might tolerate our departure, but how could we possibly escape their wrath if we thus repay their hospitality?'

'Repay?' answered Langoisse, scornfully. 'Do you think we owe them a debt? They brought us here for their own purposes, to learn from us what happens in the outer world, and in return they offer us arrogant lessons to demonstrate the folly of our ways and the vanity of our ambitions. Do you think that because I have so little Latin I cannot understand what is happening here? Your friend has called this a paradise of fools, and so it is, though they think we are the fools while theirs is the paradise. I will seek out the lonely ones, who will not be missed when they are put to sleep, and will never see who it is that thrusts the knife into their bodies.'

'I have thought of that,' Noell confessed, 'but I fear that it will not work. However lonely they seem, there is none who would not be missed, because each must be visited every day, to receive his allotted donation of blood. Do not think that their victims would hesitate to betray you; they would not pause for an instant before raising a hue and cry. If you try to do it that way, you will surely destroy us all.'

This objection made the pirate pause and scowl, and he seemed to realise the truth of what Noell had said. 'Mayhap we must leave, then,' he said, 'and find a vampire in another place, who may be safely used. Had we but known this last year, I'd have bade poor Selim go mad much sooner, and given him strict instruction as to how to wield his knife. We must pray that Heaven will give us another opportunity.'

'Langoisse,' said Noell, pleadingly, 'I beg you to be careful. The vampires of Africa are very unlike the ones which rule in Gaul and Byzantium, but I think that any man who deliberately wounded one would be treated no less cruelly, by the tribesmen if not by the vampires themselves. You did not see how the Egungun which came to meet us in the forest behaved when they found Ghendwa hurt. I think we might all have been slaughtered then, had not Ntikima interceded on our behalf, and I still fear for the boy, because none of us has seen hide nor hair of him since we first arrived here. Were we to castrate a vampire, finished or unfinished, I think it would be reckoned an insult so grave that all Africa would hound us to our deaths. Should we ever see Gaul again, I'll help you start your rumour, but I have wondered long and hard whether I dare raise a hand against the vampires of Adamawara, and have so far decided that I dare not.'

Langoisse looked at him long and hard, with more than a trace of the old fire in his eyes, but in the end he lowered his accusative gaze.

'Nay, Master Cordery,' he said. 'I cannot name thee coward on that account. What you know may be too precious to risk in the kind of adventure which I proposed. I'll bide my time – you have my word on't. In the meantime, you must call upon my help to make ready for the journey home. Neither the forests nor the grasslands, nor a legion of savages, can prevent our winning home, if we are truly determined.'

Noell shook his head, tiredly. 'There are too many enemies,' he said. 'And we no longer have your guns. We have looked for them, but they are nowhere to be found. I do not even know where the donkeys are kept, if they are still alive.'

Langoisse's expression became bleaker, and Noell knew that the truth had cut a path clean through the pirate's hopes and dreams. 'Aye,' he whispered. 'I had forgotten the guns. I have lain too long in this wretched bed, and must get up now, to play my part in this endeavour.'

'Do not hurt yourself,' said Noell, surprised by his own sincerity. 'You have been very ill, and I would not like to see you increase your troubles by driving yourself too hard.'

'Master Cordery,' said the pirate, in a cold low voice 'I think that you misread me. I have greater strength than you suppose.'

ELEVEN

When Noell next took himself into the forest outside Adamawara it was not so much to carry forward his studies as to give him space for further thought concerning the matters which he had broached with Langoisse.

That all of them desired to quit Adamawara in the coming dry season he took for granted, but it seemed that he must also take it for granted that not all of them were able. He dared not go alone, or with only Ngadze for company; that would leave him scant chance of success, and in any case he could hardly bear the idea of leaving Quintus behind – or Leilah, if the truth be acknowledged. But when he asked himself what chance there was of making an elixir to make aitigu of them all, he had to answer that he could see none at all, unless he was prepared to deal in such wild and dangerous fantasies as had sprung at once to the pirate's mind.

While he sat, and pondered, he heard a noise behind him, and turned in a flutter of alarm, fearing to see Egungun walking there, although it was brightest daylight.

It was not Egungun, but Ntikima, whom he had not seen for nearly a year. The boy was standing beside the crooked bole of an ancient tree, higher up the slope. Ntikima seemed taller than before, and held himself more like a warrior. His expression was very serious, his eyes shadowed in the gloomy light beneath the canopy of the tree. Noell greeted the boy with feeling, and told him how anxious he had been for his safety. He asked whether Ntikima had suffered much from the silver death, and what the present state of his health was, but received no immediate answer. It was obvious to Noell that this was no chance meeting of old fast friends, but something which touched the fate of both of them.

'I have been in Iletigu,' said Ntikima, finally. 'I was taken there because I am Ogbone, and once met Aroni in the forest, who made me a promise which the elemi are bound to keep. I have seen and touched Ekeji Orisha, and have watched the gods descend to earth.'

'Will you be an elemi yourself?' asked Noell, standing to face his visitor, but shy of reaching out to touch him, because of his manner.

'Once, I hoped that I would be,' replied the boy. 'I was to be a magician and a healer.' He paused, then added: 'I owe a debt, Noell Cordery, and have come to pay it.'

Noell felt an unnatural calm, as though a coldness had stolen into his heart. He knew only too well that the debt which Ntikima owed him was the debt of a life, and that if Ntikima had come to pay it now, his life must be in dire danger. 'Have the Ogbone decided, then, that Egungun must come to find me once again?' he asked.

'I am Ogbone,' said the boy. 'I know what Ogbone knows. Ifa has spoken to the babalawos, to tell them that you mean to do wrong in Adamawara, and that you have already offended against the most sacred taboos.'

Noell fought a momentary impulse to laugh. Had Ifa, then, been eavesdropping inside his head? Had his conversation with Langoisse been overheard? 'Is there any defence against this judgement?' he asked.

Ntikima shook his head.

'The priests of Ifa have juggled the palm nuts,' he said, 'and they have spilled the secret blood. Yesterday was ajo awo, the day of the secret, and the babalawos huddled their shaven heads in urgent conference. Ekeji Orisha is troubled by what you have told the elemi, and has said that there is a kind of poison in your words. The ancestors in Ipo-oku are disturbed. Egungun will come, and I must put myself before you, as you once placed yourself in front of me.'

There was something new and unexpected in the way that Ntikima spoke of the priests and the gods. It was a tone which Noell had not heard in his voice before. Ntikima's was not now the voice of a devout believer, but the voice of one who had begun to doubt his idols.

When he was in Burutu, thought Noell, *he was completely Ogbone, in his thoughts and in his heart. But now that he is in Adamawara, there is a little of Burutu in him, kept secretly in his soul, which has given him eyes to see. It is not just the debt of life which he owes to me, but a clearness of vision. Without that, I do not think he would be here, come to warn me against the risen dead.*

'What is it that I need to do?' asked Noell, aloud.

'You must leave Adamawara,' Ntikima told him.

'I cannot leave alone.'

'Not alone. You must take the others with you – all those that you wish to save. Even the white babalawo is in danger now.'

'It cannot be done. Langoisse has not the strength, nor Quintus. They could never cross the lifeless forest, let alone the plain beyond, the uplands and the forest.'

'To stay is to die very soon,' Ntikima assured him. 'You must take whatever risks there are. I cannot promise to deliver you safely, but I will do what I can.' He paused, as if uncertain how much more he dared to say, and then went on: 'I do what I must, but if I do not act cleverly, they will kill me too, as they would have killed you when

you took my place. Shango saved you then, and I must pray that he
will extend the same mercy to me, but you must do as I say.'

For a moment, Noell took leave to doubt what was being said to
him, but the boy bore himself now with an authority more profound
than the earnest confidence which he had had in days gone by, when
he had told them what he knew of Adamawara and the Uruba gods.

Though he had never quite realised it before, Noell saw that it was
not Ghendwa but Ntikima who had brought them to Adamawara. It
was Ntikima who had laid down the lure with his innocently-told tales;
it was Ntikima who had told the Ogbone about the man the tribesmen
called the white babalawo. All along, they had been moved by Ntikima,
and now he was urging them on again, perhaps to their deaths. Trust
in providence had become Quintus's watchword; was this black youth
a personification of the providence which had had them in its charge
all along?

'By telling me this you place yourself in danger,' said Noell.

'I am already in danger,' said Ntikima, flatly. 'I owe as great a debt
to you as that which I owed to Aroni. I must forsake Aroni, and must
trust myself to Shango now.'

Precisely what this might mean, Noell was not sure, though he
knew it was a change of allegiance for which he had every reason to
be thankful. Did not Ntikima, who saw with clearer eyes now, know
that it was Langoisse's bullet which had struck Egungun down, not
Shango's thunderbolt? Or did the boy still believe that it could be one
thing *and* the other?

'Do you know where they have hidden the donkeys?' asked Noell,
and quickly added: 'We will need the guns and powder, too.'

'I will do what I can,' the boy replied.

Noell did not look away from Ntikima's eyes while he paused for
half a minute, wondering whether he dared to say more. In the end,
he felt that he had to. 'My friends will die,' he said, 'unless they
become aitigu. We are told there was once a medicine whose secret was
forgotten. Is it really forgotten?'

The boy was neither startled nor offended by the question, but Noell
knew that it was too much to hope for that he might offer the reply
which would save them all. 'It is forgotten,' he said. 'It has been put
away, and there is nothing I can do to make you stronger than you
are. Will you hear what I can do?'

Noell nodded his head in weary assent.

'Can you find your way here in the dark of night?'

'Yes.'

'Two nights hence, you must come, soon before first light. I will
need as long to make preparations. I will try to bring the donkeys, and
some food, but you must gather whatever you can. Keep the secret
from your servants, and at all costs from Aiyeda and the man who

wears the turban. You will not find me here, but do not wait. Go with all speed when dawn comes, and put your trust in Shango.'

Noell would have asked further questions, but when he opened his mouth the boy suddenly raised his hand.

'Remember,' he said, insistently. '*Trust Shango!*'

Ntikima turned away, running with some urgency. He was swallowed up by the forest. Noell shook his head, and threw away a clot of earth which he had been kneading in the fingers of his left hand. To his own surprise, he felt as much relief as fear, for confusion now was banished by necessity. He knew what he had to do. All awkward questions could now be set aside, in favour of trust in Ntikima's wit and wisdom.

Trust Shango? he repeated, ironically. He could not even trust in his own God, and could hardly hope that a single idol from a heathen flock might serve where the Lord of All could not. But Shango had spoken before through the barrel of a musket, and perhaps that was all that Ntikima meant. 'Well then,' he murmured, as he began to stride purposefully toward the wall of rock and its hidden gateway to Adamawara's Eden, 'perhaps we must try for the treasure after all, in Langoisse's way, and damn all consequence that might attend the quest!'

He wasted no time, upon his return, in communicating what had been said to him to his friends, but in view of the need for secrecy he had to tell them as carefully as he could. He had no opportunity to bring them all together to agree upon the making of a plan.

Langoisse, who was still confined to his room though no longer in his bed, was the easiest to find. Noell saw by the way that he reacted that the news of their rumoured danger was like an animating spark, drawing the pirate suddenly to an unspoken resolve, but he had not time to counsel caution, and did not really care to. Langoisse was ever a man, as Noell knew, to take the devil's risk when all was to be gained and nothing lost. On this occasion, Noell did not feel disposed to try to stop him.

Noell said nothing to Quintus, when he eventually found him, to warn him of what Langoisse might do. And when he had told them all to be ready – except Ngadze, whom he dared not trust entirely – he found business of his own to be about. He set about the gathering of a pack which he could to take with him when the time came. But when he sat alone at sunset on the day which Ntikima had designated for their flight, he had to face the pangs of his conscience, which tugged him in two different directions. He had to tell himself that he had not urged Langoisse to any crime, and that what the pirate would do must be to his account alone; but he had to tell himself that Langoisse would surely execute the task all the more cleanly and cleverly if left to himself, unencumbered by a feeble accomplice, because he did not like to think that he had sent the other man to do a foul job unaided.

Oh God, he said, in an entirely unaccustomed moment of prayer, *give me strength, I beg of you, to take action on my own behalf, in future. Let me not live my life entire without ever once grasping a nettle, and deciding for myself what must be done.* No sooner had this plea been uttered, though, than Noell was chiding himself again, for theatricality and for taking in vain the name of a deity in whom he did not believe.

'In any case, it probably matters not,' Noell whispered to himself. 'If I fail to make an elixir of life, if Ntikima fails to pay his debt, if every one of us must die, in Iletigu or in the lifeless forest . . . well, then, what mattered Noell Cordery's little life in the great pattern which unfolds within the shadow of eternity? 'Twas only one more useless thing among millions.'

There was no comfort at all to be found in these thoughts, and Noell was glad when Quintus came into his room, to sit with him while they waited. All preparations were made, but their conversation was about innocent things, lest they be overheard. Noell was sure that the monk could not suspect what Langoisse had gone to do. Neither of them went to his bed when the sun was gone; they sat instead over a lighted candle, uneasy and afraid.

Noell went to Leilah's room at one point, to make certain that all was well with her, and was astonished and annoyed to find her gone. He had not expected that the pirate would take her with him on such a mission as this, and he could not think of any other reason why she should not be there. He cursed the coldness which had grown between them, and made him leave her so much alone that he no longer knew her part in their adventure, but there was nothing to be done about it now. He could only return to Quintus, and wish the hours away.

He almost began to wish that naught would pass except the hours, and that Langoisse would come to him empty-handed, but he never quite gave way to that failure of resolution. And when the night was well advanced, with the stars standing out as bright and sharp as they ever did, Langoisse did come to him, with something precious cradled in his hand.

'It is time for you to make your elixir,' he said to Noell, 'and make haste to cheat the devil of our death. Be quick, for I do not know whether the semen of a vampire is as incorruptible as the remainder of his flesh.'

Noell dared not glance at Quintus, to see what the holy man's reaction might be to this speech, but he took what Langoisse gave him, and was astonished to find it not a mass of bloody flesh, but only a small stone jar, with thin white-yellow stuff inside it, which looked more like spittle than aught else.

'What is it?' he demanded.

'What thinkest thou?' returned Langoisse, in a fever of anxiety. 'It is stuff to make vampires, if you have told me true. But we need blood to nourish it, do we not, ere we even begin? Hurry, Master Alchemist, I beg of you!'

Noell, mystified, stared at the several droplets of fluid, which were already beginning to dry out. The fluid was milky, like the ejaculate of any common man. It was by no means the 'semen black as night' which Guazzo had mentioned, but Langoisse would surely have made no mistake. He knew that this must, indeed, be the semen of a vampire.

Langoisse was right: there was no time for questions or for hesitation.

Nevertheless, Quintus asked in an icy tone: 'What have you done, Langoisse?'

'I have bought us the chance to live instead of die,' replied Langoisse, 'if God has made Noell Cordery clever enough to do it.'

Ignoring the tart exchange, Noell quickly added some water to the stuff in the jar, and then opened the box which contained the parts of his microscope. He took from it the keenest of his knives, and without a pause for fear or thought he slashed at his own left arm, drawing a line of blood across the white flesh above his wrist. Deliberately, he spilled as much of the blood as he could into the jar.

'I know what is needful,' said Langoisse, quickly. 'Take mine too.' He produced from his belt a pointed dagger, but Noell shook his head, and looked among his own things for a second scalpel, which he moved through a candle-flame before holding it ready.

While Langoisse held out his forearm, Noell drew the blade of the knife along the length of a blue vein. The pirate did not cry out, but clenched his teeth and hissed in alarm as blood gushed from the long cut. Noell caught the blood in a drinking cup, and as the cup filled he tipped in the contents of the jar which Langoisse had brought him. This mixture he swirled about, adding salted water from a bottle.

'What is't?' said Quintus, in an angry tone, but stifled the question half-asked as his reason caught up with his astonishment. Noell glanced at him, trying to apologise with his eyes for the fact that he had said nothing, deliberately concealing from the monk what he and Langoisse had said to one another on this subject.

'I can only hope that no other substances are vital,' said Noell to Langoisse, speaking rapidly but with assurance. 'Pray, if you will, that we have what we need.'

He turned to look Quintus in the eye. 'No time,' he said, with a hint of apology. 'Decide now, I beg thee, whether thou art in this with us, or whether thou wouldst rather seek the merciful arms of thy loving God. I can promise nothing, but wilt thou try with us the power of the rite?'

Quintus stared at him so gravely that Noell was certain that he would refuse. But instead, the monk bared his own arm. 'Let God decide,' he said, with a strange lightness. 'If He does not want me to be a vampire, no doubt He will have his way.'

Trust in providence! thought Noell. Without undue pause, he passed the blade of the blood-stained knife through the candle flame for a second time, and then he scored Quintus's arm exactly as he had scored Langoisse's. He placed the cup on the table-top, and Quintus let the blood run over his skin to drip from his wrist into the mixture.

The pirate looked from one to the other, first at the monk, and then at the mechanician's son, but he did not speak until the flow of blood had eased. Then, he said: 'We will be brothers now, will we not? Past hatreds are dissolved, whether forgiven or not. Whatever becomes of us, we are akin.'

Noell took up the cup, and weighed it briefly in his hand. Then he offered it to Langoisse, remembering as it was taken from him how the Lady Cristelle had once offered her blood to this man, who had refused it once, and then taken it at another time. He remembered, too, how the same lady had asked to drink *his* blood, and how he had refused her, in spite of her distress.

Langoisse did not hesitate. He was quite ready for this moment, and no thought of what the cup contained could give him pause. He dipped his fingers in the bloody mixture, then clapped his hand upon his arm, and rubbed away at the wound, gasping at the pain but not shirking in the least. Then, he took his own dagger and made a cut upon his breast, and rubbed his fingers there too.

These touches were painful, and Langoisse made a face, but he was avid to press as much of the mixture as he could preserve into his wounded flesh. 'Well, Master Cordery?' he said. 'Dost take the draught with me?'

Noell was not entirely prepared, for his thoughts were in turmoil and his heart was racing in his breast. Nevertheless, he found sufficient composure to hold out the cup, steadily enough, to Quintus. The monk reached out, to take some of the mixture on his fingertips, and then – with much more delicacy than Langoisse had shown – touched it to the wound upon his arm, tracing the length of the cut, moving his sticky fingers slowly back and forth.

Noell, to his alarm, felt nauseous, though he remembered that when he had watched the rite in Iletigu, it had been Quintus and not he who had sought to hide his eyes.

He put his fingers to the rim of the cup, and was about to draw what remained there on to his fingers, when he was interrupted by a sudden thought. 'Leilah,' he whispered.

'What of it?' replied the pirate, very quickly, and with unseemly roughness.

'She should be here!'

Langoisse made no reply, but reached forward with his bloodied hand to press Noell's fingers to the cup, forcing him to take the slimy stuff whether he would or no. Then the pirate snatched the cup from him, and ran his own fingers greedily around the bowl, trying to scrape up every last drop of what it had contained.

The pirate looked at him, and fiercely said: 'I brought you life, Master Cordery. Use it, or be damned!'

Noell hesitated a moment more, crushed by the pirate's apparent cruelty in leaving his mistress behind. Then he gave way to the rushing pressure of events, and clasped his fingers tightly about his arm, digging his nails into the wound which he had made, biting his lip against the great surge of pain which made him shudder with distress.

When that surge finally eased, and he opened the tear-filled eyes which he had closed against the hurt, Noell watched Langoisse lick his bloody fingers, one by one.

'I wish I'd sweet Madeira wine to soothe the taste away,' the pirate said. 'We might drink a toast to the endurance of our souls, and the hope that our bodies might remain intact until the end of time. Brothers, Master Cordery, kin we are, and naught can change it now.'

Then, and only then, did Noell ask the question which he had not been able to ask, because it was not *seemly*. 'How, Langoisse?' he whispered. 'How did you get the semen?'

'Why,' said the pirate, 'what does it matter how? Did you care, when you put it in my mind that I might steal it? Were you careful to say how I might and might not go about the task, when you told me that we must quit this place? Oh no, my brother in blood . . . you did not care then, and you must not ask me now.'

Noell was hurt by the taunt. The pain of his self-inflicted wound was far greater than he had anticipated, and there was a sickness too which churned in his gut, unexpectedly.

'There is no time for this,' said Quintus, reasserting the command which he had long ago surrendered to his protegé. 'I will bandage your arms, and you must bind mine. If we become vampires, the wounds will no doubt heal, but if we do not, they will need protection. And then we must make haste, to get out of this place. Will you fetch Leilah, Langoisse, when I have bound your wound?'

'Oh aye,' said Langoisse, fingering the second wound which he had made upon his breast. 'Bind me well, father, for we have a longer way to go tonight than we may imagine. I'll fetch my little darling, and the black man too, for we must make sure to count among our party a sufficient source of blood. I suppose Ngadze will come, though he has not been forewarned?'

'I hope so,' said Quintus. 'I believe that he is homesick now. At any rate, I do not think he will raise an alarm.'

Noell, to his shame, felt his gorge rise again, as he realised this implication of what he had done, and knew that he should have considered it before. But the thought that Langoisse had withheld this elixir from his mistress, because he might need her for his vampire's prey, was so appalling in its callousness that Noell could not find words to voice his pain. He had so bravely used the pirate to serve his end, and never thought how Langoisse might serve his own. And to mock him too, with these claims of brotherhood in crime!

The thought that he might now become a predator, to use Ntikima and Ngadze as Ghendwa had once used them, was more hurtful than he could have imagined. He fought to control himself, and suffered Quintus to bind his arm while the pirate left the room, swaggering in a fashion which Noell had not seen for many years.

'What have I done?' asked Noell, of his dearest, yet untrusted, friend. 'What have I done?'

Quintus did not immediately reply, but looked at him hard-eyed, knowing that he had not been told, that he had not been trusted, that his judgement had not been sought. He was hurt, and Noell could see that hurt in his ancient face; he was injured by the knowledge that Noell had been ashamed to tell him what was in his mind.

'Only time will tell,' replied the man of God. 'Perhaps thou hast delivered us from all that threatens us. Perhaps thou hast failed in everything, save to hasten us to uncomfortable death.'

TWELVE

When they hurried through the dark corridors and across the open space atop the ridge, none tried to hinder their going. While they found their way down a winding cleft to reach the outer slopes of Adamawara, they were forced to go most carefully, with only the light of the stars and a crescent moon to guide them, but all the five came safely down, and by the time they were among the trees dawn was near to breaking.

The four donkeys which they had brought safely to Adamawara a year before were waiting patiently, tethered to a tree, but there was no sign of Ntikima. There were packs on the donkeys' backs, containing food and blankets; in one there were four muskets, with powder and shot, and Noell was glad to see them, though not as cock-a-hoop as Langoisse. Noell looked all around, wondering why Ntikima was not there, but it was necessary to make all speed in getting away. When Kantibh or Aiyeda discovered that they had gone, a chase was sure to ensue.

They took the donkeys, each of the four men guiding one while Leilah lagged behind, and they began to make their way down a steep slope, which led them to the north-west, away from the country of the elemi. Noell looked back but once, as much to catch a glimpse of the gypsy as to look at the hard grey heights, but it was the sternness of the mountains which called forth an echo in his soul.

Farewell to the Garden of Eden, he thought, sarcastically, *and on, if we can, to the land where the sons of Cain cry havoc.*

He was not sorry to be gone from Adamawara, but could not help feeling anxious about the uncertainties of the way that lay ahead. As the company progressed under the shadow of the forest canopy, whose end they would not see for many days, he wondered whether a man who was becoming a vampire could feel the change inside him, and what feeling that might be. In his own self, he felt no different at all, but did not know whether this was a sign that his makeshift elixir had failed.

Quintus was the one who led the way, taking his direction from the sun. They had only the vaguest notion of the route they must follow, despite the attention they had paid to the way they had come, but their resolve was to keep as straight as they could until they came out of the evil forest and into the lands of the Sahra, where they might find food. If the Sahra would help them, and offer them the same hospitality as before, then they would be able to equip themselves to cross the first of the grasslands before it had dried into a firetrap. Then, of course, there would be the Fulbai to face, and though they had only a few guns and donkeys, they were an attractive target for thieves.

Though they were safe from the silver death, having suffered its ravages once and recovered, the lifeless forest was still a daunting prospect, with its unnatural trees, its oppressive silence, and its uneven ground. The donkeys made slow progress despite the thinness of the undergrowth, but they were able to continue long into the afternoon, taking brief rests every hour, because the shade and the altitude kept the sun's heat from becoming too troublesome.

It was not until the sun was sinking in the west that they stopped to rest, and while Noell pulled off his boots wearily in order to inspect his feet, which had been so softened during his time in the city that they were blistering badly, he looked anxiously back along their path for any hint that Mkumkwe warriors were on their trail.

He could see no immediate indication of pursuit, and turned his full attention to his feet. As he inspected the tender spots, wincing with the discomfort, he wished fervently that he had the vampire trick of quieting pain. Langoisse came to sit beside him, and remarked that his elixir seemed so far to have failed them.

'We must wait and see what happens,' said Noell. 'If we become vampires, well and good. If not, then I will have more work to do when we return to Gaul. Perhaps there are many foul concoctions yet to test before the secret is found.' Langoisse went away.

Leilah came to Noell, then, and took Langoisse's place beside him while the pirate went to help in the building of a fire, where the water

for supper would be set to boil. Noell wondered whether it was wise
to risk the making of the fire, but he knew that the passage of five
humans and four donkeys would make too obvious a track to be missed.
If the Mkumkwe came after them, they would know which way to
come.

He did not doubt that they would come – but when? And where
was Ntikima?

'Hast thou forgiven me, then?' asked Leilah.

'Didst need forgiveness?' he asked, in surprise. 'If anyone has been
betrayed, surely it was thee?'

She stared at him, and he wondered if she knew what had happened.

'Did Langoisse tell you nothing?' he asked, in a whisper full of pain.
'I made an elixir last night, with his help, but he would not bring you
with him to try it, and . . . .'

Suddenly, he read in her eyes what he should have known from the
very beginning – what he should have understood not yesterday but
several days before. He knew then why Langoisse had taunted him,
and saw how very stupid he had been. He asked himself, bitterly, how
in all the world he had avoided knowing, when he had seen what
Langoisse brought him in the little jar.

'*You*' he whispered. '*You* procured the semen.'

'Thou didst not know?' she asked, far less anxious than he about his
ignorance. 'But 'twas thee who explained to Langoisse how the vampire
ladies of Gaul were made by their lovers' discharge. I thought thou
must have known that he would send me whoring after Kantibh, and
were bitter with jealousy, despite the pretty vampire lover who came
so often to thine own bed.'

Noell felt a sudden impulse to laugh, as he realised that Langoisse
had not brought her to their meeting because she had already had taken
her ration, in less elaborate fashion than they, of that which might
make her immortal. And the pirate had let him believe that he sought
to use her for his prey!

'The man has the devil's sense of a jest,' he muttered, hardly knowing
whether to cry in delight or curse his stupidity.

'Kantibh was nothing but whoring,' she told him, defiantly. 'I did
as I was commanded.'

'I too,' replied Noell, 'though my whoring after secret wisdom seems
to have come to naught. Perhaps the dark gods have their part to play
after all, and do not like us for our presumption.'

They were silent for a while, watching as the sun went down, and
darkness fell upon the forest like a cloak. Then Ngadze called out to
them, complaining that they must eat, and Noell put his boots back
on. He stood up first, and reached out a hand to help her rise. She took
it, eagerly enough.

'I have forgiven thee,' she whispered, though she would not meet his eyes.

'And I thee,' he replied, and squeezed her hand within his own before letting go so that they might walk to the fire and join in the meal.

They posted a guard when they went to sleep. First Ngadze stood watch, and then Noell. Langoisse was still exultant with the fire that had come back into his weary frame, but Noell knew the pirate would need every minute of his rest, and Quintus too. He was resolved for his own part to stay awake all night, if it should be necessary.

He had lost all track of time, and perhaps had dozed a little, when he saw the lights dancing in the forest, and knew that their pursuers had not rested at all, but had come after them even through the night.

He moved the musket which lay across his knees, then reached out to stir Ngadze with its butt.

'They are upon us,' he whispered, 'and we must fight.'

Ngadze looked out into the night, and tried to count the pinpricks of light which moved between the trees. 'Egungun?' he asked.

'Does it matter what masks they wear?' said Noell. 'You are Ibau, and Egungun belongs to the Uruba.'

The black man shook his head, fearfully. 'The Ogbone have given Egungun to all their peoples,' he said. 'If Egungun come, we all must die, white and black alike, for this is their own land, and none can stand against the risen dead, wherever they appear.'

'Take up a gun,' said Noell, 'and wake the others. We stood against them once before, and brought Shango to our aid. We must do the same again.'

He tried to make a rough wall from the packs, that they might lie behind a crude redoubt and rest the muzzles of their guns upon it. But when he saw the great ugly masks lit by the torches which their pursuers carried, he wondered what use his powder and shot would be. These were Egungun, to be sure, and in such numbers that five men, well-armed or not, could hardly hope to stand against them. As they approached, bearing spears as well as torches, they seemed to him a mighty host, sent against them by Shigidi.

We stopped them before, he told himself, *with but a single shot.*

Somehow, he did not think a single shot would be enough, this time.

'Trust in Shango,' he murmured. Then Ngadze knelt beside him, and Quintus on his other side. Behind him, he heard Langoisse say: 'Wait until they are close, and aim not at the masks, but at the unprotected bodies beneath.'

There was a clearing around their camp, and a huge rounded rock just beyond its edge, with withered trees beside it. When the Egungun came around the rock they gathered there, forty yards away, raising their torches and their spears in threat. Noell counted them as they emerged to form a great long line. There were thirty-five in all.

'Wait,' said Langoisse, in a whisper. 'Take careful aim, and do not waste your shots, for the love of Heaven!'

But as he spoke, another figure appeared, on top of the great rock, lit by the fire of the torches which the Egungun carried. This one was not the same as the others, but had a painted body, and wore a mask more gorgeously endowed, on which the jagged whiteness of lightning stood out from a night-black ground. The eyes which were set in the mask held such a measure of wrath that even the white men drew breath at their awesome stare.

'*Don't fire!*' whispered Noell, with sudden urgency. 'For the love of God, hold still!'

Noell had seen this figure once before, in the rite which he had watched in Iletigu. He had known it then for the representation of a god – a god who had more power in Adamawara than any other, save only Olorun. *This* god had made Adamawara. Noell knew now what Ntikima had meant when he had said that they must put their trust in Shango.

The Egungun took one pace forward, and then a voice rang out behind them, magnified by a cone of wood in the mask's wide mouth, calling them to halt. And halt they did, for they were not at that moment men of the Mkumkwe, but the risen dead come back to call the living to account: subjects not of the elemi but of the gods. And the one upon the mound was not Ntikima at all but Shango, god of storms and master of thunder and lightning.

The Egungun turned, and the figure high above them began to beat upon a drum, while its magnified voice howled out an incantation, whose syllables rose and fell like the wind howling in a storm. The Egungun bowed low, as they were bound to do by their nature, and they knelt, and they listened to what it was that they were ordered to do.

Noell counted his heartbeats while the strange shrieking filled the air, keening in such an eerie fashion that he could hardly believe the sounds were produced by a human throat. On and on went the strange song, neither prayer nor invocation, in a language which Noell did not know, and somehow did not ever want to learn.

Beside him, Quintus was whispering an appeal of his own, in the Latin of the Roman church. Even Langoisse made the sign of the cross, and Ngadze shivered in superstitious terror, as he had before when he watched the gods at work in the world of men.

Leilah put her hand on Noell's shoulder, as though the fingers could make a bridge between their souls, to carry courage in whichever direction it was required to flow. And on the hill, Shango spoke, and extended the spell of his protection to those he sought to save, in spite of the elders of Adamawara. The Egungun listened, and listened well.

When it was over, the Egungun lifted off their masks, and cast them down upon the ground, so that the torchlight fell upon their painted faces, which no longer seemed ferocious, but only ugly. It was a company of men, and not the risen dead, who went away into the forest, singing to themselves a sad lament. They sang because they had met a god in the forest, who had commanded them to be less than they were, and they would never again be the same.

When they had all gone, Shango came down from his throne, and walked slowly to the white men's fire. Then he took off his bright and savage face, and became Ntikima.

'Once,' said the boy, 'I was pledged to Aroni, fated to learn the plants of the forest and become a great magician. Now, I am Shango's, and must shave my head and wear the beads which are the colour of blood. And when I am old, I might return to Adamawara, to be made his elemi in Ogo-Ejodun.'

Then he sat by the fire, and shivered, while they gave him some food.

The next day was no different, in any important respect, from the first, save that they now were six, and no longer five. The straps of Noell's pack chafed, and the blisters on his feet made him limp as he walked. His throat was perpetually dry because he rationed his water very meanly, not knowing when they next might reach a stream or pool. Again, they forged on during the hot afternoon, intent on reaching the far side of the forest in as few days as possible.

By comparison with the slow headway they had made when coming in the other direction, they did well, though Langoisse was sick and Quintus tired. Again, when they stopped for the night, Leilah came to Noell as he sat by himself, some way from the tents. This time, she was in a different mood. She did not avoid his eye, but wanted him to look at her, and though she said nothing, he was not long in doubt as to her implication.

In the bright glare of day it had not been obvious, but in the shadows, and the flickering light of the fire, there was a definite lustre in her skin. Her complexion had always been smooth, but the smoothness now was taking on that extraordinary perfection and sheen which marked Berenike's skin, and advertised what she was.

'I feel strange,' she said. 'My hurt is not hurt any more, though I feel the blood coursing in my body as never before. Dost thou . . . ?'

'Nay,' replied Noell, hollowly. 'I have no such feeling.'

He looked then at his hands – both the palms and the backs – and found them wrinkled and rubbed. When he put his fingertips to his face, he could feel the sweat, and the many blemishes he knew to be there. When he touched his bandaged arm, the wound burned beneath his touch. He was as he had always been, stricken with all the manifold signs of common mortality.

He wanted to ask her how many times she had been with Kantibh, and whether the time she had brought his semen in her mouth for Langoisse to bring to him was the first or one of several, but he could not bring himself to speak of it. It could not matter, in any case. Even if he could make himself hope a little longer, hope would neither help or hinder him. Hope was irrelevant. The change would come, or it would not.

'And now thou wilt love me,' she told him, in a low voice, 'because I am a vampire lady, as Langoisse always promised me. And I will have thy blood to sustain me, will I not?'

He looked at her, not knowing what to say or to think.

'Langoisse?' he asked.

'No sign,' she said. 'But I do not think he likes me enough to offer me his blood. I am no longer his, and I have no use for him.' Her voice was so serene, her manner so thoughtful, that Noell wanted to laugh, but he dared not.

'Quintus?' he asked. He looked about him, searching for the monk, and found him tending to the donkeys. He hobbled across the space between them, somehow feeling far more frail than he had felt all day, and took his friend by the arm, turning him so that the ruddy light of the setting sun, filtering through the curling leaves, caught his features and made them shine. Quintus had always seemed to be carved from polished wood, his tanned skin stretched and sealed. It was hard to judge the beginning of a difference, but he was suddenly sure that it was there.

'Quintus?' he said, again, and stopped, not knowing how to ask the question. But the monk knew what it was.

'Aye,' he replied, softly. 'I think 'tis so. I am not sure, yet, but I must pray for my soul, that it may be worthy of such a body. The souls of so many clearly are not.'

'Langoisse?' asked Noell, but Quintus shrugged his shoulders.

'I do not know,' said the monk. 'But I could not think, when we began, that he could come so far and still be on his feet. He will have his dearest wish, I do believe.'

'But *why*?' asked Noell, in a fearful whisper. 'Three took the elixir. How can some receive the gift, and not another? For the love of God, Quintus, what is *wrong* with me?'

'I do not know,' said Quintus. 'Believe me, Noell, I would trade places with thee, if I could.'

They came eventually to the place where they had found the bodies of the dead men, whose skin had become stretched upon their bones when the flesh had withered and wasted away, under the heat of the sun.

There was one more body now to be counted in that strange group. Like the others, it had not been attacked by scavengers, and had been left to decay slowly, after the peculiar fashion of things in this mysterious forest. They had no difficulty in recognising Selim the Turk, whose madness had brought him here to die.

It seemed that the Turk belonged in this company, for as the flesh upon the other faces had dried out and shrivelled, their noses had become shrunken and distorted, as his had been. He no longer seemed a monster cruelly set loose in a world of more perfect beings, but a murdered creature among murdered creatures, worthy of pity. Langoisse knelt before the body for a few moments, to whisper an improbable prayer; then they went on.

They came, in the fullness of time, to the pleasanter forest where the trees were not so twisted; where flowers grew, and insects flew, and birds sang. The further they went, the more birds there were, and many other living things which they were glad to see. They found water here in abundance, and were able to forage for food.

In due course they came out of the forest altogether, and on to the high plain where the Sahra planted their fields and kept their cattle. The chiefs of the Sahra villages made them welcome, and feasted with them, and danced to celebrate their passing, as they had always done for the elect of Adamawara, who were made of finer flesh than themselves.

And so it was to be in other lands through which they passed on their long and weary way. News of their progress went ahead of them, often, because there was something momentous in their arrival in each new place: they had come from Adamawara, and some of their party were vampires.

There was no way for those who made them welcome to know, or to understand, what sadness and bitterness there was in at least two of their hearts. Noell renewed his endeavour to make himself a vampire, with the means which he now had readily to hand, but his further attempts to overcome his mortality were no more successful than his first.

And when they came, at last, to a place which they could count a destination, it was still the same. Two of those three who had sworn themselves brothers in blood were vampires; and one was not.

PART FIVE

The Blood of Martyrs

'A prince, so long as he keeps his subjects united and loyal, ought not to mind the reproach of cruelty; by setting good examples he will achieve a better end than those who, in being merciful, permit disorders to arise; for disorders injure the whole people, while a prince's executions offend only individuals . . .

'If the question is posed, whether it be better to be loved than feared or feared than loved, the ready answer is that it is better to be both; because it is difficult to unite these qualities in one person, however, it must be said that it is much safer to be feared than loved if one or other must be chosen . . . men have less scruple in offending one who is beloved than one who is feared, for love is preserved by the link of obligation which, owing to the baseness of men, is broken at every opportunity for their advancement; but fear preserves by the dread of punishment, which never fails.'

(Niccolo Machiavelli, *The Vampire Prince*)

PROLOGUE

The de-ciphered text of a letter received by Sir Kenelm Digby in London in the summer of 1660.

Malta, May 1660

To my dearest friend, Sahha!

No glad tidings have ever been more welcome to me than the news that England is liberated from the Imperium of Gaul, that Richard and his Norman knights are banished, and that a Parliament of new vampires now presides over a British Commonwealth. The knowledge that my home is free lightens my heart, and I am greatly glad that the victory was accomplished without the shedding of overmuch blood. That Richard accepted the untenability of his position in the face of your manoeuvres allows me to believe that all his prating and posturing in the name of the chivalric ideal, by which Gaulish vampire knights have ever sought to glorify themselves, has in it a core of sincerity and reason.

What has happened in England gives me hope for the future of Gaul entire, and I pray that the end of Charlemagne's empire might now be accomplished without such a carnival of destruction as would plunge all Europe into an age of darkness and despair.

I know that in hands such as yours, the elixir whose secret I made known will be used wisely and justly. It will bring the world nearer to a condition in which all men will have reasonable hope that when they have long enough borne the trials and tribulations of frailer common flesh, the chance to be immortal will not be denied them. With the aid of this secret which is secret no more, I believe that England will become a great nation in the remade world. Now that the existence of the new Atlantic continent has been determined, the opportunity is there for British mariners to create an empire more glorious than any that was ever devised by Attila's kin, and this is the work which must be yours in the centuries to come.

While the northern nations still fight to throw of the yoke of Charlemagne's rule, and the southern princes are beset from all sides by their enemies, your people and mine must build a New Atlantis in the west, as Francis Bacon prophesied. Of all the nations in Gaul and Walachia, Britain alone stands to emerge from the present conflict strengthened.

My heart is warmed by your urging that Quintus and I should return to England, now that she is free. I am sure that Langoisse could bring us safely through the hostile waters which stand between us, but I do not feel that the time is right for us to quit our station here. We have promised a great deal to the men of this island, and they have treated us most generously. Without the conversion of the knights of St. John to our cause, the secret which we brought to Europe might have been more effectively suppressed. To leave these allies now would seem an unkind desertion, and I would not like to do it. Your invitation to the Order of St. John to bring its knights to London is considered most generous by the Grandmaster, but the Pillars of the order could no more think of abandoning Malta, which has been their home and stronghold for a hundred and thirty years, than you could have thought of deserting England while the battle to force Richard into exile was yet to be fought.

The reasoned omens say that Malta's direst hour may now be fast approaching; the knights of St. John will not shirk defence of their tiny realm, and I will do everything in my power to help them. I am an Englishman first and always, but my loyalty now must be to those who befriended me in an hour of desperate need. I spent too great a fraction of my life in leaving action to others; now I am become a man who takes credit for his ambitions I must take my stand with those who have served my ends.

You are probably in a position to gather far better intelligence than we of the disintegration of Gaul and Walachia, and what response the emperors plan to make. A few of the younger princelings have secretly offered support to our cause, because they see in our rebellion an opportunity for advancement which they could never have had while the older immortals held their power. For most of them, of course, our ideals are simply a convenient mask to put upon their ambition, but while they use us, we may also use them. There are many printing presses, and common men enthusiastic for their use no matter what the risk. We set out to disseminate the secret of the elixir so widely throughout Christendom that it could never again be put away and hidden, and we have found such a host of allies that I know the work is done. Unless miracles come to my aid, I will not live to see Charlemagne and Attila capitulate, and the old order absorbed into the new; but I will die knowing that such a capitulation is inevitable, and that I have helped to bring the great day forward.

We continue to hear rumours that our exploits have so annoyed the vampires of Gaul and Walachia that they intend to raise a great Armada of ships at Cagliari, Naples and Palermo, bringing galleys from Spain, Italy and France into a fleet which will overwhelm our own forces and land an army to devastate the entire island. The pope has now excommunicated the entire Order of St. John, and declared anathema against them, proclaiming Malta to be a nest of vile pirates. This shows singular ingratitude, given that it was the Knights of St. John and their navy which mastered the Turks in the Mediterranean, and have helped keep Europe safe from a seaborne invasion for a hundred and fifty years, but it is no more than we expected.

Villiers de l'Isle Adam, as Grandmaster and guardian of the Order, is by no means unperturbed by these threats, but he stoutly declares that the knights are well used to such ungrateful treatment, and would expect no more from a false pope who is naught but a gaudy puppet of the godless vampires. It is because he has long held such an opinion that the Knights Hospitallers were so readily won to our cause. La Valette, who is the greatest naval commander in Christendom – as even Langoisse admits – has said that if this Armada comes, then Malta will withstand its siege just as it withstood the great siege of 1565, when Suleyman the Magnificent failed to destroy it. Then, the Order had less than a hundred vampire knights; today Malta has four hundred vampire fighters within the Order and a further three hundred without, not one of whom will easily surrender the privilege of longevity to fire and the sword.

Our enemies have tried to frighten us by promising to send Vlad Tepes himself against us, and your own Coeur-de-Lion with him, at the head of a new crusade of Gaulish knights. I cannot pretend that we are not disturbed by such possibilities, but I know that our allies cannot be terrorised into any renunciation of the path which they have taken. If Attila and Charlemagne themselves were to emerge from their seclusion to put on their armour the men of Malta would gladly take the field against them.

Langoisse and la Valette have done their best to convince our followers that it is not the greatness of heroes which determines the outcome of battles, no matter what the balladeers and romancers may claim. They insist that our fleet, which has such a preponderance of sailing ships, with their cannon mounted broadside, is a great force to be reckoned with at sea, and will not easily be defeated by any armada which consists almost entirely of Spanish and Italian galleys. Our hunters of the sea, they say, can destroy ships without needing to send out boarders, while the galleys – which have only oarsmen at their flanks – can hardly make effective defence of themselves.

Alas, I cannot share their optimism, though I am no man of the sea. I fear that we have far fewer good cannon than we need. Langoisse and la Valette are well used to battles in which only a few ships are involved, but I fear that if what we hear is true, then the coming battle of Malta might be the greatest conflict of ships that the world has yet seen. We discount the stories which say that an army of three thousand vampire knights will be raised, because we believe that such a number could never be spared from the war in the north, but whatever force sets out against us will be intended to make a clear and unmistakable demonstration that Attila's empires will deal harshly with their enemies.

I must enter a renewed plea here, though I know that you have already told me that you cannot answer it. If only your new Parliament could send us two hundred Sussex cannon made from Sturtevant's iron, I might be prepared to believe that we could stand off any fleet which the world could muster against us. I do not ask for the aid of Britain's fleet, which is the chief defence of our island nation, but if a few cargo ships could bring such guns to add to our artillery, it would make a reckonable difference to our strength.

As things stand now we have been forced to send emissaries to Tunis and Tripoli asking for support. My darling Leilah asked to be our ambassador, but we dared not send a vampire among the Mohammedans, and so we used liberated prisoners who once were oarsmen in Christian galleys. We have made representations to the sultans on the grounds that we are the enemy of their enemies, and hence might be reckoned friends, but the hatred which the Turkish sea-captains have for the knights of Malta will make them most reluctant to come to our aid. I think it more than likely that the Turks will bide their time, rejoicing meanwhile that Christendom is being torn apart by its internal struggles.

Sometimes, I too wonder whether the grey sages of Adamawara might not have been right to conclude that the world of the unfinished is too violent to permit any future but its own destruction. But I avoid despair; I remain convinced that the elders of that mysterious valley are themselves incomplete, having sheltered themselves all too well from the ambitions of civilisation. If I have ever known a truly finished man – by which I mean a man in whose nature and temper there lies the seed of a finer world – then that man is my friend Quintus. I know that you too are that kind of man, and it is to your like – to men of science and men who love justice – that I look for hope that the future of mankind will be bright.

Despite my continued labours, I still have no clue as to why the elixir will not work upon my own flesh, nor that of those few unfortunate others who share my stubborn mortality. Perhaps that God, in which Quintus and you believe so firmly, loves this miserable unbeliever so ardently that He cannot bear to delay the moment when I shall be delivered into His care. Or it may be that He wishes to hurry me into the care of that Other, whom the Gregorians assert to be the parent and master of the vampire race. I cannot tell.

In any case, I have become reconciled to the fact that I belong to that company which is marked for early death. With things as they are in Europe, I believe that there will be many vampires who will precede me to the grave, for there is burgeoning violence everywhere now that common men are hungry for the blood of those who have preyed upon them for a thousand years.

The deterioration in my eyesight has continued, and although I wear spectacles at all times, save when I am at my microscope, I cannot obtain proper relief. I believe that I must have some disease which is affecting the interior of my eye, and I think that I might soon go blind. I cannot help but consider this a suitably ironic fate. I remain convinced that all diseases are caused by tiny living agents which penetrate the body and disturb its operation, and yet I have not identified with confidence even a handful of such creatures, despite the aid of the instrument which you forged for me so long ago. I have tried since coming to Malta to obtain better and more powerful combinations of lenses, in the hope of looking yet deeper into the heart of things, but it seems that these agents, if they do exist, are determined to strike back at me, and frustrate my quest.

In spite of these difficulties, I have continued with experiments with the transformed semen which vampires produce, and have not contented myself with attempts to enhance the power of the elixir. I dare not say now what I think I may achieve, but I am embarked upon a series of investigations which may give us more power over the forces of life and death. Quintus knows what I am doing, and the Grandmaster too, but I have not told many others, because

I think that it would alarm them, and because I fear to fail. I have retired to Mdina in order to carry out this work, and I think that la Valette and his fighting men have not been sorry to see me leave the region of the Grand Harbour, for I have such a reputation as wizard and alchemist as makes me fearful in spite of my frailty. Vampires dislike to be in the company of ugliness, and I have to say that no one could now believe that I was once the worthy son of the handsomest man in England.

Quintus is not with me just now, having gone to the south of the island to examine a stone unearthed at Marsa Xloqq, which carries an inscription in two different tongues – one the Greek which he already knows, the other a tongue which is foreign to him, which may be the language which the islanders spoke when they were part of the empire of Carthage. If Quintus is right about its nature, that stone was lost long before St. Paul was driven here by tempestuous Euroclydon and shipwrecked on the island. It is a link to a more distant past than any vampire of the order remembers.

Quintus has said to me that the strange stone circles which can be found on the island are as ancient as any in England, and he has been fascinated too by certain bones exhumed from the caves of Ghar Dalam, which the islanders claim to be the bones of giants. Gigantic they certainly are, but Quintus believes them to be the bones of elephants rather than men, and wonders if the Carthaginians brought such beasts here when they were the island's governors. Immortality has made him not one whit less avid for the wisdom and understanding which he has always craved, and I cannot believe that he will ever fall into the kind of waking dream which claimed so many vampires in Adamawara. I can say with confidence that in the centuries of life which stretch before you, there will be time enough for all the matters of state and science to which your ambition and your curiosity bid you. A man such as you, I think, would not waste a single day of life no matter how long he might live, nor be led to desolation by the tedium of eternity.

Write to me again as soon as your duties will give you time. Send me news of your new parliament, and of the Commonwealth which you have built in England, and of the progress of explorations in Atlantis. Tell me all that you can which is good and bright and hopeful, for that is the kind of news which we desperately need.

Remember, I beg you, to pray for all of us, that we might prevail against the assaults of Gaul and Walachia.

Fare well, my friend, and be happy.

Noell Cordery

ONE

The Voivode Vlad the Fifth – whose scribes signed him Dragulya, and who was known to the world as Vlad Tepes, the Impaler – returned in a poor temper from the council of war to his lodgings on the outskirts of the city of Naples.

There had been a time, perhaps two hundred years earlier, when the news that Vlad Tepes was in a poor temper would have set his entire entourage trembling, and struck terror into the heart of anyone who might have incurred his wrath. Those were the days in which he had earned his name, and earned it full well, first in putting down the only serious rebellion which Attila's empire had ever faced, and then in his historic victory over the Turks who had taken advantage of Walachia's trouble to mount an invasion. Vlad's army had clashed with the army of Mohammed II at the Danube, and had won a great victory for Attila, for Walachia and for Christendom.

Dragulya's enemies then had been treated utterly without mercy, and he had been a man ever eager to find more enemies, whose opposition to his will could be quickly snuffed out. His dark fame had been spread throughout Europe by the poet Michael Beheim, who had carried blood-curdling tales of his deeds to all the courts in Walachia, causing more anxiety than relief to Attila's long-lived princes, who feared that this upstart might outshine them all in the emperor's favour.

Centuries had passed since Dragulya had last planted a forest of stakes whose sharpened points were to be driven remorselessly into the bodies of his enemies. He was by no means averse to arranging the odd impalement, but he had lately kept the habit within the bounds that might be expected of a civilised man, and usually did it somewhat in the spirit of a jest – for he liked to think himself a very humorous man, after his own fashion.

His followers nowadays liked to tell the tales of his most famous jests – when he had had the caps of a group of cardinals nailed to their heads because they would not doff them in his presence; or when he flayed the soles of Mohammed's faithless messengers and let goats lick salt from the raw wounds – and they laughed more freely at such incidents than once they had. In those times when Dragulya's cruel jokes were of more common occurrence, and were feared as fates which might befall any visitor or member of his household, none had taken much pleasure in the telling of the stories, though that had not prevented their being told.

The response of his servants now to news of his annoyance was a very ordinary determination to be careful, and Dragulya, when he saw it, regretted that he had not better maintained his reputation for horrors. His opinion was that if he and others had more diligently followed the examples he had set in his treatment of the Turks, the enemies which were within Attila's empire would not be so eager to make their bid to topple it. This opinion had been brought to the forefront of his mind by his meeting with the man sent by Charlemagne to be his partner in the enterprise which faced him. If Richard the Norman had ever honestly won the right to be called Lionheart (which Dragulya doubted) then he had surely lost it during the last year.

When Dragulya had removed his quilted armour, which he had been forced by protocol to wear despite the oppressive heat, he sent immediately for Beheim, who was now his friend and adviser. That had been one of his kinder jests, for when the minstrel had first been brought to Dragulya's court he had fully expected the Impaler to drive a pointed stick up his arse and stand him up in the courtyard to die – uncomfortably slowly – as his own weight dragged his guts downwards about the point. Instead, it had been something else entirely that the noble prince had stuck into his anus, and instead of being killed he had been made immortal. And why? Because the princes of Gaul, inspired by Charlemagne, all had their minstrels to flatter them with music and wit, and Vlad Tepes had desired a minstrel to suit his own peculiar temper – a poet who would celebrate the power of his wrath as he wished to hear it celebrated.

Perhaps, thought Dragulya, now, *there was not difference enough in choosing to be painted a monster instead of a hero. To accept a flatterer at all was to admit a Gaulish weakness that should have been condemned.*

Michael Beheim came not hurriedly in answer to his master's summons, but not because he was apprehensive of the voivode's mood. He had learned through the long years that what Dragulya most valued in him was his insolence – an impudence which he alone was licensed to possess – and he always liked to be lazy in responding when he was called. On this occasion, though, his late arrival was greeted by a scowl more ominous than was usual

'How went the celebrations?' asked the poet of the warlord, uneasily.

Dragulya was relaxing in a lukewarm bath, with only his face and beard protruding from the scummy water. He did not seem very relaxed as yet, and his eyes – as Beheim might have described them in his poetic manner – were smouldering with anger. 'We met to plan a campaign,' he growled, 'not to celebrate a victory.'

'Most certainly,' replied Beheim. 'But the victory is never greater than in the planning, nor the celebration more joyous than in the anticipation. We poor artists, who can only tell the stories of battles once they have been fought, cannot paint so fabulous a picture as the schemes of the generals who have yet to take the field. Or am I wrong, and was there naught in your meeting with great Lionheart but strife and mistrust? That would be a pity and a vexation, not least for Blondel and I, who must tell it differently when our time comes to sing the praises of your triumph, when Malta is destroyed?'

The voivode raised his hand above the surface of the water, and brought it down again to make a dull splash. 'Lionheart!' he exclaimed, with disgust.

'You do not like Prince Richard,' observed Michael Beheim, deliberately calm in his statement of the obvious.

'The man is a fool! He has done the empires of our kind more damage with one act of monumental cowardice than all our enemies have inflicted in a thousand years of warfare. It is bad enough that this fool must be foisted on me, but intolerable that he looks at me with a distaste which he cannot conceal. He speaks to me with condescension, as if he believes me to be stupid. You could never guess, to hear this Richard talk, which one of us had lost his crown and accepted exile from his homeland. I do believe he takes a certain pride in his retreat, thinking that his reluctance to shed English blood reflects some noble regard for the cattle over which he reigned, and a degree of civilisation which we of the East are too crude to savour. *Civilisation!* I could not believe that this was a man who once fought the Mohammedans as fiercely as any, and I swear that his cursed Blondel must have told far bolder lies in singing his master's praises than ever you told of me.'

'But he has brought a thousand vampire knights to Cagliari,' Michael Beheim pointed out. 'We hardly dared to hope that the West could spare so many, with the Dutch and the Danes in open revolt, and all of Gaul in turmoil. Who else could Charlemagne send, when all his other princes are so urgently occupied? These Norman are not cowards, for all that they departed England without attempting to fight against unreasonable odds – and the slur upon their honour will make it all the more vital for them to distinguish themselves in the coming fight. I think they will serve us well, my lord.'

'Ach!' said Dragulya. 'I do not believe that these self-elected heroes know how to fight. I no longer trust their accounts of those crusades which once they fought. Their code of chivalry makes me sick with its vanities and posturings. Their tournaments have accustomed them to play at fighting instead of making war; of their thousand knights there can only be two hundred who have ever been in battle, and they like all the rest are spoiled by dreams and illusions. They have brought their warhorses and lances, but they leave nearly all their muskets to be carried by common soldiers, because they do not consider it honourable to bear such arms. Nor are all his common soldiers armed with guns – he has brought four hundred common men who are trained to fight with longbows!'

'Longbows, my lord?'

'Oh yes! Perhaps Richard was a fine fighter when the business of war was all swords and longbows, but he does not truly belong to our world. How else do you think he could have woken up one morning to find that those English cannon which are said to be the finest in the world were aimed against him instead of being set to defend him? Betrayed by his own mechanicians, unable or unwilling to keep a check on his common generals – the man is an imbecile! And then to surrender his citadel without a fight!'

'If the reports are true,' said Beheim, drily, 'all the vampire knights in England would have been slaughtered to a man, had he resisted.'

'*So be it!*' cried Dragulya. 'They'd have taken ten thousand commoners with them – and what those commoners had done would be a crime against nature which Gaul could punish in due course with a hundred thousand executions and the burning of every city in England. What Richard did made it not a crime and a blasphemy but a victory in ordinary war, and gave the message to the world that common men *could* fight against vampires, iron against iron. We have lost our standing as a legion of demons, and have become mere men of hardy flesh. We have lost the greatest ally we ever had – the dread of superstition – and it was Richard the Norman who betrayed us.'

'If he had stood his ground and submitted to annihilation,' said Beheim, 'England would still be lost to Gaul, and where would Charles have found a thousand knights to add to our strength in this coming conflict? Would you rather the Spanish and Italian ships were manned by the common scum of Europe?'

'I'd have none of them!' replied Dragulya, without hesitation. 'I'd rather fight with my thousand vampire Walachians, and a like number of my own common men, than have that number matched by any that Charles might give me. Attila was a fool to divide his empire with the Roman general in the days of the first conquest. In Gaul they still consider theirs the true empire, and Walachia a nest of barbarians. They have laughed at us behind their hands even while our kinsmen have built Khanates in India and Cathay, while our armies have defended Byzantium against the Sultans, and while our merchants have made safe the trade routes that connect them with the East. Attila should have sacked Rome, made one empire out of all the world, and proved himself a greater man than Alexander.'

'But Attila is not a man as great as that,' the poet reminded him, gently, 'as you know full well.'

'He was old before I ever knew him,' the voivode replied. 'Aye, and mad too. But in his own day . . . he was not always the stricken creature that he now is . . . I do not believe it.'

'If he had not been mad before he was made a vampire,' said Beheim, 'then likely he would not be mad today. No doubt he was a fiercer fighting man in the days of his conquests, but he was not a man who might really rule the world. It is not he whose authority has secured the fortunes of Walachia, but men like Frederick Barbarossa and your own father – aye, and men like yourself. Yours is the real power, and the true wonder is that you proclaim allegiance to Attila while you wield it. But still, that is history. What of tomorrow? You surely do not fear to lose this crusade against the Order of St. John, no matter how poorly Richard may support you?'

'Oh no,' said Dragulya, sarcastically. 'We cannot lose. Has not the pope himself come to bless our fighting men? The new vampires which this troublesome alchemist has made with his elixir cannot stand against an army such as ours – there can be no doubt of it. But who will be the real victors? Who will drink a full measure of strength and power in the blood of the defeated, now that England is lost to Gaul and Charlemagne's empire is crumbling like a house of cards? It is too late, Michael, too late.'

'The victory, my lord, will be measured by the songs of praise which are sung by such as I,' said Beheim, though he knew that the voivode had not his future fame in mind. 'If we sing it loudly enough, we may yet cast doubt upon the ambitions of our enemies, and turn the tide for Charles and for Walachia.'

'Our armies are combined to tell the world that Gaul and Walachia will stand together against a common enemy,' said Dragulya, 'but I fear that we will tell a different story to those who watch keenly. Even our friends may see a competition between Richard and myself, to see how we will answer those who stand against us, and even our victory might show us divided. We cannot destroy the secret which this Maltese alchemist has given to the world – we can only seek to use it more efficiently than our enemies, and in so doing we must give away our power by degrees. We are too late now to make an example of destruction sufficient to terrify the world.'

'Then march your men back home again. I for one would thank you if I had not to set foot on these creaking ships.'

'That I cannot do,' replied the voivode, rising from his bath and wrapping a cloak about himself. 'It would seem infinitely worse to turn around than to go on, and would surely encourage a rebellion in Walachia like the one which has already taken root in Gaul. We must take what small advantage is left for us to take, or our world might easily shatter, instead of submitting to a gradual decay which will let us keep our power for a while.'

'I have never seen you so concerned with seeming, my lord,' said the minstrel, unhappily. 'In the past, you have left the seeming of things to me, and have attended to the doing. I fear, sire, that long life is making you into a statesman.'

'I am a vampire prince,' retorted Dragulya, relating himself to the book by Niccolo Machiavelli, which was even more admired in the east than in the author's homeland. Indeed, the Voivode Vlad V *was* a vampire prince, who had learned to use cruelty and destruction most carefully. Even in his youth, when his wrath had held greater sway over his actions, he had always appreciated the virtue of being feared. Now, if his conscience troubled him at all, it troubled him because he had grown indolent in his cruelty, and had taken insufficient care to strike terror in the hearts of common men.

'You are the perfect model of a prince,' confirmed Beheim. 'But my lord, Richard is a prince too, if only according to his title. It would be as well, I think, if at the end of this campaign the two of you can stand together, to show the world that the vampire princes of Gaul and Walachia will act as one to put down these rebellions.'

The voivode sighed, acknowledging that his servant had the right of it. No matter how much he despised Richard, and no matter how monstrous it was that the Norman should presume to despise him, the battle had still to be fought, and the demonstration to be made. He finished drying himself, and stood naked for a moment, examining his body.

Dragulya's form was huge and powerful, massively muscled, as befitted a fighting man. Many vampires, satisfied with their immunity from pain and wounding, did not trouble to work their muscles over-hard. Though they never grew fat, they often grew soft, less strong than they might have been. Dragulya had never yielded to such temptation, for his strength was an obsession with him, and he despised all weakness. His father, Vlad III, called Dragul, had set his son a fine example in that respect, until the rebels had murdered him. But if this Vlad were to perish, he knew that he would be succeeded by his brother, Radu the Handsome, who was a man of very different kind. Radu was soft, more like the Norman Richard than Vlad his brother, both in appearance and in character.

Thought of Radu made Dragulya scowl again, as it always did. The Khanate was overfull of younger brothers and ungrateful sons, resentful that they had not power and must wait for centuries to get it, careless in their preparation to receive and use it. Was the world really worth preserving, he wondered, for the likes of Radu?

'What truly preserves our empires,' growled Dragulya, 'is the fact that they have so many enemies without, against whose menace we can close our ranks. Enemies within can only hurt us, even if we can destroy them.'

Beheim did not have to ask him what he meant. The empire of Walachia was united in hatred of the Turks, and in the constant need to fight them. That common enemy not only distracted attention from rivalries between the princes of the East, but offered hope to the two groups of men who might otherwise have been unduly troublesome:

the most powerful commoners, who could hope to distinguish themselves in that conflict and earn conscription to the vampire ranks; and the vampires who had elder kinsmen, whose hope of succeeding to positions of power and privilege lay in the warlords' exposure to constant danger from the alien foe. Enemies within were far more likely to seduce those groups to their own causes than to encourage loyal sentiments.

While his master dressed, Beheim poured wine from a flask into two crystal goblets, and waited patiently. He wondered whether Blondel de Nesle might at that very instant be making a similar offering to Richard. But if rumour were to be believed, the Norman prince preferred a different offering, and rarely drank wine if he could have blood instead. Dragulya seemed to find no pleasure in taking blood – except when he took it with a sword. While other vampires made an indulgence of necessity, Dragulya was plainly resentful of the need which made him in one small way dependent on those of weaker nature than himself.

The voivode took the goblet from Beheim's hand, and stared moodily into its depths.

'No gift from the pope, I assure you,' murmured the minstrel. The pope's experiments in the use of poison as an instrument of the art of diplomacy had made his name notorious.

Dragulya raised the vessel as if to make a toast, and then hesitated. He looked at his faithful minstrel, as he always did when he required inspiration in matters of ironic propriety.

'To the frustration of the enemies of Walachia?' suggested Beheim. 'Or perhaps we should rather offer up a prayer that God might guide the arrows of Richard's ridiculous bowmen?'

Dragulya managed only the thinnest of smiles. 'To the frustration of the enemies of Walachia,' he said, with a snarl. 'And let the arrows fly where they will, to wreak such tiny havoc as they may!'

TWO

Richard, deposed Prince of Grand Normandy, was in no better temper than Vlad Dragulya when he left the council of war. He went likewise from the conference to his lodgings, and likewise summoned his friend, the minstrel Blondel de Nesle. He also sent for his astrologer.

Blondel was of greater importance to Richard than Michael Beheim to Dragulya. Richard would have said that it was because he was a warmer man, who knew the true value of friendship; Dragulya might rather have observed that it is more difficult for a prince to find a mirror for his nobility of spirit than a mirror for his ferocity.

The popular account had it that Blondel de Nesle had become Prince Richard's most trusted confidant because he had helped to secure his release when he was briefly imprisoned in Walachia following the Third Crusade, but in fact the story was false, invented by Blondel himself as part of a romance whose main function was to conceal the true reason for that imprisonment. In Blondel's version, Richard had been imprisoned by the Walachian Archduke Leopold because Leopold was jealous of his successes in fighting against Saladin. As Blondel had made the story famous, Richard would have recaptured Jerusalem had it not been for the perfidy and faintheartedness of certain Walachian allies, whose imprisonment of the Norman prince simply set the seal on their betrayal. In fact, the Walachians had been angered by the fact that Richard, exhausted by his long and fruitless campaign, had made a treaty with Saladin and set forth to return home, abandoning the war against the Mohammedans to the armies of Attila. Over the years, Blondel's version had come to be accepted as truth in Gaul, where the heroic reputations of Charlemagne's princelings were carefully maintained in song and celebration.

Blondel's myth-making had created for Richard a past altogether more glorious than the real one, giving an uplifting account of his appointment to the throne of Grand Normandy which glossed over the bitter disputes which had led to his brother Geoffrey taking control of French Normandy and Anjou. Blondel was already planning an account of the present campaign according to which the contrite Walachians begged the Lionheart to take part, regretting their past ingratitude, and in which Richard's answer to their plea was a gesture of magnanimity quite without parallel. In truth, Charlemagne still held Richard partly responsible for the bad feeling which had soured relations between Gaul and Walachia for several centuries; and the fact that the so-called Lionheart had surrendered the Tower of London to the revolutionary army without a fight had placed the Prince of Grand Normandy still further from the light of royal favour. This new crusade was to be a last chance of redemption, an opportunity to heal the breach between the empires and open the way for Walachian troops to come to the aid of the beleaguered warlords of Gaul.

In view of all this, Blondel was not in the least surprised to find Richard in a state of high anxiety following his encounter with the Impaler.

'The man is a monster,' Richard told him. 'An upstart barbarian brute with shaggy hair and oaken limbs. He poured scorn upon my bowmen, who have served me faithfully for nigh on five hundred years. The man is hardly more than two centuries old, and yet he professes himself an expert in all the arts of war, as if firepower were everything.

When I told him that I had brought the finest knights of Christendom to this crusade he begged leave to correct me, and said that I had only brought the oldest!'

The prince removed the last of the chain-mail armour which he had worn for his historic meeting. He was perspiring freely, unused to the Mediterranean sun which blazed above in the cloudless sky. 'This Dragulya is a butcher, not a warrior. I had hardly believed that he could have earned the foul reputation which has preceded him, but now that I have seen him I would credit the worst account of his brutality. He affects to despise me for what happened in London, though he has no notion what it is to be on an island, cut off from allied armies by a vicious sea. He seems to blame me, too, because this petty alchemist of Malta was Norman by birth, and because I nursed his father as a mechanician in my court. There are no traitors in his own land, since he cleared them out by spitting them all on wooden stakes, and he wonders that the rest of the world will not deign to follow his black example! As if I had never put a traitor to death!'

'The world knows well enough how you deal with traitors, my lord,' purred Blondel. 'Even the naughty English celebrate your fortunate escape from assassination by burning Guy Fawkes in effigy, on every fifth of November.'

'It is a custom which they are unlikely to continue now,' retorted the prince, and added: 'more's the pity.'

'We will restore it,' said the minstrel. 'And we may, perhaps, set aside other days for celebrating the fall of your enemies. We'll let the commoners burn effigies of Cordery, too, and the popinjay Digby who calls himself Lord Protector of the English race. We'll see them all in Hell, and make carnivals of the anniversaries of their deaths. That way, my lord, we'll make the people rejoice in our salvation and our justice, and give thanks for our preservation. When the day comes that you return to London in triumph, and England's mortal youth has been eaten up by war, then the new vampires will be revealed for what they are – usurpers infinitely more wicked than the good men they have briefly displaced. The commoners will sing in the streets to welcome you home, when you return. And if they sing not loudly enough – why, I'll swear that they did, and time will make it true in the hearts and memories of your mortal subjects.'

'Oh yes,' said Richard, bitterly, 'but first we must board these cursed galleys, and trust their captains to batter a way past the pirate fleet, and force a path across this cursed island – not fighting mere Mohammedans, mark you, but vampires who no more feel pain or fear injury than we do. This will be a harder fight, my friend, than any we have seen before.'

Blondel de Nesle was too careful a man to ask whether his master was afraid. He knew the answer, anyhow. Richard was afraid, and in extremity desperately so. The days were long gone when the prince was young, when he had fully deserved the fame of his boldness and recklessness. There had been a time when he was quite fearless in battle and truly expert in the arts of war. His elevation to immortality had given him such zest, and such an enormous appetite for battle, that he had readily earned the reputation for fierceness which made him Charles's favourite for a while. But as time had gone by, in the Holy Land, Richard had come to realise how precarious his immortality really was. Two severe wounds had brought home to him the fact that he could be killed, and might live forever if and only if he successfully avoided destruction.

By the time he had turned back from Jerusalem, Richard was a changed man, who no longer had the heart for a real fight. That had become obvious on the journey home, when the prince had fallen prey to the common vampire anxiety about being at sea. Few vampires could bear to have the ocean beneath them for long, but Richard had conceived a special anxiety which haunted him still, and which made the prospect of the coming campaign an ordeal indeed.

Richard was still a mighty man in pretended fighting; there was none better in the tournaments of which he was so earnestly fond. With a weakened lance, and safe in the knowledge that no one really intended to kill him, he would throw himself into the conflict as if he really believed that he was the legendary Lancelot reincarnate. But in his heart of hearts he was, like so many other vampires, a coward. The rewards which vampirism had bestowed upon his body had made him all the more anxious not to lose the precious gift of life.

In Blondel's most secret opinion, Vlad Tepes had every right to despise the Norman prince, provided only that men spoke the honest truth when they claimed that Dragulya had retained the full measure of his own courage. Blondel had never seen the fierce Walachian, and he knew too much of the power of minstrels to trust entirely the image which Beheim had built for the voivode. For all he knew, the tales of Dragulya's battles were as inflated as the tales of Richard's. He was not impressed by the bloodcurdling accounts of the Impaler's actions in the aftermath of his victories. Impaling the defeated by the thousand – especially when so many were women and children – did not require bravery. If anything, such an appetite for blood was more likely to signify fear.

Despite this opinion, Blondel did not, on his own account, despise his master. He understood only too well the way that Richard saw the world. Blondel was a vampire too, and knew how great a coward he was himself, though he would never have confessed the fact. He always gave himself parts in his own songs and stories which implied that he was nearly as fine a hero as his master.

Richard's astrologer Simon Melcart joined them, then, full of news about the terrible state of the city of Naples – a fever pit, he said, such as only rude Italians could bear. Melcart did not have to consult the stars, it seemed, before advising his master that they should all return forthwith to Cagliari. Alas, that was no part of the plan which the Walachian warlord had hatched. Richard's ship was to sail with that part of the armada gathered in the Bay of Naples, to meet his own ships and join those now lodged near Palermo only when the whole fleet was gathered for the approach to Malta.

'Tell me,' said the prince to Melcart, in a tone more threatening than imploring, 'what you have calculated regarding the outcome of the battle.'

'A victory!' proclaimed the astrologer, seating himself opposite the prince. 'No doubt of it. A great victory!'

The prince looked for water to drink, but there was none on the table. As Melcart had said, Naples was afflicted at the present with an epidemic of fevers, and its water was not considered safe to drink by the physicians. He called instead for ale, and Blondel heard a servant scurrying upon the stair, made anxious by the petulant tone of the cry.

Blondel curled his lip slightly as he watched the two men sitting together at the table. The astrologer was very confident, it seemed. His kind were usually more cautious in their prophesies, not liking to commit themselves too far lest they be wrong. Richard was not the kind of man to kill a messenger simply because he bore bad news, but he was not inclined to be generous to bearers of good news who proved to be incorrect. This astrologer was new, his predecessor having fallen fatally from favour by failing to warn his master of the impending coup which had driven the vampires from Grand Normandy.

That sin of omission had not weakened the prince's faith in the reading of the stars; it had merely made him lament all the more the loss of his dear John Dee, who had possessed – as Richard believed – all kinds of arcane and secret knowledge which he had failed to tell to the prince only because of his unfortunately treasonous sympathies. Richard, like most of the vampire princes in Charles's empire, had an insatiable appetite for news of the future, and was far more enthusiastic to count the successes of his seers than their failures. He had maintained a perfect fascination for the strange experiments carried out in the Martin Tower by that wizard Earl of Northumberland who was once his prisoner. For his own part, Blondel had been far more impressed by the mechanical wizardry of Simon Sturtevant and the elder Cordery.

'What of my own fortunes?' growled the king.

'Secure,' Melcart assured him. 'You will distinguish yourself in the field, as ever before. A good star stands watch over your sword, and Mars in Sagittarius promises that your archers will give the finest possible account of themselves. Arrows will determine this conflict, I declare, and the glory must be yours, for the Walachian prince has only muskets and cannon.'

'A tragedy it is,' murmured Blondel, 'that the zodiac has no musketeer, to lend heavenly assistance to Dragulya's artillery. We might need those guns against the vampires of St. John, and not a constellation in the sky may bless their aim!'

Melcart favoured the minstrel with a dire look, but ignored the interruption. 'I have cast the horoscope of the rascal Cordery, which I am able to do most accurately because we know the hour and place of his birth. That horoscope is full of darkness. Death's shadow reaches out to claim him, and there is fire for him, on the earth and in Hell.'

'Oh, aye,' said Blondel. 'The pope took cognisance of that, no doubt, when he ordered that Cordery be brought to Rome for the Inquisition, even though the pontiff is a holy man and not a black magician.'

'There is naught that is black in my art,' said Melcart, stiffly. 'God made the stars as he made the earth, and there is meaning writ in his entire Creation, if we have the wit to learn the signs.'

'And are you sure that you have more wit than Noell Cordery, Master Melcart? After all, 'twas he who learnt the magic of making vampires, though no doubt 'twas written in the stars that his elixir would not cure his own mortality.'

'His magic is not the one which God gave to us,' retorted Melcart, 'It is black, and against nature. Had he known how to read the stars he would most certainly have known that he had traded away his soul in return for his vile elixir, and that the devil would brook no delay in reclaiming the debt.'

"'Tis a mercy, then, that the pope intends his inquisitors to break the alchemist's spirit and to save his soul,' said Blondel, in a lower voice. He said no more than that; it was not for him to speculate as to which of the two magics for making vampires might be against nature. And who was he to complain, when he surely owed his own immortality to the pleasant aspect which had caught the Lionheart's lustful eye? Blondel was not a modest man, but knew that he did not owe his high position to his poetic skill. He knew how easily he might have been replaced by such a wordsmith as Master Shakespeare, had the playwright only had a greater fairness of countenance to supplement his flattering histories of vampire aristocracy, and his dark and bloody tragedies of common mortality.

"'Tis a mercy indeed,' said Melcart, not entirely sincerely.

'This is not a time for quarrelling,' said Richard, sternly. 'We will have time enough to judge whether Melcart has the skill which his predecessor pretended. Let him be, Blondel.'

'Quarrelling, sire?' complained Blondel, with careful lightness. 'I would not quarrel with good Simon, or with the kindness of the stars. I only wish that Edmund Cordery might have saved us all the trouble which now we face. Had he only troubled to consult his friend the wizard earl about his son's future, good Harry Percy would surely have foretold both their tragic deaths, and dissuaded him from treason. If we had only had Melcart then, my lord, we might have strangled Noell Cordery in his cradle, captured the cursed Langoisse, and saved the beauteous Ladies Carmilla and Cristelle to grace the court with their presence for a thousand years.'

'Peace, Blondel, I command you' said the prince, impatiently. 'I'll not scorn any help which I can find, so hold your scalding tongue lest it burn your own fair lips. God will decide this battle, after his own fashion; we merely seek to gain such insight into his intention as he might permit, in order to shape our prayers. I'll pray for the fortune of our arrows, and you will do the same, whether you like it or not.'

Blondel bowed. 'As my prince pleases,' he replied.

Richard always prayed for the fortune of his arrows, because he traced his own inheritance to that remarkable shot which plunged into Harold's eye, and won the sovereignty of the British isle for William the Bastard, for Normandy and for Gaul. The Normans loved their bowmen as much as they loved their tourneys and their flattering minstrels, and even Charles thought the bow a lucky weapon for his kin. Whatever Norman astrologers found in the house of Sagittarius when they calculated their charts was always interpreted to the credit of their masters, and Melcart was simply following in the pathway of tradition.

Blondel would rather have placed his faith in good English cannon made of Sturtevant's metal – if only Richard had not been forced to leave his cannon behind when he sailed away from London. He had been forced to come here with a great insufficiency of basilisks and culverins. It was touching, in a way, that the common bowmen of Richard's army had shown such loyalty as to bring themselves to exile, but Blondel was under no illusion that these were any longer the cream of Britain's fighting men. Their prestige within the realm had been so closely bound up with their royal patronage that to stay in the new England would have been a steep fall for all of them. If a man were to search for honest omens, the one which spoke the fate of Grand Normandy was surely the simple fact that England's cannoneers had taken Kenelm Digby's side in the short-lived Civil War.

'And let us not forget,' said Richard, without undue enthusiasm, 'to pray for our allies the Walachians, that their musket-balls may also fly to good effect.'

'Amen,' said Simon Melcart, and the minstrel also, before Richard bade them leave him alone with his thoughts and his God.

Those thoughts were so bitter that Richard could not bear to be alone with them for long. Though Vlad Dragulya had raised his ire there were others aplenty on whom it might be turned. Richard saw himself

as a man betrayed, by his fellow men and by his ideals, and the fact
that he had lost Grand Normandy hurt him infinitely more than his
scornful enemies and friends imagined. He had truly believed in the
divine right of vampire princes, in the God which had supposedly
ordered the world to the advantage of his kind, and in the mission
which that God had supposedly given to the vampires, to civilise and
bring splendour to a world once racked and rent with all the horrors
of mortality.

Where now, he thought, *is the reward of all our effort? What now becomes
of the glorious world which we sought to make of the estates of Gaul? It is
given to darkness, and the immortality which was our privilege is cast recklessly
to the meanest and most ignoble. Where now is hope, on earth or in the
heavens? What can our arrows avail, against such enemies as these?*

He picked up a small printed pamphlet which lay upon the table. It
was an ill-looking thing, unbound and printed on the poorest stock of
paper; it had not the appearance he would have imagined for a sorcerer's
book of evil, but it had already cast an evil spell upon the world. It
told how to compound an elixir from the semen of vampires and the
blood of men, which could then be taken into the body in any of several
ways, to make common men into vampires. It was a way far simpler
and less solemn that the one which Attila's kin had always used to
favour those they loved, and those who had served them most loyally.

To Richard, the pamphlet was an unholy thing, which reeked far
more of evil than the Gregorian heresies which called the vampires
devil's kin and demon-possessed. The true nobility of his own station,
Richard thought, was assured by the fact that his own vampirism, and
that of many whom he had converted, was based in love and affection,
and not in the cold calculation of men like Noell Cordery.

There was one way, and one way only, to relieve the anguish of his
bitterness, and so he went to his bedchamber, which was the most
luxurious part of the villa which had been given him to use in Naples.
There he called out for the youngest of his servants, who had eyes of
Mediterranean blue and yellow hair, and would one day make a handsome vampire knight.

Richard, deposed prince of Grand Normandy, called *Coeur-de-Lion*,
picked up the silver dagger which he kept beside his bed, and lifted it
to the level of his eyes, which were thus reflected in the polished blade.
They were remarkable eyes, coloured coppery red instead of the near-
black which was typical of vampires.

Eyes of fire, he said, silently. *Brave eyes. The eyes of a hero; a man born
to rule.* Gently, he licked his lips, anticipating the sweet warm taste of
blood.

THREE

Noell Cordery sat on a three-legged stool, watching his cauldron warming gently beside the fire.

He was in a windowless room with benches on either side which were strewn with jars and alembics, lamps and candle-trays, clamps and files. It was a perfect alchemist's den, save for certain embellishments not often associated with such places: the cages housing little ragged dogs or big brown rats, which gnawed incessantly at the wire mesh which confined them; the mops and the ammonia used in cleaning; the microscope upon the table. All these things were necessary, for his alchemy, and there had betimes been other things, which to the casual observer might have signalled his involvement in still blacker arts: cadavers to be dissected; limbs removed by surgeons; bottles and phials and jars and goblets and gourds and wineskins, all containing naught but blood. He had become the most earnest student of blood in all the world, and would have said that he knew more of its mysteries than any man alive . . . and yet, not enough.

Not near enough.

He had tried to see to the very core of human nature, to find and understand the animating soul, but when he added up the sum of his discoveries, he could only count himself a failure. He had discovered the elixir of life, but he knew not how it worked, or why it sometimes did not work.

Though the room was a cellar, and was usually cool, the fierce heat of the summer and the fire burning in the grate had combined to banish its coolness and take a soothing grip on Noell's tired bones. The heat conspired with lack of sleep to send him off into a trance-like state where memories and associations floated into his mind like the rags and tatters of discarded dreams.

Watching the cauldron, he remembered the kitchen in the monastery at Cardigan, where once he had laboured to pay for his keep. He remembered the taste of the puddings which cooked to moist perfection while those cauldrons seethed above the fire, whose like he had not tasted since.

He remembered another cauldron, too, which had featured in a play which once he had seen in the Tower of London, while he was still a small boy. Around the rim of that magical vessel, three witches had cackled and canted, while sending some mortal princeling to his fated end. He could remember so little of his youth, now. It had been such a carefree time, now overlain in memory by a deal of pain, which had etched more powerful impressions on his soul. But certain fleeting lines of that once-beheld play now lingered near the threshold of consciousness, and he frowned as he tried to recall them.

Double, double, the witches had said, *toil and trouble*. Once that was remembered, the couplet was not too difficult to complete: *Fire burn, and cauldron bubble*. They were words he might easily address to his own cauldron – which contained, he felt sure, a more awful admixture of sinister things than ever those poor hags had chuckled over. But his own cauldron was not to be boiled, only warmed in gentle fashion, to protect what was within it. He could not remember the recipe which was quoted in the play to make the audience smirk in disgust at the witches' nastiness, but he had read all the best books of recipes and other magical prescriptions. He knew the *Compendium Maleficarum* of Guazzo, the so-called *Clavicula Salomonis*, the *Ars Magna* of Ramon Lull, the book of black magic falsely attributed to Cornelius Agrippa, the works of Marcello Ficino, and countless other works of occult art. He knew well enough what kind of ingredients witches and sorcerers were reputed to use in their potions. He had tried more of them than he cared to count, but had found them all quite impotent.

I have potions more powerful than those of which the playwright spoke, he thought, *and I deal not in petty fate but in liquors to give long life to mortal men, and in poisons to steal it back again*.

That playwright, serving vampire masters, had written dramas of recent history to flatter the vampires – which Noell had never bothered to see – but had saved his greater art for tragedies set in more distant ages, which dwelt upon the perils of mortality, and spoke forthrightly to crowds of common men. Noell could remember very little of the play which was now in his mind, but he did remember something of its climactic speech, which had made of life a walking shadow, strutting upon a stage for a few brief moments before it was snuffed out like a candle. He struggled to piece the phrases together in their proper order, but could not, though he thought he had captured the beginning.

His lips framed words which he did not speak aloud: *Tomorrow, and tomorrow, and tomorrow . . . creeps in its petty pace*, but his memory failed; it had been too long, and his younger self had not known how to listen as fully as he might.

More memories arose then to crowd the others away – memories of other dark and airless rooms, with hardly a breath of coolness, where fever was always near. He hated his memories of Adamawara more than any, though he could not really say why, for nothing so very dreadful had happened to him there, and it was there that Berenike had taught him the love of women. But it was a realm where he had not belonged, because its people were bizarre, and the supernatural world which they created with their fears and hopes was horrid and alien.

His journey to Adamawara and the time which he had spent there he remembered now as his season of blood, his ejodun, when he had stretched himself upon the altar of sacrifice and given up his health and strength in exchange for a perverse wisdom whose potency was denied to few save for himself. He had drunk the blood of man, and yet had failed to make it just and right that he had done so. He thought of his mortality now as a kind of punishment – the vengeance of God – though he never could decide on the precise form of his sin.

The door of the cellar opened, screeching on its hinges, and he started, suddenly sitting upright, ready to make a guilty denial if he were to be accused of having fallen asleep. But no such accusation came; it was only Leilah, the most loyal of all his servants and helpers.

He had a great many servants and helpers now, for he was a man who had immortality in his gift, if not in his bones. Every week he created more vampires, but his time was running out – his candle-life fluttering in the cold draught of Gaul and Walachia's enmity – and he knew that the vampires he had made might not be enough, when the Grandmaster of the Order had nothing with which to arm his further recruits but bows and daggers. There were no more cannon to be positioned, no more muskets to be given out, and even arrows were in short supply.

'It is late,' said Leilah. 'Thou must go to thy bed, and sleep. Thou hast a dozen apprentices to watch over the work.'

'Oh no,' he said. 'The work needs no attention now – even the new and desperate work, which goes on alongside the old. All is still, but I do not like to go away just now. Is there news?'

'Langoisse and la Valette sent fireships into the harbour at Palermo, aided by a kind wind. They did fair damage among the close-packed ships, but the enemy is too many to be defeated by such means. They came back into the Grand Harbour some hours ago, and they say that all the galleys must now be at sea. They are making ready as fast as they can to set to sea again, and will go forth tomorrow on their last great expedition, to do what damage they can.'

'What of the Mohammedans?'

'The ghazi are at sea in the south, creeping in closer the while, but they only want to watch. The sultans will fight on their own account when we have wrecked the Gaulish fleet for them.'

'No word from other friends?'

'None.'

Noell bowed his head, relaxing his weight again upon the stool. The defending fleet had already been supplemented by a handful of English privateers, who had sailed to join the battle on their own account – heroes all, given the odds, though they would take their ships away when the fight at sea was settled. Such allies could not be asked to drop anchor in order to join the fight on land, where great armies of vampire knights would oppose one another for the first time. None could blame the sailors for staying away from that gory circus.

Noell had clung to the very faint hope that a part of Kenelm Digby's navy might after all have come to join the knights of St. John, but he had always known it as a romantic illusion. In his heart he was not sorry that his friend had chosen to be prudent. The safety of England had to be paramount in Digby's thoughts, and England would be all the stronger for standing back from this dire battle. It was a pity that more English cannon could not have been spared.

Leilah put her gentle hands on Noell's shoulders, and looked him in the face. His eyes were so weak that even with the lenses to aid them he could not bring her face into proper focus, and that was a cause of sorrow to him. But if there was one thing in his memory that would remain forever sharp and clear it was the lustre of her skin, and the brightness of her eyes, and the lush blackness of her hair.

He hoped that she would remember him as well, if fortune let her live and preserved her honest soul through the centuries which she surely deserved. He hoped for this memorial above all others – that when she lay with future lovers, their caresses would always recall his own.

Leilah was clad now almost as she had been when he first saw her, in leathern male attire, but she wore no tricorn hat and carried neither pistol nor poniard. Noell ran his hand along the sleeve of her jacket, slightly surprised by its texture. It was with something of a shock that he realised why she needed to be dressed in this fashion.

'You have come to say goodbye,' he whispered.

'Not yet,' she told him. 'I came to bring you away, so that we might make our farewells more comfortably, and in a better place.'

'A better place?' Noell looked up and around at the gloomy walls, his failing eyesight barely able to pick out the bottles and beakers on the shelves, the books and the manuscripts, the tools and instruments. But his attention was caught by the brass barrel of the microscope which Kenelm Digby had made for him so long ago, gleaming in reflected firelight.

This is my better place, he thought, *for this is where the alchemist belongs, in his witch's kitchen, brewing the essences of life and death, juggling with destiny and God's dark secrets.*

Nevertheless, Noell suffered himself to be taken up from his stool, and led to the doorway, where Quintus was waiting. Noell was glad to see him, for he did not want to leave this room unguarded, despite that no vital work still remained to be done. There was none among his legion of apprentices he could trust wholeheartedly to keep his vigils for him, but he trusted Quintus now as always.

Noell grasped the monk's hand as he came to the doorway, and clutched it hard, conveying more by that wordless message than any instruction could have done. The monk's grip was firmer by far than his own, the hand corded with strong muscle. When they had lived in Burutu, Noell had been the younger man, in the prime of his life, tall and lean and handsome. Now he was the older by far, not in terms of elapsed years, but in every appearance.

The fevers which had visited Noell in Adamawara, and the potions which the elemi had fed to him, had left their mark on body and soul alike, and while Quintus had flourished with the breath of life, Noell had shrivelled and weakened without it. It was sometimes easy to imagine that the few donations of blood which Noell had made to Quintus over the intervening years had achieved a transfer of vitality, but Noell did not begrudge his friend the strength which those donations had helped to secure in him. After all, Noell Cordery was the creator who had breathed that life into Quintus and thousands more, and when he was dead, he would be revered as a saint by some, no matter how many there would be who would call him a devil.

'I will pray for you,' promised Quintus, as Noell began to mount the steps beyond the door.

'Pray for us all,' Noell told him. 'Pray for our shipmasters, our artillerists, and our bowmen. Pray for our cannonballs and our arrows. Pray for England, and New Atlantis, and for generations yet unborn. This night of all nights we cannot have too much of prayer, for we will need a miracle to deliver us from destruction.'

He let Leilah lead him up into the open streets of Mdina, but when she turned to take him to her own lodgings he would not go with her, and brought her in the opposite direction, to the church which was the first place of Christian worship on the island. On this site had stood the house of Publius, made first bishop of Malta by St. Paul himself, when that saint was shipwrecked on the island in the company of St. Luke, some thirty years after the crucifixion of Christ. The church which stood here now was not the one which Publius had built, but a grander one built to replace it by the Norman, Roger of Sicily – for this island, like Britain, had suffered a Norman conquest in the eleventh century, when the Imperium of Gaul had set its limits at their furthest bounds. What kin that Roger had been to Richard *Coeur-de-Lion*, or to Charlemagne, Noell did not know, though *The Vampires of Gaul* would no doubt have told him had he cared to consult it. He had not opened that book in ten years and more, having spent his life so far outdating what was writ in it that no one could produce a new and full edition.

Within the church there was a great deal of light. The sun was bright behind the stained glass, and near a thousand candles had been lit within the last twenty-four hours, when nearly every man, woman and vampire in Mdina had passed through the cathedral to offer special prayers. At this hour of siesta the benches were almost deserted. Only half a dozen kneeling figures could be seen – women wearing the *ghonnella* to hide their features and their feelings. Noell did not kneel, but sat upon the hindmost bench, while Leilah sat beside him. They were both virtual strangers here – he an unbeliever, she still a pagan unbaptised.

'Have we come to pray?' asked the vampire lady.

'I am too proud to pray,' he told her. 'I could not do it in my youth, and if I cannot do it honestly I would rather leave it to those who can. I will not beg for the protection of my soul, nor the preservation of my flesh. Not now.'

'We could find more comfortable lodgings to spend our final hour together,' she said.

'Dost thou want my blood?' he asked her, but not bitterly.

'Nay,' she said. 'I have had blood enough, and before this affair is done there will be so much blood spilled upon the sea that the ocean will run red from Sicily to Tripoli.'

'You must sail away across that bloody sea,' he told her. 'When the galleys have broken through, and their vampire knights pour on to the island, you must force Langoisse to set forth for England. Langoisse is insufficiently cooled by his immortality, and I fear that he will bring the *Spitfire* back to land, to join the hopeless fight. He yearns still to settle his account with Richard, and there's none in all the world who can turn him aside, save for thee. I look to you to save him from his own hot head, and keep his ship for other work.

'She will go to England,' Leilah promised. 'I will make sure of it, even if I must perforce become her captain.'

Noell was silent for a moment, so she spoke again. 'Langoisse still says that the galleys may not get through, that his broadsides will cripple and destroy them, and keep them from the harbours.'

'In a battle fought at sea,' said Noell, 'a single sailing ship will always outrun a single galley, and may blow it to smithereens with a sufficiency of cannon-shot. But we are talking about hundreds of galleys, which will not even try to fight our ships at sea, but will crowd together, doggedly making for land so that they may discharge their cargoes of horses, men and muskets. The mighty defences around the Grand Harbour will hold them for a while, but galleys will land men at St. Paul's Bay and at Marsa Xloqq; the fortresses there have not the guns to prevent them. The real battle will be fought when those armies converge on the walls of Mdina, where Durand must hold them, or the day is lost. It does not matter much what will happen then – the *Spitfire* must go to England, and there thou must make preparation to fight again in defence of that realm.'

'There is some secret,' she said, 'which thou wilt not tell to me, though Quintus knows. It is not entirely for England's sake that thou wouldst bid me go away, nor only because thou art fearful for my life.'

'It is in the nature of a secret,' Noell replied, 'that it be kept.'

'Even from me?' she questioned, making no secret of her own sense of injury in the way she spoke.

'Even from thee,' he told her. Then, to avoid the accusation of her gaze, he rose to his feet again, and walked down the aisle toward the altar, where the great silver frontal blazed with the glory of the myriad candles. She followed him, but did not try to catch him up, until he paused beneath the painting of Mary, Mother of Jesus, which tradition ascribed to St. Luke. Noell stared up at the Madonna, blinking his tired eyes. He tried to move his spectacles into a better situation, but still the image was blurred.

'She has not the beauty of a vampire lady,' he said, knowing that it was true even though he could not see her. 'No human woman has. It is a foul trick for fate to play on common men, to give the greatest beauty to a different race, and a race which never could bear children. It is a jest so silly that only the Gregorians seem able to explain it. Pity the common men who will always love thee, my lovely child, and pity the mothers of future men, who can never be entirely loved.'

'Come home,' said Leilah. 'Come home and sleep, for whatever secret thou art guarding will keep better if thou wilt only let it rest.'

She took his arm in hers, and gently urged him back along the aisle. As they left the church, the stiffened silken hoods all turned in measured fashion, as the women interrupted their praying to watch them leave – *creeping*, thought Noell, *in our petty pace . . .* and then he remembered half another line, about the candles which lighted fools their way to dusty death. Behind him, the air was full of candlelight, mingled with the coloured sunbeams streaming through the great windows of pictured glass.

Noell wondered what the world would be like when all men could become vampires, once they had fathered the children on whom they would have to feed. *As mothers suckle their infants,* he thought, *so must the infants suckle their parents.* It would be, he supposed, a world less strange to itself than it seemed in his wild imagination.

'Wilt thou kiss me, now?' asked Leilah, as they stood in the hot sun outside the sanctuary of the church.

'I will,' he said, taking her in his arms for what he believed would be the last time. He hugged her close to him, and remembered that he had done that long before she had become a vampire and his lover, when she was only a girl, a stranger in a strange drear land. But he had not kissed her then, poor fool that he was . . . and he had been too proud in those days to offer his blood to a needy vampire.

He kissed her now, and told her that he loved her.

But when she told him in her turn that she loved him he thought that he might be a poorer fool now than he had been in his long-lost youth, for he was old and infirm, sightless and decayed, and yet could make himself believe such tender words, though they were spoken by a creature as beautiful as the sun.

'I cannot preserve myself,' he whispered to her, 'but I would not mind that, if only I were certain that thou wert safe. Preserve thyself, I beg thee, for my sake as well as thine own, for in thine eyes and in thine heart are all the immortality I need or care to have.'

She wept, then, giving the lie to all who said that vampires could not weep, and to any who believed that those who felt no pain could feel no pity. Indeed, could he have looked deep into her human soul just then, Noell Cordery would have understood that his mistress was filled with such a burden of pity and sorrow as would take three hundred years and more in its discharging, and would never leave her empty, if she lived until the end of time.

FOUR

The great sea battle which was fought to defend the rebel island of Malta against the combined might of Gaul and Walachia was not fought in any narrow region of the sea, but rather took the form of a series of battles scattered in time and space. The greatest and closest conflict, however, took place some three to twelve miles north-west of the island on the day before the invasion.

That wind which the islanders called the *gregala*, and classical writers Euroclydon, was by now blowing laterally across the course of the war galleys. Their square sails had caught more of the wind in the early part of their journey, and the captains had allowed it to carry them more to the west than might otherwise have been desirable, so that their legions of oarsmen now had their hardest work to do. The Maltese sailing ships, which had more square sail, and triangular sails too, could make more use of the wind, but given its present alignment could not exploit it to the full. Although the wind was brisk, the caravels and galleons of the Order of St. John could not greatly outrace the enemy ships which they sought to destroy.

The biggest galleys were not placed close together in the Imperial ranks, but had galiots and bergantins in between, packed so closely that their oars were oft within a dozen yards of touching. Their captains knew that la Valette would try to run his ships between their lines, slaughtering their oarsmen with the fire of side-mounted cannon, but were determined to prevent it if they could. The galleys had their best cannon mounted forward, and had spurs there which could serve as boarding bridges at the closest quarters, but even though they had little at their vulnerable flanks but oarports and musketeers, still they must protect themselves from fatal broadsides by clever sailing and such armour as ships could mount.

Aboard the *Spitfire*, in la Valette's first squadron, Langoisse stood on his bridge, measuring the gaps in the rank of enemy ships which was fast approaching. He was shading his eyes from the sun, but needed no telescope to judge the situation. Leilah was standing by his side, relaxed and patient. Langoisse had such a surge in his veins as he had not felt since the days when first he took to piracy. His years as a vampire had subdued his capacity for excitement, but had not dried it up entirely.

'God's blood, my sweet,' he said to her, when he dropped his arm, 'we've the odds against us this time. But how those frightened vampire knights must be huddling 'neath the decks, waiting for the storms that we'll unleash!'

She made no reply, but fixed her stern dark eyes upon him, and simply by her staring gave him heart. She looked so young, more like the wondrous slave-girl he had freed than the tall grave woman she had briefly become, before she went to Kantibh to secure what Noell Cordery had asked for, and her own immortality besides.

The fleets were closing quickly, and the leading ships of the knights of St. John could not yet turn aside despite the fact that by turning westward they could better catch the wind. They must keep their bows to the enemy guns, and try to sail through the hail of fire to get amongst the galleys, riding over the oars if they had to. The Imperial fleet outnumbered their own by six or eight to one, and Langoisse knew that their only hope lay in crippling sufficient ships to break the formation and scatter the galleys to the west and to the east. Some would undoubtedly reach Malta no matter what, but if the enemy vessels were sufficiently strung out, and la Valette's defenders remained in good enough condition to harry them, then the galleys might not be able to mass for a sustained assault upon the Grand Harbour, or for a massive landing of troops at St. Paul's Bay.

Langoisse called instructions to the helmsman. He did not have to bellow yet, for the noise of the wind in the rigging was muted, and the men waited quietly by their stations. Already they were crouching, because they knew that the fore-mounted guns of the galleys were certain to open fire first. All the men knew this business well, for some had been with Langoisse since his pirate days, and all the rest had served their time as naval men or privateers. He had a few Maltese aboard, but the bulk of his crew was French or English, and Cordery had made vampires of three-quarters of them.

'Oh for fierce Selim by my other hand,' murmured Langoisse, glancing again at Leilah. 'How he'd have loved the fury that's to come!'

The *Spitfire* had only one rank of cannon to either side, and they were mostly light bronze guns. She was a small ship by comparison with la Valette's flagship, the Great Carrack of Rhodes, which had two gundecks to either side and the best iron cannon in the fleet. The flagship was lying back with the other big galleons, in the hope that the more slender vessels could bring the Imperial formation into sufficient disarray to allow the bigger ships and more powerful cannon to pick their targets and work at reasonable leisure.

Some of the ships which trailed in Langoisse's wake were hardly bigger than arab dhows, and carried only the light swivel-mounted guns which the Spanish called esmerils, but even these vessels might serve to disturb the oarsmen on the smaller galiots and break the ranks of the invaders into more ragged lines. Once those ranks were broken, it was possible that the galleys would get in one another's way while the raiders wrought havoc. If the oarsmen were only slaves and convicts, they would have little muscle on their arms or stomach for the fray, but Langoisse was too wise not to know that Dragulya and Richard would have searched the whole of Spain and Italy for strong freemen, who would do the job for pay, and grit their teeth under fire.

Langoisse looked down at the waves which lapped the flanks of the Spitfire, and wished devoutly they were higher. A violent storm could do more damage to the enemy's scheme than all the cannon in his squadron; but the sky was brilliant and cloudless, the sea blue and benign.

As he looked forward again to mark the gap in the enemy line towards which he was aiming, and then looked around to see how the other ships in his squadron were scattering, he felt the thrill of excitement still growing in him, until it seemed that his breast was banded tight by a great shackle. In his earliest days as a reaver he had known this thrill as a kind of fear, but had learned to reinterpret it as exhilaration, and a kind of bloodlust. Now, it was merged with that other blood-hunger, and he licked his dry lips and thought of the land, and those whores which had sprung up by the hundred in Valetta and Mdina, to make whatever donation of their being the brave men of Malta required.

He drew the sabre from the scabbard at his waist, and raised it high, as a signal to his men. Leilah, beside him, drew her twin pistols, to show herself equally ready.

The bombard mounted in the bow of the nearest galley, which was ahead of them and slightly to starboard, boomed for the first time, and a stone shot splashed into the water a hundred yards away. Langoisse smiled, preferring to regard the shot as one less which might be aimed at the walls of the Grand Harbour or St. Elmo's fort.

Though they were making no more headway than half a dozen knots apiece the ships closed with what seemed to be great rapidity, and more guns opened up, from the galley which had fired first and from the smaller galiot to the Spitfire's port. When the captains of these two

ships had observed that Langoisse intended to go between them they
had moved toward one another in the water, so that the passage had
narrowed, but Langoisse did not care about that. The *Spitfire* had
impetus enough to splinter their oars, and as long as neither ship could
bring its spur to bear on his narrow bows he would be safe.

The galiot was turning as the *Spitfire* swooped, whether trying to
come into his path or get better aim with her guns he could not tell,
but she was trying to turn against the wind, and she could not do it.
Perhaps her oarsmen were not responding with all due courage to the
urging of their foremen, no matter how loudly the drum was beaten,
or how frequently the lash teased their shoulders.

An iron cannonball tore at the foremast rigging, and another skittered
across the deck, splintering wood, but the galley's bombard could not
touch them now, and it was only the lighter guns that had their reach.
Langoisse shouted to his own artillerists, and the *Spitfire's* light bow-
gun replied, while the musketeers stationed in the rigging began to fire
at the oarsmen.

The galiot, which now had no chance at all to intercept the *Spitfire's*
rush, tried to turn again, and lost all of its forward impetus, so that the
galley to starboard was suddenly a whole ship's length ahead, with the
caravel coming up abeam. Langoisse cried out in jubilation at this happy
result, and reached high with the sabre while he measured the seconds
to time his broadside.

When he howled the order to fire, the starboard gunners leapt to
their work. The cannon bucked in a ragged line. The galley's deck was
far higher than the caravel's, with two ranks of oarsmen two to an oar,
and though the musketeers on her deck directed fire down on to the
Spitfire's deck, the cannonballs which smashed into the galley's body
did tremendous damage, much of it dangerously close to the waterline.
Langoisse cheered, and Leilah too, though they could see half a dozen
of their own snipers and fire-monkeys sprawling wounded. A musket
ball tore splinters from the wheel and the helmsman recoiled in fear,
but that had been a lucky shot, for that station was the best-protected
of all.

Leilah fired her pistols at the galley's castle as it passed astern, no
more than thirty feet distant, and Langoisse looked back for a moment
to see how great a disarray his shots had caused. But there was no time
for celebration, for the floundering galiot was alongside now to port,
and his artillerists had already begun to fire. These shots struck higher
upon the smaller ship, and probably killed more men though they did
less damage to the hull.

Another hail of musketfire came in retaliation, and two more men
fell aboard the *Spitfire*, while Langoisse cursed. These were Italian ships
that he was facing, but he saw now that they carried Walachian troopers,
who were the best musketeers in the world, by no means to be

discounted even when firing from the decks of ships. The *Spitfire*, much more lightly manned than the enemy ships, could not afford to lose its fighting men at such a rate.

Langoisse damned his luck, but did so under his breath, for what he was truly lamenting was the loss of that hope he had secretly nurtured, that he might be fortunate enough to find the ship which carried the flower of Norman knighthood, so that he might spit his broadsides at Richard's ancient swordsmen and turn the princeling green with the fear of the sea's blue deeps.

Again, Langoisse found pause to regret the clement weather, which allowed the flat-bellied galleys to lie level in the water, while the caravel yawed and rolled. He shouted orders to the seamen, and now he had to exercise his lungs to their fullest effect, for the riot of cannonfire was loud. His men knew what to do, and responded quickly to his signals, putting on more sail as they canted to catch the wind.

The second rank of enemy ships was close upon the heels of the first, but not close enough yet to reach the *Spitfire* with their bombards as she gained speed. Light fire came from the stern of the galiot in the first rank, and the galley which lay to her north-west, but it did no harm, and by the time the ships of the second rank were in range, the square sails were furled again and the *Spitfire* had come right about to repeat her dash at a gap in the ranks.

Langoisse could see, however, that this would be far the more dangerous passage, for here were two great galleys, not turning an inch as he came to meet them, and their sides were crowded with Dragulya's musketeers. Their culverins were in the bows, but stations had been made for esmerils between the oarsmen, so these ships could make some measure of reply to the blasts of his own cannon. He felt a cold sensation in his breast as he realised that the enemy had made this preparation to meet him, and knew that those gunmen would be the best Walachia had. He had hoped to find this hastily-assembled warfleet ill-fitted for the conflict, but contests between trader galleys and neatly-sailed pirates had been going on for far too long, and the masters of this armada had anticipated the threats which they had to meet.

In all the years he had been a pirate, harrying merchantmen in the Mediterranean, Langoisse had never met an enemy with such a sting as this, and though the best of his men were used to assaults against heavily-defended ships, they could never have faced the kind of fire that would now be directed against them. Had Langoisse the seahawk seen a prize as well-defended as either of these ships, he'd have let it go, with only a tear of regret, but he was not fighting now for spoil.

As the *Spitfire* swept into the passage between the galleys Langoisse marked how huge they seemed, and how crowded. He cried to the snipers in the rigging to get down, for it seemed all too likely that there was no good they could do, and they would make too ready a target for Dragulya's men. His artillerists were all uninjured, and the shots from the galleys' guns which hit the ship did little damage, but when the broadsides were fired all hell was let loose.

The *Spitfire's* cannonade did terrible damage to the lower oar-decks of the great ships, but the men on their upper decks had hardly flinched, having anticipated that Langoisse would fire low across the water. A hail of shot was launched from both sides, peppering the decks of the caravel, and though the ship took hardly any damage from the musketballs, the men were by no means so fortunate. His own artillerists could manage no more than a single blast to either side while Langoisse took the *Spitfire* through the corridor between the ships, but the enemy had musketeers by the hundred, and two or three weapons to every man.

Leilah fired at the galley which was to port, but her pistols were useless at the range she had, and Langoisse grabbed her by the shoulders to force her down below the barrier to the side of the bridge. He ducked too, but had to leave her when the helmsman, despite the protective screen around the wheel, was struck in the neck and fell without a sound. Langoisse knew that there must be marksmen aboard the galleys who had been allotted this target, but there was no alternative save to take the wheel himself, so that he could bring the ship to port as soon as she was in open water again.

He looked wildly about, trying to gauge the damage that his own fire had done, and was glad to see that great holes had been ripped in the sides of both galleys. He knew that dozens of oarsmen must be slain, their oars broken, but he also knew that those ships would have oarsmen to spare, and that the destruction he had wrought might easily prove futile, unless they began taking in water too quickly. He laughed aloud at the thought of the consternation which would spread among the clever musketeers if their ship did begin to go down, but he knew that hours must pass before that could happen, and he knew that there might easily be plenty of time to take the gunners to another ship, unless la Valette could bring forward his bigger ships to sink the stricken vessels.

While the *Spitfire* was safe for a while, running again before the wind, near a mile in front of the third rank of galleys, Langoisse called out for a report on the condition of his fighting-men.

The news, when it came, was not good. Though the ship, hit only twice by cannonballs, was hardly hurt at all, he had lost fourteen men, either dead or too sorely wounded to do their work even though they were made of vampire flesh. One more passage like the last might leave him too few cannoneers to man the guns. One man, sent scurrying up the rigging, called down to him that he could see a ship afire, but that her blazing sails marked her for a friend, and that he could see two ships locked by a spur. From this, Langoisse judged that those who had sailed with him were faring no better than he, and probably worse. He knew then that the battle would be lost. Of the four ships upon which he had fired, none could certainly be counted out of the subsequent action – it was entirely possible that all four could continue to Malta, in reasonable formation, and there land troops wherever the Lionheart and the Impaler wanted to deploy them. It was possible that one or two of the other lighter ships had caused greater distress, but the likelihood was that la Valette's galleons would have to face the might of the galleys virtually intact.

The ships of the armada would not find it so comfortable to face the galleons' broadsides, but if they followed the same strategy they had shown just now, their musketeers would surely win the day for them. Although the galleys were slow and ponderous by comparison with the sailing ships, they were well enough armoured to defend themselves against all that la Valette could do. Langoisse did not doubt that the Knights of St. John would give a mighty good account of themselves at sea, but there could be little doubt now that the real defence of Malta would rage around the walls of the Grand Harbour, and eventually about the walls of Mdina itself.

'Take the wheel!' Langoisse commanded Leilah, and when she had done so he leapt to the deck to muster his men, bidding seamen to the unattended guns, making ready for one last co-ordinated blast. He jumped up to a position in the rigging to measure the progress of the ship, and shouted to Leilah to make a steady passage between the two great galleys which lay before them.

This time, though, the galleys deliberately came apart, so that he would face only one when he went between them. This gave him a choice, and he elected to attack the ship on the port side, because his guns were slightly stronger on that side. It also allowed him to bring a full complement of artillerists to those guns, but the move was not all to his advantage, because he knew full well that this might be his last real chance to cripple a ship, and he would rather have fired at two close together.

Cannon-shot carried away part of the lateen sail and brought down part of the rigging, but too late to keep the *Spitfire* from her line. The bronze cannon boomed in ragged sequence, their shot tearing yet again into the hull of the galley. Then the musketeers struck back, and his own men began again to fall. Langoisse himself was scored in the left side, and though his vampire flesh could not be too badly damaged by such a blow, he knew that it was a sign of the end. Almost all of his injured men were vampires, but even vampires could not fight on if they were hit full in the body or the head, and almost all would lapse eventually into the deep sleep which was necessary for their artful bodies to make repair.

Langoisse controlled the pain in his scratched ribs, then slashed at his flesh with a dagger to remove the musket-ball before forcing the wound to close with insistent fingers. His senses reeled, but he took hold of himself and made himself move about the deck to take stock of the damage, showing himself to his men to seal their resolve.

Leilah, meanwhile, was trying to turn the ship to port again, perhaps intending to loop around and bring the *Spitfire* back alongside one or other of the galleys in the third rank, to fire yet another broadside. But with the ropes and sails so damaged, the caravel was limping in the water, and might be easy prey even for a galley's gunners. She could make speed now only if she ran before the wind, and Langoisse called for more square sail, shouting to Leilah to run to the west, and bidding the starboard gunners to fire at the bows of any galley whose course they crossed.

Then he began to go to the wounded, one by one, to see what might be done to ease their condition, and to see whether he had men enough to repair the damage, and put the *Spitfire* back in fighting trim.

He bent over a common man who was shot in the belly, lying on his back on the deck. Strangely, the poor fellow seemed to feel little pain, though he did not have the vampire trick of command. His eyes were open, and he stared unblinking into the bright-lit sky.

'Is it over?' he asked, when he saw the face looming above him.

'Nay,' said Langoisse. 'By God, it is *not* over, nor will it be while I've a gun to fire or a blade to swing. But I beg your pardon, for I fear you've lost your chance at immortality.'

'Aye,' said the man, 'but I had the hope, and that was more than I was born to.'

Langoisse stood up, and left him, running back to the bridge and shouting as he went. Even as he ran, though, he knew that the fervour which still had him in its grip was not exultation, nor lust for blood, but a desperate kind of fear.

He had lost the knack of lying to himself.

But the man is right, he told himself, *and he hath a better wisdom than my traitorous feelings will allow to me. I have the hope, and more than I was born to, and I will not own this fear which tries to hurt me. I've business yet with these enemies of ours, and I'll have the measure that they owe me, if I pay for it in vampire blood!*

FIVE

While the biggest galleys that Italy and Spain had lent to his use were bombarding the walls of the Grand Harbour, drawing fire not just from Valetta but from Fort St. Angelo and Kalkara, the advance guard of Dragulya's army was taken by smaller ships into the harbour at Marsa Mxett, past the guns of Fort St. Elmo and Fort Tigné. The fire to which these two fortresses subjected the invading ships was by no means slight, but these vessels had sustained relatively little damage in the battle at sea, and Dragulya's captains were under orders not to hesitate in sending his musketeers, even his vampire knights, to help with the oars during the critical hour of their passage.

From his station by the spur of the galley *Cockatrice* the voivode watched impassively as the cannons blazed in ragged sequence on the ramparts of Tigné. A great cloud of purple smoke roiled around the towers, soaring at first from the guns in the updraft above the cliff, then swirling and sinking as the particles cooled and moved into stiller air. Aboard the ship, the battle seemed all noise: the whine of cannon-balls hurtling through the air; the splashing of shot which hit the water, sending up great sheets of spray; the splintering of wood where the missiles struck home. His own cannon made no reply, but his snipers in the rigging fired upwards at the cannoneers. Dragulya could see that there was little chance of hitting such targets, but the musketfire made the artillerists anxious, and helped a little to spoil their aim.

For the time being, there was no doubt that the *Cockatrice* and her companions had the worst of it; while she ran under the guns of the forts she was a target, and must stand up to the bombardment. The cannon-shot was taking its toll upon her upper decks, where the sailors bore the brunt of it, but most of Dragulya's fighters were shielded, waiting below with the oarsmen, and the bronze cannon of Tigné had not the weight to smash the decks to smithereens, as some of the bombards of the Grand Harbour might have done.

The mainmast was shattered by a lucky shot, and sent wreaths of rigging everywhere. Half a dozen of his musketeers were sent flying, to land on the deck, dead or wounded. Dragulya was little troubled by that, but he cursed the panic which then broke out among the horses of his troop, which had to be on the deck ready for the assault upon the waterfront. Though they were educated not to waver under fire, the animals did not like the shifting decks beneath their feet. When they broke the rope which confined them on the deck they pranced back and forth, causing great confusion to the seamen and the soldiers alike. There had not been space aboard the warships for the ostlers who normally tended the animals, and the voivode shouted orders now to bring more soldiers from below, to help restrain the maddened beasts.

While Dragulya watched the drama unfold he saw a huge bay leap from the deck into the troubled water, where it struggled to swim, its forelegs beating the brine into foam. Mercifully, few others followed its example; crazed as they were, the horses were more afraid of the water than the littered deck.

The ramparts of the forts, high above the decks of the ships which slid between them in tight-set single file, were shadowed now that the sun was setting over the island. Their crenellations stood out in sharp silhouette, and every time a cannon fired the flash of the powder seemed all the brighter, and the roar of the gun all the more ominous.

The *Cockatrice* was passing now from the most dangerous zone, surging through into calmer water and cooler air. To Dragulya, it seemed that the harbour ahead was curtained with thin wreaths of descending smoke released by the dying wind. According to the legends of the Greeks, whose nation marked the southern boundaries of the Khanate of Walachia, this was supposed to be the mouth of one of several rivers which girdled that underworld to which the dead must go. As the *Cockatrice* made slow headway toward the darkened creek which fed the bay, the voivode could understand why credulous men might fancy that to be the case. To him, though, the dark and shrouded waters ahead were welcoming, a gateway not to the afterlife but to the damnation of the rebels of Malta.

Three galiots had already passed the guns of the forts, and were drifting now from the mid-channel, waiting for more ships to come through to gather for the landing. One at least was in a parlous state, lying very low in the water, her castles shot to pieces, but Dragulya could see his fighting men lining her upper deck, all the more anxious to depart the ship and run riot along the shore.

He looked towards the shore, measuring its extent in the murky light. As he had expected, the wharves and piers were thick with men, but he knew that they would be a thin line of defence. The island was too large, and its fighting men too few. Were he facing half or a third of the Order of St. John it would have been well-nigh impossible to land, but with all their forts and bays to guard, there could be no more real fighters arrayed against him here than a twelfth or a fifteenth part of their total force, perhaps augmented by some of Cordery's new vampires and certain Gaulish traitors who had taken refuge here when the island broke from the empire.

There was no way to tell in this light how many of those he must face might be vampires, but Dragulya could see contingents of cavalry to either side of the bay, with pitched banners which bore great crosses after the fashion of crusader-knights. Which of the eight pillars of the order was directing operations against him Dragulya could not tell, but he did not care. What concerned him more was the order of his own troops, who might have to fight on foot *en masse* if the horses could not be sufficiently calmed. He scanned the decks of the galiots, but they had few horses aboard, and he had to call to the sea-captain on the bridge to ask what difficulties they had aboard the ships now under the guns. He waited while messengers ran back and forth, but was glad to see that the animals on the *Cockatrice* were under better control.

The voivode called for the musketeers to come to starboard and form ranks, ready to fire upon the north shore when the moment came for the *Cockatrice* to run into the shallower water. For the moment, the oarsmen were resting easy, no doubt believing themselves to be in the final stages of exhaustion. They knew by now that they were out of the firing line, and had come safely to the end of their hazardous journey. The fear which had lent its force to their efforts was spent now, and the greater number of them would be collapsed like broken dolls. They had a few more pulls to make, to guide the galley closer to the shore, in the face of musket-fire, but more ships would have to come through before the assault began.

Dragulya leapt down from the spur, and ran the length of the deck to the stern of the vessel, where he could see what progress the following ships were making. He clenched his fist as he watched, his eyes following the line of vessels as it marched dutifully into the range of the spitting cannon.

He hoped that the pilots who had been brought to him in Naples, claiming to know these waters well, had given advice which could stand the proof to which it now must be subject as the shipmasters struggled to bring the leading vessels into formation, edging closer to shore. His vampires wore very light armour, but his common men were more heavily clad, and could not go through the water. He knew that the balance of power here was more likely to be settled by the firepower of his common musketeers than the courage of his knights.

In all likelihood, his vampires would be evenly matched against the vampire knights of St. John. He had to keep in mind, too, that the defending forces would have more young vampires, who had learned to fight in a modern way. His own batallions had still a great number of vampires who had first learned their skills in a world of swords and arrows, though his forces were not nearly so ill-equipped for contemporary warfare as Richard's men, who were hamstrung by their education in an out-dated code of chivalry, and still did their mock-fighting with lances. He knew from his own experience how difficult it was for a fighting man to adapt his reflexes to the changing arts of combat. He did not believe, however, that the new knights of Malta had guns enough to have become expert in their use, and when he measured the fire that was coming now from the nearer side of the bay he was confirmed in this opinion. Malta had not the armaments to defend itself, no matter how many of its people had tasted the alchemist's elixir.

The *Cockatrice* wheeled slowly in the water as the sea-captain and the steersman made way for other ships coming up astern. Most of the oars were still laid to rest, the remainder gentle in the water. Dragulya called to his men to fire when they had the range, to sow what consternation they could along the shore. The ship must wait until the following vessels were almost upon her, so that the invading fleet could discharge the greatest possible number of men at one time, rather than dispatching a trickle of soldiers at well-grouped and steady opponents, but the galleys must not become too crowded in the water. If one vessel were to go down, to block the channel with a waterlogged hulk, it would create great difficulties for the remainder. Dragulya knew the virtue of patience, yet he dared not wait too long, and his gut seemed twisted with the tension of the wait.

The firing was sporadic, with the greater number of men on ship and shore conserving their powder and shot; all knew that they were set for a gruelling night, and were in no hurry to expend their best. The knights of St. John made only a desultory reply to Dragulya's gunners, though they had more to gain for the moment by inflicting casualties before the invaders set foot on shore. The voivode could see that the captains on the shore were trying to summon reinforcements, arranging themselves as best they could to harry the attackers once the assault began in earnest. These were hardened soldiers which he had to face, and not the kind of rabble that he had often routed with cruel ease.

The other galleys of the squadron still came one by one through the channel between the forts, battered and broken but not completely crippled. The one disaster which Dragulya really feared – the destruction of a ship which would split his force in two – had been avoided long enough. Despite the hail of cannonfire, and the battering which a few of the galleys had already taken in the fight with la Valette's galleons, the ships which ran the gauntlet continued to pass, one by one, and now it was time to begin the landing. Every vessel which had come through the neck of the bay to join the cluster in the quiet water was a further nail in the coffin of the rebellious order, and Dragulya smiled in the knowledge that the men on shore must feel that as keenly as he.

The hulls of the galleys which were massed close to the north shore, ready to discharge their cargo, were creeping ever closer now to the wharves where pirate ships and traders had earlier been berthed. The tired oarsmen had been roused to their one last effort. Dragulya ran toward the spur, where his men were already gathering.

The men on the quayside were drawing back from their firing positions, which were too exposed to be held at the range which now separated them from the shipboard musketeers. There were not sufficient numbers on the shore for any attempt to be made to board the ships, and the defenders preferred to fight from the buildings. That was not entirely to the voivode's liking, for he never liked to attack a force which was scattered and hidden behind stone defences, but he had expected it. His captains knew what faced them, and how to carry such a fight to the enemy, when they had marshalled sufficient numbers on land.

Dragulya paused to help the men who were struggling to hold the horses, shouldering his way between the nervous animals regardless of the danger of being struck by a kick. He shouted orders, making his way to his own mount, a bulky black animal which noticed his arrival and became quieter than the rest. It was not a very quick horse, but it was steadfast under fire, and Dragulya trusted it to go ashore even over a narrow wooden bridge. If necessary, he knew that he could jump from deck to pier, if only the galley could be brought to a proper rest. He was glad to see that now the ships were almost all in quiet water the horses were allowing themselves to be calmed, and he knew that he would have enough of a mounted troop to lead when the moment came.

Closer and closer to shore edged the *Cockatrice*, under fire that was pouring now from dozens of upper windows in the buildings on the harbour-side. Though his own musketeers were firing more steadily now, he knew that theirs was far the more exposed position, and that these next minutes would be desperate. Further delay could only be damaging. The starboard oars were withdrawn as the ship came in to the quay, and Dragulya measured the distance of the pier as it lessened by degrees.

When he looked around he saw that at least half his troop had managed to get mounted, though some who had done so were wrestling to control their steeds and might not be able to use their weapons to full effect. Nevertheless, Dragulya knew, nothing alarmed an enemy so much as a cavalry charge, and so he drew his sword and prepared to lead the attack. He called to the lookouts in the rigging for advice on the condition of the other ships, and was told that they were coming safe to the shore, though not all had the benefit of a wharf at which to land. If fortune favoured him, Dragulya would be able to land two hundred horses and the greater part of a thousand infantrymen in a matter of minutes – sufficient, he hoped, to overwhelm the defenders on the shore.

As soon as the wooden hull began to scrape upon the stone, the seamen began to throw mooring ropes at the capstans, leaping from the decks to secure them, while others brought up bridges. Dragulya screamed to his men to begin the charge, and forward they went in a hurrying tide, every man anxious to get among the buildings, seeking cover from the fire which poured from the lofts and attics.

Dragulya spurred his horse, and clattered over a wooden causeway, turning to the left as he reined in, hugging the wall while he waited for others to group about him. There was too much confusion to allow accurate measurement of the progress of his men, but with the fervour of battle all around him Dragulya did not give himself pause. He was set to race away from Tigné with he knew not how many followers at his heels.

The guns became less vital now, as the loaders could not keep up with the human flood which erupted from the decks of the armada. Dragulya knew that when the Walachian horsemen first clashed with the cavalry of the defenders it would be lances and swords that would do most damage, once the initial volleys had been loosed. He did not bring the musket from its holster beside the saddle, but began to slash with his sword at the figures on the wharf, who ran to cut him down.

The noise of the battle was tremendous, but it did not take long for Dragulya to realise how thin the enemy lines actually were. The cavalry from the south shore of the bay would doubtless hurry around to meet his men as they cut inshore, with their infantry behind them, but they would be too late to help those few who were now trying to stem the tide of the invasion. These were mostly common men, who would die as easily as common men always did.

Cutting and slashing, Dragulya steadied his horse, then sent his entire troop coursing along the pavement, heading inland. The defenders had strung a low barricade across their path, between a warehouse and the lip of the wharf, and two dozen men crouched behind it, aiming their guns. But they could not co-ordinate their fire, and when the horsemen hurtled towards them, seemingly invulnerable to all that they could do, most of them scattered, running away in a hopeless search for better vantage points.

Dragulya threw himself forward, and urged his mount into a great leap which easily cleared the barricade, while his swirling sword cut the heads of two defenders who could not scramble out of the way. He felt some kind of blade nick his leg, but knew that no serious damage had been done. He wheeled about, slashing to left and right, but then heard a mighty explosion as a musket went off just beneath him, and was thrown as the horse, its head near blown to bits, collapsed in a heap.

His left leg was caught in the stirrup, and the horse landed partly across him, but his leg did not break, and he pulled himself from under it, quelling the wave of pain which the jarring impact sent all through his body. Had all the defenders stayed their ground, there might have been one at hand to strike a blow that might have changed the course of the war, but he had already done enough to save himself, and his companions were hurdling the barrier now to surround him with friends.

As he closed off the greater part of the pain, letting himself feel just sufficient to tell him where his hurt was and give an edge to his wrath, Dragulya knew that the battle was already half-won, and that nothing now would stop his troops landing in their thousands through the night. The men on shore could not possibly stand against the relentless tide and the bloodthirst of Attila's kin. By the time the horsemen from the south shore rounded the bay and came to the aid of their fellows, they would meet the legions of Walachia in the fullness of their strength and fury, and could only expend their charges hopelessly against the power of his guns.

Dragulya stood aside while Walachian horsemen poured past him, to race along the cobbled quay. He took advantage of the pause to lift the point of his sword to his mouth, and lick blood from the blade. The taste of it on his tongue renewed his excitement despite the dampening effect the suppression of his pain had had.

For Dragulya, the taking of blood had never been a pseudosexual experience, reserved for pleasurable self-indulgence. He would take the blood of servants by necessity, but he always preferred the blood of an enemy. The earliest vampires of Europe, he was convinced, had been such fierce and indomitable warriors because they used their blood-hunger to drive them on in battle, ever-eager for new conquests. He despised the vampires of Gaul who had made that inner drive into a softer kind of lust, building it into their crass mythology of courtly love. In his thinking a vampire must be a predator: an eagle to feed on human carrion, not a lover to fondle and caress those whom nature commanded him to use.

The voivode called out to a horseman who had paused near the broken barricade, wheeling around with blood gouting from a bullet-wound in his neck. The man was a vampire, yet even so he did not find it easy to close off the wound, and he was swaying in the saddle, ready to fall. Dragulya came swiftly to his side and took the stricken man in his arms as he slid from his mount. He took the fallen man's weight with ease, and laid him close to the wall, where he would not be trampled, holding meanwhile the rein of the horse, which waited, wild-eyed but still. Then Dragulya pulled himself up into the saddle, from which vantage point he could look again along the line of the shore, dim and grey in the fast-fading twilight, swarming with horses and men and alight with the fervour of battle.

Drunk with elation, Vlad Dragulya stabbed the sky with his bloody sword, howling now at his captains and his cavalrymen. He spurred his new mount back along the wharf to a pier where he could see the channel where his last few ships still laboured under the tired guns of the defending forts. Neither Tigné nor St. Elmo were bright-lit now, and he knew they must be sending men along the cliff's edge to join the fight along the harbour's edge. But there was nothing they could do; they might as well set out to defy the surge of the tide. Like great crashing waves Dragulya's fighting men were bursting upon the quays in tens and hundreds, irresistible as they carried destruction into the shops and warehouses of the waterfront.

Hundreds of his common men were dying, and no doubt there were vampires falling who would never rise again from the long sleep, but the day was safe for Walachia now, and Malta was set to fall.

Dragulya galloped off, to catch with his sword more gore for his tongue to taste, to feed the thirst which burned in his belly and his brain. Michael Beheim, he told himself, would make such song of this as to warm the hearts and heads of the huns and their descendants for many years to come, while the ruins of this rebel isle would rot into foul and unlamented dereliction.

SIX

Richard the Norman, called *Coeur-de-Lion*, stood atop a small hill a mile from the walls of Mdina, and watched the soldiers of Walachia march out of the east like a great column of dark ants. The cavalry came two abreast, the foot soldiers three, and in between each company came wagons which bore the loot of Pietà, including all the cannon seized from those forts and barricades which had fallen to the assault. These cannon would be added to the ordnance brought by the Spanish and Italian cargo ships which had sailed with the war-galleys. All would be brought to bear upon the walls of Mdina, and would demolish them by degrees.

From where he stood Richard could count thirty of the wagons, and he knew that there would be hundreds more arriving through the afternoon and the subsequent night. What losses Dragulya had sustained in taking Pietà, Richard did not know as yet, but as he watched the army in its approach he judged that the knights of St. John had not inflicted half as much damage as they might have hoped to do. These soldiers were neither exhausted nor demoralised.

There was something about the mechanical regularity of the marching of the Walachians, and the metronomic precision of their drummers, which brought a shiver to Richard's heart, though these were his friends and not his enemies. In the plan which he and Dragulya had with difficulty agreed, provision had been made to take Valetta should its defenders risk everything in support of their brethren in Marsa Mxett, but Richard judged now that the knights of St. John had taken the less bold course, and allowed the city to come under siege. Perhaps their commanders imagined that they might yet escape by sea, if la Valette's pirate navy could bring relief.

Richard's troops had not reproduced such unholy order in their own marching, but had come more raggedly from the north of the island. They had met substantial opposition, but such was the force of their numbers that the defences had crumbled very rapidly. There had been many skirmishes on the shores of St. Paul's Bay, and a long exchange of cannonfire between the galleys and certain pestilent sailing ships which harried them throughout the difficult disembarkation; but there had been insufficient cannon on the shore to keep them back, and far too few vampires to oppose the immortal knights of Grand Normandy. The defenders had retreated towards Mdina, and would now be adding their strength to the walls of that notable city.

The greater fraction of Richard's army had not yet been involved in a serious battle. Dragulya's men, meanwhile, had passed through the flame in storming the defences of the Marsa Mxett and sacking Pietà; yet here they were, in obvious good order and apparently cheerful heart, ready to complete a great circle about the walls of Mdina, to seal a siege from which there could be no escape. Even Richard, who thought the Walachian soldiers rough and rude, could not help but admire their discipline and their tenacity of purpose.

A party of horsemen moved away from the head of the Walachian column, attracted toward the Norman banner which flew over Richard's tent. Meanwhile, two riders approached from the south, one of them bearing a lance from which a white flag flew – messengers from Mdina.

Richard's gaze moved from the one group to the other, his coppery eyes patiently measuring their respective progress. It was the messengers who arrived first, the unencumbered man leaping from his mount and bowing low before the prince. He held out a scroll of parchment which Richard's brother and lieutenant, John, took from his hand. John passed the parchment immediately to Blondel de Nesle, who wrenched it open and scanned it quickly.

'No surrender,' said the minstrel, tersely.

Richard was not satisfied with that. 'Read it,' he commanded.

Blondel looked up at his master briefly, then shrugged his shoulders. 'To Richard the Norman,' he read. 'Your knights have no more business here than in England, unless they have come to join our cause. You may lay down your arms and enter the city as a friend, else you must take your men from Maltese soil, and never return. Stay, and you will pay dearly for every Maltese life you seek to take.'

'Whose signature does it bear?' asked Richard, bleakly.

'There are three,' Blondel told him. 'Sceberra, Baron of Castel Cicciano; Inguanez, Baron of Diar-il-Bniet and Bukana; Durand, Seigneur de Villegaignon. They are all nobles of the city, I believe. No mention of Cordery.'

'And yet it is Cordery's voice which I hear in the words,' replied the prince, 'speaking of England and not Grand Normandy. Still, I have given him the chance which his countrymen gave to me. I owe no debt to him now.' The Norman prince turned to watch Dragulya's party arrive on the ridge of the hill. As the voivode dismounted, Richard looked at the quilted armour, now stained, torn and dirty, for signs of injury. It was clear that any wounds which Dragulya had sustained were trivial. The Walachian's stride, as he approached, was as arrogant as ever.

'What have you there?' asked Dragulya, his black eyes darting sideways to study the sweating horses which the messenger and his escort had ridden from the city gate.

'I sent to the city offering terms of surrender,' Richard told him. 'This is their refusal.'

Dragulya took the parchment from Blondel's hands, and glanced at it briefly. Then he looked hard at Richard, displeasure lining his face with a scowl. Without a word he passed into the Norman's tent. Richard was at first surprised, then frowned at what seemed to him insulting impoliteness. He followed the voivode quickly, and not in good humour.

As soon as they were out of sight of the watching crowd Dragulya rounded on the Gaulish prince, no less wrathful himself. 'What does this mean?' he demanded. 'By what right do you send messages to our enemy, before my forces arrive? This is no part of the plan which we decided.'

'Plan?' answered Richard, taken aback by the other's fury. 'Our plan was to conquer this island, and put down its rebellion. I sent to the city to offer terms of surrender, to secure that end. The Maltese must realise that the city cannot stand against us; the knights of St. John are defeated, most of them penned helplessly in Valetta. Our own cannon, together with those which we have captured, will soon be arrayed against the walls of Mdina, which are not thick enough to stand against such fire for more than a day. If they had been prepared to give up Cordery, and swear allegiance to the empire, our work would be done.'

'Our work would be done!' Dragulya, shaking his head, threw the parchment down. 'As it was well done, no doubt, that you quit the nation over which you lately ruled. Did the rebels there send you a message, asking you meekly to take your leave? No doubt they did, and inflicted thereby such damage on your empire as a thousand cannon never could.'

'I was betrayed,' Richard told him, coldly. 'The Tower had already fallen. Had I fought, it must have cost the life of every loyal knight in the realm. Yes, if you will, I thought to offer the people of Mdina the same gentle consideration which my enemies offered me. Their adventure is over, and they must know it. I suppose that you would gladly impale them all – man, woman and child – and are so thirsty to be about such work that you are deaf to any cry for mercy. You seek to make an example of these people . . . an example, no doubt, which will last in men's memories for a thousand years, to set a tariff which you'll essay to exact on every challenger of Attila's rule. But this is Gaul, my lord, and there are many in that city who were recently loyal to Gaul. Many have been sucked into this rising against their will. I warn you now, Dragulya, that I will not lend my name to the wanton slaughter of innocents. I have a code of honour to uphold, and I am glad to say so.'

'Prince,' said Dragulya, calmly, 'we are here for precisely the reason that we must sign both our names to the things which we must do. Gaul and Walachia must act together now; they must be seen to have one mind and one heart. Otherwise, the world of which Gaul and Walachia are parts will crumble into the dust. We must stand together, and we must above all else be merciless. We must destroy Noell Cordery, and those who gave him shelter, and every man who has been his follower. We must make a festival of that destruction – a mighty spectacle to burn its lesson into the minds of men and vampires alike. Immortality is no longer our own preserve and firm guarantee of our authority. We must fight more fiercely now than we ever have ·before, to secure our rule. Yes, we must destroy them, every one. We cannot extirpate this evil which the alchemist has brought into our world, but we must do all that we can to contain its force. The new vampires must submit to us instead of forming ranks against us, and they will only do that if we show them what fate awaits them should they dare to practise rebellion.'

'We cannot rule by fear alone,' replied Richard, insistently. 'Our empires are only safe while the great majority of men consent to our authority. What we have taken by force we must hold, at least in part, by persuasion. We must show that we are fit to rule, not only by our strength, but by the justness of our conduct and the honesty of our contracts. We can destroy Malta, and Britain too, but there must come a day when destruction is finished, and common men and vampires will live again in peace. There has been too much hatred in the world these last thousand years, and it is that hatred as much as Noell Cordery's discovery which has brought us to this field.'

'I know that,' the voivode said, his voice a hard, icy whisper. 'I know that very well. But we must secure our empire now, and that we cannot do, save by setting such terror abroad in the world as the world has not yet seen. We cannot rule by fear alone, but without fear we cannot rule at all. That is why we must use our power to the utmost, not simply to bring these rebels to defeat, but to bring them to a Hell which others in their train will do aught to avoid. Aye, it means slaughter; it means tortures which go beyond pain to inspire as sickening a dread as we can. This is no ordinary war, my fire–eyed friend, but a holy war, in which there can be no relenting. We have a thousand years of life before us, you and I, and we may spend that millennium as rulers of our empires, if we have the strength and the stomach for the task. But you must not dissent from that which I must do! Unless you join with me and share the riot of violence which I unleash, you have already cracked the mask of implacable iron which we must show to the waiting world.'

Richard did not answer this. He felt, in truth, that he had no answer to give this cruel creature which could possibly satisfy or calm him. Honour, he believed, was something which had to be felt before it could be understood, and Dragulya was no man of feeling. The wintry east was not fertile soil for the summery conventions of propriety which Charles had tried to teach his empire, and a man content to bear the name of Impaler could never comprehend the heritage of a Lionheart. And yet, he wondered, how could he openly declare his opposition to the voivode's plans? He had hoped to use the few hours of advantage he had in reaching Mdina to bring about a *fait accompli* – a surrender offered and accepted – which would force the Walachian to fall in with his scheme, but that chance was lost. Perhaps the bold defenders might now be deemed responsible for their own vile destruction, and Richard, having offered them a chance to save themselves, could justifiably stand aside and lend his name to whatever Dragulya planned.

And yet . . .

Blondel de Nesle appeared within the tent then, entering with some trepidation.

'What do you want?' asked Richard, waspishly.

'Another messenger is coming, my lord.'

Richard, surprised, glanced quickly at the Walachian warlord, but Dragulya said nothing, and his rugged face was quite devoid of expression.

'Have the nobles of Mdina relented, then?' asked Richard.

'Oh no, sire,' said Blondel. 'This messenger approaches from the west, not from the direction of the city gates.'

At this news, even Dragulya permitted himself a raised eyebrow, expressing curiosity.

Richard hurried from the tent, and looked to the west, where a lone rider carrying a white flag was cantering across the parched grass in front of the serried ranks of Richard's forces. Though he could hardly be unaware that a thousand pairs of eyes were upon him, the rider looked neither to the left, where the invaders were, or to the right, where the walls of the city stood above the terraced fields. His horse was obviously tired, slow in its paces despite the urging of hands and heels, and it was plain that he had come some way to bring whatever message he had.

'What manner of man is that?' asked the voivode, shading his eyes from the sun in order to view the rider more clearly. Certainly, the approaching rider was no ordinary herald. The messengers from the city had been neatly and gaudily dressed, as befitted servants of a Gaulish court, but this man was clad in a torn and bloodstained shirt, with dark britches such as sailors wore, and the white flag which he bore was tied to a broom-handle instead of a lance. His fair hair made it apparent that he was no vampire, and the manner of his riding implied that he was no practised equestrian.

The commanders of the invading army waited patiently on their hill while the rider came to them. When the man slowed his horse to a walk in order to come up the slope Richard could see that his eyes were glazed with barely-controlled fear. This messenger knew that he was among enemies, and did not entirely trust to the safe-keeping of his banner.

'Who are you?' asked Blondel, who moved forward to meet the messenger when he saw that John, lounging against the pole which bore the Norman flag, was staring with open contempt, disdainfully refusing to recognise the man.

The man on the horse made no reply to Blondel's question, and favoured John with a glance as mocking as the stare which the princeling aimed at him, before looking over Blondel's head at the two warlords who stood side by side before the tent. He did not attempt to come any closer, but took from his shirt a folded piece of paper.

Blondel, though he presented to the visitor a most ungrateful expression, reached up to take the paper. He unfolded it, and read what was written there. Then he scowled, and turned to look at Richard, plainly very uncertain as to what must be done.

'Bring it to me,' said Richard, sternly. He could not have explained why he did not ask Blondel to read the message aloud, but he had an awkward feeling in his breast, which told him that this might be a matter best dealt with quietly. Blondel brought the paper to his master, and handed it over without a word.

Richard looked at the paper, and read the words written thereon.

To Richard the Norman, called Lionheart,

I had hoped to meet thee upon the sea, but missed thy ship among so many. I could not bring myself to go away and not see thee, and so I would beg leave to come to meet thee on the land. Once upon a time thou wouldst not fight me, because thou wert a prince of that realm which thou wert pleased to call Grand Normandy, and because I was not a vampire. Thou art a reigning prince no longer, nor am I a common man. I therefore challenge thee to meet me, before the walls of Mdina, so that all the knights of Malta and all the knights of England may bear witness to the settlement of our debt of honour.

The paper was signed: *Lucien Villiers, called Langoisse.*

Richard looked up, into the staring eyes of Blondel de Nesle, who was watching him anxiously. He did not look around, at the Walachian warlord who stood close by. What Dragulya would have him do, he felt sure, was to have the messenger seized and bound, and then to send a large party of knights and commoners to scour the western reaches of the island for this arrogant miscreant – and having found him, to murder him most expeditiously. Perhaps that would indeed be the wisest course.

But Richard hesitated, nevertheless.

For nearly sixty years the story had been repeated in his realm that a cocksure pirate had branded him a coward. It mattered little to the resentful English that a vampire was quite right, and honour bound, to decline a challenge from a common man; and that a prince of the realm could not legitimately be challenged at all. The slackmouths were happy to repeat the pirate's slander, and laugh behind their hands because all the Norman navy could not catch the clever sea-dog, nor put an end to his nuisance.

Richard had never quite been able to put Langoisse out of his mind, and the thought of him was never pleasant. That this creature should choose to repeat his challenge now was a typical audacity, and he knew that if he did not answer it forthrightly, and could not capture the pirate before he put to sea again, this tale would be added to the other, cursing him in the fictions of the common folk for as long as he might live.

We have a thousand years of life before us, you and I. Dragulya's words echoed in his mind. A thousand years, to bear the consequences of every decision, to regret every error that a man might make.

And there was honour, too. Whatever the voivode Dragulya said, it was not merely the power of the vampires of Europe which had to be saved, but their hegemony. If he was not free to do aught but set his signature to the slaughter which Dragulya intended, he was at least free to handle his private affairs in any way that he wished.

Mdina, he thought, *has asked to be delivered to whatever fate will fall upon it; so shall it be. But first I'll show this dark eastern legion how a prince of Gaul conducts himself, and what nobility the knights of Charlemagne have given to the world.*

Without saying anything to Dragulya, Richard walked forward, past Blondel, to the waiting horseman.

'Tell your master,' he said, 'that I will meet him, as he asks, before the walls of the city. Tomorrow morning, after dawn.' With his hand he pointed to a tract of land which lay between the camp of the invaders and the city.

'I must have your word that there will be no treachery,' said the rider, uneasily.

'No treachery,' said Richard. 'I will come alone – mounted, armoured, and bearing no weapon but a sword. I doubt that your master has the use of a lance, and I would not have him come to the field bearing some ill-fashioned broomstick.'

The rider bowed his head a little, then turned his horse, and urged it into motion with greater alacrity than necessity demanded.

Richard did not wait for Dragulya to bid him back to the tent, but strode into its shade with such haughtiness that he did not seem to care whether the Walachian followed him or not.

But when the voivode came in pursuit, there was no anger in his manner or his voice. 'What have you done, O noble prince?' he asked, mildly.

'It is a private matter,' replied Richard.

'I have no doubt of it,' replied Dragulya, 'but I beg you to let me know what noble rival it is that you intend to meet on the morrow.' His voice was sarcastic, but gentle enough.

Richard passed the paper to him, but said as he did so: 'There is a history in this matter which you do not know.'

'I know it,' said Dragulya, softly, as he read the letter. 'I think they tell tales of my famous jests even in England, and tales of your own exploits are not unknown in the courts of Walachia. The kitchen-lads in your lost Tower of London probably tell the tale of how I set some noble robbers to boil in a cauldron, and the servants in my own great houses are gluttonous for rumours of the Barbary pirates and their histories. A man like this Langoisse should have been put out of his misery many years ago, and I pray that you will not let him tarry upon this earth a moment longer than is necessary.'

Richard was startled by the other's sudden willingness to play with words, and was more wounded by that levity than he could have been by the wrath which he had expected.

'I will defeat him,' he promised. 'You may be sure of that.'

'Oh yes,' said the Walachian, with contempt which showed through the polite veiling of his tone, 'this silly madman rides to his death, I know. I do not suppose that he doubts it, else he is a greater fool than any I have known. He must hate you very much indeed.'

'I think he does,' said Richard, 'though the fault was always his. In truth, I am not the guilty party.'

'It is ever our own faults,' observed Dragulya, 'which distress us most. This Langoisse must have many, to have chosen such a name.'

SEVEN

All night long the road from Valetta to Mdina was thronged with men and horses, wagons and artillery. There was nothing in the procession to give the least encouragement to the defenders of the city, who had a clear view along the road from the ramparts. Dragulya knew that their sentries posted in the dome of the cathedral could see for several miles, and he was well aware that they could see nothing but what must teach them the futility of their cause. Those Walachians who had been wounded when the Grand Harbour had been stormed were safely left in the hospital which had been the *raison d'être* of the Order of St. John.

Dragulya knew that the appearance of the legion creeping along the road was to some extent a sham. His forces had not troubled to storm Fort St. Elmo and Fort St. Angelo, and had indeed encouraged the vampire knights arrayed against him to take shelter there, where they might be bottled up by a relatively small force. But that did not affect what Durand's men could see, and what they saw was a great army of fit and ready fighting men, come to destroy them.

The voivode was prepared to gamble that the knights of St. John who had been set to defend Valetta, no matter how sincere their support might be for Cordery's cause, would be well content to wait in their strongholds rather than launch themselves into a suicidal assault on a far superior enemy. With la Valette and other important commanders still at sea the knights defending the Grand Harbour had leaders likely to float with the tide of affairs. Just as the courts of Gaul were full of incipient traitors in the form of ambitious men whose dreams of glory were frustrated by the longevity of their masters, so the Order of St. John must have high-placed underlings who coveted the title of Pillar or Grandmaster, and would turn their coats again if the chance were offered. Dragulya knew that he could manipulate such foes as cynically as he pleased, and take care of them at his leisure. His immediate concern was to see Mdina crushed and Noell Cordery secured.

Dragulya went to his tent in the early hours, but he slept only for a short while. He had Michael Beheim wake him again before sunrise, because he was anxious to be present when the upstart pirate attempted to pay off his ancient score against the prince of Grand Normandy. He looked to this affair to afford him some amusement, and he had some preparations of his own to make in respect of the duel.

In the cold darkness before the dawn the voivode rode on a tour of inspection of his troops, who were occupying the land to the east and south of the city. He told them to build their fires high, so that the fighting men in the besieged town could witness the tightening of the strangling knot by which they were contained.

When he was satisfied with what was being done he selected out a score of his best musketeers, and bid them form a guard around him, to accompany him to the barren strip of land which lay between Richard's famed bowmen and the walls which they were appointed to storm. He arrived there, with these men, while the attendants were putting Richard's armour on, and hooding his horse.

Dragulya watched these preparations with cool disinterest.

Richard had put on a helmet of chain-mail, and a coat made of light overlapping scales of the new iron which Simon Sturtevant had first made half a century ago. That iron was stronger than any cast iron had previously been, and it made fine cannon, but Dragulya thought it far too heavy for a vampire's armour. A vampire, though far less prone to fatal hurt than a common man, was not one whit more powerful, and heavy armour slowed a vampire knight just as much as a commoner. Dragulya would far rather risk a cut and preserve his own agility, but this was the fashion in which Richard had been trained to fight, and there was no use in the Walachian offering advice for which he would not be thanked.

Dragulya judged from Richard's face that the deposed prince had not slept at all. His copper-coloured eyes were restless, and his lips were tightly pursed. It needed two men and a deal of patience to get him up into his high saddle, though the charger he was to take into the duel was as quiet and biddable as could be expected. Finally, they handed him the weapons which he was to carry: a great broadsword, carefully edged on either side, and a shield marked with his coat-of-arms. The sword, like the armour, would be of Sturtevant's metal, and would not break or easily lose its edge – but Langoisse would surely be armed likewise, and would not suffer any crucial disadvantage.

When Richard moved to take the field, Dragulya and his men moved casually in front of the rank of bowmen, taking up the best position from which to watch the fight. Because the ground was rising, they blocked the view of the men behind them, but Dragulya dismounted, and commanded his men to assume a kneeling position, their guns laid to rest upon the grass, with the result that they were not too much in the way.

Richard's bay walked carefully away, to a distance of fifty yards or so, before the prince reined in and turned to face the west. He was almost close enough to the walls to be reached by the best of their artillery, but it would have taken a miracle to aim such a shot, and none was fired. All eyes – those on the walls as well as those in Richard's battle-lines – turned to the west, looking for the pirate. When he came,

Dragulya observed, he would find his royal adversary standing within the arc of the rising sun, limned by its silver light.

'Would it not have been wise to stop this, my lord?' asked Michael Beheim. 'Should Richard fall, it would serve our cause ill.'

'Perhaps,' said Dragulya. 'But I have wondered, while studying this bold crusader, how ill it might serve our cause should he live for another hundred years. This victory of which we are certain will be his as well as mine, and though I will determine its violence while our armies are united, he might go back to Gaul a stronger man, his reputation redeemed. It has occurred to me that it might be better for all of us were Richard to be a casualty of the war. If he seeks to make a martyr of himself, I am inclined to let him.'

'A martyr might serve the cause of chivalry as well as a living prince,' murmured Beheim, 'unless Blondel falls with him.'

'I do not think so,' answered Dragulya. 'He might be a martyr to the cause of chivalry this morning, but when we have stained these terraces with the blood of ten thousand Maltese, his martyrdom will be counted to the cause of Attila's wrath. Let us wait to see what will happen before we decide what it will mean.'

They had not long to wait, for Langoisse did not let the dawn precede him by many minutes. He approached at a wary canter, on a grey stallion which looked every inch a warhorse, though it was not protec-tively hooded as Richard's was. The pirate wore no armour, and his thick leather jerkin had no sleeves, exposing the bright red cloth of his shirt along his arms. In his right hand he carried a sword much lighter than Richard's, with a hemispherical handguard where Richard's had only a bar. In his left he had no shield, but was carrying a white banner. This had brought him safely through the ranks of Richard's artillerists.

Dragulya judged by the way Langoisse held himself that the pirate had sustained a wound in his side, but it did not seem likely to affect his sword-arm.

When he saw Richard waiting, Langoisse cast his flag of truce aside, and steadied his horse.

'The man is but a fool,' said Michael Beheim, in a disappointed tone.

'Which one?' asked Dragulya, drily.

'Now that you ask me to choose, I am torn,' admitted the minstrel. 'But it was the pirate I had in mind this time. He could have escaped the destruction which will fall upon those who are trapped in Mdina; he had only to sail away, and take up his former life. He is a vampire now, and should be more wise than to throw his life into a dicing-pot in such stupid fashion.'

'Whichever loses is the greater fool,' said the voivode, watching the two combatants as they faced one another, pausing while Langoisse rested his horse. 'Richard is a fool for taking the risk at all, but if he wins, it will make a great difference to his pride. The ignominy of losing Britain has probably hurt him more than he guessed when he let it go, and he would dearly love to be a hero again. The battle for Mdina could not suffice, and he does not like the thought of its aftermath. If he wins, Blondel will make a flattering legend for him.'

'I know that art only too well,' said Beheim, 'but I will not beg you to give me like opportunity. Such an act as this would seem stupid in a man like you.'

'Never fear,' said Dragulya. 'It is a Gaulish glamour which these two seek, which would mean little in our way of weighing a man. Our saying has it that he who is careful with his blood is careful with eternity, but theirs is different; they shrug their shoulders and declare that even a vampire dies, while a legend lasts forever. They have never quite forgiven themselves their own immortality. But hush now, Michael, the thing begins.'

Richard and Langoisse walked their horses slowly forward until they stood no more than a dozen yards apart. No word was spoken or signal exchanged, but each man urged his mount into a trot, the prince's bay accelerating a fraction faster than the pirate's grey. The mounts converged at a canter, each rider steering to ensure that he would pass on the other's left, so that their swords could engage one another. Richard had to raise his high, so that its weight would help him in the downward sweep, but Langoisse drew his own weapon back, ready to stab if he could.

Richard had the taller horse, and was himself as tall as the pirate, so he had no need to seek further height than he already had, but Langoisse stood up in his stirrups as they came together. Richard's hooded horse kept straight, but the pirate's was not trained for this kind of work, and shied away, as much from the plated hood as the descending blade. The shy took Langoisse out of range of the sweeping blade, but he had not the slightest chance to put in any blow of his own, and there was a murmurous jeer from the great crowd as the combatants carved at the empty air as if in play.

Langoisse was quick to turn his horse, and guide it quickly behind the other, so that he came up alongside the armoured man on his left hand side. Had Richard had no shield he would have been forced to turn, to make his heavier mount buffet the lighter one, but instead he simply lashed out with the shield as Langoisse came to strike, hoping that the greater advantage of the exchange would fall to him. The pirate's sword glanced lightly off the prince's shield, but neither man was unbalanced.

Now Richard turned his mount, wheeling to the left and raising his shield to take a second blow, but Langoisse, seeing what would happen if the bay made the turn complete, made the grey run through, and took a space of a dozen yards before turning him. Richard, in consequence, interrupted his own turn, and again the men and their horses faced one another, standing quite still.

'Time has not calmed thee, then?' said Richard, not unpleasantly. 'Thou wert ever a fluttering presence, darting hither and yon, with no steadfastness at all.'

The words, spoken so low that they could not have been intended to be heard by any other ear, though Dragulya heard them, were no taunt. Indeed, they might have been taken to conceal a great compliment, in using the intimate form of address; but Richard knew, as Langoisse had when addressing his challenge, that more than one interpretation of that mannerism was possible. Richard, despite the cohort of vampire ladies which his court must have for appearance's sake, saved the intimate form of speech for his intercourse with other men – and that had been the half-forgotten origin of the ill-feeling which led to this quarrel.

'Nor has time awakened thee,' replied Langoisse, speaking loudly, more conscious of the watching crowd. 'For thou'rt as slow and slumbrous as ever was, as leaden in thought and character as a turtle in a stagnant pool.'

Richard's temper was not hot enough, at any rate, to ignite with ire at such an insult, and when the prince came forward again he came steadily, with arm well-balanced and sword tight-aimed. Langoisse found his horse reluctant to respond, and had first to win that battle of wills before he was ready to contend with the real conflict. His victory over the animal was too slow, and this time he could not avoid Richard's blade entirely, but could only wriggle so that it skidded down his back. While he did so, though, he thrust with all his might at the prince's side.

The force of Richard's blow was much the greater, and Dragulya knew that Langoisse must have felt his skin uncomfortably flayed from his ribs as jerkin and shirt were cut to ribbons. The fact that he was already hurt there would make the new cut more troublesome. Nevertheless, it was the pirate's blow which was better aimed to wound deeply, and it was straight enough that the scaly armour could not deflect it. Langoisse's blade penetrated to a depth of an inch and a half between Richard's third and fourth ribs. In the meantime, the horses, brought together by the thrusts, clashed saddle to saddle, bruising the legs of both fighters and causing such a rebound that for a second or two it seemed that one or other mount might fall.

This time it was no jeer which was voiced by the watching men, but a cry of excitement. Little blood was spilled, but these fighting men knew well enough that the hurt of a vampire was never accurately signified by gory stains, and no one doubted that these earnest blows had provoked real consequence.

Langoisse, anxious lest his mount was not long to be trusted in this affair, wasted not a second in commanding the grey to close again with all possible expedition, and while Richard's heavy-laden beast was labouring for balance, the pirate managed another dart with his blade, this time aimed at the prince's groin, below the hem of his coat of armour. Again the blade went home, though it was only the tip which bit, and Richard, though he could not raise his own sword to deal a fatal blow, was able to bring his shield crashing across, smiting the pirate in the face and hurling him backwards, unsighted and markedly dazed.

Had the grey stallion crumpled then and dropped his man, none could have said that the beast was entirely to blame, but it seemed rather that panic lent the unpractised horse greater strength and wit, for it brought its master away quite cleverly, charging on to take him out of reach while the bewildered bay did nothing, waiting for the urging of the bridle.

There was a full minute's pause, while the separated combatants collected themselves, put hands upon their damaged parts, and disciplined their minds to make the pain remote. Langoisse had to blink his eyes to clear his vision, but he was looking away from the sun now, and had no longer to contend with its brightness.

From where he watched with Michael Beheim, it seemed to Dragulya that Richard had had the best of it, and though neither fighter had yet sustained a dangerous wound, Richard had been less disturbed by the first exchanges. But when the two horses came together again, it was the prince of Grand Normandy who seemed less easy in his adjustment for the clash.

It was at this moment that the difference in training between the horses became plain. The grey would not suffer itself to be guided into another close pass. It tried hard to turn away, and when Langoisse wrenched forcefully on the reins to prevent it from so doing it threw up its head, and reared up on its hind legs. This left Langoisse hopelessly exposed, his sword-arm waving uselessly, open to be cut all along his right side.

But Richard never got in the one blow which might have ended the contest, for one of the grey's flailing hooves caught the armoured bay full upon the iron hood. The hood came loose. The shaped metal, held from falling by its strap, moved so as to prick the bay in the eye, whereupon the horse cried mightily in pain, leapt up in the air, and quite deliberately tossed its heavy rider.

Richard, cumbersomely armoured, with one arm anchored by his weighty shield, had no chance at all to control the horse, and fell lumpenly to the ground. The jarring impact must have knocked all the wind from his lungs, and every man watching knew it. The soldiers who were close by, Walachians and Normans alike, cried out in distress.

Richard must have known full well how desperate was the need to

THE EMPIRE OF FEAR

raise himself to his feet, and he must have fought to fetch air into his lungs though it seemed that a vice had been tightened about his gasping throat. The nearest watchers could hear and see the effort in his face, and those who had themselves been direly winded at some time knew what a terrible pain would be in his chest, capable of defying for a moment his vampiric power of control. Though this straining would last no more than a few seconds, it left him helpless in the meantime, and Langoisse came quickly at him to take advantage.

The pirate did not attempt to dismount, or even to calm his horse, but simply used the length of loose rein which remained outside his clutch, whipping it back and forth to scourge the horse's neck, while he forced the angry beast full-tilt towards the fallen man. The flying hooves rained down on Richard's fallen body as he struggled to rise, hammering at the armoured torso and the mailed head.

Richard managed to raise his shielded arm just a little, and must then have felt the air returning to his lungs in a great gasping flood, but it was too late. An iron horse-shoe struck his temple with such force that consciousness was blasted out of him, and he fell flat again.

A great roar went up from the watching men: dismay from Richard's bowmen and Dragulya's musketeers, eerily echoed in the triumphant calls of the guardians of the distant walls.

Langoisse leapt clear of his mount; it was hard to judge whether he stepped down or whether he was thrown, but he landed on his feet, and bounded quickly to the stricken prince, to stand over him. Without pause, he raised his sword two-handed, and brought it down in a mighty chopping motion, almost as if it were an axe. It would surely have broken had it been cast from poorer iron.

Then Lucien Villiers, called Langoisse, reached down to seize the severed head of Richard the Norman, to whose disfavour he traced the origin of every misfortune which had blighted his long and arduous life; and he held that trophy high aloft, wordlessly yelling his delight to the deep blue vault of heaven.

He was facing the walls of Mdina, so the volley of shots which was fired by Dragulya's musketeers took him full in the back.

The marksmen were good enough, and the range so short, that the bullets nearly tore Langoisse in half, and while the cheering that had begun upon the walls of the city was still fading away in shock and alarm, the musketeers ran forward to make sure that even though the pirate was a vampire, he would never recover from his wounds.

Dragulya watched them at their work, admiring their thoroughness.

'A fool,' said Michael Beheim, 'as I claimed.'

'A legend, though, in the Norman way of thinking,' answered Dragulya, ironically. There was nothing in his voice to indicate that he would have preferred it if the prince had emerged the victor. 'We must not forget the legend, which will last when even vampires are gone to their graves.'

EIGHT

The bombardment of the walls of Mdina continued all through the day and long into the night. Though the artillerists of the city replied as best they could, few of their guns had the range of those which the enemy had brought from Italy, whose number was now greatly swelled by cannon which Dragulya's men had captured in Pietà and Kalkara. The cavalry and infantry of Gaul and Walachia were camped well behind their cannoneers, beyond the range of any of the city's weapons. It was plain to the defenders that this host need only delay its attack until their cannon had opened up half a score of breaches into which they might pour to be well nigh certain of victory. The men whose task it would be to meet the eventual assault – vampires and common men alike – laboured hard to repair what damage they could, and grew wearier while they worked.

Seigneur Durand, who commanded the Maltese batallions inside the city, was urged by some of his captains to lead a company against the besieging forces, in order to carry the fight to the enemy. This he steadfastly refused to do. To charge the ranks of Dragulya's musketeers would be suicidal, and Durand knew how necessary it was that the outnumbered defenders should have the benefit of whatever barricades could be erected in the damaged sections of the wall. His men, whether mortals or vampires, did not like to labour under the cannonfire, struggling to pile up massive blocks of stone wherever the walls were shattered; but that was by far the best work they could do to make the task of their enemies as difficult as could be.

The Barons Sceberra and Inguanez had not yet given up hope that the knights of St. John from la Valette's fleet and the forts of the Grand Harbour might contrive to regroup and assault the besieging forces from the rear. Nor had they altogether ruled out of account the possibility that the Mohammedans might yet decide to strike a blow for themselves against this awesome Christian army. Durand, though he knew such hopes to be frail indeed, did not entirely discourage their optimism. He knew that there was nothing to be done save to fight to the death. He had travelled to Byzantium in former days, and had once seen Dragulya there; he was one of the few who fully understood what the Maltese had to face in the Walachian warlord.

When the guns finally ceased their blasting, the silence seemed no less menacing than their deafening roar, for it promised no mercy and mocked the people of the city with an invitation to sleep for an hour or two before the dawn. There could be no sleep, in any case, for the soldiers in Mdina, who must continue their efforts to maintain the fortifications. While they toiled they knew that their adversaries were obtaining refreshment denied to themselves.

Noell Cordery had removed himself from his laboratory, where the work was finished, to the residence of the archbishop which stood beside the cathedral. There he had a bedroom under the eaves, where he would wait for the outcome of the conflict. It was not that he was standing aside, to leave everything in the hands of others; he had done his part, and the real consequences of the battle, as they extended across the years and the centuries, would be the consequences of his actions and his decisions.

Because the cathedral was at the very edge of the town, looming above the wall, it had suffered several blows from stone and iron shot hurled by Dragulya's bombards; but this was perhaps the strongest point of all the town's defences, and the damage was slight. From the topmost floor of the residence it was possible to look out over all the great array of the attacking forces, and Noell had been drawn to the window while the guns were firing, like a moth drawn to a flame. He had looked long and soberly into the comfortless darkness, while the night itself seemed to speak with a terrible voice, spitting flame and exhaling smoke, hurling destruction at the wall. The city came to symbolise, in his estimation, the world of men beleaguered by the despot Death. The cannonade put Noell in mind of Shango, the Uruba god of storms, whose voice was the thunder. Shango had fired destructive bolts at the earth far greater than those which were tossed by Dragulya's cannon, attended by lightning infinitely more fearful than the powder-flashes which erupted from the firepans of these bombards. But in the end, Shango was only a boy in a fabulous mask; a mere charade.

There was a charade in this too, for all the real murder that was going on. Attila's empires were in the process of being unmasked; the idols of vampire hegemony were being cast down.

Even when the guns had stopped, Noell could not tear himself away from his window, though he could see very little of what was happening. His short sight made the fires of the besiegers blur into amorphous ribbons of light, and he could not make out the lines of their tents. For all that he could truly see, he might as well be looking through the earth and into one of the brighter regions of Dante's inferno.

Perhaps, he thought, this was the region reserved for the vainglorious; he had certainly been guilty of vaulting ambition, and now it seemed that the fall awaited him which the scriptures promised to those of haughty manner.

Now that the die was cast, and there was nothing more to do but await the unfolding of the drama, he was not very tired. He seemed to have passed beyond exhaustion, into a fatalistic inertia. All the events which lay in wait for him now were mapped out as neatly and as carefully as Durand's observers had mapped out the lines of the besieging forces, and there was nothing in that map to give him pleasure or relief.

Durand's charting of the enemy's dispositions had been necessary in order that the defenders would know where they faced vampires and where they faced common men, because the bloody arrows which were the last of all their hopes ought not to be wasted in mere slaughter. The mapping had been carefully done, with great attention to detail. So, it seemed, had the mapping of his own future been done with precision and care by fate or by God, or whatever other force it was that impelled today into tomorrow, and brought the form of history out of the readiness of time. Were he to consult that map of his fate, Noell supposed, he would see little in the way of symbols and contours. A few scratchmarks signifying fear and pain, a rude cross to mark the moment of his death, a straight road to take his shade to hell or oblivion; that would be all.

He had wondered whether he might take poison, to avoid the stake and the fire which Dragulya presumably had ready for him. He did not want to die in agony, most certainly not in public agony, for he still remembered with a chill of terror that tale his father had told while they had supped with Carmilla Bourdillon, of how Everard Digby had met his horrid death. Thus, it seemed, all martyrs must perish – if one could believe what was written in the legends of the saints. There was nothing to stop him taking poison. He was apothecary enough to prepare a draught which would give him easeful release, and as an unbeliever he had little fear of the wages of self-murder. And yet, he could not or would not do it.

What a wreck of a man I am, he said to himself. *And what a poor thing my life is, to show itself in such a meagre map.*

He had watched Langoisse die, despite his weak vision, and had wept when the gunmen cut him down. Was that, he wondered, a true hero's death? No doubt there would be many tellers of the tale who would have it so: the pirate had destroyed the prince, in honest combat, and had then been treacherously slain. But was not the whole history of Malta's rebellion written in that little allegory? Had not Noell Cordery's elixir put an end to Attila's empire of superstition and dread, only for that empire to strike back with merciless force at its slayer?

'Oh, Langoisse,' murmured Noell, aloud. 'Thou wert free to flee this tragic isle . . . to go to England, where the true future is. Thou wert a fool to let the past restrain thee, and haul thee back to settle such a silly score.'

His heart ached, with all sincerity, for the pirate. He had hated Langoisse once, for what had happened to poor Mary White, and to Cristelle d'Urfé, but that hate had long been denied further nourishment, and had perished in his soul. He had not forgotten Mary, nor Cristelle, and would have felt ashamed had he been able to reckon their two deaths irrelevant, even in the face of such extravagant killing as he had lately seen and was yet to see; but his old bitter rage had been overlaid and hid by warmer feelings. Perhaps he had learned – better than Langoisse, it seemed – the futility of nursing such subtle poisons as hatred.

Noell was anxious for the *Spitfire*, but the mere fact that Langoisse had returned was assurance that the ship had not been sunk, and he did not believe that the pirate would have imperilled his crew in order to follow his fatal ambition. Leilah should be safe, and ought now to be on her way to London, to the protection of Kenelm Digby and his parliament. That, at least, was a cheering thought which should have lightened the burden of his despair, but his spirits were too deeply sunk.

'Come away from the window, my friend.'

The voice cut through his reverie, making him start. Quintus had entered the room without his being aware of it, and he asked himself sarcastically whether his hearing was going the way of his sight. *So much evidence of mortality!* he said, under his breath. *Will anything remain of me for Dragulya to murder?*

'You are ill,' said the monk, when Noell made no audible reply to his plea. 'You must rest.'

Noell had already turned his tired eyes towards the monk, and was measuring with his enfeebled gaze the candle-lit features and dirtied white robe. Quintus, who had been old before he was made a vampire, was not now the model of a doughty warrior, but there was a strength in his wiry limbs and in his shining eyes which could not be mistaken.

'You were once a kind of father to me,' said Noell, meditatively, 'and yet it is I who seem far the older now. Indeed, I am older than I look, thanks to all my fevers and agues and infirmities, while you have the polished, unconquerable health of your kind. Perhaps you should call me sir, as surely befits the station of my rotting flesh, when you try to usher me away from confrontation with my destiny.'

'I have always thought of thee as a kind of son,' said Quintus, softly, 'the only kind which I might have. If I had feared to lose that consciousness in becoming immortal, then I was anxious in vain. Not all the undying lose their power of affection, though once I thought that perhaps they must.'

'An undying Quintus could never lose affection,' agreed Noell. 'Nor

Leilah, nor, in his own peculiar fashion, Langoisse. I have my doubts
about the greater number of those others, whether they be on the far
side of the wall or the near. You have not surrendered your pity – nor
ever could, I think – but I think that is because you have also refused
to surrender the prerogative of pain. You might ignore a wound in
your own flesh, but never a wound in another's, and the pain of the
world will e'er be upon your shoulders. If all men were like thee, my
friend, there'd be no need for all of this, but thou art a man alone – a
better man than I, I do believe.'

While he made this speech, Noell allowed Quintus to take him by
the arm, and lead him across the room to a chair which was set beside
the fire. There he sat, and Quintus sat opposite, so that they faced one
another across the hearth.

'I do not know about that,' answered the monk, belatedly. Then,
after a pause, he went on: 'It seems to me, still, that if this is the world
there is, then God's handiwork is in it. I do not pretend to understand
what manner of creature man is, or why he is beset by so many traps
and temptations, but I know there is a purpose in its somewhere. I can
no more fathom that purpose than you have fathomed the mysteries
which you have sought to understand, but faith I have that all men
have the chance to see the light of good and reason, and that more than
we might sometimes imagine have something in them worthy to be
saved. We have done God's work, you and I, and not alone. What we
do today we do with loyal and hopeful heart, and there are many like
us in the vast wide world.'

Is this a final bid for my salvation? asked Noell of himself. But he did
not answer in such terms. 'Aye,' he said, instead, 'if there's a God, then
it must follow that His will is somewhere in this awesome chaos,
though 'twould take a wiser man than I to guess precisely where.
Sometimes, my bitter head explains to my hopeful heart that all of this
was but a tiny jest of our Creator, such as He played on faith-besotted
Job. One day, perhaps, he spake to a favourite angel, and said: "I will
make men immortal, to prove to them that the gift of eternal life would
only serve to make them strive much harder to destroy one another!"
He's a merry wight, our loving God, who gave us a span of life that
we might readily spoil in sin, and will make us pay for our pleasure in
the infinite fires of damnation.'

He was not surprised when this reply did not please the priest, but
the monk only frowned a little, surely more in sorrow than in anger.

'Do not be misled by thought of the morrow's battle,' Quintus said,
his voice still gentle, not querulous or uncertain in the least. 'It will be
the day on which many men die, and a terrible price will be paid for
what you have given to the race of common men, but it will not be
the end of this history which you and I have dared to turn upside-
down. The secret which we have made known will give long life

to millions of men, and Dragulya knows even now – as Attila and Charlemagne know – that the days in which a tiny handful of men could hoard in miserly greed the treasures of youth and long life are dead and gone. The empire of the few is already crumbled, and the empire of the many is at hand. You have given the common men of future generations a freedom which Attila's empires would ever have withheld, and the revenge which Dragulya intends to take is but a testament to your triumph.'

'A sad and blood-stained triumph,' murmured Noell, 'still to be further polluted by our Parthian shot.'

Quintus bowed his head a little, and now his reply had not such certainty of resolution. 'Do not regret it, my friend. There is nothing you or I can do to halt it, for Sceberra and Inguanez would not now be asked to sacrifice their people timidly. These Maltese are unbending folk, with a great and special courage, which will ever lead them to strike back at an enemy who would destroy them, even in the moment of their destruction. Attila's empire is foredoomed to crumble, but the bolts from Durand's crossbows will bring it all the sooner into dust, and save the lives of many future men.'

'I know that,' answered Noell, with a sigh. 'All my bile against the wicked empire has been poured into the making of this thing, and left me empty of spite, but I am not about to complain against its justice now. Yet you and I will likely die tomorrow, and there is something in that circumstance which urges me now to think of further things than the fall of Gaul and Walachia. What I have loosed will not be put away so easily, and the empires which come after Gaul and Walachia might find that I have placed upon their own affairs a curse which will not be easily lifted.'

Quintus hesitated. 'My son . . . ' he said, but was not allowed to proceed.

'I am not, after all, your son,' said Noell, clasping his hands tightly, 'but another man's. I know that I have done what my father would have wished of me, and for his sake I am not ashamed to own to it, but I still cannot be sure that what my father did was moved by concern for his fellow men, or by the anguish thrust upon him by his vampire lover, and while I cannot be sure of him, how can I be sure of myself?'

As he finished this speech he stood up again, turning first one way and then another as if he did not know what to do with his derelict body. Then he strode back to the window, while Quintus came quickly from his seat to follow him.

'Thou hast had vampire lovers yourself,' Quintus reminded him, 'who have not led thee to anguish.'

'They never broke my heart.'

'I knew Edmund Cordery,' said the monk. 'He was not a man with a broken heart. He had the stoutest heart of any man in England, braver than any Lionheart, worth ten of any vile impaler of the weak. He loved your mother, too; you must remember that.'

Noell passed his hand across his tired brow, and shivered in the cold breeze which blew through the unglazed window. Quintus tried to take him by the arm again, to lead him back to the chair where he might rest, but this time Noell shook off the hand and gripped the sill of the window as if to bind himself to it while he stared impotently into the night.

'It is another of our kind creator's jests,' said Noell, remotely, 'that we common men are made of clay so stupid that no common woman can ever possess the attractions of a vampire lady. Beauty, alas, is in the eyes of beholders, and we are drawn to that beauty which only vampires can possess. For me, there has never been aught to put in its place, and I sometimes despise it in myself. I pray that my father was a different man, but what is my blood was once his, and I dread that my sins were once his also.'

'My son,' said Quintus, more urgently now but without raising his voice, 'you must absolve yourself from this imagined sin. It is not evil to own desire. I wish I knew whether the beauty of vampire women were a gift of God, or Satan's trap, or a mere accident of happenstance, but I cannot tell. Your father loved the Lady Carmilla, perhaps as well as you love Leilah, but the fact that you could not love Leilah until she became immortal is to be excused as a mystery of your heart. It is not a matter for damnation, and it surely is not a proof that your father could not have loved your mother, or that his wrath against the empire of Gaul was not honestly found.'

'Nevertheless,' said Noell, 'I wish that I could know myself with sufficient certainty to absolve myself of evil. I wish I could say that I knew, without the shadow of a doubt, that what I have done was done for good and noble reasons, and not from some foolish motive so twisted and cunning that I cannot trace its tanglements within my soul.'

Noell paused, listening for a moment to the faint noises which drifted from the streets below – sounds which had earlier been masked by the roaring of the guns. Then he went on. 'My friend,' he said, awkwardly, 'you know what it is that I have done, and perhaps you alone have the power of foresight to know what it will mean, not just to the war we must fight tomorrow, but to the world which our heirs must make out of the dereliction which we leave to them. I beg you to tell me whether there is any absolution from this sin. I ask you not for God's forgiveness, nor even for your own – I ask you whether children yet unborn, when they grow to understand what I have done, will call me saint or devil?'

'They will call thee martyr,' said Quintus, with all the assurance of which he was capable, 'and they will weep for you with all the pity that is in the world.'

'All the pity that is in the world,' echoed Noell. 'But how much pity can there be, in a world which has conquered pain?'

'The world will always have such pity as it needs,' Quintus promised him. 'Always and forever. And whatever the race of man becomes, with your gift of remaking itself, it will not lose love, for that is too precious a thing to be abandoned.'

Noell listened to these words, and repeated them to himself while he stood rigidly, clinging to the stone sill. Then, after a while, he slowly relaxed himself, and Quintus reached out again to help him bear his weight. The monk did not try to guide him away from the window this time, but put his arms around him to make him warm.

'Dear God, Quintus,' said Noell, with half a sob in his voice, 'I am so afraid to die. I do not think I can do it well at all.'

'Thou couldst not be a better man,' whispered his friend, 'if thou shouldst live a thousand years. Do not care about the manner of thy dying, for it is the way that thou hast lived which determines what thou art.'

'But dost thou see,' said Noell, softly, 'that this is what I do not know? I ask of myself, how have I lived? I ask of myself, have I done what is right? And I cannot tell. Quintus, *I cannot tell!*'

The monk only clasped him harder in his arms, until Noell came in his own good time to the understanding that within this stern embrace was all the answer that he needed. He did not need to believe in God, but he needed to believe in himself. In the end, it was simply a matter of faith.

NINE

Dragulya watched the long assault on Mdina from the hilltop, where his tent was pitched alongside the one where Richard the Norman's body lay. Beside him was the man who now had command of the Norman troops, and might by Charlemagne be reckoned prince of Grand Normandy: Richard's brother John.

John was by no means as imposing as his brother, being much slighter of build and carrying himself rather less arrogantly, but Dragulya liked him a little better, for he seemed calmer of mind and quicker of wit. Where Richard had all-too-obviously disliked the voivode, John gave the impression that he liked him. Dragulya did not care whether the appearance was true or not; in either case, it signified that John was the more cunning statesman. Then again, there seemed nothing squeamish about John, who seemed utterly indifferent to any contemplation of human suffering. He was the kind of man who would appreciate the humour of Dragulya's jests.

Michael Beheim was still by his master's side, too, watching with him while the walls of Mdina crumpled under the trumpeting of the bombards. Blondel de Nesle was not to be seen, though. It seemed that John did not like his brother's dear friend as well as he might, and Blondel had been sent to stay by his dead hero, to mourn and perhaps to count the cost of chivalry.

In the afternoon, the watchers on the hill saw the Walachian cavalry charge three times at a huge breach in the wall which Durand's musketeers and artillerists fought desperately to defend. Less than a quarter of the troop were vampires, but their bravery was not lessened at all by the fact that so many stood to die. John exclaimed in ironic admiration of the recklessness of men possessed by the ambition to be vampires, but Dragulya never mocked his own men, even in secret. Indeed, he felt for them as he watched them surge forward on each assault, his heartbeat accelerating as he willed them on. When men and horses fell, bloodied and screaming, he gritted his teeth with anger, for these were his men, and every blow struck at them was aimed at the heart of his empire, and his power.

John was right, no doubt, to argue that ambition to be made immortal drove them on, transforming the fear of death into a burning fury, but that was good and right. That was a foundation of loyalty far more secure and trustworthy than any love or admiration. Dragulya's common followers feared him, but they knew from the experience of eight generations of their antecedents that he was scrupulously fair in dispensing rewards. If they served him well, then they would win their place in the secret ceremonies of their masters, and join them in the ranks of vampirekind. So Dragulya watched his common soldiers, measuring their mettle, determined that many here today would become allies to share the centuries with him.

Though their horses were climbing the hill, against heavy fire, the riders drove them on with the passionate fierceness of those who had accepted the ultimate gamble: their mortal lives against the prize of immortality. In doing so, they earned the respect of the watching warlord, who knew the worth of any man who would willingly seize such odds. In his eyes, these were the best of humankind, the ones whose values accorded with the realities of existence. What else was mortal life for, but to use as a stake in the great lottery?

Though one in four of their number was cut down during the first two charges, the remainder of the valiant company went for the third time at the ragged ruin of the wall, and this time found the cannon exhausted and the musketeers falling away. The breach could not be held. Even John gave a cheer when the horsemen attained their end, balling his fist within his sequined gauntlet.

'Now,' murmured Dragulya. 'Now it begins, in earnest.'

With each turn of the cavalry the supporting infantrymen had crept closer behind, well within the range of the defending cannon but no longer fearful of their fire. They were ready now to run forward in great waves, vampires and common men together, to sweep into the streets of Mdina. A great roar went up from these ranks when the cavalry broke through, and they swarmed up the hill yelling in triumph and exultation. Dragulya muttered an invocation in his own tongue, and drew a curious glance from John, but the would-be prince of Grand Normandy ventured no more ironies. Dragulya had erased the last vestiges of honest superstition from his thinking a hundred years before, but he was still inclined to mutter spells and incantations in such moments as this, out of habit and excitement, and in the knowledge that they could do no harm.

In the far distance, Dragulya could see other signs of the battle's impending climax. The longbowmen which Richard had brought from Normandy had moved into a position from which they could fire over the north-western wall into the town. Their shieldbearers had made them a wall of wood and iron behind which they crouched, rising in unison with arrows notched to loose volley after volley to skim the ramparts. They were within the range of enemy guns, but they drew little fire in return, either from cannon or crossbows. The defenders plainly had the opinion that they had less to fear from these relics of the past than from artillerists and musketeers; but this disregard was a boon to the bowmen which they were exploiting to the full. In declining to mount an effective defence against them, Durand's men were allowing the archers to make full use of their skills, and their arrows were more accurate than musket-shot. The defenders were not ashamed to use their own wooden bows to what effect they could, but there was no way that the Maltese bowmen could match the massed ranks of Richard's men arrow for arrow.

Dragulya requested that John should send a courier to tell the bowmen that his own men would soon be within the city wall, and that the hail of arrows must cease for fear of hitting friend instead of foe. Then it would be the turn of the Norman vampire knights, who must ride for the city gates as soon as they could be opened. John did as he was bid, willingly. The heir to Grand Normandy's throne was quite content to act as second-in-command to the Walachian warlord; Dragulya doubted that Richard would have shown the same deference or the same willingness to carry out the agreed plan.

A messenger came from the south, where another contingent of Dragulya's cavalry were trying to force a second breach. His news was that they had come under heavy fire, but that the cannons' power had been sapped by lack of powder and shot. Such opposition as was now to be faced seemed likely to come mainly from crossbows. The courier reported that many were injured, vampires and commoners alike, but few fatally.

Dragulya received this intelligence with a mirthless smile. Crossbow bolts could not long delay a company of vampires, and it was plain that the defenders of Mdina no longer had the resources to make further resistance.

This town had stood fast against a Turkish troop a hundred years before, with the same Durand in command, and that had been written down as a great victory for Gaul against the fiercest of its foes. But Dragulya knew full well that the Turkish army had been little more than a pirate band, numerous enough but essentially ill-armed and ill-disciplined. Those walls, and the guns set to defend them, had not been built to stand against the force which now assailed them – a force which could have taken any city in Gaul.

'They should have agreed to my brother's terms of surrender,' said John laconically. "Twould have saved a deal of trouble, and a great many Maltese lives.'

'There is naught like fire and threat of death to increase the worth of mercy,' Dragulya told him. 'Had Durand given in without a fight, any sparing of life which we did would be clemency in debased coinage. Now, we may burn whatever in that stony citadel can be put to the torch, and impale as many of the knights and their friends as will give the others appropriate pause for thought. Those we take back into the Gaulish fold will be tearful with gratitude, chastened and loyal. Rome will send its inquisitors to the cathedral, and Charlemagne will place a group of his favourites as Grandmaster and Pillars of the Order. Under their governance, every man, woman and child on the island will learn to curse the memory and name of Noell Cordery. We'll make him the kind of demon which Gregory sought to make of Attila and Aetius.'

'It is very necessary,' said John, judiciously. 'It is a lesson they must be taught, and must be seen to learn – a lesson in fear and authority. My brother could not see the logic of such a case, but we might now forgive him that, for he belonged to a more innocent age, which may now be buried with him. He liked to be loved, even by the people who were only his by conquest, and never understood why they did not pay full credit to his nobility. His ideas were shaped too much by minstrels, and he believed too much in the flattery offered by his courtiers. Perhaps he was not often enough in the company of women to learn the possibilities of perfidy.'

'And you are very different, no doubt, though you were born just a little later?' said Dragulya, who understood well enough that this was a speech carefully calculated to win his favour and approval.

'It is the duty of an heir apparent to learn from the deficiencies of his predecessor.'

'And will you lead the Normans to conquer England for a second time?'

'Perhaps I will,' replied the other, 'if Charles is pleased to order it. I could do it, with help from Geoffrey, who will be a better friend to me than ever he was to our elder brother, but Britain is a dreary isle, when all is said and done. There are other conquests to be planned, now that we know of the New World in the west. We must carry the Imperium hastily to the lands of Atlantis and Hy-Brasil, lest they fall instead to the legions made by Master Cordery's elixir. We need now to fight the British and the Dutch in the farthest corners of the world, and on their own soil as well.'

'I wish you well of it,' said the voivode, drily. 'As I wish you well in the defence of Gaul against the Mohammedans. The gilded days of old will indeed be interred with your foolish brother, but the age of iron which is to come will be hard enough to bear.'

'We are victorious here,' said John, boldly. 'There is nothing that cannot now be achieved by the combined might of Gaul and Walachia. The new world will be ours, like the old, and we'll hold it all the tighter now that this rebellion is crushed.'

'I have said that I wish you well of it,' repeated Dragulya. 'We have a thousand years to fight for, you and I, and we will preserve what we can of our dominion. But take care lest your ambition outreach your grasp. Vampire has now been set against vampire for the first time since Attila defeated the legions of Rome. The making of vampires is known now to be a matter of machinery and not of magic, and all the commoners in Europe know now how little more than men their masters truly are. This day is won, and a forest of sharpened stakes will warn the world that our empires will not readily give way to rebellion. But the world is not ours by right, little princeling, and our might is revealed now for what it truly is. There is a darkness come to Gaul and Walachia, eager to quench the light of our glory, and our empires are under a siege which can never finally be lifted.'

John looked into the voivode's eyes while this bitter oration proceeded to its end, but when it was over, he tore his gaze away, to stare with grim countenance at the walls of Mdina, swarming with men whose shouts of pain and exultation were clearly audible now that the guns were hushed.

The Walachian foot-soldiers had full command of the broken wall, whose defenders had been driven back by the cavalry, and the men who were marching up the hill to fill the breach were no longer under fire. Dragulya's attention, drawn back to the battle, moved to the city gate, and he tried to picture in his mind's eye the progress which his men must now be making, along the inside of the wall. No doubt the Maltese were fighting, with their swords and their crossbows and such muskets as they still had powder to fire, but they could make no stand now, as the streets were flooded with men, and chaos reached its angry fingers into every corner and hidey-hole.

'Come to your horse,' said the voivode to the prince, in a much kinder voice. 'It is time for us to seek out your troublesome Master Cordery, and make him safe. We must ride beneath our banners into this wretched city, that we may be seen by all as its destroyers, you in your white-clad armour and I in my black quilt: Gaul and Walachia side by side.'

'United and unconquerable,' agreed Prince John, too quietly for his words to seem ironic.

So they went to their horses, Dragulya to a mount as black as he could find, John to a grey, so that when they went side by side they might strike as fine a picture as any tale-teller might imagine. Each brought three dozen vampire knights into a company with which they would make their charge. All of Dragulya's had muskets, and were trained to use them from horseback, but those which John had inherited from his brother had been too long accustomed to the play of tourneys, and they carried naught but their broadswords in their hands.

These fighting men walked their horses down the hill to ford a small stream, and then began to climb the planted terraces, taking a diagonal course towards the city's largest gate. The fighting about that gate was fierce now, but Dragulya had sent so many vampires across the wall to prepare his way for him that the defenders – no matter how many had partaken of Cordery's elixir – would be vastly outmanned as well as outgunned.

The Norman vampire knights, amassed ahead and ready for their own charge, surged suddenly forward as the gate began to open. It seemed for a moment that all resistance had ended, but then from the walls to the west of the gate a sudden hail of crossbow bolts met their charge. Though this was unexpected, and the range was close, these were no mortal men, and their mail protected them from peripheral blows even when their shields were passed or splintered. Those who fell as their horses poured into the gateway were a mere handful, and the exultant cries of the Normans mingled with the loud greetings of the Walachians within the wall.

'The way is clear, my noble prince,' called Dragulya to his companion, as he urged his horse into a canter.

John, who had an armoured helm upon his head, raised his sword in a high salute to the Walachian warlord, and urged his own horse more rapidly forward.

As they came to the gate there seemed to be no resistance left at all, but when they drew near, five men with crossbows appeared from hiding on a roof which overlooked the open space within the gate. As these ambushers released their bolts, Dragulya's musketeers returned their fire, and Norman musketeers who had occupied the walls joined in with them. At least four were hit by these volleys, but all five must have been vampires, for only two fell mortally hurt. The other three reloaded, and fired again.

There was no doubt that these five had been stationed to make targets of the warlord and the prince, for one of the first five shots took Dragulya in the arm, while another whistled past his face. One more struck John's shield, and another hit the Norman's nearest companion hard enough to carry him from his saddle.

The bolt which had hit Dragulya went clean through the flesh of his right arm and stuck fast. The pain struck at him like lightning before he could tense himself to control it, forcing him to grit his teeth. He fought to keep his balance on the horse, and when the animal was still he reached across with his left hand to snap the bolt behind the head. Then he dragged the shaft backwards from his arm and threw it aside. The flow of blood was stanched very quickly, but the muscle was so badly torn that the arm would be useless for two days or more, and Dragulya cursed his luck.

The second shots launched by the would-be assassins all found targets, but not the ones intended. John, sheltering behind his shield, deflected another bolt so that it hit a Norman knight in the upper leg, but he had taken sufficient force from the shot to make it less damaging than a direct hit. The knight pulled it out immediately, ignoring the extra damage which he would inflict by dragging it back against the barb, and howled his contempt at the enemy. A second bolt hit one of Dragulya's men full in the face, smashing through his cheekbone to cause a very ugly wound, but one which would not be fatal to a vampire. The third of these shots hit John's grey horse behind the ear, and it went down like a slaughtered ox, killed instantly.

Dragulya smiled grimly, not only because the remaining three snipers were now felled by bullets which would likely kill them, vampires though they were, but because he could not find it in himself to be entirely displeased by John's ignominious tumble. No doubt the prince would quickly find another horse, but in the meantime, Dragulya could ride on alone, past the Great House of the Inguanez family, along Villegaignon Street, and then around and about, to see what havoc his men were making. He had done his bit, he thought, to stage a pretty picture of union, and now he had a chance to stain his sword with the blood of conquered men, before he must come at last to the great Cathedral itself, where he would wait for the humiliation of his enemies to be completed.

The last of the vampire assassins rolled from the roof which had been his station, and Dragulya called out an order to one of his foot-soldiers to mark the man, if he was still alive, for impalement.

As the Walachian moved to obey, though, he had to sidestep as something else clattered down the roof to fall beside the Maltese vampire. It was a pot of some kind, which shattered when it hit the stone pavement, red liquid bursting out of it and drenching the recumbent man.

'What is that?' demanded Dragulya.

The foot-soldier shook his head in puzzlement, but John was on his feet now, livid with anger at his fall, and he strode past the voivode's black to look at the man who had shot his grey, and at the stain which had splashed over him.

'It looks like blood,' he said, his voice grating with anger at the humiliation of his fall.

'Wait!' said Dragulya, but John had already bent down to smear his fingers upon a shard of the pot, and lifted them to his lips. He sniffed the liquid first, then tasted it with his tongue. He turned around to look up at the voivode, who licked his own dry lips, but not with any imagined relish.

'It is only blood, my friend,' said the heir to Grand Normandy. 'Only common blood. The streets are full of it.'

The warlord made no reply aloud, but murmured to himself, beneath his breath: 'Aye, and so they are. But is there a reason, I wonder, why they have gathered it in pots which stand beside their archers?'

He remembered, then, how Edmund Cordery had died.

TEN

Noell Cordery offered no resistance when the Walachian soldiers burst into his room in the archbishop's residence.

He was standing by the window, despairingly watching the tumult, and there was such a desolation in his heart that he could hardly bear to turn to look at them, but they had to be faced.

The first of the invaders, a fair-haired common man with an ugly face, crazy with excitement, seemed ready to put him instantly to the sword. Doubtless the soldier saw only an old man wearing spectacles, whose plain clothes had no badge of rank to make him any different from many others equally helpless. Noell, in fact, moved as if to offer his breast to the Walachian's sword, and was waiting for the blow when a vampire captain shoved the common man aside, cursing him in his own tongue. Then Noell knew that it might not be so easy to die. The vampire did not know him yet, but feared to make a mistake.

The soldiers made him a prisoner, and took him away, showing him to others they had captured, until someone was found who was persuaded to name him. Until then, they treated him roughly, but when they knew who he was they became more careful. Noell saw the Walachian captain stare at him with fear and loathing, and with great puzzlement; clearly he did not look the part of a master alchemist and black magician.

His hands were bound tight behind him with a curtain sash, but first he was taken back to the chamber where they had found him, while the captain looked about the room, sorting through the papers on the desk as though to evaluate them – though he probably knew no written English, and seemed unable to speak even a few words of the language.

After a few moments of pretence, the captain instructed his men to gather up everything, and bring it with them. Then he led Noell away again, to bring him from the residence to his fated meeting with Vlad Tepes.

He did not need to be taken far, for Dragulya had made his head-quarters in what was called the Palace of the University, where the Commune of the Maltese islanders had convened to exercise those rights and privileges which were guaranteed to them by the Grandmaster of St. John. The Palace had been the principal magisterial court in Mdina, where the Maltese received whatever justice was offered to them by their own nobles, and Dragulya plainly thought it apt that he should use the place for the court where he would pass sentence on the defenders of the island, who had sought to separate it from the Imperium of Gaul and make it the cradle of a New Order.

That emergent order seemed now to be dead in its womb, a corpse to be dissected by Dragulya's wooden stakes, but Noell, disheartened though he was by what he saw in the bloody streets, knew that the appearance might yet prove deceptive.

The voivode was waiting in a small chamber beside the main hall of the palace, where he had made himself comfortable. He was not alone, but those who were with him were not fighting men, being nobles of a different stripe. When the captain told the warlord who his prisoner was, Dragulya received the information impassively, and told the soldiers to leave him and withdraw.

Noell's spectacles had slipped down a little from the bridge of his nose, and despite the fact that the distance was not great, he could not quite bring Vlad Tepes into proper focus. He had the impression that here was a huge and handsome man, with long hair and a flowing beard to show off very obviously that glossy sleekness which marked him a vampire. He could see, too, that the Walachian seemed to be holding his right arm crookedly against his chest, as though it was hurt and the hand could not be properly used. He wondered whether Dragulya was surprised to find him as he was, weak and imperfect, marked by age and illness and all the deficiencies of common flesh. But Dragulya must have known that he was an unlucky man, immune to immortality.

'I am glad to meet you, Master Cordery,' said the voivode. His English was lightly accented.

'I had hoped to avoid the occasion,' answered Noell. 'I do not expect that it will have a happy outcome.'

'You need not fear the stake,' said the warlord. 'I am asked to take you back to Rome, in order to deliver you there to the officers of Alexander's inquisition, who will obtain your confession to crimes of sorcery, intercourse with the devil, and other maleficia. They will try to treat you more gently than some, I believe, for they will be a little anxious that you do not die under question. They would prefer it were you to walk alive to the place where they will burn you as a heretic, and will try to make you sufficiently penitent to condemn yourself before you burn.'

Two of the others who were present were bold enough to come to the warlord's side to inspect his prisoner curiously. They were smaller, slimmer men, whose clothes had not been stained by the toil of battle. Because they had the sleek black hair and dark eyes characteristic of vampires they seemed almost indistinguishable to Noell's blurred vision. One of them, seeing his condition, turned away and fetched him a chair, holding it for him so that he might sit down. Noell did not thank him.

'This is my friend, Michael Beheim,' said Dragulya, referring to the man who had not moved. 'The one who has your comforts more fully in mind is Blondel de Nesle, but perhaps you know Blondel?'

Noell looked at the man who had fetched him the chair, and said: 'I saw you several times, when I was very young. No doubt you have not changed, but my sight is feeble.'

If Blondel smiled, Noell could not see it.

'Do you know what has become of my friend, a monk called Quintus?' asked Noell of Dragulya. He had little interest in discussing the more awful aspects of his own intended fate, but he was anxious for news of the monk.

'If he is not dead, then he will go with you to Rome,' said the voivode. 'Vampires may burn with common men, if they are proven heretics. I have not seen him yet, but you will understand that he cannot escape. You had your chance to sail away, and perhaps you were foolhardy not to take it.'

'Perhaps,' said Noell, 'you will understand why I thought that you could not harm me. My life has already brought me to the edge of death.'

'I could hurt you still, if I wished,' Dragulya told him. 'I have no doubt that the pope's kind officers will do what they can to make your remaining time on earth unpleasant. It was a pretty jest of fate that such a physician as you have become could not cure himself of the curse of pain. I think the Romans will take ample time to laugh at it.'

'Still,' said Noell, keeping his voice quite level, 'they cannot hurt Quintus. They might kill him, but they cannot hurt him. And I think I have placed many other men beyond the reach of the agonies which you intend to inflict. Did you find room aboard your galleys for a cargo of pointed stakes, or will your carpenters strip the island of its every tree? I fear that it has not very many.'

'I have what is needed for my work,' replied Dragulya, sounding almost as though he were mimicking the calmness of his prisoner's tone. 'It falls to me to deal with the Maltese, and the rebel hospitallers, to punish them for their part in what you have done. You know, of course, that Langoisse was killed?'

'I saw it done. Has his ship been captured or sunk?'

'I do not know. I have heard no such report, but the sea is still calm, and if the vessel sailed away from the western shore, there is no reason why it should not reach another port.'

Dragulya seemed honest enough in making these answers, and there was no sign of personal animosity in his cultured voice. If anything, there was a note of courteous curiosity, as if the impaler wondered what manner of being it might be which could appear before him in such meek and feeble guise, yet had caused him so much trouble.

'What of Sceberra, Inguanez and Durand?' asked Noell.

'The Baron of Castel Cicciano is beyond our immediate reach: not yet dead, but in a sleep from which I will not trouble him to awaken. You must count me lenient in that, though it is not for mercy's sake that I give him an easy death. He is not sufficiently important. My men are sharpening stakes for the other baron and for the Seigneur de Villegaignon.'

Noell shook his head in sorrow. 'What point is there in impaling vampires?' he asked, with more contempt than bitterness. 'They can cancel out the pain, and will merely go to sleep with the stakes inside them. Their death will be as easy, in its fashion, as Sceberra's. Your methods, prince, are out of date.'

Dragulya came closer to him then, and reached out to move his spectacles, apparently having become aware that Noell could not see him clearly. He adjusted them, gently and neatly, in spite of the fact that he was using his left hand. When they were better-balanced, he looked his adversary straight in the eye.

Noell had to look upwards in order to meet the vampire's gaze. He offered no thanks, and was determined to meet Dragulya's dark stare as stoutly as he could. But he looked away, eventually, glancing at Michael Beheim and Blondel de Nesle, whose faces were clearer now. They seemed fascinated by him, and by his conversation with Vlad Tepes.

'You have never seen a man impaled, I think?' said Dragulya, with calculated delicacy.

'No,' answered Noell. 'But I have seen a vampire tortured, and I know how little the pain means, once the effort is made to contain it. I know that it serves no purpose.'

'A common man impaled need not die quickly,' said Dragulya, softly. 'The stake is driven into his arse, so that the point lodges in his entrails. When it is carefully set upright, the man's weight drags him very slowly down around the pole, so that the point inches upwards inside him, tearing the liver and the stomach, until it reaches the cavity where the lungs are. I have known men survive until that cavity is pricked, but they usually die before that, of loss of blood and the ravages of pain. If they writhe, the agony is worse but death comes quickly. I have seen men who knew that, and who understood it, throw themselves about most violently, though the pain must have been so terrible as to tear their souls to shreds. I have seen men bite their tongues clean through in such state, but I thought them brave men, after their fashion.

'For a vampire, though, it is different. A vampire can control the pain, as you say. It is an effort, of course, but it can be done and a vampire on the stake does not writhe about. Instead, he must stay as still as he can; it is part of his exertion of control. He does not bleed as much inside as a common man does, and cannot die from that loss of blood. He may, if he is fortunate, fall into the deep sleep because of the pricking of his lights, but I have seen that it rarely happens that way. The very skill which a vampire's flesh has in self-repair begins to heal the organs around the shaft which penetrates them. A vampire impaled, therefore, might live for weeks instead of hours, quite conscious of what is happening, while the point of the stake works up through the torso to the neck. He can be kept from the sleep of escape if he is fed with blood and water from a sponge on the end of a stick.

'I have seen impaled vampires, in the fullness of time, tilt back their heads so that the point of the stake might emerge again through their mouths, with their internal organs adapting all the while to the spit which runs right through them. They control the pain, *but they cannot unlearn the knowledge of what is being done to them*. It is a subtler form of torture than you might understand, but we are made of subtle flesh, and those who seek to torment vampires must be very clever.

'I have sometimes wondered, watching vampire flesh make such accommodations, what ingenious shapes human flesh might be induced to assume, if we only had the patience and the art to shape it. What deformities one might force upon a man! I have men who are skilled in the art of impalement, through practice and interest, but it has always been in my mind to attempt more elegant experiments. In the past, I have always been frustrated by a lack of vampires on which to exercise my arts, for we have ever been most careful of our own kind, but you

have changed the world to help me in my work, and the beneficiaries
of your elixir will surely supply me with such raw material as I need.'

Throughout this speech Dragulya looked very steadily into Noell's
eyes, waiting patiently for him to turn away again, but he would not.
When the voivode finished, Noell continued to look at him, voicing
no response at all.

'You see,' said Dragulya quietly, 'what your endeavours have
wrought. You have set vampire against vampire, and you have forced
us to learn how direly we might treat one another, to secure our empire.
You have added greatly to the sum of human misery, have you not?'

'The harm which you do is on your conscience, not on mine,' Noell
told him.

'Is it, Master Cordery?'

Noell realised that Dragulya was very serious in this debate, and was
not simply seeking to horrify his prisoner. Dragulya was genuinely
angry with him, and was earnest in wanting to make his argument
clear.

The voivode went on: 'Is your conscience, Master Cordery,
untroubled by anything which you have done, or any consequence of
the rebellion which you have fostered? Do you reckon yourself a saintly
man, Master Cordery, condemned by your frail flesh to die like the
martyrs of old on their crosses and pyres, all for the love of Jesus? But
the world goes on, Master Alchemist, and what you have begun will
extend over centuries, touching the lives of generations of men. You
have upset the world, and it will never be the same. Had you not come
to Malta, many men who now lie dead in the streets would still be
alive. Had you not done your work, many men who will this night be
perched on wooden needles would instead be drowning such petty
sorrows as they had in pleasant wine. Do you not believe, Master
Physician, that they will die cursing you with all the harrowed breaths
they take? Believe it, I command you, for I know that 'twill be so.'

Noell looked at him steadily, saying nothing, and waiting.

'Have you no defence?' asked the voivode.

'It is not I who needs a defence,' Noell told him. 'You are the tyrant,
the oppressor, the torturer. Malta has never harmed you; its citizens
sought only freedom from the Imperium of Gaul. We are not the killers
or the crucifiers. You are a poor fool if you think to make me guilty
of the sins which you will gladly commit. You believe that this forest
of death which you intend to plant will show the world how foolish
men are to seek out the freedom and longevity which your kind have
denied them, but in fact it will show them how vicious and how godless
you really are. It will show them how desperately the world cries out
for the smashing of your empire. I have done what I could to secure
that end, and would have done more. I weep for every drop of blood
that is shed in this cause, but to do other than I have done would have

been a betrayal of the unborn: a treason against humankind as great as the one which Attila himself committed, and which your kind has brutally carried forward down the years. I am not to be made ashamed, Vlad Tepes, by such as you. I have done all that I could to destroy you, and I still have hope that I have done more than you imagine.'

As he spoke the last few words, Noell lowered his gaze at last, to look at the voivode's injured arm. Dragulya looked down also, then reached across with his left hand to feel the upper part of his right arm, as if searching for some mysterious sign.

'I had hoped that you would tell me,' Dragulya aid, coolly. 'But I would not have you think me devoid of imagination. I was wounded, as you must have guessed, by a bolt fired from a crossbow – a bolt which was bloody before it struck me. I had not quite understood the disposition of the defenders' arms while the battle was in progress, for it seemed to me that you aimed cannon at common men and arrows at vampires, in defiance of the logic of the situation. I wondered, for a while, whether Durand had made some inexplicable error. Then, I saw your bloody bolts scattered on the ground, and the pots in which your marksmen anointed them, and I began to suspect that there was reason in what had been done.

'I remembered what Richard had told me of the manner in which your father died, and I asked myself then whether a man who could devise an elixir of life might not also conjure up an elixir of death. I realise now that we, who have always made vampires with our magic, have taken too readily for granted the alchemy which you have used to copy us. At first, we did not believe that your elixir was anything but a mask, and assumed that you were only buggers like ourselves, mysteriously prolific. We have suffered, I think, for our complacency. Will you tell me, Master Alchemist, what damage your arrows will do?'

'In all honesty,' said Noell, smoothly, 'I do not know. We have had no chance to test what I have made, except on rats which I first made immortal, and then destroyed. I cannot pretend to understand all that I discovered in Adamawara, and most of the secrets of my alchemy are secrets still. Human semen is not the only seed which can combine with that other seed to become that which makes men vampires, and I think there is more than one way in which human semen can be remade. What I have tried to do is to combine the seed of vampirism with seeds of disease taken from the bodies of suffering men, in the hope that those seeds of disease may gain the power to destroy vampires, as certain plagues in Africa are known to do. I am myself so vulnerable to contagion that I have been forced to be circumspect in this work, but I could not let Quintus and my Maltese apprentices do everything alone, and I have been the planner and director of this work. I have tried to murder you, Vlad Tepes, though with a slighter shaft than the one which I expected you to prepare for me.'

'Your father failed,' said Dragulya, coldly.

'He killed Carmilla Bourdillon.'

'And the plague which he loosed claimed thousands of common lives in London. If the Gaulish knights carry sickness back to every part of Charlemagne's empire, and my Walachians to Attila's, a million common men might die, and no more than a handful of vampires. Which is the greater monster, Master Cordery: a prince who impales a thousand guilty men to keep the peace, or an alchemist who might slay a million with fever, making no discrimination between friend and foe? How do you plead to the charge, Master Cordery? If Vlad Dragulya is to be reckoned a demon in disguise, how may the world reckon you when you have set abroad a greater plague than any the Europe has known before? Will you still imagine yourself the martyr? Are you even now a saint unjustly condemned to burn?'

'I am no saint,' Noell told him, quietly, 'and others must judge the cause in which I am become a martyr. It is a poor martyr, I know, who sheds the blood of others in addition to his own, but we have been a race of martyrs, we common men, who have given too much of our blood in these last thousand years, to feed a race of tyrants and torturers. I say again that I do not know what I have done, but it is the vampire knights of Europe who are the first and principal targets of the arrows which I poisoned. If you would save the vampires and commoners of Gaul and Walachia from the danger of plague, you have only to stay in Malta, and bear that burden entirely by yourselves. I beg you to do it, for without the men of your wondrous army, assembled to humble this tiny island with a vast display of strength, neither Gaul nor Walachia can defeat the enemies which wait within.

'Attila, they say, is mad, and Charlemagne not the man he was. Their day is done, and the shadow of eternity falls darkly now upon a future no man can know. I have tried to be one of its makers, and have done everything that I could to contrive a true lottery, so that every man alive might strive to take a noble part. If I have set free such forces of destruction as will spoil the world entirely, then I will offer my soul to suffer in Purgatory for every innocent soul struck down by what I have unleashed. My prayer, though, is that I have destroyed Vlad Tepes, and hundreds of his vampire knights, and in bursting the iron bonds of the vampire empire might save a hundred lives for every one that will be lost.'

Dragulya took a step back, away from him, and Noell felt as if a burden had been lifted from him. Dragulya's accusations had hurt him more than he had expected, and had honestly tested his faith that what he had done could be justified. He felt illimitably tired now, and could not believe that he would have sufficient endurance to survive a journey in chains to Rome and the subsequent attentions of Alexander's inquisitors. He felt too delicate to withstand any pain or pressure, and was almost ready to laugh at any threat.

'If you had only stayed in London,' whispered Vlad Tepes, whose eyes were burning now, as if with the onset of a fever. 'Richard would never have had you killed. He was a prince, you see, who so liked to be loved, and could always be tempted by a handsome youth. Perhaps his way of making you a vampire might have succeeded where your own elixir failed, but in either case you'd be a noble of the English court today, a creature of silks and powders, devoted to masques and courtly dances. You might have had the world at your feet, with fine and lovely vampire ladies to make up for your mortality.'

'I have had a better life than that,' said Noell, simply.

'You will not think so, when they light the fire.'

Noell laughed, not bravely nor with contempt, but only because he saw a kind of jest in it: an absurd example of the wit, whether God's or the devil's, that was in and of the world.

He was glad to see that Dragulya looked to his left, at Michael Beheim, because he did not understand.

'Oh yes,' said Noell, with a sudden dash of spite. 'Look to your arokin, to whom you have entrusted that history which tells how foul you are, despite the lies and legends which are woven into it. But I tell you now, Vlad Tepes, that Shigidi is coming, and he will come to you as readily as he comes to me!'

'He is raving,' said Michael Beheim, as casually as he could.

So Noell turned to Blondel, to whose credit he had noted one small gesture of kindness, and said: '*Y Gwir yn erbyn y Byd.*'

He was pleased to see that Blondel, and Blondel only, knew what that motto was, and what it meant. The Walachians had to look at the Gaulish minstrel, and wait for his translation. He paused before giving it, to tease them just a little, but eventually deigned to speak.

'The Truth,' said Blondel, ironically, 'against the World.'

EPILOGUE

T he de-ciphered text of a letter received by the Lord Protector of the British Commonwealth, Sir Kenelm Digby, in the summer of 1663.

My Lord,

You have asked for a full description of Noell Cordery's end, which I made shift to witness at your command, and I will give it, though I think that its details can only bring you pain.

One the sixth day of June I went alone and incognito *to the great square in the Vatican. There was a considerable crowd gathered, its people in a strange mood – some capering as with delight, others anxiously quiet. In the confusion I could not overhear much, but what was said was in much the same temper as the gossip of the streets whose currents I have previously reported to you. Few of the commoners here genuinely believe Cordery responsible for that plague which has lately come to Italy and Spain, though it is paradoxically accepted that he had something to do with the deaths of Vlad Dragulya and the Norman pretender. Cordery's reputation as a magician has become very considerable, but the Roman Churchmen have taken every opportunity to assure their subjects that the power of his curse is now nullified.*

When the waggon bearing the two men was brought into the square there was much cheering and jeering, and for some minutes the clamour was so great that no single voice could make itself heard. The monk, Quintus, looked about him all the while, but Cordery's head was bowed. When I reached the closest distance which I could attain I was able to see that his lips were swollen, tinged as if with gangrene, and that his hands were wrecked, the nails having been torn away and small bones wrenched away with pliers. The monk, presumably because he was a vampire, bore no obvious marks of torture, but his tongue had been cut out before the cart set forth, to prevent his speaking to the crowd.

I saw Cordery's head lift when the cart stopped, so that he might take in at a glance the high pyre, the platform, and the stake to which he would be secured. I swear, sir, that he laughed a little, but I think it more likely that he was partly maddened than entirely brave, for he had nothing of that desperate liveliness one sometimes sees in the men condemned to hang at Tyburn.

Cordery had to be carried up to the platform, being plainly unable to walk, though the monk was forced to climb the steps himself. They were chained to their respective stakes, loosely enough that they would be able to move their arms and legs, to make a display of fighting the flames, for these Romans love to see their victims dance.

The crowd became quiet while a Cardinal of the Holy Office read out a confession signed by Cordery, proclaiming that he was a subject of the devil, who had wrought great evil in the world, of which he now repented most sincerely. It ended with his thanks for those who had helped him to a true repentance, and the wish that he be not allowed to tarry in the world, lest he injure it further. This declaration was not so very impressive, for the Inquisitors never consider their job properly done unless a convicted heretic is persuaded to condemn himself out of his own mouth. This, it seems, Cordery could not be brought to do.

Afterwards, the light was set to the flames. I had not thought Cordery to be capable of much movement, but in fact the licking of the flames about his body made him writhe most horribly, and he released one awful scream of agony. The vampire, of course, remained still, with eyes to heaven upraised, beyond the reach of any pain.

The pyres burned quickly, for the wood was dry, and the bodies were soon consumed. When the flames sank lower it was still possible to see, held by the stakes, blackened and twisted forms: mere skeletons held together by shrivelled flesh. The noise had grown again by this time, to become tremendous, and it did not entirely slacken when the Cardinal tried for a second time to speak to the crowd. There were some there who wailed woefully that the wizard had hurt them while he screamed, by supernatural means, but there were soldiers moving in the crowd to silence such unruly claims.

I heard that there was another Englishman somewhere in the throng, but I was not told his name, which makes it impossible to think of seeking him out. I was told that this man said to another that when the Cardinal pointed to the blackened corpses, and shouted to the world that these were enemies of mankind, justly destroyed, one or other of the skulls turned creakily upon its shrunken neck, and said distinctly: 'Thou liest!' I think this an unlikely tale, but it is nevertheless bound to be oft-repeated, as such tales ever are, and I cannot say for certain that it is false.

Your most humble servant,

P

PART SIX

The World, the Flesh and the Devil

I that in heill was and gladness
Am trublit now with great sickness
And feblit with infirmitie:–
   Timor Mortis conturbat me.

Our plesance here is all vain glory,
This fals world is but transitory,
The flesh is bruckle, the Feynd is slee:–
   Timor Mortis conturbat me.

The state of man does change and vary,
Now sound, now sick, now blyth, now sary,
Now dansand mirry, now like to die:–
   Timor Mortis conturbat me.

(William Dunbar, *Lament for the Common Man*)

ONE

It was the thirteenth of June in the Year of Our Lord 1983. An early spell of warm weather had come to Nova Scotia and the window of Dr. Chadwick's waiting-room was open to welcome a gentle sea-breeze, faintly scented with the odours of dying wrack and recently-landed fish.

Michael Southerne sat in the waiting-room, on a low plastic-upholstered sofa, with his lame leg stretched uncomfortably in front of him. He was clutching his walking stick in his right hand, his knuckles whitened by the tension. His pale eyes were restless, and his gaze fluttered along the array of electron-micrographs which decorated the wall to his left.

There was a freeze-dried fracture-section of a liver cell, resembling a cratered lunar landscape. There was a great shoal of spermatozoa, with red rings identifying the transformed Y-chromosome sperms which were the agents of emortality. There was a gigantic nucleus in the process of division, its tangled skeins of chromosomal material treading the paces of the dance of life. These few candid poses before the magical camera which saw to the very heart of Creation told a marvellous story of nature's ingenuity and man's power of discovery.

Michael felt that the receptionist was watching him covertly, though when he turned to face her she was always looking down at her work. Her typewriter was switched off, and she was studying some papers, but her attention was seemingly divided, probably because his presence made her uncomfortable.

She was not a finished woman, only a commoner like himself. She was probably no more than twenty years old, but that would make her all the more sensitive to the stigmata of his deformity. She was still, for the time being, a creature of frail flesh, and must hate to be reminded of its frailty. She surely knew how he had come by his injuries, and must be uncomfortably aware that the same thing might happen to her every time she crossed a road or got into a car. That, of course, was not the *true* horror of his fate. The true horror, for Michael Southerne, was that he could not put away his frail flesh to become a finished man.

He had applied for early transformation, not so much because of his damaged leg (which still allowed him to walk, after a fashion) or because of the constant pain (which the morphia controlled), but because the traumatised tissues in his repaired ankle had lately produced a cancerous tumour. Though the surgeons had quickly removed it, the probability was high that other tumours would form, and the cancer might eventually spread to other tissues. In these circumstances, premature finishing had been deemed entirely proper, and he had taken the course of treatment.

It had failed.

It was no wonder, Michael thought, that the receptionist was discomfited by his presence. In a world of physical perfection he was crippled and ill; in a world of the undying, he was condemned.

There might, of course, be hope for him yet. Chadwick was the leading genetic scientist in Nova Scotia, perhaps the best which the entire Atlantean continent had to offer. If there was any help to be found, it would be found here. But Michael knew more than most about the recent triumphs and limitations of the science of life. His own father was one of Darwin's protegés: a pioneer of the deciphering of the genetic code; one of the excavators of that marvellous dust which had come to earth as the great meteor of Adamawara.

It had been during the few brief moments when he spoke to his father on the transatlantic telephone, and was distant witness to his alarm, when it had really come home to him what an awful predicament he was in. To die at nineteen or twenty, in a world whose oldest inhabitants had been born in the time of Christ, suddenly seemed the cruellest of imaginable fates. Had he only known that he must remain unfinished, how much better care he would have taken of his perishable body!

There was no comfort at all in the knowledge that had it not been for the accident, he might easily have lived to see the day when genetic science would discover a cure for Cordery's syndrome, and eliminate the perversely stubborn residue of common mortality from the human world. Indeed, the fact that he, of all people, should have been badly hurt in a road accident now seemed a particularly vicious irony.

Michael was roused from his uneasy reverie by the sound of a buzzer beneath the receptionist's desk. She smiled brightly as she told him to go in. She could even bear to watch his clumsiness as he hauled himself to his feet, forced to prop up his weight with the stick before he could hobble to the inner sanctum.

Chadwick rose and came to the door as Michael entered, and put out a hand to help him, but Michael evaded it He made his uncomfortable way to the chair by the desk, and eased himself into it.

Chadwick took his own seat, and picked up the file which lay on the desk before him. He opened it – a gesture more symbolic than utilitarian, for there could be no further need to refer to it.

'When will your father be here?' he asked.

'Tomorrow,' Michael told him. 'He flies out of Heathrow this evening.'

'Would you prefer him to explain all this to you? He could do it as well as I, and you might find it more . . . relaxing.'

'On the contrary,' said Michael. 'I'm sure that he would find it nerve-wracking, and that would make it more difficult for me. I know that you can't offer me much help – only an explanation of what it is that's wrong – but I'd like to have that if I may, so that I can meet my father on more equal terms, so that we both know what it is we're talking about.'

'I see,' said Chadwick, sounding as if he didn't see at all. 'Well, perhaps you could help a little by telling me what you already know about the biology of emortality.'

'Not a great deal. Despite my parentage, I'm very much a layman in these matters. I hadn't planned on going into medicine, or genetic science. I hadn't any particular career plans at all, in fact. Now it seems that I won't need any.'

Chadwick seemed embarrassed by his tone. The doctor's black hair was shorter than was fashionable, and had an odd streak of grey in it, which was something very rarely seen in finished men. It made him look very venerable, though he could hardly have been more than ten years finished – forty or forty-five years old, in strictly chronological terms. 'Yes,' he said, awkwardly. 'I'm sorry.'

'No need,' said Michael distantly. 'My fault. I'm not answering your question, am I? I know what everyone knows. The DNA responsible for the finishing is one of several chromasomids which, thanks to the recent work of my father and others, we now know to have been carried to earth by the Adamawara meteor, about thirteen thousand years ago. Several of the chromasomids can attach themselves – by means of a biochemical link which is not entirely clear – to the Y chromosomes of humans and a few other mammalian species. They can only do it, though, when the Y chromosome is isolated from its partnering X in a spermatozoan.

'There are other chromasomids too, which do bizarre things in association with very primitive organisms; a few have transformed protozoa or fungi into parasites capable of infecting people, as in the case of the disease which used to be called the silver death. It's the ones which combine directly with the human Y chromosome which are most interesting, especially the one which is responsible for emortality.

'Emortality is the result of a benign 'disease' which promotes cellular self-repair and obliterates the effects of aging. All the transformed sperms become incapable of fertilising ova in the normal way, but they can still colonise the tissues of a man or a woman when taken into the bloodstream. It matters relatively little how they get into the blood – direct application to an open cut and intravenous injection work perfectly well, though I believe the European vampires, who believed that it was all a kind of magic, passed it on by unorthodox sexual intercourse.

'Once having colonised the host body, the transformed sperms undergo some kind of crucial change which enables them to produce packets of DNA – including replicates of themselves – wrapped up in a protein coat. These metaviruses resemble ordinary viruses, and can infect other cells within the body, but they don't carry their own DNA into the nucleus of the infected cells. Instead they set up a kind of independent construction unit in the place where protein manufacture goes on. There they operate to make the cell better able to repair itself, and resistant to damage, infection or the chemical changes associated with aging. This means that the body, once 'finished', can repair all of its cells very efficiently. Side-effects are various: obvious changes in skin-tone, hair and eye-colour, and of course the drastic slowing down of sperm-production in males and the prevention of ovulation in females. Is that about it?'

Chadwick managed a wan smile. 'Shorn of a little of the jargon, that's about it. I don't want to complicate the picture with too much talk of vagrant cytogenes and augmented ribosomes, though you'd probably be able to understand me. There are only a couple of essential features of the system which are relevant to your case.

'Finishing, in this sense of the word, is a double-vector process. The DNA which enables human beings to be remade as sterile emortals has to take a complicated route to its sites of operation. The first vector is a Y chromosome, with which it fuses to become a passenger in a transformed sperm. That carries it into the body, where it must transfer to the second vector, becoming part of the metavirus which distributes it through the tissues where it will do its work.

'Even then, the system isn't complete. The finishing DNA, once set up as part of a cytogenetic complex, produces a number of enzymes, including the one which is commonly called the vampire enzyme. We're still not sure whether this enzyme has a useful role to play in promoting emortality, but we think that it does. One of its side-effects is to prevent the manufacture of a protein molecule present in the bloodstream of common men and women, which is essential, albeit in very tiny quantities, to the feedback system regulating the production of hormones like thyroxin and adrenalin.

'A finished person can only be sustained if he or she has some regular external supply of that molecule. The only reliable recourse which our ancestors had was to drink or otherwise transfuse a little of the blood of common men and women on a daily basis, which is why emortals used to be called vampires. The equivalent molecule in most other mammals – sheep, cattle, and the like – is sufficiently different to be useless; only chimpanzees and gorillas are closely enough related to us to make their blood a viable substitute. Nowadays, of course, we extract the relevant molecule on a commercial scale from blood donated by humans and by chimpanzees, though we hope to move over in the near future to manufacturing techniques based in genetic engineering.

'I don't know exactly why the system has these peculiar properties. Nobody does, though your father may be able to offer some speculations, on the basis of his investigations of the other alien DNA found in the environments surrounding the Adamawaran crater. What's important with respect to your problem is that there are three ways in which the process of transformation can break down, two connected with the vectors and one with the operation of the established cytogene. All three can be causes of Cordery's syndrome -- effective immunity to emortality.

'Sometimes a body will react against the transformed Y-chromosome sperms, so that they can't easily implant in the tissues. We've found that we can usually overcome that eventually, by trying one tissue after another until we find one less likely to react. In these cases, once colonisation has been achieved, the rest of the process is unimpeded.

'In the second set of cases, the host's immune system produces antibodies which successfully act against the metavirus particles which ought ultimately to become cytogenes, preventing them from penetrating cells or drastically slowing down their colonisation of the body. The metaviruses are very delicate, of course, and are entirely host-specific. This too can now be overcome, though not without difficulty, by removing tissue containing implanted sperms, growing it *in vitro*, and exposing it to light irradiation. The great majority of the any metavirus particles produced are simply denatured, but a few remain viable, with mutated protein coats which are immune to the antibodies. This can be a laborious business, and a lot of patients have died while we were still trying to bring it off, but sheer persistence tends to pay off eventually.

'Unfortunately, our tests seem to indicate that in your case the third cause is effective. Vagrant cytogenes are operative within your tissues and ought to be getting on with their job. Unfortunately, they aren't. Somehow – we don't understand exactly how – your body is switching off one or more of the cytogenes, including the one which produces the vampire enzyme. We think that it may be a single mutant gene on one of your own chromosomes, which affects the mechanism determining whether other genes are active or inactive in particular specialised tissues. The mutation is seemingly irrelevant to the ordinary functioning of your body but it seems to be preventing the augmentation of nature which the Adamawaran complex usually provides. We have no way of countering this at present, though we hope that one day soon we might be able to identify rogue genes of this kind, and cancel out their effects. Until we know exactly what it is that the gene is doing, we're impotent to intervene.'

As Chadwick finished speaking, he spread his arms a little, palms open, to express his helplessness. He did not need to add that although progress in biotechnology was very rapid, there was no way to estimate

whether a breakthrough of the relevant kind could reasonably be anticipated within the next ten, twenty or fifty years.

In the meantime, Michael's condition could only be expected to
deteriorate. Now that his damaged tissues were producing cancers –
cancers which the vagrant cytogenes in his cells should have been able
to destroy – he was in a race against time. In that race, as in all others,
he was handicapped . . . lame . . . crippled.

'Do you understand all that?' asked the consultant, anxiously. 'It
is complicated, I'm afraid, and one can't get away from the jargon
entirely.'

'Yes,' said Michael. 'I can follow the argument. I do understand.'

'I'm very sorry.'

'I know. Thanks.'

'It's important that you don't give up hope. We still have all the
resources of ordinary medicine at our disposal. We can control the pain,
and check up regularly to see that the cancer doesn't recur. Even if it
does – caught early enough, there are effective treatments.'

'Yes, of course,' said Michael. But his weak blue eyes told him that
the consultant was aware of the inadequacy of what he was offering.
The doctor posed in his businesslike fashion, beneath his insouciant
grey streak, knowing that he might live to see the year 3000, provided
only that mankind could refrain from nuclear self-annihilation. With
that certainty to arm him, he was trying with absurd earnestness to
reassure his patient that he might, with luck, live to be sixty or seventy
years old, lame and hurt, essentially outcast from the human
community.

And what could Michael say, in the face of this miserly measure of
reassurance, but: 'Thank you. I know you can't do more.'

'There is hope,' Chadwick insisted. 'Improvements in gene-mapping
may soon open the door to the complete analysis of the human genome.
It's a Herculean task, to be sure: vast quantities of DNA, hundreds of
thousands of genes. But there are thousands of men working on it.
Then again, we're slowly finding out how the controlling mechanisms
work: the ones which switch particular genes on and off in specialised
cells. You must think of the progress we've made since you were born.
Every year brings new discoveries. Your father . . . '

It was as though the doctor expected some kind of gesture of forgiveness – something which would release him from the obligation of
searching desperately for more hopeful phrases and incantations of
encouragement. 'Are the tablets working?' he asked, switching to a
different tack, in search of safer conversational ground.

'Oh yes,' said Michael. 'I don't have to take them all the time, now
– only when the pain is bad. No side effects, unless you count the
nightmares.'

'That's good,' said the doctor.

Michael said nothing in reply, but stared with his pale eyes. The eyes which added one more item to the list of his stigmata. Only common men had eyes of blue, the colour of the sky-reflecting sea.

Chadwick waited, his hands still groping feebly in the air, as though hopeful of finding a series of healing passes which would work by occult power. There was nothing more that he cared to say.

'Thank you, Dr. Chadwick,' said Michael, again. He said it flatly, without warmth.

Thank you, he thought, as he rose with difficulty to his feet, and leaned again upon his stick.

Thank you, he thought, as he passed through the door which the doctor gratefully opened for him.

Thank you, he thought, when he glanced very briefly at the receptionist, who smiled to see him depart.

He did not know who or what it was to whom he owed these muttered, bitter, and sarcastic thanks, but he offered them anyhow, because they did not seem to be in short supply. And after all, everyone was quite sincere in feeling sorry for him, quite sincere in trying to help him, and he only had himself to blame if it was in fact too late for their feelings and their actions to do him any good.

TWO

When the twilight had faded Michael turned on the reading light beside his bed. He picked up a book which he had begun to read a week before, and had quickly laid aside: a history of the Second World War. His interest in it had been awakened by the celebrations commemorating the fiftieth anniversary of the war's end, but enthusiasm had quickly waned when he found that the book contained a great deal of political commentary and very little description of the more melodramatic phases of the conflict. He did not want to read about diplomatic niceties; he wanted descriptions of the major cities of Europe and Africa laid waste by the bombers which had deluged them with fire and poison gas.

Having taken up the book he read half a page, but the paragraphs only served to remind him why he had stopped, and he threw the book back on to the bedside table with a sigh.

There was a knock at his door, and he moved his legs reflexively as though to swing them from bed to floor, so that he could answer the knock. The shock of pain reminded him that such reflexes had become

anachronistic, unsuited to his present state of being. He called out an
invitation instead.

He was slightly disappointed when he saw his father come in; not
because he did not want to see his father – quite the reverse – but
because he was curiously hurt that his father had waited for the knock
to be answered. That small politeness seemed to Michael to be a symbol
of the distance which had grown so quickly between them since the
elder Southerne had become emortal, two years before the accident.

Thomas Southerne was a tall man, who had always been strong and
handsome. He was more handsome still now that his hair was black
and sleek, and his skin pale and lustrous. In a way, though, a part of
his former strength seemed to be gradually draining out of him, now
that he did not need to preserve his fitness by trial and exercise.

Michael knew that he had once looked very like his father – very
like, that is, the common man that his father had been – but the scars
inflicted by the shattered windscreen distorted his face now, just as his
lame leg distorted his gait.

The older man was carrying an open bottle of wine, and two glasses.
He held them up to display them, and said: 'Good claret. I brought it
from Europe. I thought you might like to share it with me.'

'I'm not supposed to drink,' said Michael, then added quickly: 'One
glass can hardly hurt; it's kind of you.'

Thomas set the glasses down on the bedside table. He pushed the
discarded book aside, after the briefest of glances at the title, and poured
from the bottle, carefully. Then he brought up the armchair from the
corner of the room, and sat down.

This was not the first time they had talked since Thomas Southerne
had returned from Europe, but the man and the boy were well aware
of the fact that the most important things still remained to be said.

'How do you feel?' asked Thomas.

'Better, I suppose. I've been worse, that's for sure.'

'No problems coming off the painkillers?'

'I'm not addicted, if that's what you mean. But it does hurt, still.
Sometimes a lot.'

'Perhaps it's too early to do so much walking. You mustn't drive
yourself too hard.'

'It's not the walking. I can bear the pain when I walk. It's when I'm
sitting still or lying down that it seems likely to drive me mad. But it's
okay. It *is* okay.'

There was a pause, while Thomas Southerne nodded, pensively. His
brown eyes, which had once been blue, met his son's.

'I talked to Chadwick on the phone,' he said. 'He told me that he had
explained the situation fully, and that you understood, but I wondered if
you were only being polite. He does find difficulty in putting things

in plain English. Did you follow what he told you about the mutated controller gene?'

'Not entirely,' said Michael. 'But it doesn't really matter, does it? Understanding the technical words which describe it won't help – words in themselves have no magic power. The simple fact is that I'm going to die, and that until I do I'll be lame, and always fighting against the pain. I can't change that with understanding, can I?'

'I don't know. Perhaps you can. Understanding is a form of power, a source of courage. If you are to be saved, it will be the growth of understanding which does the trick. We learn so much more with every year which passes. We're beginning to learn how the vagrant cytogenes do their work, and once we've mastered it intellectually, the chance will be there for us to devise new biotechnologies. Understanding *can* change things, Michael, or open the way for things to be changed. It may not happen soon, but you're still in your teens, and you'll have the best of medical care. We may make an emortal of you yet, and all the pain won't have been in vain.'

'It's not so hard for you to discount the pain,' said Michael. 'It's not so easy for me to bear it.'

'That's not fair, Michael.'

Michael gulped wine from his glass, feeling suddenly close to tears, and not liking himself for that weakness. 'Oh no!' he complained, in an irrepressible fit of ill-temper. 'You understand, of course. You remember what it was like to be young. You're not yet three hundred years old, as cold as stone. Who feels no pain can feel no pity – isn't that what they say? You're not there yet, are you? Not *yet*. You can still imagine how I feel.'

Thomas sipped from his own glass, parsimoniously. 'It isn't true, Michael,' he said. 'Emortals don't become emotionless, unless they cultivate callousness. That saw is just one more old wives' tale, like all the rest.

'But that's not the point at issue, is it? I do know that you're hurt, in more ways than one, but it really is important that you don't give up hope, because giving up is one way to make sure that all your fears come true. I don't say that what has happened to you isn't horribly bad, because it is. It seems so much worse because we live in a world, now, where everyone expects to become emortal. You must remember, though, that there are many parts of the world where one person in two dies before achieving emortality, and where two emortals in three die by violence before they reach that mean three score years and ten which even common men are promised. Be glad you were born today, when there is hope, and not a hundred years ago, when you'd have had two world wars to survive, and not the slightest hope of any cure for your condition. I know how difficult it is, Michael, but . . . '

'You *don't* know!' Michael fought, with only moderate success, to control his tears.

Thomas Southerne shook his head, in dismay but not in anger. 'I've been in Africa, Michael. I've been in the rain forest and the deserts, as well as the cities. Do you think I haven't seen suffering enough? Do you think I haven't seen people less fortunate even than you?'

'No,' said Michael, softly. 'I suppose you have. But the Africans have made their own mess. They had emortality long before the rest of the world, and what did they make of it? They have no one to blame for their troubles but the stupid superstitions to which they clung too long. They might have created a whole society of emortals before Rome was built, if they had only used the gift more wisely, but instead they created Ogbone, and a race of castrated ancients, and set their faces against the very possibility of progress. What did I do, to deserve the loss of the chance to live forever?'

'You must not despise the Africans,' said Thomas. 'Not even the Ogbone. We owe our own emortality to what you call their stupid superstitions. If the organic material which rode to Earth inside the Adamawaran meteor had fallen among other men, what would it have brought but a series of plagues? Not just the silver death – the seed of emortality itself would only have killed men, because they would never have known what else it was they needed in order to live. It was because some Africans offered sacrifices to their gods, because certain of their holy men drank human blood, that they found the secret of eternal life. Without that, the gift was worthless, and might have destroyed mankind instead of securing such salvation from death as we enjoy.'

'Securing salvation? Has it secured salvation? Is that the lesson we learn by understanding history, do you think? I've heard it said that eternal life has only been a challenge, to make us devise better ways of destroying one another. I've heard it said that were it not for emortality, we'd have been well content with clubs and spears, instead of devising such means of slaughter as we used in the two world wars – and the nuclear weapons we'll use in World War Three, in the face of which all men are truly equal.'

'If that's true,' Thomas pointed out, gently. 'Then you've not lost so much, after all.'

'Perhaps I haven't. Perhaps that's what I ought to tell myself, to keep my spirits up. Beneath the shadow of the hydrogen bomb, everyone is mortal, and no one's pain counts for much.'

'You can tell yourself that if you wish,' his father said. 'But I don't think it's the right way to go about it. As a means of avoiding despair, it hasn't much to recommend it, has it? It's just a matter of trying to see your own misfortune mirrored in the condition of the world. You've been brought face to face with the possibility of your own death, but that shouldn't let you to take comfort in contemplating the holocaust. If you want to find lessons in history, I wouldn't have thought it was hard to discover the moral that nobody ever quite knows what will happen next, and that it's never out of order to hope.'

Michael drained his glass, and held it out for more, though Thomas had not yet finished his own. The older man took the bottle from the table, and filled up his son's glass.

'I suppose you're right,' conceded the boy. 'But I can't help feeling, sometimes, that there's a certain irony in this world crisis which we hear so much about. You've found, thanks to your excavations in Adamawara, that emortality was indeed a gift from outside the Earth – a kind of miracle, brought to a species which had not yet come near to the spontaneous evolution of any such privilege. But how have we always used that gift? How, for that matter, have we used all those other privileges that we have, which we presumably did evolve for ourselves – our clever brains and our keen eyes and our skilful hands? Why, we've used them to bring ourselves cleverly and skilfully to the point of annihilation. If the gift had a giver, how he must weep to see what has become of it!'

'We have not yet destroyed ourselves,' said Thomas Southerne, evenly. 'And we have accomplished a great deal with our clever brains, our keen eyes, and our skilful hands.'

'Of course,' Michael mused, 'there are those who argue that the gift *was* sent to us – that the Adamawaran meteor was a missile hurled, if not by God, or some idol of the Africans, then by friendly aliens whose only wish was to help us become just a little more godly ourselves. No doubt you've heard such speculations?'

'I've heard them,' his father agreed. 'Put like that, they sound a little silly. But if there was no giver, still there was a gift. If there was no God, still there was a kind of miracle. Some of my colleagues still don't believe that the Adamawaran DNA is of extraterrestrial origin – they still want to argue that there is far too much of coincidence in the hypothesis that DNA might independently evolve on more than one world, and too much imagination in the hypothesis that it first came to earth from elsewhere in the universe. They propose that the meteor sparked off a chain of mutations, by radiation or chemical pollution. They suggest that it stretches credulity far less to believe that it was some spontaneous doubling or recomplication of the Y chromosome itself which produced the Adamawaran chromosomids, than to believe that the DNA is alien but that it was nevertheless capable of fertile combination with human DNA.'

'It sometimes seems to me,' said Michael, 'that all such explanations stretch credulity. Not just the ones which aspire to tell us how men became emortal, but those which aspire to tell us how men became men, or how that hot primeval soup gave rise to life at all. I'd rather trust a monkey with a typewriter to produce the works of Shakespeare than a single world to produce a biochemistry as complicated as ours in a few billion years.'

'You're not alone in that. The elder Darwin has said to me that it is clear proof of design and the hand of God; and even Charles, who worked so damnably hard to expel the deity from the scheme of things, finds the circumstance of the fusion of the alien DNA with the human Y chromosome so remarkable as to give him pause for wonder. He has exchanged letters with Svante Arrhenius, and they are now involved in earnest debate with astronomers and cosmologists about the possible extraterrestrial origin of life on Earth.'

'But I can't believe in paternal aliens either,' Michael added, contemplatively. 'The monkey Shakespeare is a likely chap by comparison with the alien philanthropist who made us a present of emortality, wrapping it ever so carefully in an interstellar missile. He would be a convenient man to have around, of course – he might earlier have sent us the genes which gave us clever brains, too, and those which are our helpful hands. Those things were also born in Africa, if the palaeontologists are to be believed, so Africa must be the bull's-eye which this alien artilleryman never misses.'

'If it were only so,' said Thomas, 'how right we would be to say: What a piece of work is man? A thing of genetic thread and patches! If it were so, though, we could only deem our makers bad and careless parents: fathers who donated their semen to a luckless womb in the course of a loveless one-night stand, then disappeared, leaving their infants to a life of struggle and strife, bereft of loving care and good advice, save that which busy Mother Nature feels she can spare.'

Michael did not laugh, but at least the flow of his tears was dammed. 'You don't give much credit to fathers,' he said, gruffly.

Thomas Southerne looked sharply at his son then, as if blame were being hurled in his direction.

Michael met the look, and instantly regretted the careless implication. He knew that he had been a late child, from his father's point of view – his mother was somewhat younger – but Thomas Southerne had delayed his own conversion until Michael was fifteen, and few would reckon that an inadequate delay. Even before his conversion, the elder Southerne had spent much time abroad, but he had never neglected his family, according to their reckoning as well as his own. When Michael had had his accident, his father had come to sit beside his hospital bed every day for a month. Michael knew that he had no legitimate grievance against his parents; they were not responsible for his accident, or for his unfortunate immunity to emortality.

'I'm sorry,' said Michael. After a pause, he added: 'I can't help feeling that in some crazy way I've let you down. It's just the one thing on top of the other, you see. The accident was bad, but I could accept one bad break. To find on top of that that I've got Cordery's syndrome, in the untreatable form, is just too much for this flesh and blood to bear. Too much, you see?'

Michael had tears in his eyes again now, though he was still trying his best to suppress them. He would have liked, in a way, to see tears in his father's eyes too. That would have given him permission to let go and weep, and it would have demonstrated that his father, though emortal, still cared for him as much as he ever had.

But Thomas Southerne had no tears in his eyes.

Emortals rarely wept, though no one really knew why. The tears simply did not come readily to their eyes. Once, it had been said that vampires could not cry, but that was not true. They had said the same about witches once; it was probably no more true of them, if there ever had been witches in the world.

'It is too much,' agreed the older man. 'And it means that you must be extraordinarily brave. You must be too good to be defeated, even by a burden like this. It isn't enough to be a common man – you have to be a hero. Common men can be heroes. It's a proven fact.'

'It's equally well proven,' said Michael, 'that some can't.'

'But you do have the choice.'

Michael shrugged his shoulders. 'What do *you* think?' he asked, shifting the conversation back to safer ground, 'about the Adamawaran meteor. If the DNA is extraterrestrial, how did it come to be the case that it could stick to a human Y chromosome as if it had always really belonged there?'

'God alone knows,' said Thomas Southerne, softly. '*So far.*'

'But what do you *believe*?'

'It's not a matter for belief. We can only speculate. The alien artillerists aren't credible, but I don't find it so difficult to believe that life, and DNA, are spread all over the known universe. I can't deny that I find it an attractive notion. The astronomers assure us that the sun is a second-generation star, and that all the heavier elements in the solar system are the wreckage of a supernova which flared up billions of years ago. Maybe life on earth is second-generation life. Maybe the space through which the solar system glides in its journey about the centre of the galaxy is impregnated with the genetic wreckage of an earlier ecosphere, or perhaps a thousand ecospheres. And perhaps the story of life on earth really is a story, which we are just re-telling, re-collecting, re-membering phrase by phrase, legend by legend. Perhaps we aren't just moving from non-existence to annihilation, by way of emortality and the atom bomb. Perhaps we are like your monkey tapping away at a typewriter, except that when he's typed "To be or not to be . . ." and then pauses for inspiration, staring into the empty darkness, he happens upon something which can cling to it, and extend the phrase " . . . that is the question". Perhaps life isn't just something that's here, in our tiny little corner of infinity, but everywhere, busily making ecospheres and species, which – even if they bloom only briefly and then wither – leave lingering traces in the emptiness: tiny molecules which busy themselves all over again, whenever and wherever they find a place to take root, always reaching further and further on, though stars explode and even the universe itself expands toward some distant oblivion.

'It's not a matter for scientific belief, Michael, but perhaps it's a matter for faith. Perhaps we have to have faith in something like that, to make sense of ourselves at all, just as our ancestors had faith in a paternal God, just as those ancient elders of Adamawara had faith in Olorun and Shango and Olori-merin. Perhaps you do have to look outside yourself – as far outside as you can – to figure out just where you fit in. Perhaps you have to ask yourself bigger questions than *why did it have to happen to me?* Suppose, after all, that the meteor *hadn't* hit Africa thirteen thousand years ago. What's thirteen thousand years in the litany of eternity but the blink of an eye: an arbitrary pause, entirely irrelevant to the pattern of the prayer? Then, Michael, you might measure your predicament in the fate of the whole human race. But the meteor might come tomorrow or never come at all, and still we'd be a part of the same vast unfolding story, still we'd have our part to play, our moment on the stage, our little legend. I don't think we need to see ourselves as an irrelevant detail, Michael. Not the earth, not mankind, not any single life that any one of us has ever lived.

'I think what I'm trying to say, Michael, is that there are all kinds of ways of finding hope, if you look hard enough for it. Sometimes, you need a little help, that's all. A microscope, or an idea.'

Thomas Southerne lowered his dark eyes, and drained the last drop of wine from his glass. He seemed embarrassed at having said so much, and a little saddened by what he had said, but there was still no trace of a tear in his eye.

Abruptly, Michael decided that he did not, after all, want to see that tear. The reassurance which he needed from his father was not some casual symptom of his heartfelt pity, but a simple reaffirmation of community and kinship, which he already had.

'Maybe you're right,' he said, uncertainly.

'Maybe I am. I'm sorry a maybe is all I have to offer. I'm sorry a maybe is all there is.'

'I can cope with a maybe,' Michael told him. And added, lest he be thought impetuous: 'At least, I can try.'

THREE

Michael Southerne had often walked along the clifftop paths which wound around the bays to the south of his parents' house. He knew the bays well, having explored all those which were within easy reach before he was twelve years old. He had returned again and again to his favourites, to search among the rock-pools for the creatures of the sea abandoned by the retreating tides.

He had been, in those lost days, an agile youth. He had had a veritable fondness for the work of scrambling and clambering over the rocks. When the tides were at their lowest he would follow the sea out as far as it went, to examine those jagged reefs which saw the light of day only once or twice a month. There he would hunt for exotic weeds and strange echinoderms, then play a joyous game with the returning waves, keeping one step ahead of them all the way to the shore, leaping from rock to rock, emotionally charged by the thrill of the chase.

He had not minded, in those days, that the sea was always cold, the wind usually bitter, the skies often leaden with cloud. He had been indomitable, warmed by his own enthusiasm for life, made safe from the elements by his fascination with the zone between the tides.

The accident had changed all that.

For a while, he had not walked the cliff paths at all, but lately he had gone back to them with a new purpose: to make his weak leg grow stronger with use. When he had first come out of the hospital he had hardly been able to manage a hundred yards across level ground, but since returning to the cliffs, and making them his training ground, he had made himself far more capable. Now he could drive himself for several miles, and often did, visiting the farthest places to which his earlier love of rambling had taken him.

Those places were very different now; he barely recognised them. Where once there had been racetracks along which he had fled before the tide, now there was a wilderness: untouchable, unreachable. His battles now were no longer with the sea, but with the pain which threatened always to return, and with the fatigue which was forever draining the spirit from his efforts.

When he first began to venture out, after his return from the hospital, he tried at first to judge his exertions so that he could return to the house on foot. He quickly came to believe that this made him cowardly, and adopted instead a policy of driving himself to the limit on the outward journey, then searching for a house or a coastguard station from which he could call for a car to pick him up.

His mother did not like this habit, worrying that he would one day overreach himself and be stranded too far from the nearest source of assistance; but his mother was emortal now and he often thought, perhaps unworthily, that she protested too much, to disguise a cold calmness which was growing inside her, taking over her mind just as the alien DNA was colonising her body. For this reason, among others, he refused to take her protestations seriously, and pursued his exertions with obsessive determination.

Michael had hoped, today, that his father might walk with him, as he sometimes had in earlier and happier days; but a man like Thomas Southerne could never entirely escape the demands of his position, and the fact that he had returned from Europe specifically to see his son had not deterred interested parties on the Atlantean continent from clamouring for his attention. So Thomas Southerne had gone to Halifax, leaving Michael to seek amusement and distraction without him, as he had so many times before. Michael masked his disappointment by driving himself all the harder, determined to break previous distance records and take himself as far from his home as he possibly could before he was forced to return.

The morning was not very cold, though the wind from the sea was strengthening and the weather forecast had promised heavy rain. The fishing boats in the village harbour had not put out to sea, which argued that the forecast might err on the side of leniency. Michael was undeterred; he had never been afraid of bad weather in his youth, and he was still prepared to be contemptuous of its threats.

By noon he had covered seven miles, and was nearing a path which he had not walked for years. He had not paused to look down at the bays beneath the cliffs, although their weed-clad rocks were being slowly exposed by a far-retreating tide in a way which once would have tempted him greatly. The path descended as the cliff-face became less steep, bringing him to a shallow strand of scree-slopes and wooded hummocks.

The downward slope carried him forward more rapidly, but the acceleration put additional strain on his poorer leg, and it began to ache. It seemed to Michael an unkind paradox that while the path was becoming easier the punishment inflicted upon his damaged muscles was increased. He stopped, and began to look about him. The sea was now a long way out to the east – a thin sparkling line upon the horizon, sharply differentiated from the crust of grey cloud which stood behind it. The greater part of the sky was clear and blue, though scudding cumulus clouds frequently interrupted the sun's light.

He looked inland, but the undulations of the ground and the clumps of trees obscured his view. There was only one house in view, nestling among the trees, and he judged that it was quite remote from the road. It was not a farmhouse, and he guessed that it had been erected in order to take advantage of the loneliness of the spot, probably harbouring some immigrant survivor of an earlier age, who had become reclusive in response to the vexatious pressures of adaptation to a world dramatically transformed by modern technology and the legacy of the two world wars. This part of New Atlantis still offered a lot of scope for such escapists, who liked a landscape unthreatened by change and modernisation.

He looked along the coast to the cliffs which raised themselves up in the south-west, like a great fortress contemptuous of his tiny strength. He was sure that he had been up the farther slope, once or twice, but could not bring the route to mind. He struggled with the recalcitrant memories for several moments before he realised, with a rush of annoyance, that he was no more than half a mile from a stream, still hidden from him by the rocks, which ran into the sea near here. Though it was by no means a river, it had cut a deep and steep-sided ditch during the millennia of its running, and even as close to the beach as this it provided an obstacle to his course. There was a bridge, but it was some way inland, and he decided that it might be more convenient to go out towards the sea, in search of a place where the waters fanned out into a delta of shallower rivulets, which he could easily ford even in his walking shoes.

With this in mind, he descended to the beach below the high-tide line, and made his way across the wet sand, selecting a way between the outcrops of rock which ran out to sea like twisted ribbons. In former years, he would not have considered the rocks to be any kind of barrier, but his injured leg was a far greater deterrent to climbing than it was to walking. In search of a way through to the stream he went farther and farther out towards the line of the returning tide. Twice he reached low rocks which seemed simple enough to negotiate, but even with the stick he could not get over them. The damp wrack made them very slick, so that there were too few footholds to help him.

Because he was concentrating on the business of continuing his course south-westward he did not notice how far he had strayed from the line of broken weed and empty shells which marked the upper reach of the tide. It was with a slight shock that he realised that the waves were bursting on rocks only ninety feet away.

He was not immediately alarmed, even though he was fully aware of how slow he had become. Even in his present state of deterioration, he could not imagine being in danger from the sea. He turned, in some annoyance, to make his way back to the wooded shore. He realised then that there was no direct course which he could follow, and that he had not the slightest memory of the route which had brought him here.

It dawned on him that his situation was hazardous. The shock of knowing that this time, a race against the ocean would be no foregone conclusion, was not totally unpleasant. There was a thrill in it, too, a sense of challenge. The awareness that his weakened body was to be put to the proof was oddly satisfying.

He looked back at the white waves breaking violently upon the rocks, and noted how far the grey pall of cloud had now extended itself into the sky. He felt that it was not simply the ocean which was hunting him, but the whole of the earth, investigating with studied impartiality his fitness to exist.

His walking-stick rattled against the pebbles as he forced himself forward, but he knew within minutes that he had not the time to retrace his steps, though he could see the irregular footprints which he had left in the glutinous sand. It mattered not that he was ill-equipped for climbing; climb he must.

He knew that if he could get to the top of a twisting ribbon of rock he might well to be able to follow it all the way to the tide-line, for although the granite ridges turned in their course, they were basically natural jetties extending like tentacles from the bedrock.

He came close to the wall of rocks which was on his left, searching for a place to clamber up. It did not look too difficult. The nearness of the sea and the violence of the waves made him hurry, but the first time he tried he could only pull himself part-way up before he slipped and fell backwards. He dropped his stick and grazed his right knee painfully. He knew that he had as much to fear from a fall as from a failure to mount the wall.

He knew how to swim, and paused to wonder whether it would be so very awful if the sea did catch up, but when he felt the gathering force of the storm-wind, and the first drops of rain, he knew that he would stand no chance at all in the water in the midst of so many jagged rocks. The merciless waves would dash him upon the brutal edges with casual contempt.

Desperate now, he tried to climb again, and again he slipped back on the wet wrack. He had not the strength to draw himself up by the leverage of his arms alone, and his feet could find no purchase. He hurried further along the wall, but the sea was gaining ground on him.

At last he found a crack wherein his feet would lodge. It was like a very narrow chimney, into which he could wedge his body so that he could raise himself up, inch by inch. He threw his walking-stick up on to the ridge, and scrambled up, with the waves lapping at his heels. He scraped his hands and bruised his elbows, and tore his trousers on the roughened stone, but with one last heave he pulled himself out of the cleft.

For a moment he lay there, but he knew how far he still had to go, and he knew that the ridge of rock would surely be far more uneven than the sand. He picked up his stick and hobbled on, aware now of dozens of bumps and abrasions. In his rush to go forward he fell, and when he had hauled himself upright, fell again. The rain was pelting now, and though the surface of the rocks had earlier been dried by the noonday sun they quickly became wet again, their slipperiness threatening more falls, any one of which might damage his injured ankle so badly that it would no longer bear his weight.

He forced himself on with gritted teeth, his stick clattering as he probed the way. Every step now seemed a victory, but his eyes, blinking away the rain as he searched the way ahead, reminded him how many such victories he would need. He reached up with a dirty hand to wipe the rain from his face, and realised with a start that the rainwater was mingled with tears. He was weeping copiously, responding as if by reflex to exertion and anxiety. He cursed himself for it, though it was one weakness which could surely never be detected by an observer.

He was aware as he pushed himself onward that he had been overtaken by the tide. Had he still been on the sand the waves would have been breaking around his knees, and he would have been in constant danger of being bowled over; but in his elevated position he was still relatively safe. The waves which broke to either side were full of sound and fury, but only a little of their froth and foam reached out to splash him.

He looked ahead, measuring the distance to the tide-line, and judged that only eighty yards stood between himself and safety. He was sure now that he could make it. He knew that he had the strength to reach the steeper rocks which would carry him beyond the reach of the clutching waves, if only he did not fall.

He stopped, the breath caught in his throat by a sudden, all-consuming dart of panic, as he saw before him the gap which interrupted the ribbon of rock, which the sea had already invaded.

It was not a big gap; even as a twelve-year old he might have jumped it, and he was not sure now that he could not. If he pushed off with his good leg, even without a run, he might project himself with sufficient force to reach the other side. But how would he land? How could he stretch out his weakened leg to cushion his landing, knowing what destruction the impact would wreak?

He had no option but to lower himself down again, and wade waist deep across the narrow channel. It would not be so hard, shadowed as he was from the breakers. He would not be in the water for more than a few seconds – just two lunging strides. That would not be so hard, but could he climb the opposite face, to regain the ridge of the reef?

Five seconds passed while he stood still on the edge, looking down at the gap. He was not trying to make up his mind, because there was no decision to be taken. There was no choice; it was all or nothing. He was simply gathering his strength and resolve.

It seemed monstrously unfair to him that he had already used up so much strength in almost winning through, only to come to this final hurdle. It was as though the world had belatedly thrown this last, most vicious trap before him, in a gesture of pure gamesmanship.

Bastard! he thought, with all the exclamatory force he could muster. *Bastard sea! Bastard rocks! Bastard leg!*

Then he threw his stick across the gap, took what grip he could with his hands, and slid forward down the miniature cliff into the water. The coldness shocked him, but as it closed over his wounded leg it seemed to have both an anaesthetic effect and a merciful buoyancy. He twisted around as he came to rest, taking one hand off the ridge behind him. He moved as far forward as he could while still keeping that contact, and then reached out towards the other side of the chasm. He needed only one lurching step to bring him close enough to grab a hold, and then it seemed easier to draw himself in closer. The water's depth was altering with every surge of the breakers – now rising around his midriff, now falling to the level of his thighs. He gripped the rock above shoulder height, struggling to find the best handhold, and then he waited for the water to recede, wanting to draw himself up while he had the surge of the wave to help him.

When the moment came, he heaved with all his might. His good foot scraped the rock face desperately, trying to find a foothold. He found one – enough of one, anyhow, to complete his forward lunge. He flailed his arm forward, trying to find a new handhold, and gripped the edge of a hollow, clinging with all his might for a moment while his legs dangled, still scrabbling for purchase. Then he was able to pull himself forward again, clear of the water and over the edge.

He lay still, on his side, for a moment, sobbing with gratitude. Then he hauled himself up, and began his ungainly walk again, leaning on his stick as much as he dared.

When he came to the steeper, lichen-covered rocks above the tide-line he did not pause, for the waves could still reach him here. The sense of urgency had gone from his flight. The breakers were behind him again, and the water on his face which he tasted with his tongue was salt no longer – neither brine nor tears, but good clean rain.

He remembered how far it was to the house which he had seen among the trees, but it did not seem to matter. If necessary, he could take all afternoon to get there, and all night too. The chase was finished, and the sea had lost. Racked with pain though he was, and soaked to the skin, he was in his own element again, as far from final defeat as ever he had been in all his life.

FOUR

When Leilah first saw the boy lying on the rocks above the beach she thought for a moment or two that he was dead, and that his body had been washed ashore in the storm, thrown up by a mighty wave.

When she came closer, though, she saw that he was bleeding. He was not quite unconscious, either, for he moved slightly as she approached, and must have heard her. When she knelt down beside him he tried to rouse himself and sit up, but the effort was too much for him. His eyes flickered as they blinked away the rain, but he obviously found it hard to keep them open, and though his jaw moved it was clearly difficult for him to pronounce words. She knew that he could not get to his feet unaided, but might be able to make his way to the house with her support. First, though, she checked his injuries, to make sure that she would do no damage by helping him to come to his feet.

'Bad foot,' he murmured, when at last he was able to make his vocal cords obey him.

She nodded, to show him that she understood.

He was taller than she, and heavy, but she managed to lift him, at first clasping her arms about his chest, until he was upright and able to put his right arm around her shoulder. He had picked up his walking stick, but he leaned on her instead as they began to hobble up the slope, back across the rocks to the path, and then to the woods. She stopped to rest once, and suppressed the pain of the pressure which the boy's dead weight put upon her back, but she had always been strong for a woman of her size, and the boy was lean and spare of frame, carrying hardly an ounce of fat. She got him into the house, then let him down on the couch, and sat down herself to catch her breath.

'Thanks,' he said, in a low tone. 'I wasn't much help. I'm sorry.'

She waved away his awkward apology.

She pulled the couch a little closer to the fireplace, where a fire had been laid but not lit. Then she set a light to the kindling, and watched the little flames run up the sides of the dried logs. She fetched a blanket and put it over the boy, though his clothes were wet through.

He had slumped back now, and his eyes were closed. She fetched some brandy, and tried to force a little into his mouth, in the hope of reviving him. He opened his eyes briefly, took a sip, and coughed, then shook his head to refuse a second draught. She brought a bowl of hot water and a cloth instead, and began wiping his face and hands, cleaning the cuts and helping to restore the circulation. Eventually, he was able to open his eyes again and to speak more clearly.

'Thanks,' he said, again, this time with more resolution in his voice.

'Can you get out of those wet clothes?' she asked.

He shook his head. 'Bad leg,' he murmured. 'Do you have my stick?'

She had put the walking stick in the hall, and told him so. 'No harm will come to it,' she assured him. 'I don't think you need it now. What's your name?'

'Michael,' he answered, then added: 'Michael Southerne.'

'Oh yes,' she said, noting now a resemblance which she had not earlier picked out. 'I used to know your father, some years ago.'

Perhaps it was the words themselves, or perhaps something in the way she spoke them, but his reaction was immediate, despite his enfeebled condition. She watched the expression which crossed his face, then reached out to restrain him as he tried to sit up. How many common men had heard such words from a vampire lady – *I knew your father, when he was young* – and had taken them as a kind of treason against their all-too-human mothers? But she had not meant it that way. Thomas Southerne had been a mere acquaintance.

'I don't know you,' said Michael, his voice a little less faint, a little more hostile.

'No,' said Leilah. 'I'm not very . . . sociable . . . any more. My name is Leilah.'

He frowned. Obviously, the name meant nothing to him. His blue eyes fixed their gaze upon her face, and when she stood up, the eyes followed her, almost as if he were reaching out to hold and restrain her. She allowed herself to be held, and stayed still, looking back at him.

She understood well enough what kinds of puzzlement were in that stare. She was dark of skin by comparison with other emortals in this part of the world, golden brown instead of alabaster white, but that would be a small matter to him. The cardinal question which must be going through his mind could only be: *How old is she? From what dark era of the foreign past has she survived?* Whenever a common man looked at a vampire lady, he wanted to know what gulf of time was there to be crossed in touch and imagination.

'I should telephone your father,' she said.

'No point,' he replied. 'He's gone to Halifax. My mother went with him, shopping. There's nobody home now.'

She looked at her wristwatch. Did he know how long he had lain on the shore? she wondered. But it was not yet five, and it seemed fairly likely that she would get no reply.

'I'll try anyway,' she said.

She crossed the room to the telephone, and picked up the directory. She imagined the half-smile which might be flickering upon his face as he noticed that she did not know the number. It had been more than twenty years since she last saw Thomas Southerne, and she had never known his telephone number. She found the number, dialled, and waited, listening to the repeated burr of the unanswered phone.

When she gave up, and turned back to her guest, she saw that he was looking carefully about the room – at the books on the shelves in the alcove beside the fireplace, at the painting above the mantel-shelf, at the brass microscope which stood above the centre of the fire, a mere ornament now.

'That looks very old,' said Michael Southerne, fishing indelicately for information.

'Yes it is,' she said. 'And rather famous, in its way. It once belonged to Noell Cordery. It was given to me by the pope – not Alexander, of course, but one of the common Pauls who succeeded him in the Vatican.' She watched him, to savour his reaction.

Oddly, he laughed in a rather sour fashion. That was unexpected. 'A coincidence,' he said, to explain his indelicacy. 'I have a disease named after Noell Cordery.'

She raised her eyebrows in surprise. 'You're very young to have attempted transformation,' she observed.

'My bad leg,' he reminded her. 'It gives me a lot of pain. I can't walk properly. That's why I was nearly trapped by the incoming tide. I had a bit of a struggle, getting to the rocks.' He frowned at the memory, and with an effort he did manage to drag himself nearer to a sitting position. She went back to him, afraid that he might hurt himself. His face was very white, and she was in no doubt that his leg must be hurting him.

'You're a long way from home,' she said. 'Did you walk all the way?'

'I limped,' he answered, curtly. Then, apparently repenting of his slight discourtesy, he said: 'Why did the pope – whichever one it was – give you a microscope that once belonged to Noell Cordery?'

'He knew how much I wanted it,' she said, quietly. 'I was rude enough to ask him for it, and he was polite enough not to refuse.' She watched for his reaction, knowing how much her statement might have given away, if he was clever enough to follow through the chain of argument. She was slightly amused, happy to tempt him into showing an interest.

He stared at her again, his blue eyes seeming a little softer now, his gaze more speculative. 'Did you know Noell Cordery, then, when he was young?' he asked. He had picked up her hint of amusement, and she found that rather engaging. There was no doubting the seriousness of the question, but the implied levity made it all the easier to answer.

'Yes,' she said. 'I knew him when he was *very* young.'

He paused for a moment, then said: 'In that case, I've never met anyone as old as you. You must remember the entire history of the continent. The entire history of the science of emortality, too – from Noell Cordery to Thomas Southerne; the bloody elixir to the genetic code. Are you mentioned in the history books?'

'Oh yes,' she said. 'The more detailed ones, anyhow. I went with Noell Cordery to Adamawara, and lived in Malta before the Armada came. I was even in Cardigan, before Noell first left Britain. But historians aren't really interested in me, except as an eye-witness to help them piece together the story. I did nothing; I was only a bystander. Perhaps that's why I'm still alive, when all the others were slain and martyred long ago.'

He smiled, but his attention was wandering. It was not that he wasn't interested, just that he was wet. 'Can you get me some dry clothing?' he asked, having become embarrassingly aware of the wretchedness of his condition.

'Yes,' she said, and in response to another flicker of curiosity which crossed his face, added: 'Not left here, I fear, by anyone you might have heard of.'

'No,' he said. 'I expect Noell Cordery's things would be threadbare by now.'

She went upstairs, to search drawers which she rarely opened, looking for attire which he might consider sufficiently masculine to wear. He was too tall for a close fit, but at least he was thin enough to find almost anything capacious. She found a shirt, a pair of jeans, and a thick pullover, and took them down to him. He had already discarded most of his wet garments, and she carefully refrained from watching him while he got rid of the rest, hiding his body beneath the blanket, and trying to hide his discomfort too. She did not offer to help him, because she felt certain that he would not welcome it. Instead, she told him that she would find some food for him, and went into the kitchen. When she came back, with buttered bread, cold meat and cheese, he had dressed himself and put aside the blanket. He was holding his hands out towards the fire, which was blazing merrily now.

'I'm sorry there's nothing warm,' she told him. 'But I've put the water on to boil. Would you prefer coffee or tea?'

'Coffee's fine,' he told her. Then, apologetically, he said: 'I'm not really hurt. I was just tired. I overdid it a bit, getting away from the tide.'

'I know,' she said. 'I checked to see if there were any broken bones. No need for a doctor, but your leg must hurt a good deal.'

He showed her a plastic bottle, which must have come from his trouser pocket. 'Pills,' he said. 'Painkillers. I don't often need them, but I always carry them.'

She nodded, and went to fetch the coffee. When she brought the cups in, she sat down beside him on the couch, pushing the discarded blanket away with her foot.

'I'll try to ring your home again in a little while, unless you'd prefer a taxi,' she said. 'I don't have a car, so someone else will have to come to fetch you.'

'It's okay,' he said. 'You're not very sociable, you say. I guess you have supplies delivered?'

She nodded, and for a minute or more they sat looking into the flickering flames, sipping coffee. Eventually, he turned to stare at her again – that same, speculative stare: curiosity commingled with fascination, and perhaps a little fear. It wasn't fear of her, but fear of that great emptiness which separated his experience from hers. He stood at the point in time which history had reached, a common boy, the product of his age. She, by contrast, was part of the thread of that history, a relic of the undead past. The understanding was growing in his mind that as a thread, she lay a little closer to the heart of the weave than most.

'You knew Noell Cordery,' he said, turning the notion over in his mind. 'You went with him to Adamawara, three hundred years before Darwin and my father. You must have been one of the very first beneficiaries of the elixir.'

'No,' she said. 'Langoisse and Quintus used the elixir. It was a man who made me a vampire, in a different way. Langoisse, my erstwhile lover, sent me out whoring, for the good of all mankind. I carried the vital ingredient back to Langoisse. He took it to Noell, without telling him exactly how it was obtained.'

'Noell,' repeated Michael, as though he found it wonderfully strange to find himself suddenly on first name terms with a man who had played a celebrated part in the making of the modern world: the man who made eternal life much cheaper to obtain, then balanced what he had given by making death a little cheaper too, even for emortals.

'I am not so very old,' she told him, gently. 'I have met men and women a thousand years older than I. Your father has been in Adamawara, has he not?'

'He has. He met some people there, I think, who claimed to have known Noell Cordery. An important Ogbone leader, who styles himself Ntikima Oni-Shango. And a chief named Ngadze. He mentioned a lady, feeble in mind, who might be one of the oldest women in the world, named . . .'

'Berenike.' Leilah cut him off, feeling a kind of eerie shiver, such as vampires were not supposed to feel. 'Poor Berenike. Lost in time and lost in mind. We are not yet ready to live forever, though we may yet learn. Ntikima saved our lives, once. I think he learned a good deal more from Quintus and Noell than he understood at the time. He is perhaps the one man who can bring Ogbone into the twentieth century, and might thereby save Africa from its present torment.'

'My father said the same,' said Michael, as if surprised to hear the judgement confirmed. 'He said that Ntikima gave him protection, too, and that he alone among the so-called elders understood what the excavations revealed about the nature of the miracle which brought the breath of life to Earth.'

'Oh yes,' said Leilah. 'Ntikima always understood. Sometimes, I envied him his understanding. Without any real knowledge, he had an admirable sense of certainty, and when he was offered real knowledge, he could take it, and build it into his way of seeing. For him, there will be no difficulty in the discovery that it was a meteor which brought eternal life to earth in alien DNA, because it cannot contradict his notion that it was a thunderbolt hurled by a god, containing the gift of another god's heart. It will be one thing and the other.'

'My father is not so very different,' observed Michael Southerne. 'He suggested to me a little while ago that there must be a great deal more than meets the eye in the coincidence which made the alien DNA compatible with the human genome. I think that he and the younger Darwin are trying to move the theory of evolution on to a much bigger stage: one which extends beyond the Earth to take in the entire universe, with a single system of life extending throughout its infinite reaches.'

Leilah remembered looking up with Noell Cordery and Quintus into the infinite sky, when she had told Ntikima that the stars were very far away; and Quintus had said that they were distant suns, and had rejoiced that God had made man incarnate on every world of every star, to fill his infinite Creation with body and spirit, in a scheme whose grandeur was beyond imagination – beyond even the imagination that a vampire had, despite that she had lived for thousands of years.

And then she thought again: *Poor Berenike! To have the breath of life without the nourishment of vision.* She spoke silently of Berenike to distract herself from the fact that she had first thought of her own inadequacies.

Aloud, she said: 'I am glad to hear it. The universe of stars is a drear and dreadful place, if we have no sense of belonging there. I do not need the kind of God which Quintus had, but it soothes me to think that the story in which I play my part is not confined within a tiny particle of stone, lost in a limitless desert of midnight dark.'

To herself, she said: *I remember him better than I thought, to speak thus for myself, for those were words that might have been his, long before I learned to speak in such a way.*

'You sound very like my father,' said the boy, rather harshly. 'I suppose emortals always think that way. I wonder whether it's true, though, or just a convenient illusion?'

She looked at him carefully, measuring his frailty in the blueness of his eyes, which spoke so frankly of mortality.

'I don't know,' she said. 'No one does. Someday soon, we may have better evidence, when we go to the stars, and discover whether life is really everywhere, and what it is like in other places, but the farther reaches of infinity will always be outside the things we know.'

'Someday soon,' he repeated, 'when we go to the stars. It will be soon for you, no doubt, but not for me. This world is all that I have, and its pain too. My part in things is unfortunately limited, like the part which Noell Cordery had to play. He and I were marked alike by our treasonous DNA – condemned to early death.'

If he was trying to make her uncomfortable, he succeeded. She could hardly bear to think of the cruel trick which fate had played on Noell. Condemned to death he most certainly had been, and to such horrid pain that a boy like this, with morphine in his pocket and a whole world to help him in his distress, could not begin to comprehend. And yet, in her own treasonous heart, she had never been able to be truly sorry that he remained mortal, for if he had not, she would not have had him for a lover.

'It was not his DNA which killed him,' she said, not without a harshness of her own. 'He was martyred by vengeful men.'

'I know. But he did offer himself for capture and for trial, didn't he? Would he not have fled Malta if he had not been doomed to death regardless? What comfort was there in life for him, once he was certain of his own mortality?'

She had to look away then, and she stood up to go to the window, to peer out at the cloudy night. The rain was beginning again, and she judged that it would be heavy.

'What comfort?' she echoed. She had always said to herself that she had been his comfort. But she had never been sure what that tiny comfort could be worth, weighed in the balance against death itself, and pain.

To Michael Southerne, she said something very different. 'I suppose there was no comfort at all,' she said. 'He was not, after all, a comfortable man, never easy in his thoughts. He could be bitter, and sad, and at times he might have worn the nickname which my pirate lover took more readily than the pirate did. I cannot tell you that he was reconciled to his fate, or that he was entirely saved from misery by some discovered faith. He never found Quintus's God, so that he might soothe himself with dreams of Heaven, nor was he ever truly convinced that he had made a proper mark on history. He did not know, when he spent his last months in producing a poison to destroy vampires, whether posterity would bless or curse him for his efforts – whether men like you would reckon him a hero or a felon. But still, he was a man who thought the life which he had worth living, and the things which he did worth doing – and he did not think that the infinity of things made any one of his achievements, or the least of his discoveries, too infinitesimal to be reckoned in the sum of existence.' She turned around, to see what his reaction would be.

Michael was silent, and gave nothing away. It was as though he deliberately wanted to give no sign, even that he had heard. That in itself, she thought, was sign enough.

'To tell the truth,' he said, after a while, 'I wouldn't know whether to count him a hero or not. I think my father would call him a great man, for his discoveries, and for the role he played in breaking an old order to make way for a new, but I don't know. I think I've become sceptical of my father's opinions, almost as a matter of habit. Do you think, then, that I should take Cordery as my model, having found myself victim to his disease? Should I shoulder my own burden nobly, and set an example to the pitiless world by demonstrating that a common man can still make his mark?'

'It sounds like good advice,' she said, refusing to acknowledge that he was being sarcastic.

'Easy enough to offer. Very easy, I suppose, for one like my father, who set out to be a man of science, who made discoveries while he still belonged to the world of pain and sickness, and who carried into his emortality a zeal for work which should sustain him for a hundred years. I'm not sure, though, that I'm as much like him as either he or I would want me to be. Tell me, how have you used your centuries of life?'

She did not mind the impoliteness, with all its veiled accusations. 'I was born a slave,' she said. 'and then I became a pirate. I have been an explorer in this great wilderness, and have tried to help a little in the making of New Atlantis. I was a spy for a while – an agent of the European emortals among the Mohammedans, carrying recipes for Noell's elixir into the nations whose rulers fought hardest of all to keep it out. That was how I earned the gratitude of popes, though it was not for Christ's sake that I did my work. I suppose that was the bravest thing I have done, but I was in London during the poison gas attacks in the last war, and I worked with those who tried to bring survivors from the rubble – emortals in coma, commoners brought close to death. Perhaps that was the nearest I have come to making myself useful to others. But what I have been all along, more constantly than any of those other things, is a mistress to common men – because that, for the most part, has been what the world I have lived in has asked me to be.'

'I wonder what advice you would give to a girl who was like me?' he said. 'A poor, plain girl who not only could not become emortal, but who could not obtain the beauty which comes with it.'

'I don't know,' she said. 'Nor do I really know what advice to give to you. I can't tell you that you should be happy with what you have, nor how to make yourself happy. I can only say that it's a mistake to believe that happiness can only come with long life and freedom from pain. I have seen men and women for whom long life became a kind of curse, who knew no better how to use it than they knew how to use the kind of life you have. I have seen common men and women who had great joy in their brief span, and felt no loss in what they never gained. Men have many shapes and sizes, and are as unalike in their tempers as they are in their noses. No path is there already, laid out for you to follow; you must find your own way. One thing I can say is that if you lose yourself in despising what you have, because others have more, then the path which you make for yourself will be all the worse for it, but I think you know that already, or you would not have fled the sea, and might indeed have been a corpse when I found you on the rocks.'

He was looking into the firelight again, still very careful in his unresponsiveness. That tendency to look away, to retreat into a private realm of thought, was something she knew well enough. Noell Cordery had had it too – and of her many lovers, it was still Noell that she remembered best of all. She always would, though fading memory had dimmed so much of her early life that she could not remember frailty or pain at all. Noell's legacy she could not lose, because he was far too much a part of what she had ultimately become, and if she lived to be as old as Berenike, she would never forget the sensation of his touch or the image of his face, which was engraved upon her soul.

Poor mortal Noell!

The sound of the rain upon the roof was greater now. It was a steady drumming which promised no relentment or release.

Shango is busy, she thought. Once known, the Uruba personifications of nature were not easily forgotten.

'You'd better try to telephone your parents,' she said. 'And tell them not to worry. There is no need for them to come for you on such a night as this. You will be all the stronger tomorrow if you stay.'

He looked at her sharply, and said: 'I don't know if they'll permit that.'

She shrugged her shoulders, and said: 'Why should they not? Can you reach the telephone without your stick, or shall I get it? Or should I help you to walk?'

He stood up, unsteadily. He could not stand quite straight, because of his injured leg, and in that small untidiness was all the weight of foul misfortune, all the pathos of mortality and pain: unkind, uncompromising, uncompensated.

'I can do it,' he assured her.

And when he tried, it turned out that he could.

FIVE

He woke before her, his mouth dry and his leg aching. The ache was worse than usual, and he knew at once that this would be one of those days when he needed help to fight it.

He sometimes wondered, when he woke on days like this, how he had been able to sleep at all. In the early days following the accident he had been quite unable to release his grip on agonised consciousness, save for the mercies of heavy sedation. Then he had gone through a period when his sleep, if sleep it could be called, was more like a waking delirium, when he felt trapped by repetitive absurdities and obsessive compulsions. Nowadays, the pain was usually much less, more sullen than fierce. Most nights, he could sleep deeply and naturally – it was almost as if his brain had found a means of self-anaesthesia, to protect whatever work it did in dreaming – but still he woke, on occasion, to find himself racked by pain.

He pulled himself up to a half-sitting position and reached for the bottle of pills which he had placed on the bedside table. He shook the capsules out into his hand and looked at them. He had a dozen left, having begun with twenty-four. He was not allowed to have more on any one prescription, though he had reason to believe that twenty-four would be quite enough to kill him, should he decide to take an overdose, so the precaution seemed merely silly.

The possibility of overdosing was one which he considered, abstractedly, every time he obtained a new supply, but he had never come close to an actual attempt to swallow a lethal dose. The knowledge that he could do it, if he chose, and that the opportunity would return with clockwork regularity, was enough to assuage the temptation. He knew that he was not simply evading decision by means of procrastination; he had found a determination to stay alive, and his contemplations of suicide were really ritual reaffirmations of that determination.

He swallowed two capsules, then took a few frugal sips from the glass of water which he had placed there in careful anticipation. It seemed suddenly bizarre that he had made room in his thoughts and actions for that small item of planning, at a time when one might expect that he would be lost in submission to a tide of emotion. It seemed, somehow, the kind of thing that an emortal would do, but not a common man.

He looked down at the small cuts which the golden-skinned vampire had made upon his breast, with a scalpel so razor-sharp that he had not felt it biting his flesh, until it was gone and the blood was oozing out in little beadlets.

When she had asked him whether she might cut him he had been filled with confusion, but now he felt that he understood. No modern vampire lady need drink blood, when she could draw the same sustenance from capsules very similar in appearance to those which he had just taken; but Leilah had lived by far the greater part of her life in a world where she must take her donations in a cruder manner, day by day.

For her, he realised, the act of love must always have involved the act of donation, for it was to her lovers first and foremost that she would have looked for such nourishment.

Though he had never before given the matter serious thought, he felt that he understood now why male and female emortals had always sought lovers among common people. He had always tacitly assumed that it was a strange kind of perversity, or perhaps evidence of what common men frequently said of vampires – that they became so cold in becoming insensitive to pain that they could not love at all, but only be loved – but now he knew the link which there was between love and common blood.

He touched his wounds gently, and did not wince at the tiny pain which his fingers caused. He was used to a regime of excruciation which made such twinges insignificant. He wondered what his father's skin might have looked like, criss-crossed by many whited scars, before the breath of life had made him living marble and erased the record of his early loves. He had never thought to look, or dared to ask.

She woke up then, and saw him inspecting the marks. 'Did I hurt thee with the knife?' she asked. 'I did not mean to cause distress.'

'Oh no,' he said. 'It was nothing at all. No, not nothing – but it had more joy in it than hurt. You must know that.'

'I am never sure,' she whispered. 'Never sure. Real blood has a taste in it that the coloured tablets never have, though I sometimes feel that it might be shameful to prefer it.'

'No need,' he said. 'No injury done.' After a pause, he went on, awkwardly: 'A man might be offended, after all, if his lover preferred another donor . . . mightn't he?' He did not say it inquisitively, but there was a hint of curiosity in his voice.

'I have always tried not to offend,' she said, ironically.

He lay back, after moving the pillow to support his head. 'It would be pointless, I suppose, to sip the blood of a vampire lover,' he said, reflectively.

'It is not the only advantage which common men have,' she told him.

He blushed then, and she saw it.

'You of all men must remember that,' she said, softly. 'When men become emortal, it is not only pain which they discard, but virility. Some say that they sacrifice something of their virility of mind and spirit, too, for though emortal men grow exceeding wise with the depth of their experience, there is a kind of creative fervour which only commoners have for their own. The greatest artists have always been common men, and even men of science have often shown greater insight while still beset by mortality.'

'I don't doubt it,' he said, the answer ready to hand because he had heard the argument many times before. He said no more aloud, now, but he did continue the thread of thought in private. *Pain is a spur as well as a curse; a useful thing to some. Perhaps my life will testify to that.* He was uncertain; it was something which he had learned to say to himself, but had not yet forced himself to believe.

She reached out to touch the wounds on his breast, as he had done himself, and he watched her golden hand as the fingers stroked him. Then she kissed him on the same place, her tongue darting between her lips as if to search for some tiny residue of blood. He shivered under the caress, and hid his embarrassment beneath a smile, while he waited until she looked up at him, from her night-dark eyes.

'Did you do it,' he asked, haltingly, 'because you pitied me?'

She did not seem annoyed, though it occurred to him after he had said it that she had every right to be. She reached up to move a lock of jet-black hair which had fallen across her face.

'No,' she answered – what other answer could she give? – ''twas not from pity. Hast thou not heard that we who feel no pain can feel no pity?'

'I don't believe that,' he told her.

'It isn't true,' she confirmed. 'I have known pitiless men, both common and vampire, but I could not see that pain had aught to do with it. Some vampires lose pity, as some lose all emotion, and memory, and reason . . . but there are vampires, too, whose hearts ache in the knowledge of the suffering of the children they once were, and that is a soreness less easily wiped out than other kinds. It is a silly saying, anyhow, for vampires can feel pain, if they let it hurt them. It is only by an effort that we blot it out.'

'Yes,' he said, quietly. 'Common men forget that, I know.'

'Men who live a long time may grow cold,' she told him, 'but only if they will not warm themselves. I do not say that any anxiously seek the cold, but many let it steal over them, unawares. They need only resist, if they would have it otherwise. Vampires can love, and the manner of their loving does not diminish the measure of their love. Our lovers grow and change, while we do not; we lose them to the march of time and replace them over and over again, but we never like the losing and always delight in the finding, and it becomes, in the end, part of the rhythm of life, like the great slow beating of the heart of God.'

'Yet you cannot do what God commanded, and love one another.'

'We can do that too,' she claimed, 'in the way that the commandment was meant. Vampires to other vampires are only friends, but friendships, like hatreds, can endure forever where erotic passions never could.'

He sighed, and slid back to a lying position, with his head cradled in the soft pillow, and his eyes staring into space. 'It's a strange world,' he said, 'to which I am forbidden entry.'

'No more strange,' she assured him, 'than the one in which thou art confined.'

'But most men come to know both, and I never will.'

She touched his chest again, then gently ran her fingers along the line of his jaw, leaning back to study him from a little further away. 'Were it not for the wars,' she said, 'there would be far more vampires in the world, and fewer common men. Now there is peace, in Europe and Atlantis, the world's new age is truly begun. Frail flesh is precious to some, and will become more precious still. I am glad that the sea drove you to my door The sea has ever been my friend, you know, and it knew what work it did.'

'I think my flesh is too frail,' he said, looking away. 'I doubt that vampire ladies compete for the favours of lame boys.'

'When you grow tired, and desert me,' she murmured, 'you'll not find your lameness a handicap in the pursuit of love.'

He lowered his eyes, even though he was not looking in her direction, and in a small voice said: 'I could not grow tired of you.' Then he dared to glance at her, anxious to judge her response.

'I believe it,' she replied, and then rolled over, to pull her naked body from the protection of the covers.

Reflexively, he looked away, to guard her privacy with his politeness, but he quickly saw that such modesty was inappropriate, and he forced himself to accept the pleasure of watching her as she dressed. She looked at him once or twice, and seemed to be pleased that he was not afraid to look.

Her clothing, which he had hardly noticed the previous evening, now seemed to him strangely severe as the garments hid her lustrous body. They were oddly masculine in their neutral colouring, and did not accentuate her figure. He swung his own leg over the edge of the bed, as if to follow her example, then winced with the discomfort. She saw his reaction, and came quickly to his side.

'Stay there,' she said, 'a little longer.'

He hesitated, but then picked his foot up from the floor, and lay down again.

'Why not?' he said. 'We have all the time in the world.' The words were slightly bitter. He wondered exactly what depth of irony he really meant to imply.

'No,' she answered him, as she paused before leaving the room. 'But we do have time enough, and all that we need for our purpose.'

She said it in such a way that he could not doubt for a moment her meaning or her sincerity. She was telling him that she would love him, as dearly as she could.

At once he began to think of possibilities to diminish his pride. Perhaps she had been lonely, and would have welcomed anyone who came to her door. Perhaps he only reminded her of some former lover. But then he began to argue against himself, and told himself that even if there were a reason of that kind, it could not have been sufficient. The fact remained that it was he and not another who was here, and the more he was with her in time to come, the more he would fill her thoughts and her days. If he reminded her now of someone else, it did not matter; one day he might have his own proud place in her memories, if he had earned it.

He recognised this confusion of thoughts and feelings, belatedly, as a symptom of elation, an echo of joy.

He closed his eyes, again, to cut out the brightness of the morning light, and secure an introspective isolation which would intensify the satisfaction that he felt.

Yesterday, he had recklessly fled the sea which sought to drown him, knowing only that he was running away from a fate which sought to claim him. Now, he knew that there was also something which, all unknowing, he had been running towards. He began to understand what kind of salvation it was that providence had thrown into his path, and what he might make of it.

Whether this might be reckoned a recompense for the life which was as yet denied him, only time could tell – but he had, like all other men, to live his life one moment at a time, with only the present certain and the number of his tomorrows perpetually obscure.

Even a man who cannot live forever, he thought, *should be glad that the breath of life has come to Earth, and that the gift of immortality is nourished by the blood of common men.*

ACKNOWLEDGEMENTS

One cannot write about an alternative history without doing a good deal of research into the relevant periods of our own history; though one has a certain licence to commit anachronisms, propriety demands that they should be knowingly committed, and that they should be connected up into a coherent pattern of their own. An understanding of our own history is necessary to the task of trying to imagine how one alteration in the state of things might extend its consequences across centuries.

Much of my research was conducted in general sources such the *Encyclopedia Britannica*, but I did make use of certain specialised texts; I owe particular debts to R. W. Southern's *Western Society and the Church in the Middle Ages*; John Francis Guilmartin jr.'s *Gunpowder and Galleys*; Howard W. Haggard's *Devils, Drugs and Doctors*; and Carlo M. Cipolla's *Guns and Sails in the Early Phase of European Expansion*.

Though I moved one or two human artifacts from the locations which they have in our world (Cardigan Abbey being the principal example) I assumed that save for the existence of the crater of Adamawara the geography of my alternative world would be identical to ours; I borrowed details of settings used in the story from Hepworth Dixon's *Her Majesty's Tower*, J. D. Falconer's *On Horseback Through Nigeria*, and Sir Henry Luke's *Malta*.

The demands of my plot necessitated some radical dislocations in human society, but still required careful manipulation of data gleaned from various sources. Although I made very substantial strategic changes in designing the mythology of the 'Uruba' which is extensively cited in the story, I am greatly indebted to the account of Yoruba religion which is given in A. B. Ellis's book on *The Yoruba-Speaking Peoples of the Slave Coast of West Africa*.

Of the characters who actually appear on stage in the novel only a few figured significantly in the idol-infested story which we have created in order to give meaning to our own past – these being Vlad Dragulya, Richard the Lionheart, and some of their associates – but other characters whose pertinent roles remain offstage were also involved in the making of our world. I took a good deal of material from two specialised texts, Gabriel Ronay's *The Dracula Myth* and R. T. Petersson's *Sir Kenelm Digby*, in order to help me construct the biographies of the equivalent characters.

Accounts of food and its consumption which are offered in Parts One and Two are largely borrowed from Peter Brears' 'English Heritage' pamphlet, *Food and Cooking in 17th Century Britain: History and Recipes*.

Literary influences on this novel are too numerous to cite, and for the most part obvious, but I ought perhaps to mention that I stole the Bardic motto from Thomas Love Peacock's *The Misfortunes of Elphin*, having no proficiency of my own in the Welsh language.

Brian Stableford, Reading, February 1988